A Fantasy Masterpiece from a Five-time Hugo Award Winner

Praise for *The Dragons of Babel*

"If you haven't read Michael Swanwick yet, you've been missing some wonderful prose. . . . Con men and ward heelers, cluricauns and hobgoblins, and a stunningly beautiful elf-woman who rides a hippogriff all entice and enrapture Will, and the reader as well."

—*The San Diego Union-Tribune*

"In *The Iron Dragon's Daughter* Michael Swanwick created what was virtually a new genre of imaginative fiction. [*The*] *Dragons of Babel* is a brilliant sequel to that book. Well written, beautifully conceived, it is one of the very few fantasy novels I can unreservedly recommend. I love everything about the book."

—Michael Moorcock

"Fusing high technology seamlessly with magic, Swanwick introduces us to a wide range of marvelous conceits, fascinating digressions, and sparkling characters. His language bounces effortlessly back and forth between the high diction of elfland and thieves' argot to create a heady literary stew. This is modern fantasy at its finest and should hold great appeal for fans of Neil Gaiman's *Anansi Boys* or China Miéville's novels."

—*Publishers Weekly* (starred review)

"Huck Finn, the Lost Dauphin, and all the hosts of Faerie pursuing Destiny through Gormenghast with neon! This is original fantasy with genuine old roots, based on honest mythology instead of genre tropes. Swanwick keeps fulfilling his promises to the reader, and then upping the ante. Fascinating, lucid, logical, and enchanting."

—Kage Baker

"I forgive you, Michael Swanwick. I forgive you for making me wait so long for this extraordinary book. [*The*] *Dragons of Babel* makes good on all the promises of *The Iron Dragon's Daughter*—and then some. So come home, all is forgiven. Write faster."

—Jane Yolen, author of
Briar Rose; Sister Light, Sister Dark; and *Pay the Piper*

"*The Dragons of Babel* will immediately capture readers' interest. . . . Earthy, bawdy, and often brutal, it's a story that will keep science fiction/fantasy fans involved til the end."

—*School Library Journal* (starred review)

"Swanwick's major accomplishment here—aside from his standard authorial equipment of finely honed prose, inventive plotting, engaging characters, and clever symbolical patterning—is to instantiate a world where BMWs and motorcycles can be parked side by side with hippogriffs and manticores without rendering either 'vehicle' ridiculous. . . . The ride you get from [Swanwick's] dragons will be like no other."

—*Sci Fi Weekly* (Grade: A)

"Witty, inventive, written with enormous flair, this is one of Swanwick's most complex and rewarding novels."

—*Asimov's Science Fiction*

"Elegant, erudite, slyly funny, hard-nosed, compassionate, propulsive, and capable of punching through overused conventions and sentimentalities and delivering the jolt that restores the form to its primal power."

—*Locus*

"Pure magic."

—*Strange Horizons*

"Swanwick continues to turn traditional ideas of Faerie life upside down while remaining true to ancient Celtic Faerie lore. This masterfully written expansion of an iconoclastic vision belongs in libraries of all sizes."

—*Library Journal*

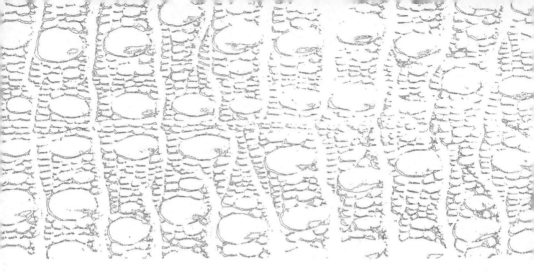

A TOM DOHERTY ASSOCIATES BOOK

New York

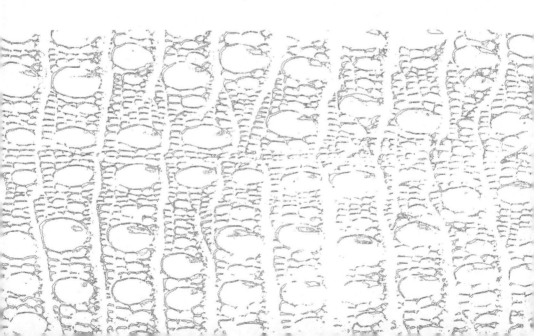

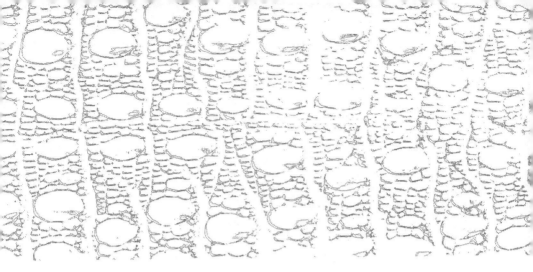

The
DRAGONS
of BABEL

Michael Swanwick

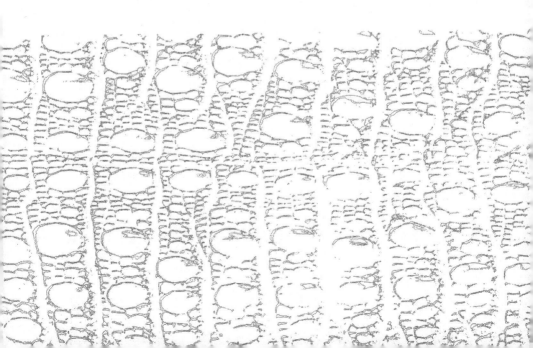

THE DRAGONS OF BABEL

Edited by David G. Hartwell

A Tor Book
Published by Tom Doherty Associates, LLC
175 Fifth Avenue
New York, NY 10010

www.tor-forge.com

Tor® is a registered trademark of Tom Doherty Associates, LLC.

The Library of Congress has cataloged the hardcover edition as follows:

Swanwick, Michael.
    The dragons of Babel / Michael Swanwick.—1st ed.
        p. cm.
    "A Tom Doherty Associates book."
    ISBN 978-0-7653-1950-0
    1. Dragons—Fiction. I. Title.
PS3569.W28D73 2008
813'.54—dc22

                                                        2007034918

ISBN 978-0-7653-3114-4 (trade paperback)

First Edition: January 2008
First Trade Paperback Edition: October 2011

10   9   8   7   6   5   4   3   2   1

For my father, John Francis Swanwick,
who gave me life

And for William Christian Porter,
who gave me something even more precious

Acknowledgments

As always, I owe thanks to more people than I have space or memory to acknowledge. However, I am particularly grateful to David Axler for assistance with folklore, Susanna Clarke for allowing me to borrow Fäerie Minor, Nick Gevers for the tokoloshe and the Jeyes Fluid, Vlatko Juric-Kokic for help with Croatian mythology, Greer Gilman for chimneysweepers and for vetting suspect passages, Boris Dolingo for introducing me to stone flowers, Ellen Kushner for the unwitting loan of Richard St Vier, and Tom Purdom for sage musical advice. The tourist brochure citation at the beginning of chapter 7 is an almost direct quote from *The Worm Ouroboros* by E. R. Eddison. The excerpt attributed to the entirely fictional *Motsognirsaga* is taken from the *Völuspa,* a part of the Elder Edda. Will's horse-charm is a compilation of Anglo-Saxon rune poems. Other poetry and songs quoted or paraphrased herein include "Scythe Song" by Andrew Lang; "When the King Enjoys His Own Again," a Cavalier ballad; "From the South," a traditional Chippewa war song; the Book of Revelations; and, inevitably, Mother Goose. Finally, special thanks are due to the M. C. Porter Endowment for the Arts for inspiring those aspects of Alcyone that I find particularly admirable.

1

East of Avalon

The dragons came at dawn, flying low and in formation, their jets so thunderous they shook the ground like the great throbbing heartbeat of the world. The village elders ran outside, half unbuttoned, waving their staffs in circles and shouting words of power. *Vanish,* they cried to the land, and *sleep* to the skies, though had the dragons' half-elven pilots cared they could easily have seen through such flimsy spells of concealment. But the pilots' thoughts were turned toward the West, where Avalon's industrial strength was based, and where its armies were rumored to be massing.

Will's aunt made a blind grab for him, but he ducked under her arm and ran out into the dirt street. The gun emplacements to the south were speaking now, in booming shouts that filled the sky with bursts of pink smoke and flak.

Half the children in the village were out in the streets, hopping up and down in glee, the winged ones buzzing about in small, excited circles. Then the yage-witch came hobbling out from her barrel and, demonstrating a strength Will had never suspected her of having, swept her arms wide and then slammed together her hoary old hands with a *boom!* that drove the children, all against their will, back into their huts.

All save Will. He had been performing that act which rendered one immune from child-magic every night for three weeks now. Fleeing from the village, he felt the enchantment like a polite hand placed on his shoulder. One weak tug, and then it was gone.

He ran, swift as the wind, up Grannystone Hill. His great-great-great-grandmother lived there still, alone at its tip, as a gray standing stone. She never said anything. But sometimes, though one never saw her move, she went down to the river at night to drink. Coming back from a nighttime fishing trip in his wee coracle, Will would find her standing motionless there and greet her respectfully. If the catch were good, he would gut an eel or a small trout, and smear the blood over her feet. It was the sort of small courtesy elderly relatives appreciated.

"Will, you young fool, turn back!" a cobbley cried from the inside of a junk refrigerator in the garbage dump at the edge of the village. "It's not safe up there!"

But Will shook his head, blond hair flying behind him, and put every ounce of his strength into his running. There were dragons in the sky and, within him, a mirroring desire to get closer to the glory of their flight, to feel the laminar flow of their unimaginable power and magic as close to his skin as possible. It was a kind of mania. It was a kind of need.

The hill's bald and grassy summit was not far. Will ran with a wildness he could not understand, lungs pounding and the wind of his own speed whistling in his ears.

Then he was atop the hill, breathing hard, with one hand on his grandmother stone.

The dragons were still flying overhead in waves. The roar of their jets was astounding. Will lifted his face into the heat of their passage, and felt the wash of their malice and hatred as well. It was like a dark wine that sickened the stomach and made the head throb with pain and bewilderment and wonder. It repulsed him and made him want more.

The last flight of dragons scorched over, twisting his head and spinning his body around, skimming low over farms and fields and the Old Forest that stretched all the way to the horizon and beyond. A faint brimstone stench of burnt fuel lingered in the air after them. Will felt his heart grow so large it seemed impossible his chest could contain it, so large that it threatened to encompass the hill, farms, forest, dragons, and all the world beyond.

Something hideous and black leaped up from the distant forest and into the air, flashing toward the final dragon. Will's eyes were wrenched by a sudden painful *wrongness,* and then a stone hand came down over them.

"*Don't look,*" said an old and calm and stony voice. "*To look upon a basilisk is no way for a child of mine to die.*"

"Grandmother?" Will asked.

"*Yes?*"

"If I promise to keep my eyes closed, will you tell me what's happening?"

There was a brief silence. Then: "*Very well. The dragon has turned. He is fleeing.*"

"Dragons don't flee," Will said scornfully. "Not from anything." He tried to pry the hand from his eyes, but of course it was useless, for his fingers were mere flesh.

"*This one does. And he is wise to do so. His fate has come for him. Out from the halls of coral it has come, and down to the halls of granite will it take him. Even now his pilot is singing his death-song.*"

She fell silent again, while the distant roar of the dragon rose and fell in pitch. Will could tell that momentous things were happening, but the sound gave him not the least clue as to their nature. At last he said, "Grandmother? Now?"

"*He is clever, this one. He fights very well. He is elusive. But he cannot escape a basilisk. Already the creature knows the first two syllables of his true name. At this very moment it is speaking to his heart, and telling it to stop beating.*"

The roar of the dragon grew louder again, and then louder still. Echoes bounced from every hillside, compounding and recomplicating it into a confusion of sound. Cutting through this was a noise that was like a cross between a scarecrow screaming and the sound of teeth scraping on slate.

"*Now they are almost touching. The basilisk reaches for its prey. . . .*"

All the world exploded. The inside of Will's skull turned white, and for an astonishing instant he was certain he was going to die. Then his grandmother threw her stone cloak over him and, clutching him to her warm breast, knelt down low to the sheltering earth.

When he awoke, it was dark and he lay alone on the cold hillside. Painfully, he stood. A somber orange-and-red sunset limned the western horizon, where the dragons had disappeared. Frogs sang from the river-marsh. In the dimming sky, ibises sought their evening roosts.

"Grandmother?" Will stumbled to the top of the hill, hindered by loose stones that turned underfoot and barked his ankles. He ached in every joint. There was a ringing in his ears, like factory bells tolling the end of a shift. "Grandmother!"

There was no answer.

The hilltop was empty.

But scattered down the hillside, from its top down to where he had awakened, was a stream of broken stones. He had hurried past them without looking on his way up. Now he saw that their exterior surfaces were the familiar and comfortable gray of his stone-mother, and that the freshly exposed interior surfaces were slick with blood.

One by one, Will carried the stones up to the top of the hill, back to the spot where his great-great-great-grandmother had preferred to stand and watch over the village. It took hours. He piled them one on top of another, and though he worked harder than he had ever done in his life, when he was finished, the cairn did not rise even so high as his waist. No more than that remained of she who had protected the village for so many generations.

By the time he was done, the stars were bright and cruel in a black, moonless sky. A night-wind ruffled his shirt and made him shiver. With sudden clarity Will marveled at last that he should be here alone. Where was his aunt? Where were the other villagers?

Will carried his rune-bag with him always, stuffed into a hip pocket. He yanked it out and spilled its contents into his hand. A crumpled blue jay's feather, a shard of mirror, two acorns, and a pebble with one side blank and the other marked with an X. He kept the mirror shard and poured the rest back into the bag. Then he invoked the secret name of the *lux aeterna*, inviting a tiny fraction of its radiance to enter the mundane world.

A gentle foxfire spread itself through the mirror. Holding it at arm's length so he could see his face reflected therein, he asked the oracle glass, "Why did my village not come for me?"

The mirror-boy's mouth moved in the silvery water of the glass. "They came." The lips were pale and tinged with blue, like a corpse's.

"Then why did they leave? Why didn't they bring me home?" Unconsciously, Will kicked at his stone-grandam's cairn, built with so great a labor and no help from anyone.

"They didn't find you."

The oracle-glass was maddeningly literal, capable only of answering the question one asked, rather than that which one wanted answered. But Will persisted. "Why didn't they find me?"

"You weren't here."

"Where was I? Where was my Granny?"

"You were nowhere."

"How could we be nowhere?"

Tonelessly, the mirror said, "The basilisk's explosion warped the world and the mesh of time in which it is caught. The sarsen-lady and you were thrown forward, halfway through the day."

It was as clear an explanation as Will was going to get. He muttered a word of unbinding, releasing the invigorating light back to whence it came. Then, fearful that the blood on his hands and clothes would draw night-gaunts, he hurried homeward.

When he got to the village, he discovered that a search party was still scouring the darkness, looking for him. Those who remained had hoisted a straw man upside down atop a tall pole at the center of the village square, and set it ablaze against the chance he was still alive, to draw him home.

As so it had.

Two days after those events, a crippled dragon crawled out of the Old Forest and into the village. Slowly he pulled himself into the center square. Then he collapsed. He was wingless and there were gaping holes in his fuselage, but still the stench of power clung to him, and a miasma of hatred. A trickle of oil seeped from a gash in his belly and made a spreading stain on the cobbles beneath him.

Will was among those who crowded out to behold this prodigy. The others whispered hurtful remarks among themselves about its ugliness. And truly it was built of cold, black iron, and scorched even darker by the basilisk's explosion, with jagged stumps of metal where its wings had been and ruptured plates here and there along its flanks. But even half-destroyed, the dragon was a beautiful creature. It was built with dwarven skill to high-elven design—how could it *not* be beautiful?

Puck Berrysnatcher bumped hips with him and murmured, "It's yours, isn't it?"

Will shrugged irritably, said nothing.

"Same one as the basilisk shot down, I mean."

"I don't know, and I don't care. It wasn't *me* that brought it here."

For a long time no one spoke. Then an engine hummed to life somewhere deep within the dragon's chest, rose in pitch to a clattering whine, and fell again into silence. The dragon slowly opened one eye.

"Bring me your truth-teller," he rumbled.

The truth-teller was a fruit-woman named Bessie Applemere. She was young, and yet, out of respect for her office, everybody called her by the honorific Hag. She came, clad in the robes and wide hat of her calling, breasts bare as was traditional, and stood before the mighty engine of war. "Father of Lies." She bowed respectfully.

"I am crippled, and all my missiles are spent," the dragon said. "But still am I dangerous."

Hag Applemere nodded. "It is the truth."

"My tanks are yet half-filled with jet fuel. It would be the easiest thing in the world for me to set them off with an electrical spark. And were I to do so, your village and all who live within it would cease to be. Therefore, since power engenders power, I am now your liege and king."

"It is the truth."

A murmur went up from the assembled villagers.

"However, my reign will be brief. By Samhain, the Armies of the Mighty will be here, and they shall take me back to the great forges of the East to be rebuilt."

"You believe it so."

The dragon's second eye opened. Both focused steadily on the truth-teller. "You do not please me, Hag. I may someday soon find it necessary to break open your body and eat your beating heart."

Hag Applemere nodded. "It is the truth."

Unexpectedly, the dragon laughed. It was cruel and sardonic laughter, as the mirth of such creatures always was, but it was laughter nonetheless. Many of the villagers covered their ears against it. The smaller children burst into tears. "You amuse me," he said. "All of you amuse me. We begin my reign on a gladsome note."

The truth-teller bowed. Watching, Will thought he detected a great sadness in her eyes. But she said nothing.

"Let your lady-mayor come forth, that she might give me obeisance."

Auld Black Agnes shuffled from the crowd. She was scrawny and thrawn and bent almost double from the weight of her responsibilities, tokens of which hung in a black leather bag pendant from her neck. Opening that bag, she brought forth a flat stone from the first hearth of the village, and laid it down before the dragon. Kneeling, she placed her left hand, splayed, upon it.

Then she took out a small silver sickle.

"Your blood and ours. Thy fate and mine. Our joy and your wickedness. Let all be as one." Her voice rose in a warbling keen:

> *"Black spirits and white, red spirits and gray,*
> *Mingle, mingle, mingle, you that mingle may."*

Her right hand trembled with palsy as it raised the sickle up above her left. But her slanting motion downward was swift and sudden. Blood spurted, and her little finger went flying.

She made one small, sharp cry, like a seabird's, and no more.

"I am satisfied," the dragon said. Then, without transition: "My pilot is dead and he begins to rot." A hatch hissed open in his side. "Drag him forth."

"Do you wish him buried?" a tusse asked hesitantly.

"Bury him, burn him, cut him up for bait—what do I care? When he was alive, I needed him in order to fly. But he's dead now, and of no use to me."

Kneel."

Will knelt in the dust beside the dragon. He'd been standing in line for hours, and there were villagers who would be standing in that same line hours from now, waiting to be processed. They went in fearful, and they came out dazed. When a lily-maid stepped down from the dragon, and somebody shouted a question at her, she simply shook her tear-streaked face, and fled. None would speak of what happened within.

The hatch opened.

"Enter."

He did. The hatch closed behind him.

At first he could see nothing. Then small, faint lights swam out of the darkness. Bits of green and white stabilized, became instrument lights, pale luminescent flecks on dials. One groping hand touched leather. It was the pilot's couch. He could smell, faintly, the taint of corruption on it.

"Sit."

Clumsily, he climbed into the seat. The leather creaked under him. His arms naturally lay along the arms of the couch. He might have been made for it. There were handgrips. At the dragon's direction, he closed his hands about them and turned them as far as they would go. A quarter-turn, perhaps.

From beneath, needles slid into his wrists. They stung like blazes, and Will jerked involuntarily. But when he tried, he discovered that he could not let go of the grips. His fingers would no longer obey him.

"Boy," the dragon said suddenly, "what is your true name?"

Will trembled. "I don't have one."

Immediately, he sensed that this was not the right answer. There was a silence. Then the dragon said dispassionately, "I can make you suffer."

"Sir, I am certain you can."

"Then tell me your true name."

His wrists were cold—cold as ice. The sensation that spread up his forearms to his elbows was not numbness, for they ached as if they had been packed in snow. "I don't know it!" Will cried in an anguish. "I don't know, I was never told, I don't think I have one!"

Small lights gleamed on the instrument panel, like forest eyes at night.

"Interesting." For the first time, the dragon's voice displayed a faint tinge of emotion. "What family is yours? Tell me everything about them."

Will had no family other than his aunt. His parents had died on the very first day of the War. Theirs was the ill fortune of being in Brocielande Station when the dragons came and dropped golden fire on the rail yards. So Will had been shipped off to the hills to live with his aunt. Everyone agreed he would be safest there. That was several years ago, and there were times now when he could not remember his parents at all. Soon he would have only the memory of remembering.

As for his aunt, Blind Enna was little more to him than a set of rules to be contravened and chores to be evaded. She was a pious old creature, forever killing small animals in honor of the Nameless Ones and burying their corpses under the floor or nailing them above doors or windows. In consequence of which, a faint perpetual stink of conformity and rotting mouse hung about the hut. She mumbled to herself constantly and on those rare occasions when she got drunk— two or three times a year—would run out naked into the night and, mounting a cow backward, lash its sides bloody with a hickory switch so that it ran wildly uphill and down until finally she tumbled off and fell asleep. At dawn Will would come with a blanket and lead her home. But they were never exactly close.

All this he told in stumbling, awkward words. The dragon listened without comment.

The cold had risen up to Will's armpits by now. He shuddered as it touched his shoulders. "Please . . . ," he said. "Lord Dragon . . . your ice has reached my chest. If it touches my heart, I fear that I'll die."

"Hmmm? Ah! I was lost in thought." The needles withdrew from Will's arms. They were still numb and lifeless, but at least the cold had stopped its spread. Pins and needles tingled at the center of his fingertips, an early omen that sensation would eventually return.

The door hissed open. "You may leave now."

He stumbled out into the light.

An apprehension hung over the village for the first week or so. But as the dragon remained quiescent and no further alarming events oc- curred, the timeless patterns of village life resumed. Yet all the win- dows opening upon the center square remained perpetually shuttered and nobody willingly passed through it anymore, so that it was as if a stern silence had come to dwell within their midst.

Then one day Will and Puck Berrysnatcher were out in the woods, checking their snares for rabbits and camelopards (it had been generations since a pard was caught in Avalon, but they still hoped), when the Scissors-Grinder came puffing down the trail. He lugged something bright and gleaming within his two arms.

"Hey, bandy-man!" Will cried. He had just finished tying his rabbits' legs together so he could sling them over his shoulder. "Ho, big-belly! What hast thou?"

"Don't know. Fell from the sky."

"Did *not*!" Puck scoffed. The two boys danced about the fat cobber, grabbing at the golden thing. It was shaped something like a crown and something like a birdcage. The metal of its ribs and bands was smooth and lustrous. Black runes adorned its sides, the like of which had never been seen in the village. "I bet it's a roc's egg—or a phoenix's!"

Simultaneously Will asked, "Where are you taking it?"

"To the smithy. Perchance the hammermen can beat it down into something useful." The Scissors-Grinder swatted at Puck with one hand, almost losing his hold on the object. "Perchance they'll pay me a penny or three for it."

Daisy Jenny popped up out of the flowers in the field by the edge of the garbage dump and, seeing the golden thing, ran toward it, pigtails flying, singing, "Gimme-gimme-gimme!" Two hummingirls and a chimney-bounder came swooping down out of nowhere. And the Cauldron Boy dropped an armful of scavenged scrap metal with a crash and came running up as well. So that by the time the Meadows Trail became Mud Street, the Scissors-Grinder was red-faced and cursing, and knee-deep in children.

"Will, you useless creature!"

Turning, Will saw his aunt, Blind Enna, tapping toward him. She had a peeled willow branch in each hand, like long white antennae, that felt the ground before her as she came. The face beneath her bonnet was grim. He danced back from her, old enough to know better than to run, young enough to feel the urge anyway. "Auntie . . . ," he said.

"Don't you 'auntie' me, you slugabed! There's toads to be buried and stoops to be washed. Why are you never around when it's time for chores?"

She put an arm through his and began dragging him homeward, still feeling ahead of herself with her wands.

Meanwhile, the Scissors-Grinder was so distracted by the children that he let his feet carry him the way they habitually went—through Center Square, rather than around it. For the first time since the coming of the dragon, laughter and children's voices spilled into that silent space. Will stared yearningly over his shoulder after his dwindling friends.

The dragon opened an eye to discover the cause of so much noise. He reared up his head in alarm. In a voice of power he commanded, *"Drop that!"*

Startled, the Scissors-Grinder obeyed.

The device exploded.

Magic in the imagination is a wondrous thing, but magic in practice is terrible beyond imagining. An unending instant's dazzlement and confusion left Will lying on his back in the street. His ears rang horribly and his body was strangely numb. There were legs everywhere—people running. And somebody was hitting him with a stick. No, with two sticks.

He sat up, and the end of a stick almost got him in the eye. He grabbed hold of it with both hands and yanked at it angrily. "Auntie!" he yelled. Blind Enna went on waving the other stick around, and tugging at the one he had captured, trying to get it back. "Auntie, stop that!" But of course she couldn't hear him; he could barely hear himself through the din in his ears.

He got to his feet and put both arms around his aunt. She struggled against him, and Will was astonished to find that she was no taller than he. When had *that* happened? She had been twice his height when first he came to her. "Auntie Enna!" he shouted into her ear. "It's me, Will, I'm right here."

"Will." Her eyes filled with tears. "You shiftless, worthless thing. Where are you when there are chores to be done?"

Over her shoulder, he saw how the square was streaked with black and streaked with red. There were things that looked like they might be bodies. He blinked. The square was filled with villagers, leaning over them. Doing things. Some had their heads thrown back, as if they were wailing. But of course he couldn't hear them, not over the ringing noise.

"I caught two rabbits, Enna," he told his aunt, shouting so he could be heard. He still had them, slung over his shoulder. He couldn't imagine why. "We can have them for supper."

"That's good," she said. "I'll cut them up for stew while you wash the stoops."

Blind Enna found her refuge in work. She mopped the ceiling and scoured the floor. She had Will polish every piece of silver in the house. Then all the furniture had to be taken apart, and cleaned, and put back together again. The rugs had to be boiled. The little filigreed case containing her heart had to be taken out of the cupboard where she normally kept it and hidden in the very back of the closet.

The list of chores that had to be done was endless. She worked herself, and Will as well, all the way to dusk. Sometimes he cried at the thought of his friends who had died, and Blind Enna hobbled over and hit him to make him stop. Then, when he did stop, he felt nothing. He felt nothing, and he felt like a monster for feeling nothing. Thinking of it made him begin to cry again, so he wrapped his arms tight around his face to muffle the sounds, so his aunt would not hear and hit him again.

It was hard to say which—the feeling or the not—made him more miserable.

The very next day, the summoning bell was rung in the town square and, willing or no, all the villagers once again assembled before their king dragon. "Oh, ye foolish creatures!" the dragon said. "Six children have died and old *Tanarahumra*—he whom you called the Scissors-Grinder—as well, because you have no self-discipline."

Hag Applemere bowed her head. "It is the truth."

"You try my patience," the dragon said. "Worse, you drain my batteries. My reserves grow low, and I can only partially recharge them each day. Yet I see now that I dare not be King Log. You must be governed. Therefore, I require a speaker. Somebody slight of body, to live within me and carry my commands to the outside."

Auld Black Agnes shuffled forward. "That would be me," she said. "I know my duty."

"No!" the dragon said scornfully. "You aged crones are too cunning by half. I'll choose somebody else from this crowd. Someone simple . . . a child."

Not me, Will thought wildly. *Anybody else but me.*

"Him," the dragon said.

So it was that Will came to live within the dragon king. All that day and late into the night he worked drawing up plans on sheets of parchment, at his lord's careful instructions, for devices very much like stationary bicycles, which could be used to recharge the dragon's batteries. In the morning, he went to the blacksmith's forge at the edge of town to command that six of the things be immediately built. Then he went to Auld Black Agnes to tell her that all day and every day six villagers, elected by lot or rotation or however else she chose, were to sit upon the devices pedaling, pedaling, all the way without cease from dawn to sundown, when Will would drag the batteries back inside.

Hurrying through the village with his messages—there were easily a dozen packets of orders, warnings, and advices that first day—Will's feet spurned the dust beneath them. Lack of sleep gifted everything with an impossible vividness. The green moss on the skulls stuck in the crotches of forked sticks lining the first half-mile of the River Road, the salamanders languidly copulating in the coals of the smithy forge, even the stillness of the carnivorous plants in his auntie's garden as they waited for an unwary toad to hop within striking distance— such homely sights were transformed. Everything was new and strange to him.

By noon, all the dragon's errands were run, so Will went out in search of friends. The square was empty, of course, and silent. But when he wandered out into the lesser streets, his shadow short beneath him, they were empty as well. A lonely breeze whispered and tickled its way past him and was gone. Then he heard the high sound of a girlish voice and followed it around a corner.

There was a little girl playing at jump rope and chanting:

> *"Here-am-I-and*
> *All-a-lone;*
> *What's-my-name?*
> *It's-Jum-ping—"*

"Joan!" Will cried.

Jumping Joan stopped. In motion, she had a certain kinetic presence. Still, she was hardly there at all. A hundred slim braids exploded from her small, dark head. Her arms and legs were thin as reeds. The only things of any size at all about her were her luminous brown eyes. "I was up to a million!" She stamped a tiny foot. "Now I'll have to start all over again."

"When you start again, count your first jump as a million and one."

"It doesn't work that way and you know it! What do you want?"

"Where is everybody?"

"Some of them are fishing and some are hunting. Others are at work in the fields. The hammermen, the tinker, and the Sullen Man are building bicycles-that-don't-move to place in Tyrant Square. The potter and her 'prentices are digging clay from the riverbank. The healing-women are in the smoke-hutch at the edge of the woods with Puck Berrysnatcher."

"Then that last is where I'll go. My thanks, wee-thing."

Jumping Joan, however, made no answer. She was already skipping rope again, and counting "A-hundred-thousand-one, a-hundred-thousand-two . . ."

The smoke-hutch was an unpainted shack built so deep in the reeds that whenever it rained it was in danger of sinking down into the muck and never being seen again. Hornets lazily swam to and from a nest beneath its eaves. The door creaked noisily as Will opened it.

As one, the women looked up sharply. Puck Berrysnatcher's body was a pale white blur on the shadowy ground before them. The women's eyes were green and unblinking, like those of jungle animals. They glared at him wordlessly. "I w-wanted to see what you were d-doing," he stammered.

"We are inducing catatonia," one of them said. "Hush now. Watch and learn."

The healing-women were smoking cigars over Puck. They filled their mouths with smoke and then, leaning close, let it pour down over his naked, broken body. By slow degrees the hut filled with bluish smoke, turning the healing-women to ghosts and Puck himself into an indistinct smear on the dirt floor. He sobbed and murmured in pain at first, but by slow degrees his cries grew quieter, and then silent. At last his body shuddered and stiffened, and he ceased breathing.

The healing-women daubed Puck's chest with ocher, and then packed his mouth, nostrils, and anus with a mixture of aloe and white clay. They wrapped his body with a long white strip of linen.

Finally they buried him deep in the black marsh mud by the edge of Hagmere Pond.

When the last shovelful of earth had been tamped down, the women turned as one and silently made their way home, along five separate paths.

Will stared after them until his stomach rumbled, reminding him that he hadn't eaten yet that day. There was a cherry tree not far away whose fruit was freshly come to ripeness, and a pigeon pie that he knew of which would not be well-guarded.

Swift as a thief, he sped into town.

William stayed out as late as he dared, creeping back into the dragon's hulk just after sundown, fearful of the great Worm's certain fury. But when he sat down in the leather couch and the needles slid into his wrists, the dragon's voice was a murmur, almost a purr. "How fearful you are! You tremble. Do not be afraid, small one. I shall protect and cherish you. And you, in turn, shall be my eyes and ears, eh? Yes, you will. Now, let us see what you learned today."

"I—"

"Shussssh," the dragon breathed. "Not a word. I need not your interpretation, but direct access to your memories. Try to relax. This will hurt you the first time, but with practice it will grow easier. In time, perhaps, you will learn to enjoy it."

Something cold and wet and slippery slid into Will's mind. A coppery foulness filled his mouth. A repulsive stench rose up in his nostrils. Reflexively, he retched and struggled.

"Don't resist. This will go easier if you open yourself to me."

More of that black and oily sensation poured into Will, and more. Coil upon coil, it thrust its way inside him. He found himself rising up into the air, above the body that no longer belonged to him. He could hear it making choking noises.

"Take it all."

It hurt. It hurt more than the worst headache Will had ever had. His skull must surely crack from the pressure. Yet still the intrusive presence pushed into him, its pulsing mass permeating his thoughts, his senses, his memories. Swelling them. Engorging them. And then, just as he was certain his head must explode from the pressure, it was done.

The dragon was within him.

Squeezing shut his eyes, Will saw, in the dazzling, pain-laced darkness, the dragon king as he existed in the spirit world: sinuous, veined with light, humming with power. Here, in the realm of ideal forms, he was not a broken, crippled *thing*, but a sleek being with the beauty of an animal and the perfection of a machine.

"Am I not beautiful?" the dragon crooned. "Am I not a delight to behold?"

Will gagged with pain and disgust. And yet—might the Seven forgive him for thinking this!—it was true.

2

King Dragon

Every morning at dawn Will dragged out batteries weighing almost as much as himself into Tyrant Square for the villagers to recharge—one at first, then more and more as the remaining six standing bicycles were built. One of the women, chosen by rotation, would be waiting to give him breakfast. As the dragon's agent, he was entitled to go into any hut and feed himself from what he found there, but the dragon deemed this method more dignified. The rest of the day, by order of his master, he spent wandering through the village and, increasingly, the woods and fields around the village, observing. At first Will did not know what he was looking for. But by comparing the orders he transmitted with what he had seen the previous day, he slowly managed to piece it together that he was scouting out the village's defensive position, discovering its weaknesses, and looking for ways to alleviate them.

The village was, quite simply, not defensible from any serious military force. But it could be made more obscure. Thorn hedges were planted, and poison oak. Footpaths were eradicated. A clear-water pond was breached and drained, lest it be identified as a resource for advancing armies. When the weekly truck came up the River Road with mail and cartons of supplies for the store, Will was loitering at the magazine rack to ensure that nothing unusual caught the driver's eye. When the bee warden declared a surplus of honey that might be sold downriver for silver, Will relayed the dragon's instructions that half the overage be destroyed, lest the village get a reputation for prosperity.

At dimity, as the sunlight leached from the sky, Will would feel a familiar aching in his wrists and a troubling sense of need, and return to the dragon's cabin to lie in painful communion with him and share what he had seen.

Evenings varied. Sometimes he was too sick from the dragon's entry into him to do anything. Other times he spent hours scrubbing and cleaning the dragon's interior. Mostly, though, he simply sat in the pilot's couch, listening while the dragon talked in a soft, almost inaudible rumble, saying things that were in themselves a kind of torture for, true or not, they could not be denied.

"You don't have cancer," the old war-drake murmured. It was, if the clock on the control panel could be believed, dark outside. By policy, however, the hatch was kept closed tight and there were no windows so, whatever the time, the only light came from the instrumentation. "No bleeding from the rectum, no loss of energy. Eh, boy?"

"No, dread lord."

"It seems I chose better than I suspected. You have mortal blood in you, sure as moonlight. Your mother was no better than she ought to be."

"Sir?"

"I said your mother was a *whore*! Are you feebleminded? Your mother was a whore, your father a cuckold, you a bastard, grass green, mountains stony, and water wet."

"My mother was a good woman!"

"Good women sleep with men other than their husbands all the time, and for more reasons than there are men. Didn't anybody tell you that? She could have been bored, or reckless, or blackmailed. She might have wanted money, or adventure, or revenge upon your father. Perchance she bet her virtue upon the turn of a card. It could be she was a worshiper of the Horned Man. Mayhap she was overcome by the desire to roll in the gutter and befoul herself. She may even have fallen in love. Unlikelier things have happened."

"I won't listen to this!"

"You have no choice," the dragon said complacently. "The door is locked and you cannot escape. Moreover, I am larger and more powerful than you. This is the *lex mundi,* from which there is no appeal."

"You lie! You lie! You lie!"

"Believe what you will. But, however got, your mortal blood is your good fortune. Dwelt you not in the asshole of beyond, but in some more civilized setting, you would surely be conscripted for a pilot. All pilots are half-mortal, you know, for only mortal blood can withstand the taint of cold iron. You would live like a prince and be trained as a warrior. With luck, you would be the death of thousands." The dragon's voice sank musingly. "How shall I mark this discovery? Shall I . . . ? Oho! Yes. I will make you my lieutenant."

Will picked angrily at the scab on his wrist. "How does that differ from what I am now?"

"Do not despise titles. If nothing else, it will impress your friends."

This was a calculated affront, for Will had no friends, and the dragon knew it. Not anymore. All folk avoided him when they could, and were stiff-faced and wary in his presence when they could not. The children fleered and jeered and called him names. Sometimes they flung stones at him, or pottery shards or—once—even a cowpat, dry on the outside but soft and gooey within. Not often, however, for when they did, he would catch them and thrash them for it. This always seemed to catch the little ones by surprise.

The world of children was much simpler than the one he inhabited.

When Little Red Margotty struck him with the cowpat, he caught her by the ear and marched her to her mother's hut. "See what your brat has done to me!" he cried in indignation, holding his jerkin away from him.

Big Red Margotty turned from the worktable where she had been canning toads. She stared at him stonily, and yet it seemed to him that there resided in her eye a glint of suppressed laughter. "Take it off and I shall wash it for you."

Her expression when she said this was so disdainful that Will almost peeled off his trousers as well, flung them in her face for her insolence, and commanded her to wash them for a penance. But with the impulse came also an awareness of Big Red Margotty's firm, pink flesh, of her ample breasts and womanly haunches. His lesser self swelled, filling out his trousers so that they bulged.

This, too, Big Red Margotty saw, and the look of casual scorn she gave him then made Will burn with humiliation. Worse, all the while her mother washed his jerkin, Little Red Margotty danced around Will at a distance, holding up her skirt and waggling her bare bottom at him, making a mock of his discomfort.

On the way out the door, his damp jerkin draped over one arm, he stopped and said, "Make for me a sark of white damask, with upon its breast a shield: argent, dragon rouge rampant above a village sable. Bring it to me by dawn-light tomorrow."

"The cheek!" Big Red Margotty cried. "You have no right to demand any such thing!"

"I am the dragon's lieutenant, and that is right enough for anything."

He left, knowing that the red bitch would perforce be up all night sewing for him and glad for every miserable hour she would suffer.

Three weeks having passed since Puck's burial, the healing-women decided it was time at last to dig him up. They said nothing when Will declared that he would attend—none of the adults said anything to him unless they had no choice—but, tagging along after them, he knew for a fact that he was unwelcome.

Puck's body, when they dug it up, looked like nothing so much as an enormous black root, twisted and formless. Chanting all the while, the women unwrapped the linen swaddling and washed him down with cow's urine. They dug out the life-clay that clogged his openings. They placed the finger-bone of a bat beneath his tongue. An egg was broken by his nose and the white slurped down by one medicine woman and the yellow by another.

Finally, they injected him with five cc. of dextroamphetamine sulfate.

Puck's eyes flew open. His skin had been baked black as silt by his long immersion in the soil, and his hair bleached white. His eyes were a vivid and startling leaf green. In all respects but one, his body was as perfect as ever it had been. But that one exception made the women sigh unhappily for his sake.

One leg was missing, from above the knee down.

"The Earth has taken her tithe," one old woman observed sagely.

"There was not enough left of the leg to save," said another.

"It's a pity," said a third.

They all withdrew from the hut, leaving Will and Puck alone together.

For a long time Puck did nothing but stare wonderingly at his stump of a leg. He sat up and ran careful hands over its surface, as if to prove to himself that the missing flesh was not still there and somehow charmed invisible. Then he stared at Will's clean white shirt, and at the dragon arms upon his chest. At last, his unblinking gaze rose to meet Will's eyes.

"*You* did this."

"That's not fair!" Will cried. "The land mine had nothing to do with the dragon. The Scissors-Grinder would have found it and brought it into the village in any case. It is the War that brought both dragon and bomb to us, and the War—surely you will acknowledge this—is not my fault." Will took his friend's hand in his own. "*Tchortyrion . . . ,*" he said in a low voice, careful that no unseen person might overhear.

Puck batted his hand away. "That's not my true name anymore! I have walked in darkness and my spirit has returned from the halls of granite with a new name—one that not even the dragon knows!"

"The dragon will learn it soon enough," Will said sadly.

"You wish!"

"Puck . . ."

"My old use-name is dead as well," said he who had been Puck Berrysnatcher. Unsteadily pulling himself erect, he wrapped the blanket upon which he had been laid about his thin shoulders. "You may call me No-name, for no name of mine shall ever pass your lips again."

Awkwardly, No-name hopped to the doorway. He steadied himself with a hand upon the jamb, then launched himself out into the wide world.

"Please! Listen to me!" Will cried after him.

Wordlessly, No-name raised one hand, middle finger extended.

Red anger welled up inside Will. "Asshole!" he shouted after his former friend. "Stump-leggity hopper! Johnny-three-limbs!"

He had not cried since that night the dragon first entered him. Now he cried again.

In midsummer an army recruiter roared into town with a bright green-and-yellow drum lashed to the motorcycle behind him. He wore a smart red uniform with two rows of brass buttons, and he'd come all the way from Brocielande, looking for likely lads to enlist in the service of Avalon. With a screech and a cloud of dust, he pulled up in front of the Scrannel Dogge, heeled down the kickstand, and went inside to rent the common room for the space of the afternoon.

Outside again, he donned his drum harness, attached the drum, and sprinkled a handful of gold coins on its head. *Boom-Boom-de-Boom!* The drumsticks came down like thunder. *Rap-Tap-a-Rap!* The gold coins leaped and danced, like raindrops on a hot griddle. By this time, there was a crowd standing outside the Scrannel Dogge.

The recruiter laughed. "Sergeant Bombast is my name!" *Boom! Doom! Boom!* "Finding heroes is my game!" He struck the sticks together overhead. *Click! Snick! Click!* Then he thrust them in his belt, unharnessed the great drum, and set it down beside him. The gold coins caught the sun and dazzled every eye with avarice. "I'm here to offer certain brave lads the very best career a man ever had. The chance to learn a skill, to become a warrior . . . and get paid damn well for it, too. Look at me!" He clapped his hands upon his ample girth. "Do I look underfed?"

The crowd laughed. Laughing with them, Sergeant Bombast waded into their number, wandering first this way, then that, addressing first this one, then another. "No, I do not. For the very good reason that the Army feeds me well. It feeds me, and clothes me, and all but wipes me arse when I asks it to. And am I grateful? Am I grateful? I am *not*. No, sirs and maidens, so far from grateful am I that I require that the Army pay me for the privilege! And how much, do you ask? How much am I paid? Keeping in mind that my shoes, my food, my breeches, my snot-rag"—he pulled a lace handkerchief from one sleeve and waved it daintily in the air—"are all free as the air we breathe and the dirt we rub in our hair at Candlemas eve. How much am I *paid*?" His seemingly random wander had brought him back to the drum again. Now his fist came down on the drum, making it shout and the gold leap up into the air with wonder. "Forty-three copper pennies a month!"

The crowd gasped.

"Payable quarterly in good honest gold! As you see here! *Or* silver, for them as worships the horned matron." He chucked old Lady Favor-Me-Not under the chin, making her blush and simper. "But that's not all—no, not the half of it! I see you've noticed these coins here. Noticed? Pshaw! You've noticed that I *meant* you to notice these coins! And why not? Each one of these little beauties weighs a full Trojan ounce! Each one is of the good red gold, laboriously mined by kobolds in the griffin-haunted Mountains of the Moon. How could you not notice them? How could you not wonder what I meant to do with them? Did I bring them here simply to scoop them up again, when my piece were done, and pour them back into my pockets?

"Not a bit of it! It is my dearest hope that I leave this village penniless. I *intend* to leave this village penniless! Listen up careful now, for this is the crux of the matter. This here gold's meant for bonuses. Aye! *Recruitment* bonuses! In just a minute I'm going to stop talking. I'll reckon you're glad to hear that!" He waited for the laugh. "Yes, believe it or not, Sergeant Bombast is going to shut up and walk inside this fine establishment, where I've arranged for exclusive use of the common room, and something more as well. Now, what I want to do is to talk—just talk, mind you!—with lads who are strong enough and old enough to become soldiers. How old is that? Old enough to get your girlfriend in trouble!" Laughter again. "But not too old, neither. How old is that? Old enough that not only has your girlfriend jumped you over the broom, but you've come to think of it as a good bit of luck!

"So I'm a talkative man, and I want some lads to talk *with*. And if you'll do it, if you're neither too young nor too old and are willing to simply hear me out, with absolutely no strings attached..." He paused. "Well, fair's fair and the beer's on me. Drink as much as you like, and I'll pay the tab." He started to turn away, then swung back, scratching his head and looking puzzled. "Damn me, if there isn't something I've forgot."

"The gold!" squeaked a young dinter.

"The gold! Yes, yes, I'd forget me own head if it weren't nailed on.

As I've said, the gold's for bonuses. Right into your hand it goes, the instant you've signed the papers to become a soldier. And how much? One gold coin? Two?" He grinned wolfishly. "Doesn't nobody want to guess? No? Well, hold onto your pizzles . . . I'm offering *ten gold coins* to the boy who signs up today! And ten more apiece for as many of his friends as wants to go with him!"

To cheers, he retreated into the tavern.

The dragon had foreseen the recruiter's coming from afar and rehearsed Will in what he must do. "Now do we repay our people for their subservience," he had said. "This fellow is a great danger to us all. He must be caught unawares."

"Why not placate him with smiles?" Will had asked. "Hear him out, feed him well, and send him on his way. That seems to me the path of least strife."

"He will win recruits—never doubt it. Such men have tongues of honey, and glamour-stones of great potency."

"So?"

"The War goes ill for Avalon. Not one of three recruited today is likely to ever return."

"I don't care. On their heads be the consequences."

"You're learning. Here, then, is our true concern: The first recruit who is administered the Oath of Fealty will tell his superior officers about my presence here. He will betray us all, with never a thought for the welfare of the village, his family, or friends. Such is the puissance of the Army's sorcerers."

So Will and the dragon had conferred, and made plans.

Now the time to put those plans into action was come.

The Scrannel Dogge was bursting with potential recruits. The beer flowed freely, and the tobacco as well. Every tavern pipe was in use, and Sergeant Bombast had sent out for more. Within the fog of tobacco smoke, young men laughed and joked and hooted when the recruiter caught the eye of that lad he deemed most apt to sign, smiled, and crooked a beckoning finger. So Will saw from the doorway.

He let the door slam behind him.

All eyes reflexively turned his way. A complete and utter silence overcame the room.

As he walked forward, there was a scraping of chairs and putting down of mugs. Somebody slipped out the kitchen door, and another after him. Wordlessly, a knot of three lads in green shirts left by the main door. Bodies eddied and flowed. By the time Will reached the recruiter's table, there was no one in the room but the two of them.

"I'll be buggered," Sergeant Bombast said wonderingly, "if I've ever seen the like."

"It's my fault," Will said, flustered. He hugged himself with embarrassment.

"Well, I can *see* that! I can see that, and yet shave a goat and marry me off to it if I know what it means. Sit down, boy, sit! Is there a curse on you? The evil eye? Transmissible elf-pox?"

"No, it's not that. It's . . ." Will flushed. "I'm half-mortal."

A long silence.

"Seriously?"

"Aye. There is iron in my blood. 'Tis why I have no true name. Why, also, I am shunned by all." He forced himself to look the recruiter straight in the eye, and saw to his amazement that the man believed his every word. "There is no place in this village for me anymore."

Bombast chewed his thumb, thinking. Then he pointed to a rounded black rock that lay atop a stack of indenture parchments. "This is a name-stone. Not much to look at, is it?"

"No, sir."

"But its mate, which I hold under my tongue, is." He took out a small, lozenge-shaped stone and held it up to be admired. It glistered in the light, blood crimson yet black in its heart. He placed it back in his mouth. "Now, if you were to lay your hand upon the name-stone on the table, your true name would go straight to the one in my mouth, and so to my brain. It's how we enforce the contracts our recruits sign."

"I understand." Will placed his hand upon the black name-stone. He watched the recruiter's face, as nothing happened. There were ways to hide a true name, of course. But they were not likely to be found in a remote river-village in the wilds of the Debatable Hills. Passing the stone's test was proof of nothing. But it was extremely suggestive.

Sergeant Bombast sucked in his breath slowly. Then he opened up the small lockbox on the table before him, and said, "D'ye see this gold, boy?"

"Yes."

"There's eighty ounces of the good red here—none of your white gold nor electrum neither!—closer to you than your one hand is to the other. Yet the bonus you'd get would be worth a dozen of what I have here. *If*, that is, your claim is true. Can you prove it?"

"Yes, sir. I can."

Now, explain this to me again," Sergeant Bombast said. "You live in a house of *iron*?" They were outside now, walking through the silent village. The recruiter had left his drum behind, but had slipped the name-stone into a pocket and strapped the lockbox to his belt.

"It's where I sleep at night. That should prove my case, shouldn't it? It should prove that I'm . . . what I say I am."

So saying, Will walked the recruiter into Tyrant Square. It was a sunny, cloudless day, and the square smelled of dust and cinnamon, with just a bitter under-taste of leaked hydraulic fluid and cold iron. It was noon.

When he saw the dragon, Sergeant Bombast's face fell.

"Oh, fuck," he said.

As if that were the signal, Will threw his arms around the man, while doors flew open and hidden ambushers poured into the square, waving rakes, brooms, and hoes. An old hen-wife struck the recruiter across the back of his head with her distaff. He went limp and heavy in Will's arms. Perforce, Will let him fall.

Then the women were all over the fallen soldier, stabbing, clubbing, kicking, and cursing. Their passion was beyond all bounds, for these were the mothers of those he had tried to recruit. They had all of them fallen in with the orders the dragon had given with a readier will than they had ever displayed before for any of his purposes. Now they were making sure the fallen recruiter would never rise again to deprive them of their sons.

Wordlessly, they did their work and then, wordlessly, they left.

"Drown his motorcycle in the river," the dragon commanded afterward. "Smash his drum and burn it, lest it bear witness against us.

Bury his body in the midden-heap. There must be no evidence that ever he came here. Did you recover his lockbox?"

"No. It wasn't with his body. One of the women must have stolen it."

The dragon chuckled. "Peasants! They'd steal the fillings from their own teeth, if they could. Still, it works out well. The coins are well-buried already under basement flagstones, and will stay so indefinitely. And when an investigator comes through looking for a lost recruiter, he'll be met by a universal ignorance, canny lies, and a cleverly planted series of misleading evidence. Out of avarice, they'll serve our cause better than ever we could order it ourselves."

A full moon sat high in the sky, enthroned within the constellation of the Mad Dog and presiding over one of the hottest nights of the summer when the dragon abruptly announced, "There is a resistance."

"Sir?" Will stood in the open doorway, lethargically watching the sweat fall, drop by drop from his bowed head. He would have welcomed a breeze, but at this time of year when those who had built well enough slept naked on their rooftops and those who had not burrowed into the mud of the riverbed, there were no night breezes cunning enough to thread the maze of huts and so make their way to the square.

"Rebels against my rule. Insurrectionists. Mad, suicidal fools."

A single drop fell. Will jerked his head to move his moon-shadow aside, and saw a large black circle appear in the dirt. "Who?"

"The greenshirties."

"They're just kids," Will said scornfully.

"Do not despise them because they are young. The young make excellent soldiers and better martyrs. They are easily dominated, quickly trained, and as ruthless as you command them to be. They kill without regret, and they go to their deaths readily, because they do not truly understand that death is possible, much less permanent."

"You give them too much credit. They do no more than sign horns at me, glare, and spit upon my shadow. Everybody does that."

"They are still building up their numbers and their courage. Yet their leader, the No-name one, is shrewd and capable. It worries me that he has made himself invisible to your eye, and thus to mine. Walking about the village, you have oft enough come upon a nest in the fields where he slept, or scented the distinctive tang of his scat. Yet when was the last time you saw him in person?"

"I haven't even seen these nests nor smelled the dung you speak of."

"You've seen and smelled, but not been aware of it. Meanwhile, No-name skillfully eludes your sight. He has made himself a ghost."

"The more ghostly the better. I don't care if I never see him again."

"You will see him again. Remember, when you do, that I warned you so."

The dragon's prophecy came true not a week later. Will was walking his errands and admiring, as he so often did these days, how ugly the village had become in his eyes. Half the houses were wattle and daub—little more than sticks and dried mud. Those that had honest planks were left unpainted and gray, to keep down the yearly assessment when the teind-inspector came through from the central government. Pigs wandered the streets, and the occasional scavenger bear as well, pelt moth-eaten and shabby. Nothing was clean, nothing was new, nothing was ever mended.

Such were the thoughts Will was thinking when somebody thrust a gunnysack over his head, while somebody else punched him in the stomach, and a third person swept his feet out from under him.

It was like a conjuring trick. One moment he was walking down a noisy street, with children playing in the dust and artisans striding by to their workshops and goodwives leaning from windows to gossip or sitting in doorways shucking peas, and the next he was being carried swiftly away, in darkness, by eight strong hands.

He fought against the bag from within, but could not break free. His cries, muffled by the sack, were ignored. If anybody heard him—and there had been many about on the street a moment before—nobody came to his aid.

After what seemed an enormously long time, he was dumped on the ground. Angrily, he struggled out of the gunnysack. He was lying on the stony and slightly damp floor of the old gravel pit, south of the village. One crumbling wall was overgrown with flowering vines. He could hear birdsong. Standing, he flung the gunnysack to the ground and confronted his kidnappers.

There were twelve of them and they all wore green shirts.

He knew them all, of course, just as he knew everyone else in the village. But, more, they had all been his friends at one time or another. Were he free of the dragon's bondage, doubtless he would be one of their number. Now, though, he was filled with naught but scorn for them, for he knew exactly how the dragon would deal with them, were they to harm his lieutenant. He would accept them into his body, one at a time, to corrupt their minds and fill their bodies with cancers. He would tell the first in excruciating detail exactly how he was going to die, stage by stage, and he would make sure the eleven others watched as it happened. Death after death, the survivors would watch and anticipate. Last of all would be their leader, No-name.

Will understood how the dragon thought.

"Turn away," he said. "This will do your cause any good whatsoever."

Two of the greenshirties took him by the arms. They thrust him before No-name. His former friend leaned on a crutch of ash wood, tense with hatred, eyes bugged.

"It is good of you to be so concerned for our *cause*. But you do not understand our *cause*, do you? Our *cause* is simply this." No-name slashed something hard across Will's face, cutting a long scratch across his forehead and down one cheek.

"*Llandrysos*, I command you to die!" No-name cried. The greenshirties holding Will's arms released them. He staggered back a step. A trickle of something warm went tickling down his face. He touched his hand to it. Blood.

No-name stared at him. In his outstretched hand was an elf-shot, one of those small stone arrowheads found everywhere in the fields after a hard rain. Will did not know if they had been made by ancient civilizations or grew from pebbles by spontaneous generation. Nor had he known, before now, that to scratch somebody with one while crying out his true name would cause that person to die. But the stench of ozone that accompanied death-magic hung in the air, lifting the small hairs on the back of his neck and tickling his nose with its eldritch force, and the knowledge of what had almost happened was inescapable.

The look of absolute astonishment on No-name's face curdled and became rage. He dashed the elf-shot to the ground. "You were *never* my friend!" he cried in a fury. "The night when we exchanged true names and mingled blood, you lied! You lied! You were as false then as you are now!"

It was true. Will remembered that long-ago time when he and Puck had rowed their coracles to a distant river-island, and there caught fish which they grilled over coals and a turtle from which they made a soup prepared in its own shell. It had been Puck's idea to swear eternal friendship and Will, desperate for a name-friend and knowing Puck would not believe he had none, had invented a true name for himself. He was careful to let his friend reveal first, and so knew to shiver and roll up his eyes when he spoke the name. But he had experienced a terrible guilt then for his deceit, and every time since when he thought of that night.

Even now.

Standing on his one good leg, No-name tossed his crutch upward and seized it near the tip. Then he swung it around and smashed Will in the face.

Will fell.

The greenshirties were all over him then, kicking and hitting him.

Briefly, it came to Will that, if he were included among their number, there were thirteen present and engaged upon a single action. They were a coven, and he the random sacrifice who is worshiped with kicks and blows. Then there was nothing but his suffering and the rage that rose up within him, so strong that though it could not weaken the pain, yet it drowned out the fear he should have felt on realizing that he was going to die. He knew only pain and a kind of wonder: a vast, world-encompassing astonishment that so profound a thing as death could happen to *him,* accompanied by a lesser wonder that No-name and his merry thugs had the toughness to take his punishment all the way to death's portal, and that vital step beyond. They were only boys, after all. Where had they learned such discipline?

"I think he's dead," said a voice. Perhaps it was No-name's. Perhaps not. It came to him as if from an enormous distance.

"Let's see." One last booted foot connected with already broken ribs. He gasped and spasmed. Somebody made a scoffing noise. "That is our message to your master dragon," he said. "If you live, take it to him."

Then silence. Eventually, Will forced himself to open one eye—the other was swollen shut—and saw that he was alone again. It was a gorgeous day, sunny without being at all hot. Birds sang all about him. A sweet breeze ruffled his hair.

He picked himself up, bleeding and weeping with rage, and stumbled back to the dragon.

3

The Last Greenshirtie

Because the dragon would not trust any of the healing-women inside him, Will's injuries were treated by a fluffer. She knelt alongside the leather couch to suck the injuries from Will's body and accept them as her own. It was only as strength returned that he was able to comprehend how young the girl was—younger even than himself. Yet when he feebly tried to push her away, the dragon overruled him. The last drops of pain drained from him, and the child stood.

It would have shamed and sickened a cockatrice to see how painfully the girl hobbled outside again.

"Tell me who did this," the dragon whispered afterward, "and we shall have revenge."

"No."

There was a long hiss, as a steam valve somewhere deep in the thorax vented pressure. "You toy with me."

Will turned his face to the wall. "It's my problem and not yours."

"You *are* my problem."

Within the cockpit there was a constant low-grade mumble and grumble of machinery that faded to nothing when one stopped paying attention to it. Some part of this was the ventilation system, for the air never quite went stale, though it often had a flat under-taste. The rest was surely reflexive—meant solely to keep the dragon alive.

Listening to those mechanical voices, fading deeper and deeper within the tyrant's corpus, Will had a vision of an interior that never came to an end but was a world in itself, all the night contained within that lightless iron body, expanding inward in an inversion of the natural order, stars twinkling in the vasty reaches of distant condensers and fuel pumps and somewhere a crescent moon, perhaps, caught in the gear train. "I won't argue," Will said. "Nor will I ever tell you the merest word of what you desire to learn."

"You will."

"Wait until the Armies of Twilight rise from the sea to overwhelm the land, and still you will be disappointed."

"Think'st so? I tell you, this very hour I will have my will of you."

"No!"

The dragon fell silent. The leather of the pilot's couch gleamed weakly in the soft light. Will's wrists ached.

The outcome was never in doubt. Try though he might, Will could not resist the call of the leather couch, of the grips that filled his hand, of the needles that slid into his wrists. The dragon entered him, and had from him all the information he desired, and this time he did not leave.

Will walked barefoot through the village streets, leaving footprints of flame behind him. He was filled with wrath and the dragon. "*Come out!*" he roared. "Bring out your greenshirties, every one of them, or I shall come after them, street by street, house by house, room by room." He put a hand on the nearest door and wrenched it from its hinges. Broken fragments of boards fell flaming to the ground. Vague shapes fled inward. "Spillikin cowers herewithin. Don't make me come in after him!"

Shadowy hands flung Spillikin face-first into the dirt at Will's feet.

Spillikin was a harmless albino stick figure of a marsh-walker who screamed when Will closed a cauterizing hand about his arm to haul him to his feet.

"Follow me," Will/the dragon said.

So great was Will's twin-spirited fury that none could stand up to him. He burned hot as a bronze idol, and the heat went before him in a great wave, withering plants, charring house fronts, and setting hair ablaze when somebody did not flee from him quickly enough. *"I am wrath!"* he screamed. *"I am blood vengeance! I am justice!* Feed me or suffer!"

The greenshirties were, of course, brought out.

No-name was, of course, not among their number.

The greenshirties were lined up before the dragon in Tyrant Square. They knelt in the dirt before him, heads down. Only two were so unwary as to be caught in their green shirts. The others were bare-chested or in mufti. All were terrified, and one had pissed himself. Their families and neighbors had followed after them and now filled the square with their wails of lament. Will quelled them with a look.

"Your king knows your true names," he said sternly to the greenshirties, "and can kill you with a word."

"It is true," said Hag Applemere. Her face was stiff and impassive, though one of the greenshirties was her own brother.

"More, he can make you suffer such dementia as would make you believe yourselves in Hell, and suffering its torments forever."

"It is true," the hag said.

"Yet he disdains to bend the full weight of his anger upon you. You are no threat to him. He esteems you as creatures of little or no import."

"It is true."

"One only does he desire vengeance upon. Your leader—he who calls himself No-name. This being so, your most merciful lord has made this offer: Stand." They obeyed, and he seized a rake that had been left leaning against one of the houses fronting the square. His grip set the wooden shaft ablaze. He tossed the rake lightly upward and caught it deftly by the tines. "Bring No-name to me while this fire yet burns, and you shall all go free." He held the brand high. "Fail, and you will suffer such torments as the ingenuity of a dragon can devise."

"It is true."

Somebody—not one of the greenshirties—was sobbing softly and steadily. Will ignored it. There was more Dragon within him than Self. It was a strange feeling, not being in control. He liked it. It was like being a small coracle carried helplessly along by a raging current.

The river of emotion had its own logic; it knew where it was going. "Go!" he cried. "Now!"

The greenshirties scattered like pigeons.

Not half an hour later, No-name was brought, bruised and struggling, into the square. His former disciples had tied his hands behind his back and gagged him with a red bandanna. He had been beaten—not so badly as Will had been, but well and thoroughly. Blood ran down from his nose.

Will walked up and down before him. Leaf-green eyes glared up out of that silt-black face with a pure and holy hatred. There could be no reasoning with this boy, nor any taming of him. He was a primal force, an anti-Will, the spirit of vengeance made flesh and given a single unswerving purpose.

All the words that the rebel-boy could not speak poured from those amazing eyes. They passed effortlessly into Will's head, and he accepted them for his own.

Behind No-name stood the village elders in a straight, unmoving line. The Sullen Man moved his mouth slowly, like an ancient tortoise having a particularly deep thought. But he did not speak. Nor did Auld Black Agnes, nor the yage-witch whose use-name no living being knew, nor Lady Nightlady, nor Spadefoot, nor Annie Hop-the-Frog, nor Daddy Fingerbones, nor any of the others. There were mutters and whispers among the villagers, assembled into a loose throng behind them, but nothing coherent. Nothing that could be heard or punished. Now and again, the buzzing of wings rose up over the murmurs and died down again like a cicada on a still summer day, but no one lifted up from the ground.

Back and forth Will stalked, restless as a leopard in a cage, while the dragon within him brooded over possible punishments. A whipping would only strengthen No-name in his hatred and resolve. Amputation was no answer—he had lost one limb already, and was still a dangerous and unswerving enemy. There was no gaol in all the village that could hope to hold him forever, save for the dragon himself, and the dragon did not wish to accept so capricious an imp into his own body.

Death, then. Death was the only answer.

But what sort of death? Strangulation was too quick. Fire was good, but Tyrant Square was surrounded by thatched roofs. A drowning would have to be carried out at the river, out of sight of the dragon himself, who wanted the mana of punishment inextricably linked in his subjects' minds to his own physical self. He could have a hogshead brought in and filled with water or, even better, wine. But then the victim's struggles would have a comic element to them. Also, as a form of strangulation it was still too quick.

Unhurriedly, the dragon considered. Then he brought Will to a stop before the crouching No-name. He raised up Will's head, and let a little of the dragon-light shine out through Will's eyes.

"Crucify him."

To Will's horror, the villagers obeyed.

It took hours. But shortly before dawn, the child who had once been Puck Berrysnatcher, who had been Will's best friend and had died and been reborn as his nemesis, and who had then raised up a rebellion that might well have ended in the dragon's downfall, breathed his last. His body went limp as he surrendered his name to his revered ancestress, Mother Night, and the exhausted villagers could finally turn away and go home and sleep.

Later, after he had departed Will's body at last, the dragon said, "You have done well."

Will lay motionless on the pilot's couch and said nothing.

"I shall reward you."

"No, lord," Will said. "You have done too much already."

"Haummgnmn. Do you know the first sign that a toady has come to accept the rightness of his lickspittle station?"

"No, sir."

"It is insolence. For which reason, you will not be punished but rather, as I said, rewarded. You have grown somewhat in my service. Your tastes have matured. You want something better than your hand. You shall have it. Go into any woman's house and tell her what she must do. You have my permission."

"This is a gift I do not desire."

"Says you! Big Red Margotty has three holes. She will refuse none of them to you. Enter them in whatever order you wish. Do what you like with her tits. Tell her to look glad when she sees you. Tell her to wag her tail and bark like a dog. As long as she has a daughter, she has no choice but to obey. Much the same goes for any of my beloved subjects, of whatever gender or age."

"They hate you," Will said.

"And thou as well, my love and my delight. And thou as well."

"But you with reason."

A long silence. Then the fire-drake said, "I know your mind as you do not. I know what things you wish to do with Red Margotty and what things you wish to do *to* her. I tell you, there are cruelties within you greater than anything I know. It is the birthright of flesh."

"You lie!"

"Do I? Tell me something, dearest victim. When you told the elders to crucify No-name, the command came from me, with my breath and in my voice. But the form . . . did not the *choice* of the punishment come from you?"

Will had been lying listlessly on the couch staring up at the featureless metal ceiling. Now he sat upright, his face cold with shock, as in that instant after being struck before the blood rushes to one's head.

All in a single convulsive movement he stood and turned toward the door.

Which seeing, the dragon sneered, "Do you think to leave me? Do you honestly think you *can*? Then try!" The dragon slammed open his door. The cool and pitiless light of earliest morning flooded the cabin. A fresh breeze swept in, carrying with it scents from the fields and woods. It made Will painfully aware of how his own sour stench permeated the dragon's interior. "You need me more than I ever needed you—I have seen to that! You cannot run away, and if you could, your hunger would bring you back, wrists foremost. You *desire* me. You are empty without me. Go! Try to run! See where it gets you."

Will trembled.

He bolted out the door and ran.

The first sunset away from the dragon, Will threw up violently as the sun went down, and then suffered spasms of diarrhea. Cramping and aching and foul, he hid in the depths of the Old Forest all through the night, sometimes howling and sometimes rolling about the forest floor in pain. A thousand times he thought he must return. A thousand times he told himself: Not yet. Just a little longer and you can surrender. But not yet.

A little longer. Not yet.

Soon. Not yet.

The craving came in waves. When it abated, Will would think: If I can hold out for one day, the second will be easier, and the third easier yet. Then the sick yearning would return, a black need in the tissues of his flesh and an aching in his bones, and he would think again: Not yet. Hold off for just a few more minutes. Then you can give up. Soon. Just a little longer.

A little longer.

He looked at the sky and could see by the position of the Scythe that there was still more of the darkness before him than behind. All his resolve, all his restraint, had filled next to no time whatsoever. He found himself weeping in self-pity. He had tried! The Nameless Ones knew, he had tried, and what had come of it? It was foreordained that he should fail and, that being so, he might as well give up the fight. And so he determined to do.

Soon.

Thus progressed the night, in continual defeat, yet with his surrender perpetually deferred. Sometimes he struck the harsh bark of the elm trees over and over again with his hands, just for the slight distraction the pain afforded him. The Scythe wheeled and dimmed unheeding of his suffering. This wasn't working! It was time he admitted it, and gave in. Time he returned to his master and acknowledged that he could no longer live without him.

Not yet.

Soon.

By morning, the worst of it was over. He washed his clothes in a stream, and hung them up to dry in the wan predawn light. To keep himself warm, he marched back and forth singing the *Chansons Amoreuses de Merlin Sylvanus,* as many of its five hundred verses as he could remember. Finally, when the clothes were only slightly damp, he sought out a great climbing oak he knew of old, and from a hollow withdrew a length of stolen clothesline. Climbing as close to the tippy-top of the great tree as he dared, he lashed himself to its bole. There, lightly rocked by a gentle wind, he slept at last.

A fortnight passed.

Two weeks after his escape, Hag Applemere came to see him in his place of hiding. She found him sitting in the shade of an oak tree at the edge of a meadow rich in milkweed, horned-god's paintbrush and Queen Mab's lace. Honeybees dutifully worked the flowers. A short distance away was a cairn not of modern make but from some long-ago time, which treasure hunters had broken into and from which they had scattered the bones. There he had slept the night before, upon a bed of field grass, while outside it had thundered and stormed. Folk avoided the cairn, for it was said to be wraith-haunted, but if so, the spirits did not bother Will.

The truth-teller bowed before him. "Lord Dragon bids you return to him," she said formally.

Will did not ask the revered hag how she had found him. Wise-women had their skills; nor did they explain themselves. "I'll come when I'm ready. My task here is not yet completed." He was busily sewing together leaves of oak, yew, ash, and alder, using a needle laboriously crafted from a thorn, and short threads made from grasses he had pulled apart by hand. It was no easy work. He had learned from it a new respect for seamstresses.

Hag Applemere frowned. "You place us all in certain danger."

"He will not destroy himself over me alone. Particularly when he is sure that I must inevitably return to him."

"It is true."

Will laughed mirthlessly. "You need not ply your trade here, hallowed lady. Speak to me as you would to any other. I am no longer of the dragon's party."

"As you wish." Hag Applemere drew her shawl about her and plomped down cross-legged before him. All in a single gesture, she had become Bessie again.

"It's a funny thing," Will said, still sewing. "You're not so many years older than I am. I can see that now. If this were a time of peace, who knows? Two years, six years down the line, I might well have grown enough to claim you for my own, by the ancient rites of the greensward and the silver moon."

"Why, Will." Bessie smiled. "Are you flirting with me?"

"If I were"—he bit the thread—"I'd be sitting closer to you. Nor would I be at needlework. I'd have a care to hold my hands free, so that they might advance my argument."

"*You're* feeling bold today." She studied him for a long, silent moment. "And you've grown, too. Physically, I mean, as well as emotionally."

"It's all that cold iron, I think. It forced my growth. Only months ago, I would have found the notion of us together unsettling. But now . . . Well, in any event, it's not going to happen, is it?"

"No," she said, "it's not." Then, cautiously, "Will, whatever are you up to?"

He held up the garment, complete at last, for her to admire. "I have become a greenshirtie." All the time he had sewn, he was barechested, for he had torn up his dragon sark, charred it, and since used strips of it for tinder as he needed fire. Now he donned its leafy replacement.

Clad in his fragile new finery, Will said, "How many would follow me, do you think, were I to show them an end to the dragon's reign?"

"None. As his creature, you are far from beloved. Puck's crucifixion weighs heavy on many a mind."

"Not even you?"

"Oh, well." Bessie blushed. "I'd follow you, yes. For what little that's worth. But I'm only me—what could *I* do?"

"You could lie." Will looked the truth-teller straight in the eye. "You *can* lie," he said, "can't you?"

Bessie turned pale. "Once," she said in a tiny voice, and reflexively covered her womb with both hands. She looked downward, avoiding his glance. "And the price is high, terribly high."

He stood. "Then it must be paid. Let us find a shovel now. It is time for a bit of grave robbery."

It was evening when Will returned at last to the dragon. Tyrant Square had been ringed about with barbed wire and harsh, jury-rigged lights that cast everything in shades of white and gray. A loudspeaker had been set upon a pole with wires leading back into his iron hulk, so that he could speak and be heard in the absence of his lieutenant. Taken together, these improvements made the square look like a concentration camp writ small.

"Go first," Will said to Hag Applemere, "that he may be reassured I mean him no harm."

Breasts bare, clad in the robes and wide hat of her profession, Bessie Applemere passed through a barbed-wire gate (a grimpkin guard opened it before her and closed it after her) and entered the black-and-white arena of the square. "Son of Cruelty." She bowed deeply before the dragon. "Your lieutenant has returned to you."

Will stood hunched in the shadows, head down, hands thrust deep in his pockets. Tonelessly, he said, "I have been broken to your will, great one. I will be your stump-cow, if that is what you want. I beg you. Make me grovel. Make me crawl. Only let me back in."

Hag Applemere spread her arms and bowed again. "It is true."

"You may approach." The dragon's voice sounded staticky and yet triumphant over the loudspeaker.

The sour-faced old grimpkin opened the gate for him, as it had earlier been opened for the hag. Slowly, like a maltreated dog returning to the only hand that had ever fed him, Will crossed the cobbled square. He paused before the loudspeaker, briefly touched its pole with one trembling hand, and then shoved that hand back into his pocket. "You have won. Well and truly have you won. Thou art victorious over all my desire."

It appalled Will how easily the words came, and how natural they sounded coming from his mouth. He could feel the desire to surrender to the tyrant, accept what punishments he would impose, and sink gratefully back into bondage. A little voice within cried: *So easy! So easy!* And so it would be, perilously easy indeed. The realization that a part of him devoutly wished for it made Will burn with humiliation.

The dragon slowly forced one eye half open. "So, boy . . ." Was it his imagination, or was the dragon's voice less forceful than it had been fourteen days ago? "You have learned what need feels like. You suffer from your desires, even as I do. I . . . I . . . am weakened, admittedly, but I am not all so weak as *that!* You thought to prove that I needed you—you have proven the reverse. Though I have neither wings nor missiles and my electrical reserves are low, though I cannot fire my jets without destroying the village and myself as well, yet am I of the mighty, for I have neither pity nor remorse. Thought you I craved a mere boy? Thought you to make me dance attendance on a soft, un-muscled half-mortal mongrel fey? Pfaugh! I do not need you. Never think that I . . . that I *need* you!"

"Let me in," Will whimpered. "I will do whatever you say."

"You . . . you understand that you must be punished for your dis-obedience?"

"Yes," Will said. "Punish me, please. Abase and degrade me, I beg you."

"As you wish"—the dragon's cockpit door hissed open—"so it shall be."

Will took one halting step forward, and then two. Stumblingly, he ran for the open hatchway. One hand closed on the short ladder up the dragon's side. Such an overwhelming sense of relief flooded through his body then that he was sure for an instant that he had re-turned too soon.

But then he let go of the ladder and stepped to the side, so that he was faced with the featureless black iron of the dragon's plating. From one pocket he withdrew Sergeant Bombast's name-stone. Its small blood-red mate was already in his mouth. There was still grave dirt on the one, and a strange taste to the other, but he did not care. He touched the name-stone to the iron plate, and the dragon's true name flowed effortlessly into his mind.

Simultaneously, he took the elf-shot from his other pocket. Then, with all his strength, he drew the elf-shot down the dragon's iron flank, making a long, bright scratch in the rust.

"What are you doing?" the dragon cried in alarm. "Stop that! The hatch is open, the couch awaits!" The words bounced from the shut-tered buildings on every side, where villagers surely listened, though they dared not speak. Then his voice lowered, tinny and harsh from the loudspeaker, but still seductive. "The needles yearn for your wrists, oh best beloved. Even as I yearn for—"

"Baalthazar, of the line of Baalmoloch, of the line of Baalshabat," Will shouted, "I command thee to *die*!"

And that was that.

All in an instant and with no fuss whatever, the dragon king was dead. All his might and malice was become nothing more than inert metal, that might be cut up and carted away to be sold to the scrap foundries that served their larger brothers with ingots to be reforged for the War.

Will hit the side of the dragon with all the might of his fist, to show his disdain. Then he spat as hard and fierce as ever he could, and watched the saliva slide slowly down the black metal. Finally, he unbuttoned his trousers and pissed upon his erstwhile oppressor.

So it was that he finally accepted that the tyrant was well and truly dead.

Bessie Applemere—hag no more—stood silent and bereft on the square behind him. Wordlessly, she mourned her sterile womb and sightless eyes. To her, Will went. He took her hand and led her back to her hut. He opened the door for her. He sat her down upon her bed. "Do you need anything?" he asked. "Water? Some food?"

She shook her head. "Just go. Leave me to lament our victory in solitude."

He left, quietly closing the door behind him. There was no place to go now but home. It took him a moment to remember where that was.

Blind Enna's cottage was at the end of a short lane half overgrown with wild honeysuckle, its scent heavy and sweet on the night air. Enna herself was down on all fours, scrubbing her stoop, when Will came walking up. "Auntie!" he cried. "I've come back!"

The old lady sprang to her feet, bucket in hand. Stricken, she moved her head slowly from side to side, as if attempting to locate him by smell alone. Those vacant eyes were black smudges in the moonlight, that ancient mouth an open and despairing pit. For an instant she stood thus. Then she dashed the water in her bucket onto the ground at his feet, as she might to drive off a carrion dog.

Will could have been no more astonished had she sprouted wings and flown away. "Why, Auntie!" he said. "Don't you remember me? I'm your nephew Will."

"Oh, I remember *you*!" the old hag said. "*And* what you've done, *and* the disgrace you've brought on your family. Consorting with dragons! Crucifying your friends! Oh, you wretched, disobedient child! You horrid little shit! You unholy imp! Were you chained at the mouth of Hell, to serve forever as Ereshkigal's mastiff, your sufferings could not suffice to unwrite your guilt!"

Will stumbled forward, arms outstretched. But, hearing the scuffle of his feet, Blind Enna flung down her bucket and darted inside the house. She was, he realized with a shock, actually afraid of him. "Go away!" she shouted, and made to slam the door.

Will was there in a stride, however, before she could close it, and his strength was greater than hers. He forced his way inside.

It was all strangely homely and familiar. Gently lit by hovering witch-fires, the great room in which he had spent so much of his youth spread itself before him, its every detail a tug at his heart. There was his bed, straw tick mattress and all, in the niche above the black stone fireplace, and there by its head the loose stone where he'd hidden away magic rings, bits of colored glass, and suchlike trash when he'd been a child—by which he meant a few short months ago. Here was the rooster-shaped teakettle that, from a defective charm, could neither crow nor whistle. Here the pious etching of a dryad being flayed alive by two of the Seven. There the large wicker basket that had served his imagination as ship and roc and cavern many a time, and the small wicker basket that had been his helmet, cauldron, and treasure cask equally often. Copper cook-pots gleamed upon their hooks. Bundles of oregano, rosemary, and thyme dried on the rafters. There were moths pinned to the lintels of every window and door.

Blind Enna retreated to her sewing corner and, brandishing her distaff as if it were a weapon, quaveringly said, "Stay away. Don't you dare try to hurt me."

Suddenly, Will was sick and weary unto death of this confrontation, of this day, of all of life and everything else. He had neither energy nor patience enough to endure any of it one moment longer. "Oh, Enna. Nobody's going to hurt anybody. That's all over and done with." And, so saying, he climbed the side of the fireplace up to his bed.

He was astonished how small it was. Though it didn't seem possible, he must have grown since last he'd been here.

When Will awoke, it was almost noon. His aunt had let him sleep late, which was unlike her, and the house was merry with sunshine and dancing dust motes. Blind Enna was nowhere to be seen. She'd left the door wide open, and that was unlike her as well. So Will dressed and washed and made a cold breakfast of bread and jam, washed down with a pint of sour beer, and went out looking for her.

It was a bright blue day and the dragon was dead. In Tyrant Square, the hammermen, clad in protective gear, were dismantling his corpse. They'd brought in a halfwit giant out of the deep hill country to do the heavy lifting. So all the village should have been joyful.

It was not.

The hostility was sharp enough to flense the flesh from his bones. A beldam hanging laundry out her attic window slammed the shutters at the sight of him. A hob rolling a cask of ale down the street would have run the thing right over his feet if Will hadn't danced away. Then, when Will cursed at him, the bastard kept on going, without so much as a glance over his shoulder. It was as if the events of the previous day had never happened at all. Bluebell sprites scowled and flounced away from his tentative smile. The Ice Tongs Man thumbed his nose and shook the reins to make his cart-horse trot. Not a soul in the village had a kindly look for their savior.

You are summoned.

Will spun around. There was nobody there.

Come. The word buzzed in Will's ear. He swatted a hand irritably at the air by his head, though he knew the action to be useless. He recognized Auld Black Agnes's voice. It was a compulsion, then, a command meant for him and him alone, which nobody else could hear. Angrily, he shut it out of his thoughts.

You cannot disobey.

"The fuck I can't."

The street before him beckoned, a gentle downslope guttered with wildflowers and emerald weeds. The way behind felt wrong, difficult, too hot, unpleasant. Hunching his shoulders, Will headed wrongwards.

Turn back.

"Fat chance," Will muttered. Leaning forward, as if into an opposing wind, he navigated the streets, going nowhere in particular but everywhere seeking his aunt. Each step was as familiar to him as the breath in his lungs. Here at the edge of town, not far from the trash pit, was the meadow, thronged with horned-god's paintbrush and Queen Mab's lace, where he had caught fire-mites in a jar when he was little. There the alley where he and his mates had cornered a manticore cub and stoned it to death. Down by the cannery was the shady spot where, all unintentionally, he had seen a russalka undressing through her second-floor window before black and leathery hands had drawn her down out of sight. All of his young life was imprinted upon the circuitry of the village streets.

Everywhere he went, he was shunned. It was as if nothing had changed. As if the dragon still rode him.

As in a sense it did.

He could not pretend the dragon had never been inside him. He could not muffle the experience. He saw the world now as the dragon had, without illusions. He saw it as it really was. The brewer who watered his beer, the tavern-keeper who needled it with ether, and the barfly who drank down the lees of any glass of it left unfinished, were all natural denizens of this place. As were the cobbler who beat his wife, the knocker who solaced her, and the dame verte who lived in the woods and for a price would give the cobbler, and whoever else wanted it, what his wife no longer would. To say nothing of the greenshirties, the neighbors and families who'd betrayed them, and he himself who'd persecuted them.

The village was a shabby and corrupt place, and he the worst of all of them: irredeemable.

And so, having no destination, he wandered by whichever ways were easiest, and so found himself confronted by the open door of Auld Black Agnes's cottage. The interior was dark and inviting.

Enter.

Lost in thought and self-recrimination, Will had let his legs carry them where they would. So it was that, they being under compulsion, he found himself facing the open door of Auld Black Agnes's cottage. The interior was dark, mysterious, inviting. With a wrench, he started to turn away.

Where else do you have to go?

He hesitated. Before the door opening into the dark, inviting, and mysterious interior of Auld Black Agnes's cottage.

Come in.

He did.

Sit down. Auld Black Agnes was sunk deep into a chintz chair with lace doilies on the arms. Her face, as wrinkled and soft as an apple left too many days in the sun, rested on her knees like a pallid spider. She gestured toward a too-small chair at the center of the parlor.

Will sat uncomfortably.

The other elders of the village moot were scattered about the room, some standing, several on folding chairs, three stiff and un-blinking as owls on the divan, and one perched shoeless on the up-right of the sideboard. On an ottoman at Agnes's feet sat Jumping Joan, still for once in her life, eyes spooked and hands folded. It only made sense. With Bessie Applemere a hag no longer, somebody would need to be trained as a truth-teller in her place. She would not speak at this moot or for many a moot to come, of course. Yet her place was important nevertheless, for without a full coven of thirteen, the village moot would not be legal.

The village elders were always true to the letter of the law.

"Tea?" Black Agnes asked.

Mutely, Will accepted a cup. He let her add milk and two lumps of sugar.

"You were late in the coming. I'd almost given up on you entirely."

"I . . . I was looking for my aunt."

The old crone lifted her beak of a nose from her cup and pointed it into the darkest corner of the parlor, where an archway led into a lightless kitchen. "Well, there she is."

With the slightest shift of Will's attention, the darkness assembled itself into his aunt. Blind Enna cringed back, as if sensing his atten-tion, and held her head as she did when listening intently. It seemed to him that her ears pricked higher. "Auntie . . . ," Will said.

Blind Enna wailed in fear. She flung her apron over her face and fled into the interior of the house.

Bewildered, Will stood. "Wait," he said. "I didn't . . . I wouldn't . . ." He had no idea what to say.

To his intense embarrassment, he burst into tears.

As if this were what she were waiting for, Auld Black Agnes said, "All right, the male elders can leave now. We'll handle this as a lady-moot."

"Be ye sure?" the Sullen Man rumbled. "Ye haven't the right of coercion without us."

"He cried," she said. "So we'll do this by persuasion."

So with sighs, mutters, and scrapes of chairs, Daddy Fingerbones and Spadefoot, the two Night Striders, and Ralph the Ferrier, followed the Sullen Man out of the room. Annie Hop-the-Frog took the forgotten teacup from Will's hand. "I don't think you want this," she said kindly. "You haven't touched a drop."

He shook his head hopelessly.

"Look at this darling boy." The matron stroked his hair. "As blond as a dandelion and every bit as foolhardy. It's always the heroes who break your heart, the seventh sons and holy fools. All those who march out to solve the woes of the world without ever asking themselves whether the world wants saving or who has the advantage of weight."

The ladies of the moot clucked in agreement.

"It's a pity that we must exile him."

Shocked, Will said, "What?"

"There's no place for you here, dear," Annie said. "You saw your aunt. The poor thing is terrified of you."

"Everyone is," the yage-witch muttered sourly. Nobody contradicted her.

"I killed the dragon!" Will cried. "I did for you a deed that not all the village put together could have done."

"That is neither here nor there," Annie said.

"I fail to see why it isn't."

"Well, exactly, dear. That's the problem in a nutshell."

"I didn't—"

"It is not what you *did* that is in question here, but what you *are,*" Auld Black Agnes said. "You despise us and our ways. You cannot see our virtues anymore; our foibles and follies fill your sight. You are filled with anger and impatience and a restless urge to be *doing* things. Yet you are young and without wisdom, and there is nobody here who will teach you it. Nor would you accept their teaching if it were offered you. So there is no choice. You must leave the village."

Every word she said rang true. Will could gainsay none of it. "But where will I go?" he asked despairingly.

"Alas," she replied, "that is of no concern to me."

Scythe Song

The first several days after leaving the village were peaceful. Will traveled south along the river road and then, where the marshlands rose up, followed that same road eastward and inland among the farms. Now and then he got a ride on a hay-wain or a tractor, and sometimes a meal or two as well in exchange for work. He fed himself from the land and bathed in starlit ponds. When he could not find a barn or an unlocked utility shed, he burrowed into a haystack, wrapping his cloak about him for a defense against ticks. Such sleights and stratagems were no great burden for a country fey such as himself.

His mood varied wildly. Sometimes he felt elated to have left his old life behind. Other times, he fantasized vengeance, bloody and sweet. It was shameful of him, for the chief architect of his ruin was dead at his own hand and the others in the village were as much the war-dragon's victims as he. But he was no master of his own thoughts, and at such moments would bite and claw at his own flesh until the fit passed.

Then one morning the roads were thronged with people. It was like a conjuring trick in which a hand is held out, palm empty, to be briefly covered by a silk handkerchief which, whisked away, reveals a mound of squirming eels. Will had gone to sleep with the roads empty and that night dreamed of the sea. He woke to an odd murmuring and, when he dug his way out of the hay, discovered that it was voices, the weary desultory talk of folk who have come a great distance and have a long way yet to go.

Will stood by the road letting the dust-stained travelers stream past him like a river while his vision grabbed and failed to seize, searching for and not finding a familiar face among their number. Until at last he saw a woman whose bare breasts and green sash marked her as a hag, let slide her knapsack to the ground and wearily sit upon a stone at the verge of the road. He placed himself before her and bowed formally. "Reverend Mistress, your counsel I crave. Who are all these folk? Where are they bound?"

The hag looked up. "The Armies of the Mighty come through the land," she said, "torching the crops and leveling the villages. Terror goes before them and there are none who dare stand up to their puissance, and so perforce all must flee, some into the Old Forest, and others across the border. 'Tis said there are refugee camps there."

"Is it your wisdom," he asked, touching his brow as the formula demanded, "that we should travel thither?"

The young hag looked tired beyond her years. "Whether it is wisdom or not, it is there that I am bound," she said. And without further word she stood, shouldered her burden, and walked on.

The troubles had emptied out the hills and scoured from their innermost recesses many a creature generally thought to be extinct. Downs trolls and albino giants, the latter translucent-skinned and weak as tapioca pudding, trudged down the road, along with ogres, brown men, selkies, chalkies, and other common types of hobs and feys. After a moment's hesitation, Will joined them.

Thus it was that he became a refugee.

Late that same day, when the sun was high and Will was passing a field of oats, low and golden under a harsh blue sky, he realized he had to take a leak. Far across the field the forest began. He turned his back on the road and in that instant was a carefree vagabond once more. Through the oats he strode, singing to himself a harvest song:

> "Mowers, weary and brown, and blithe,
> What is the word methinks ye know . . ."

It was a bonny day, and for all his troubles Will could not help feeling glad to be alive and able to enjoy the rich gold smell that rose from the crops and the fresh green smell that came from the woods and the sudden whirr of grasshoppers through the air.

> "What is the word that, over and over,
> Sings the Scythe to the flowers and grass?"

Will was thinking of the whitesmith's daughter, who had grown so busty over the winter and had blushed angrily last spring simply for his looking at her, though he hadn't meant a thing by it at the time. Later, however, reflecting upon that moment, his thoughts had gone where she'd earlier assumed them to be. Now he would have liked to bring her here at hottest midday with a blanket and find a low spot in the fields, where the oats would hide them, and perform with her those rites that would guarantee a spectacular harvest.

A little girl came running across the field, arms outstretched, golden braids flying behind her. "Papa! Papa!" she cried.

To his astonishment, Will saw that she was heading toward him. Some distance behind, two stickfellas and a lubin ran after her, as if she had just escaped their custody. Straight to Will the little girl flew and leapt up into his arms. Hugging him tightly, she buried her small face in his shoulder.

"Help me," she whispered. "Please. They want to rape me."

Perhaps there was a drop of the truth-teller's blood in him, for her words went straight to Will's heart and he did not doubt them. Falling immediately into the role she had laid out for him, he spun her around in the air as if in great joy, then set her down and, placing his arms on her shoulders, sternly said, "You little imp! You must never run away like that again—never! Do you understand me?"

"Yes, Papa." Eyes downcast, she dug a hole in the dirt with the tip of one shoe.

The girl's pursuers came panting up. "Sir! Sir!" cried the lubin. He had a dog's head, like all his kind, was great of belly but had a laborer's arms and shoulders, and wore a wide-brimmed hat with a dirty white plume. He swept off the hat and bowed deeply. "Saligos de Gralloch is my name, sir. My companions and I found your daughter wandering the roads, all by herself, hungry and lost. Thank the Seven we . . ." He stopped, frowned, tugged at one hairy ear. "You're her *father*, you say?"

"Good sir, my thanks," Will said, as if distracted. He squatted and hugged the child to him again, thinking furiously. "It was kind of you to retrieve her to me."

The lubin gestured, and the stickfellas moved to either side of Will. He himself took a step forward and stared down on Will, black lips curling back to expose yellow canines. "Are you her father? You *can't* be her father. You're too young."

Will felt the dragon-darkness rising up in him, and fought it down. The lubin outweighed him twice over, and the stickfellas might be slight, but their limbs were as fast and hard as staves. He would have to be cunning. "She was exposed to black iron as an infant and almost died," he said lightly. "So I sold a decade of my life to Year Eater to buy a cure."

One of the stickfellas froze, like a lifeless tree rooted in the soil, as he tried to parse out the logic of what Will had said. The other skittishly danced backward and forward on his long legs and longer arms. The lubin narrowed his eyes. "That's not how it works," he rumbled. "It can't be. Surely, when you sell a fraction of yourself to that dread power, it makes you older, not younger."

But Will had stalled long enough to scheme and knew now what to do. "My darling daughter," he murmured, placing a thumb to his lips, kissing it, and then touching the thumb to the girl's forehead. All this was theater and distraction. Heart hammering with fear, he fought to look casual as he took her hand, so that the tiny dab of warm spittle touched her fingers. "My dear, sweet little . . ."

There was a work of minor magic that every lad his age knew. You came upon a sleeping friend and gently slid his hand into a pan of warm water. Whereupon, impelled by who-knew-what thaumaturgic principles, said friend would immediately piss himself. The spittle would do nicely in place of water. Focusing all his thought upon it, Will mumbled, as if it were an endearment, one of his aunt's favorite homeopathic spells—one that was both a diuretic and a laxative.

With a barrage of noises astonishing from one so small, the sluice gates of the girl's body opened. Vast quantities of urine and liquid feces exploded from her nether regions and poured down her legs. "*Oh!*" she shrieked with horror and dismay. "Oh! Oh! Oh!"

Her abductors, meanwhile, drew back in disgust. "Pfaugh!" said one of the stickfellas, waving a twiggish hand before his nose. The other was already heading back toward the road.

"I'm sorry." Will smiled apologetically, straightening. "She has this little problem . . ." The girl tried to kick him, but he nimbly evaded her. "As you can see, she lacks self-control."

"*Oh!*"

Only the lubin remained now. He stuck out a blunt forefinger, thumb upward, as if his hand were a gun, and shook it at Will. "You've fooled the others, perhaps, but not me. Cross Saligos once more, and it will be your undoing." He fixed Will with a long stare, then turned and trudged heavily away.

"Look what you *did* to me!" the little girl said angrily when Saligos was finally out of sight and they were alone. She plucked at the cloth of her dress. It was foul and brown.

Amused, Will said, "It got you out of a fix, didn't it? It got us both out of a fix." He held out his hand. "There's a stream over in the woods there. Come with me, and we'll get you cleaned off."

Carefully keeping the child at arm's length, he led her away.

The girl's name was Esme. While she washed herself in the creek, Will went a little way downstream and laundered her clothes, rinsing and wringing them until they were passably clean. He placed them atop some nearby bushes to dry. By the time he was done, Esme had finished too and crouched naked by the edge of the creek, drawing pictures in the mud with a twig. To dry her off, he got out his blanket from the knapsack and wrapped it around her.

Clutching the blanket about her as if it were the robes of state,

Esme broke off a cattail stalk, and with it whacked Will on both shoulders. "I hereby knight thee!" she cried. "Arise, Sir Hero of Grammarie Fields."

Anybody else would have been charmed. But the old familiar darkness had descended upon Will once more, and all he could think of was how to get Esme off his hands. He had neither resources nor prospects. Traveling light, as he must, he dared not take on responsibility for the child. "Where are you from?" he asked her.

Esme shrugged.

"How long have you been on the road?"

"I don't remember."

"Where are your parents? What are their names?"

"Dunno."

"You do have parents, don't you?"

"Dunno."

"You don't know much, do you?"

"I can scour a floor, bake a sweet-potato pie, make soap from animal fat and lye and candles from beeswax and wicking, curry a horse, shear a lamb, rebuild a carburetor, and polish shoes until they shine." She let the blanket sag so that it exposed one flat proto-breast and struck a pose. "I can sing the birds down out of the trees."

Involuntarily, Will laughed. "Please don't." Then he sighed. "Well, I'm stuck with you for the nonce, anyway. When your clothes have dried, I'll take you upstream and teach you how to tickle a trout. It'll be a useful addition to your many other skills."

There were armies on the move, and no sensible being lingered in a war zone. Nevertheless they did. By the time the sun went down, they had acquired trout and mushrooms and wild tubers enough to make a good meal, and built a small camp at the verge of the forest. Like most feys, Will was a mongrel. But there was enough woods-elf in his blood that, if it weren't for the War, he could be perfectly comfortable here forever. He built a nest of pine boughs for Esme and once again wrapped her in his blanket. She demanded of him a song, and then a story, and then another story, and then a lullaby. By degrees she began to blink and yawn, and finally she slid away to the realm of sleep.

She baffled Will. The girl was as much at ease as if she had lived in this camp all her life. He had expected, after the day's events, that she would fight sleep and suffer nightmares. But here, where it took his utmost efforts to keep them warm and fed, she slept the sleep of the innocent and protected.

Feeling sorely used, Will wrapped his windbreaker about himself, and fell asleep as well.

Hours later—or possibly mere minutes—he was wakened from uneasy dreams by the thunder of jets. Will opened his eyes in time to see a flight of dragons pass overhead. Their afterburners scratched thin lines of fire across the sky, dwindling slowly before finally disappearing over the western horizon. He crammed his hand into his mouth and bit the flesh between thumb and forefinger until it bled. How he used to marvel at those fearsome machines! He had even, in the innocence of his young heart, loved them and imagined himself piloting one someday. Now the sight of them nauseated him.

He got up, sourly noting that Esme slept undisturbed, and threw an armload of wood on the fire. He would not be able to sleep again tonight. Best he were warm while he awaited the dawn.

So it was that he chanced to be awake when a troop of centaurs galloped across the distant moonlit fields, gray as ghosts and silent as so many deer. At the sight of his campfire, their leader gestured and three of them split away from the others. They sped toward him. Will stood at their approach.

The centaurs pulled up with a thunder of hooves and a spatter of kicked-up dirt. "It's a civilian, Sarge," one said. They were all three female and wore red military jackets with gold piping and shakos to match. "Happy, clueless, and out on a fucking walking tour of the countryside, apparently."

"It's not aware that there's a gods-be-damned war on, then?"

"Apparently not." To Will, she said, "Don't you know that the Sons of Fire are on their way?"

"I have no idea what you're talking about," Will said shakily. Then, gathering his courage, "Nor whose side you are on."

One centaur snorted in disdain. A second struck the insignia on her chest and cried, "We are the Fifth Amazons—the brood mares of death! Are you a fool, not to have heard of us?"

But the third said, "It does not matter whose side we are on. The rock people come, the dwellers-in-the-depths from the Land of Fire. Even now they climb toward the surface, bringing with them both immense heat and a fearful kinetic energy. When they arrive, the ground will bubble and smoke. All of *this*"—she swept her arm to take in all the land about them—"will be blasted away. Then will the battle begin. And it will be such that all who stand within the circuit of combat, no matter what their allegiance, will die."

"Come away, Antiope," said the first, who was older than the other two and, by the tone of authority in her voice, the sergeant. "We were told to clear the land of any lingering noncombatants. Our orders do not require us to rescue idiots."

"What's this?" said the second. She knelt. "A child—and a girl!"

Will started forward, to snatch Esme away from the centaur. But the other two cantered sideways into his path, blocking him. "Look at her, Sergeant Lucasta. The poor little bugger is as weary as a kitten. She doesn't awaken, even when I pick her up." She handed Esme to her superior, who held the sleeping child against her shoulder.

"We've wasted enough time," Sergeant Lucasta said. "Let's go."

"Should we douse the fire?" Antiope asked.

"Let it burn. This time tomorrow, what fucking difference will it make?"

The second centaur packed up Will's gear with startling efficiency, stowed it in leathern hip-bags, and started after her commander. Then the youngest of the three seized Will's arm and effortlessly lifted him onto her back. She reared up and hastily he placed his arms around her waist. "My name is Campaspe." She grinned over her shoulder. "Hang on tight, manling. I'm going to give you the ride of your life."

So began their midnight gallop. Up hill and down they sped, past forests and farms. All the world flowed by like a billowing curtain, a thin veil over something vast, naked, and profound. Will tried to imagine what lay beneath and could not. "Will all this really be destroyed?" he asked. "Is it possible?"

"If you'd been through half the shit *I* have," Campaspe replied, "you would not doubt it for an instant. Rest quiet now, it's a long ride." Taking her at her word, Will lay his cheek against Campaspe's back. It was warm. Her muscles moved smoothly beneath him and between his legs. He became acutely aware of the clean stench of her sweat.

"Hey! Sarge! I think the civilian likes me—he's getting hard!"

"He'll need to mount a stump if he expects to stick it to you," the sergeant replied.

"At least he won't need any petroleum jelly!" Antiope said.

"That was . . . I didn't . . ." Will said hastily, as they all laughed.

"Oh, really?" Campaspe's eyes and teeth flashed scornfully. She took his hands from around her waist and placed them firmly on her breasts. "Deny it now!"

Horrified, Will snatched his hands away, almost fell, and seized Campaspe's waist again. "I couldn't! The Nameless Ones forbid it!"

"It would be bestiality for me too, little ape-hips," she laughed. "But what's a war for, if not to loosen a few rules here and there? Eh, Sarge?"

"Only fucking reason *I* know."

"I knew a gal in the Seventh who liked to do it with dogs," Antiope said. "Big ones, of course. Mastiffs. So one day she . . ." And she went on to relate a story so crude that Will flushed red as her jacket. The others laughed like horses, first at the story and then at his embarrassment.

For hours they coursed over the countryside, straight as falcons and almost as fast. By slow degrees, Will grew accustomed to Campaspe's badinage. She didn't mean anything by it, he realized. But she was young and in a war, and flirted out of nervousness. Once again he lay his cheek against her back, and she reached behind her to scratch his head reassuringly. It was then that he noticed the brass badge on her shoulder, and twisted about so he could read it. An image had been worked into the badge, a thin line of moonsilver that glimmered clear and bright by the light of Selene, showing three sword-wielding arms radiant from a common point, like a three-limbed swastika. Will recognized the symbol as the triskelion of the Armies of the Mighty. And he was in their power! He shuddered in revulsion and fear.

Sergeant Lucasta, galloping near, saw this and shifted the slumbering Esme from one shoulder to the other. "So you've caught on at last," she said. "We're the wicked baby-eating enemy. And yet, oddly enough, we're the ones clearing you away from an extremely danger-ous situation, rather than your own fucking army. Kind of makes you think, don't it?"

"It's because he's a civilian, right, Sarge? Not much sport in killing civilians," Campaspe said.

"They can't fight and they can't shoot," Antiope threw in. "They're lucky if they know how to die."

"Fortunately, they have us to do all those things for them." Sergeant Lucasta held up a hand, and they slowed to a walk. "We should have joined up with the platoon a long time ago."

"We haven't missed 'em," Antiope said. "I can still see their spoor."

"And smell their droppings," Campaspe added.

They had come to a spinney of aspens. "We'll stop here for a bit and rest," the sergeant said, "while I work this thing through in my head."

Campaspe came to a halt and Will slid gratefully from her back. She took a thermos of coffee from a harness-bag and offered him some.

"I . . . I have to take a leak," he said.

"Piss away," she said carelessly. "You don't need *my* permission." And then, when he started into the woods, "Hey! Where the fuck do you think you're going?"

Again Will flushed, remembering how casually his companions had voided themselves during the night, dropping turds behind them even as they conversed. "My kind needs privacy," he said, and plunged into the brush.

Behind him, he heard Campaspe say, "Well, la-de-da!" to the ex-treme amusement of her comrades.

Deep into the spinney he went, until he could no longer hear the centaurs talking. Then he unzipped and did his business against the side of a pale slim tree. Briefly, he considered slipping away. The woods were his element, even as open terrain favored the centaurs. He could pass swiftly and silently through underbrush that would slow them to a walk and bury himself so cunningly in the fallen leaves of the forest floor that they would never find him. But did he dare leave Esme with them? Centaurs had no bathroom manners to speak of because they were an early creation, like trolls and giants. They were less subtle of thought than most thinking creatures, more primal in emotion. Murder came to them more easily than spite, lust than love, rapture than pity. They were perfectly capable of killing a small child simply out of annoyance with him for evading their grasp.

Esme meant nothing to him. But still, he could not be responsible for her death.

Yet as he approached the spot where he had left their captors, he heard childish laughter. Esme was awake, and apparently having the time of her life. Another few steps brought him out of the aspens, and he saw Sergeant Lucasta sitting in the grass, forelegs neatly tucked under her, playing with Esme as gently as a mother would her own foal. Will could not help but smile. Females were females, whatever their species, and whatever their allegiance, Esme was probably as safe with these lady cavaliers as anywhere.

"Again!" Esme shrieked. "Please, again?"

"Oh, very well," Sergeant Lucasta said fondly. She lifted her revolver, gave the cylinder a spin, cocked the hammer, and placed it to the child's forehead.

"*Stop!*" Will screamed. Running forward, he snatched up Esme into his arms. "What in the name of sanity do you think you're doing?"

The sergeant flipped open the cylinder, looked down into the chamber. "There's the bullet. She would have died if you hadn't stopped me. Lucky."

"I *am*," Esme said. "I *am* lucky!"

The centaur snapped the cylinder shut, gave it a spin, and all in one motion pointed it at Esme again and pulled the trigger.

Snap! The hammer fell on an empty chamber.

Esme laughed with delight. "For the sake of the Seven!" Will cried. "She's only a child!" He noticed now, as he had not before, that Campaspe and Antiope were nowhere to be seen. This did not strike him as a good omen.

"She has the luck of innocence," Sergeant Lucasta observed, holstering her revolver. "Twenty-three times I spun the cylinder and fired at her, and every time the hammer came down on an empty chamber. Do you know what the odds are against that?"

"I'm not very good at math."

"Neither am I. Pretty fucking unlikely, though, I'm sure of that."

"I *told* you I was lucky," Esme said. She struggled out of Will's arms. "Nobody ever listens to me."

"Let me ask you a question, then, and I promise to listen. Who is he"—she jerked a thumb at Will—"to you?"

"My papa," Esme said confidently.

"And who am I?"

The little girl's brow furrowed in thought. "My . . . mama?"

"Sleep," said the centaur. She placed a hand on the girl's forehead and drew it down over her eyes. When she removed it, Esme was asleep. Carefully, she laid the child down in the grass. "I've seen this before," she said. "I've seen a lot of things most folks never suspect. She is old, this one, old and far from a child, though she thinks and acts as one. Almost certainly, she's older than the both of us combined."

"How can that be?"

"She's sold her past and her future, her memories and adolescence and maturity, to the Year Eater in exchange for an undying present and the kind of luck it takes for a child to survive on her own in a world like ours."

Will remembered the lie he had told the lubin and experienced a sudden coldness. The tale had come to him out of nowhere. This could not be mere coincidence. Nevertheless, he said, "I don't believe it."

"How did you come to be traveling with her?"

"She was running from some men who wanted to rape her."

"Lucky thing you chanced along." The sergeant patted the pockets of her jacket and extracted a pipe. "There is only a limited amount of luck in this world—perhaps you've noticed this for yourself? There is only so much, and it cannot be increased or decreased by so much as a tittle. This one draws luck from those around her. We should have rejoined our companions hours ago. It was good luck for her to be carried so much farther than we intended. It was bad luck for us to do so." She reached into her hip-bags and came out with a tobacco pouch. "The child is a monster—she has no memory. If you walk away from her, she will have forgotten you by morning."

"Are you telling me to abandon her?"

"In a word? Yes."

Will looked down on the sleeping child, so peaceful and so trusting. "I . . . I cannot."

Sergeant Lucasta shrugged. "Your decision. Now we come to the second part of our little conversation. You noticed that I sent my girls away. That's because they like you. They don't have my objectivity. The small abomination here is not the only one with secrets, I think." All the while she spoke, she was filling her pipe with tobacco and tamping it down. "There's a darkness in you that the rookies can't see. Tell me how you came to be traveling by yourself, without family or companions."

"My village cast me out."

The sergeant stuck a pipe into the corner of her mouth, lit it, and sucked on it meditatively. "You were a collaborator."

"That oversimplifies the matter, and makes it out to be something that was in my power to say yea or nay to. But, yes, I was."

"Go on."

"A . . . a dragon crawled into our village and declared himself king. It was wounded. Its electrical system was all shot to hell, and it could barely make itself heard. It needed a lieutenant, a mediator between itself and the village. To . . . give orders. It chose me."

"You did bad things, I suppose. You didn't mean to, at first, but one thing led to another. People disobeyed you, so they had to be punished."

"They hated me! They blamed me for their own weakness!"

"Oh?"

"They wouldn't obey! I had no choice. If they'd obeyed, they wouldn't have been punished!"

"Go on."

"Yes, okay, I did things! But if I hadn't, the dragon would have found out. I would've been punished. They would've been punished even worse than they were. I was just trying to protect them." Will was crying now.

For a long moment the sergeant was silent. Then she sighed and said, "Killed anyone?"

"One. He was my best friend."

"Well, that's war for you. You're not as bad a sort as you think you are, I suspect. In any case, you're neither a spy nor an agent provocateur, and that's all that really concerns me. So I can leave you behind with a clean conscience."

"You can what?"

"You're far enough from the epicenter now that you should be safe. And we'll never rendezvous with our platoon unless we ditch the luck-eater." She unholstered her gun and pointed it at the sleeping child. "Shall we try the monster's luck one last time? Or should I shoot it up in the air?"

"In the air," Will said tightly. "Please."

She lifted the gun and fired. The report shattered the night's silence, but did not awaken Esme.

"Lucky again," Sergeant Lucasta said.

Summoned by the gunshot, Campaspe and Antiope trotted back to the spinney's edge. They received the news that the civilians were to be left behind without any visible emotion. But when Will bade them farewell, Campaspe bent as if to give him a swift peck on the cheek, and then stuck her tongue down his throat and gave his stones a squeeze. Antiope dumped his gear at his feet and playfully swatted him on his aching bum.

The sergeant, too, leaned down as if to kiss him. Will stiffened involuntarily. But instead, she said, "Listen to an old campaigner: Trouble will follow you so long as the child is in your care." She straightened. "Keep the lodestar to your left shoulder, and then at dawn walk toward the sun. That will take you east—there are refugee camps just across the Great River. Best not dawdle."

"Thank you."

"Let's go, ladies—this war isn't going to fucking well fight itself!"

The cavaliers cantered off without so much as a backward glance.

Will gently shook Esme awake, shouldered his pack, and took her hand. They walked to the dawn and beyond, ever eastward. When Esme tired, he picked her up and carried her. The sun was still low in the sky when he could carry her no longer. Ranging away from the road, then, he found a junk car in a thicket of sumac and made beds for them on the front and back seats.

For a time, he slept.

In the village, before driving him out, the lady-elders had made Will a bundle of sandwiches and placed a cantrip on his knapsack to alert and alarm him should anybody meddle with it in his sleep.

So now Will found himself sitting bolt upright, fully awake and staring at his knapsack. Saligos de Gralloch had opened the driver's side front door and had both hands buried to the hilt in it. He grinned like a hound. "Ye're up, young master. That's good. There don't seem to be any gold in here."

"What happened to your stickfellas?"

"We had a falling out. I had to kill them. Lucky I chanced on you—otherwise I'd be all by myself."

"Not luck," Will said. "You broke a pin or button in two when you first found the child and hid half among her clothes, against the chance of her slipping away from you. Then, today, you followed the other half here."

"That's very sharp for one who's just woke up," Saligos said appreciatively. "I note, however, that you didn't say 'my daughter,' but 'the child.' So you're not her father after all. I know my peasants. There's got to be some gold on you somewhere, even if it's no more than a single coin to lead you back someday to the crock you buried out behind your croft."

"Nope. Sorry."

"That's too bad." Casually, Saligos removed his belt. "You interrupted something yesterday. So, before I make sure as you haven't hid the stuff somewhere about your person, I'm going to tie your wrists to the steering wheel. You can watch while I do *her*"—he nodded toward Esme, still asleep in the back seat—"good and hard."

Will felt the dragon-darkness rising up in him, and this time, rather than fighting it down, he embraced it, letting it fill his brain, letting its negative radiance shine from his eyes like black flame.

The lubin's lips curled back in a snarl. Then he gasped as Will lunged forward and seized him.

Will squeezed the creature's forearms. Bones cracked and splintered under his fingers. "Do you like it now?" he asked. "Do you like it now that it's happening to *you*?"

Saligos de Gralloch squirmed helplessly in his implacable grip. The lubin's lips were moving, though Will could not hear him through the rush of blood pounding in his ears. Doubtless he was pleading for mercy. Doubtless he whimpered. Doubtless he whined. That was what he *would* do. Will knew the type only too well.

First the dragon-lust turned the world red, as if he were peering out through a scrim of pure rage, and then it turned his vision black. When he could see again, Saligos de Gralloch's mangled body lay steaming and lifeless on the ground beside the car. Will's fingers ached horribly, and his hands were tarred with blood up to his wrists. The lubin stared blindly upward, teeth exposed in a final, hideous grin. Something that might be his heart lay on the ground beside his ruptured chest.

"Papa?" Esme, awakened surely by the sound of what he had done, cranked down the back seat window, and poked out her head. "Are you all right?"

Sick with revulsion, Will turned away and shook his head heavily from side to side. "You should leave," he said. "Flee me—run!"

"Why?"

"There is something . . . very bad in me."

"That's okay."

Will stared down at his hands. Murderer's hands. His head was heavy and his heart was pounding so hard his chest ached. He was surprised he could still stand. "You don't understand. The dragon left a bit of himself in me. I can't get rid of it!"

"I don't mind." Esme got out of the car, careful not to step on the corpse. "Bad things don't bother me. That's why I sold myself to the Year Eater."

He turned back and stared long and hard at the child. She looked so innocent: golden-haired, large-headed, toothpick-legged, skin as brown as a berry. "You don't have any memory," he said. "How do you know about the Year Eater?"

"The horse-lady thinks I have no memory. That's wrong. I only forget people and things that happen. I remember what's important. You taught me to tickle trout. I remember that. Somebody else taught me how to undo a sleep spell." She turned her back on what remained of Saligos. "But by this afternoon, I'll have forgotten *him* and what you had to do to him as well."

Then she led Will to a nearby sump to wash his hands. While he did so, she laundered his shirt, whacking it on a rock until every last trace of gore was gone from it. Wordlessly, she began to sing the tune he had been singing when first he saw her. Despite all that had happened, she was perfectly happy. She was, Will realized then, as damned and twisted a thing as he himself. Nobody could blame him were he to leave her behind.

Then again, perhaps they belonged together, so freakish were they both.

He honestly did not know what was the right thing to do.

At noon, the land behind them turned to smoke. Not long after, an enormous blast reverberated across the land, so loud that refugees crouched in the road with their hands over their ears, and no one could hear properly for an hour afterward. All of the western shire was swallowed up in a deep and profound darkness punctuated by transient gouts of flame as farmhouses and silos were engulfed in molten rock and exploded. Those who had lived within eyeshot raised their voices in anguished shrieks. In an instant, all the generations of lives beyond counting that had been written onto the land were erased from it. It was as if they all, the cherished and the forgotten alike, had ceased ever to have been.

The giants that rose up out of the smoke burned bright as the Holy City itself, hotter than the forges of the sunset. By gradual degrees they darkened and cooled, first to a magma glow, then to a gray barely distinguishable from the clouds. There were two of them, and they carried cudgels. They still shone a ruddy red when they began to wheel and turn upon each other. They were great shadowy bulks, lost in the sky, when their cudgels were hauled as far back and high as they would go.

The giants' motions were slow beyond the eye's ability to discern. But if Will looked away for a few minutes and then back, their positions would be subtly altered. Over the long course of the morning, their cudgels swung toward each other. At noon, they connected. For as long as it would take to count to thirty, the silence was absolute. Then the blast rolled across the land. Will saw it coming, like a great wind making the trees bow down before it. He grabbed Esme and flung them both into a ditch, and so evaded the worst of it.

They walked many miles that day, though the Great River held itself ever distant and remote. Sometimes they rested, but only briefly. More, Will did not dare. At last, around sundown, Esme began to cry for weariness. Will stooped and, with a grunt, picked her up. His legs did not quite buckle.

"*Hush,*" he sang to her, "*hush, ah, hush.*" It was the song of the scythe on a hot summer's day. "*Hush.*" She was just a child, after all, whatever else she might be.

Eventually, Esme fell asleep on Will's shoulder. He plodded along for a while, and then a truck driver slowed down and offered to let him sit on the tailgate along with four others, just because Esme looked particularly small and weary. The driver said he was going all the way to the camps, and that with luck they would be there by morning.

So, really, she paid for herself.

5

The Crows of Camp Oberon

Camp Oberon stank of overflowing latrines and pitchpenny magicks. The latter were necessary to compensate for the former. Glamours as fragile as tissue paper were tacked up on almost every tent flap, so that walking down the dirt lanes between canvas dwellings Will caught sudden whiffs of eglantine, beeswax, cinnamon, and wet oak leaves, felt the cold mist of a waterfall, heard the faint strains of faraway elfin music. None of it was real, or even convincing, but each was a momentary distraction from his surroundings. Whitewashed rocks picked out borders to the meager flowerbeds planted about the older tents.

The camp was situated on a windswept ground high above the Aelfwine. Its perimeters were patrolled but it had no fences—where could anybody go? Thrice daily a contingent of yellow-jackets herded the refugees into mess tents for meals. Between times, the old folks coped with boredom by endlessly reminiscing about lives and villages they would never see again. The younger ones, however, talked politics. "They'll be shipping us East," a kobold said knowingly at one such impromptu discussion, "to the belly of the beast, the very heart of that dire and kingless empire, the Tower of Whores itself. Where we'll each be given a temporary ID card, fifty dollars, a voucher for a month's housing, and the point of their boots in our backsides for putting them to such expense."

"They could of saved themselves a shitload of expense by not destroying our fucking homes in the first place," a dwarf growled. "What's the fucking point?"

"It's their policy. Rather than leaving enemies at their borders, they absorb us into themselves. By the time we've found our feet through pluck and hard work, our loyalties have shifted and we become good, obedient citizens."

"Does this work?" Will asked dubiously.

"Not so far." The kobold got up, unbuttoned the corner flaps of the tent, and took a long piss into the weeds out back. "So far, all it's done is made them into the most contentious and least governable society in existence. Which surely has something to do with their sending their armies here to solve all our problems for us, but fuck if I know what." He turned back, zipping his fly.

"This is just venting," somebody said. "The question is, what should we *do*?"

From the depths of the tent, where it was a darkness floating in darkness, an uneasy shimmer that the eye could perceive but not resolve into an image, a ghast said, "A trip wire, a bundle of matches, and some sandpaper can set off a coffee can filled with black powder and carpet tacks. A pinch of chopped tiger's whiskers sprinkled into food will cause internal bleeding. A lock of hair tied to an albino toad and buried in a crossroads at midnight with the correct incantation will curse somebody with a slow and lingering death. These skills and more I might be convinced to teach to any interested patriots."

There was an awkward silence, and then several of those present got up and left.

Will joined them.

Outside, the dwarf pulled out a pack of cigarettes. He offered one to Will and stuck a second in the corner of his mouth. "I guess you ain't no fucking patriot, either."

Will shrugged. "It's just . . . I asked myself, if I was running this camp, wouldn't I be sure to have an informer in a group like that?"

The dwarf snorted. He was a red dwarf, with the ginger hair and swarthy complexion of his kind. "You suspect our beloved Commandant of unethical methods? The Legless One would cry in his fucking beer if he could hear you say that."

"I just think he'd have somebody there."

"Ha! There were ten in the tent. In my experience, that means at least two snitches. One for money and the other because he's a shit."

"You're a cynic."

"I've done time. Now that I'm out, I'm gonna keep my asshole clenched and my hand to the axe. Knawmean?" He turned away. "See ya, kid."

Will ditched the cigarette—it was his first, and he was certain it was going to be his last as well—and went off in search of Esme.

Esme had adapted to the Displaced Persons Camp with an intense joy that was a marvel to behold. She was the leader of whatever gang of children she fell in with, every adult's pet, and every crone's plaything. She sang songs for the bedridden patients in the infirmary and took part in the amateur theatricals. Strangers gave her old kimonos, bell-bottoms, and farthingales so she could play at dress-up and shooed her back whenever she started down the road that led to the cliffs overlooking the Gorge. She could feed herself, a sweetmeat and a morsel at a time, just by hopping from tent to tent and poking her head in to see how everyone was doing. It made things easier for Will, knowing that she was being lovingly watched over by the entire camp. Now he followed the broken half-shilling he carried always in his pocket straight to its mate, which he'd hung on a cord about Esme's neck.

He found her playing with a dead rat.

From somewhere, Esme had scrounged up a paramedic's rowan wand that still held a fractional charge of vivifying energy and was trying to bring the rat back to life. Pointing the rod imperiously at the wee corpse, she cried, "Rise! Live!" Its legs twitched and scrabbled spasmodically at the ground.

The apple imp kneeling on the other side of the rat from her gasped. "How did you do that?" His eyes were like saucers.

"What I've done," Esme said, "is to enliven its archipallium or reptilian brain. This is the oldest and most primitive part of the central nervous system and controls muscles, balance, and autonomic functions." She traced a circuit in the air above the rat's head. Jerkily, like a badly handled marionette, it lurched to its feet. "Now the warmth has spread to its paleopallium, which is concerned with emotions and instincts, fighting, fleeing, and sexual behavior. Note that the rat is physically aroused. Next I will access the amygdala, its fear center. This will—"

"Put that *down*, Esme." It was not Will who spoke. "You don't know where it's been. It might have germs."

The little girl blossomed into a smile and the rat collapsed in the dirt by her knee. "Mom-Mom!"

Mother Griet scowled down from her tent.

There were neighborhoods within the camp, each corresponding roughly to the locale of origin of its inhabitants, the camp officials having long ago given up on their rationalized plans for synthetic social organization. Will and Esme lived in Block G, wherein dwelt all those who belonged nowhere else—misfits and outcasts, loners and those who, like them, had been separated from their own kind. For them, Mother Griet served as a self-appointed mayor, scolding the indolent, praising those who did more than their share, a perpetual font of new projects to improve the common lot. Every third day she held a pie-powders court, where the "dusty-footed" could seek justice in such petty grievances as the Commandant deemed beneath his attention.

Now she gestured imperiously with her walking stick. "Get in here. We have things to discuss." Then, addressing Will, "You, too, grandchild."

"Me?"

"Not very quick on the uptake, are ye? Yes, you."

He followed her within.

Mother Griet's tent was larger on the inside than it was on the outside, as Will discovered when he stepped through the flap and into its green shadows. At first, there seemed to be impossibly many tent poles. But as his eyes adjusted, the slim shapes revealed themselves to be not poles but the trunks of trees. A bird flew by. Others twittered in the underbrush. High above floated something that could not possibly be the moon.

A trail led them to a clearing.

"Sit," Mother Griet said. She took Esme in her lap. "When was the last time you brushed your hair, child? It's nothing but snarls and snail shells."

"I don't remember."

To Will, Mother Griet said, "So you're Esme's father. A bit younger than might be expected."

"I'm her brother, actually. Esme's easily confused."

"No kidding. I can't get a straight answer out of the brat." She pulled a hairbrush from her purse and applied it vigorously to Esme's hair. "Don't wriggle." Mother Griet turned to Will, her pale blue eyes astonishingly intense. "How old is she?" Then, when he hesitated, "Is she older than you are?"

"She . . . might be."

"Ah. Then I was right." Mother Griet bowed low over the child's head. The trees around them wavered and the air filled with the smell of hot canvas. Briefly it seemed they were sitting in a tent like any other with a wooden platform floor and six cots with a footlocker resting by each one. Then the forest restored itself. She looked up, tears running down her cheeks. "You're not her brother. Tell me how you met her."

As Will told his tale, Mother Griet dabbed away her tears with a tissue. "Let me tell you a story," she said when he was done. In her lap, Esme flopped over on her back and grinned up at her. The old crone gently stroked her cheek.

"I was born in Corpsecandle Green, a place of no particular distinction, save that it was under a curse. Or so it seemed to me, for nothing there endured. My father died and my mother ran off when I was an infant and so I was raised 'by the village,' as they say. I flitted from house to house, through an ever-changing pageant of inconstant sisters, brothers, tormentors, protectors, and friends. When I came of age, some of these turned to lovers and husbands, and they were inconstant, too. All was flux: Businesses failed, pipes burst, and creditors repossessed furniture. The only things I dared hope might endure were my children. Oh, such darlings they were! I loved them with every scrap of my being. And how do you imagine they repaid me for it?"

"I don't know."

"The little bastards grew up. Grew up, married, turned into strangers, and moved away. And because their fathers had all five wandered into the marshes and died—but that's another story, and one I doubt you'll ever hear—I was left alone again, too old to bear another child but wanting one nonetheless.

"So, foolish as I was, I bought a black goat, gilded its horns, and led it deep into the marshlands at midnight. There was a drowning-pool there, and I held it under until it stopped struggling, as a sacrifice to the genius loci, begging that puissant sprite for just one more child. Such a wail I set up then, in my need and desire, as would have scared away a dire wolf." She stopped. "Pay attention, boy. There might be a test afterward."

"I *was* paying attention."

"Yeah, right. Well, exactly at dawn there was a rustling in the reeds and this child emerged, this beautiful child right here." She tickled Esme, who squirmed and laughed. "She didn't know who she belonged to and she'd forgotten her name—not the first time she'd done so, I warrant—so I named her Iria. Do you remember any of this, little one?"

"I don't remember anything," Esme said. "Ever. That way I'm always happy."

"She sold her memory to the—"

"Shush!" Mother Griet said fiercely. "I *said* you weren't bright. Never mention any of the Seven indoors." She returned to her brushing. "She was like this then, every dawn her first one ever, every evening moon a new delight. She was my everything."

"Then she's yours," Will said with an unexpected pang of regret.

"Look at me, boy, I could die tomorrow. You don't get free of her that easy. Where was I? Oh, yes. For ten or twenty years, I was happy. What mother wouldn't be? But the neighbors began to mutter. Their luck was never good. Cows dried up and cellars flooded. Crops failed and mice multiplied. Sons were drafted, unwed daughters got knocked up, gaffers fell down the cellar stairs. Refrigerator pumps died and the parts to fix them went out of stock. Scarecrows spontaneously caught fire.

"Suspicion pointed the good villagers straight at the child. So they burned down my house and drove me from Corpsecandle Green, alone and penniless, with no place to go. Iria, with her usual good fortune, had wandered off into the marshes that morning and missed her own lynching. I never saw her again—until, as it turns out, these last few days."

"You must have been heartbroken."

"You're a master of the obvious, aren't ye? But adversity is the forge of wisdom, and through my pain I eventually came to realize that loss was not a curse laid down upon me or my village, but simply the way of the world. So be it. Had I the power, the only change I'd make would be to restore Esme-Iria's memory to her."

Esme pouted. "I don't want it."

"Idiot child. If you remember nothing, you learn nothing. How to gut a fish or operate a gas chromatograph, perhaps, but nothing that *matters*. When death comes to you, he will ask you three questions, and they none of them will have anything to do with fish guts or specimen retention times."

"I'm never going to die."

"Never is a long time, belovedest. Someday the ancient war between the Ocean and the Land will be over, and the Moon will return to her mother's womb. Think you to survive that?" Mother Griet rummaged in her purse. "No, so long as you never die, this happy forgetfulness is a blessing." She rummaged some more. "But nobody lives forever. Nor will you." Her hand emerged triumphant. "You see this ring? Ginarr Gnomesbastard owed me a favor, so I had him make it. Can you read the inscription on the inside?"

Esme brushed the hair out of her eyes. "Yes, but I don't know what it means."

"*Memento mori.* It means 'remember to die.' It's on your list of things to do and if you haven't done it yet, you haven't led a full life. Put the ring on your finger. I whispered my name into it when the silver was molten. Wear it and after I'm gone, whatever else you forget you'll still remember me."

"Will it make me grow up?"

"No, little one. Only you can do that."

"It's not gold," Esme said critically.

"No, it's silver. Silver is the witch-metal. It takes a spell more readily than gold does, and holds it better. It conducts electricity almost as well as gold, and since it has a higher melting point, it's far superior for use in electronic circuitry. Also it's cheaper."

"I can repair a radio."

"I bet you can. Go now. Run along and play." She swatted the little girl on the rump and watched her scamper away. Then, to Will, she said, "Your hands are bleeding from a thousand cuts."

He looked down at them.

"It's a figure of speech, fool. Each cut is a memory, and the blood is the pain they cause you. You and the child are like Jack and Nora Sprat; she forgets everything, and you remember all. Neither is normal. Or wise. You've got to learn to let go, boy, or you'll bleed yourself to death."

An angry retort rushed to Will's lips, but he bit it back. He had dealt with old ladies like her before, and argument never helped. If he wanted to tell her to buzz off, it would have to be done politely. He stood. "Thank you for your advice," he said stiffly. "I'm leaving now."

Though it had been a long walk to the clearing, three strides took him out through the tent flap. He stood blinking in the sunlight.

Two yellow-jackets seized his arms.

"Garbage duty," one said. Will had been pressed into such service before. He went unresisting with them to a utility truck. It grumbled through Block G and out of the camp and when the tents were small in the distance, slowed to a halt. One soldier shoved a leather sack over Will's head and upper body. The other wrapped a cord around his waist, lashing him in.

"Hey!"

"Don't struggle. We'd only have to hurt you."

The truck lurched, clashed gears, and got up to speed. Soon they were driving uphill. There was only one hill overlooking Camp Oberon, a small, barren one atop which stood the old mansion that had been seized for the Commandant's office. When they got there, Will was prodded through passages that smelled musky and reptilian, as though the house were infested with toads.

Knuckles rapped on wood. "The DP you sent for, sir."

"Bring him in and wait outside."

Will was thrust forward, and the bag untied and whisked from his head. The door closed behind him.

The Commandant wore a short-sleeved khaki shirt with matching tie and no insignia. His head was bald and speckled as a brown egg. His forearms rested, brawny and stiff-haired, on his desk. Casually, he dipped a hand into a bowl of dead rats, picked up one by its tail, tilted his head back, and swallowed it whole. Will thought of Esme's plaything and had to fight down the urge to laugh.

Laughter would have been unwise. The Commandant's body language, the arrogance with which he held himself, told Will all he needed to know about him. Here was a pocket strongman, a manipulator and would-be tyrant, the Dragon Baalthazar writ small. The hairs on the back of Will's neck prickled. Cruelty coupled with petty authority was, as he knew only too well, a dangerous combination.

The Commandant pushed aside some papers and picked up a folder. "This is a report from the Erlking DPC," he said. "That's where your village wound up."

"Did they?"

"They don't speak very highly of you." He read from the report. "Seizure of private property. Intimidation. Sexual harassment. Forced labor. Arson. It says here that you had one citizen executed." He dropped the folder on the desk. "I don't imagine you'd be very popular there, if I had you transferred."

"Transfer me or not, as you like. There's nothing I can do to stop you."

"Bold words," the Commandant said, "for somebody who was conspiring with subversives not half an hour ago. You didn't know I had an ear in that meeting, did you?"

"You had two. The ghast and the dwarf."

The Commandant sucked his teeth in silence for a long moment. Then he rose up from the desk, so high his head almost touched the ceiling. From the waist down, his body was that of a snake.

Slowly, he slithered forward. Will did not flinch, even when the lamius circled him, leaving him surrounded by loops of body.

"Do you know what I want from you?"

Yes, Will thought, I know what you want. You want to put your hand up inside me and manipulate me like a puppet. You want to wiggle your fingers and make me jump. Aloud, he said, "I collaborated once, and it was a mistake. I won't do it again."

"Then you'll leave by the front door and without the courtesy of a bag over your head. How long do you think you'll last then? Once word gets out you're friendly with me?"

Will stared down at his feet and shook his head doggedly.

The Commandant slid to the door and opened it. The two yellow-jackets stood there, silent as grimhounds. "You can stand in the foyer while you think it over. Knock hard when you've made up your mind; this thing's mahogany an inch thick." The lamius smiled mirthlessly. "Or, if you like, you can leave by the front door."

The foyer had a scuffed linoleum floor, an oliphaunt-foot umbrella stand, and a side table with short stacks of medical brochures for chlamydia, AIDS, evil eye, and diarrhea. Sunlight slanted through frosted panels to either side of the front door. There were two switches for the overhead and outside lights, which made a hollow *bock* noise when he flicked one on or off. And that was it.

He wouldn't become the Commandant's creature. On that point he was sure. But he didn't want to be branded an informant and released to the tender mercies of his fellow refugees either. He'd seen what the camp vigilantes did to those they suspected of harboring insufficient solidarity. Back and forth Will strode, forth and back, feverishly work-ing through his options. Until finally he was certain of his course of action. Simply because there was nothing else he *could* do.

Placing his palms flat on its surface, Will leaned straight-armed against the table. Like every other piece of furniture he had seen here, it was solidly built of dark, heavy wood. He walked his feet as far back as he could manage, until he was leaning over the table almost paral-lel to its surface. He wasn't at all sure he had the nerve to do this.

He closed his eyes and took a deep breath.

Then, as quickly as he could, Will whipped his hands away from the table and clasped them behind his back. Involuntarily, his head jerked to the side, trying in vain to protect his nose. His face hit the wood hard.

"Cernunnos!" Will staggered to his feet, clutching his broken nose. Blood flowed freely between his fingers and down his shirt. Rage rose up in him like fire. It took a moment or two to calm down.

He left by the front door.

Will walked slowly through Block A, wearing his blood-drenched shirt like a flag or a biker's colors. By the time he got to the infirmary, word that he had been roughed up by the yellow-jackets had passed through the camp like wildfire. He had the bleeding stanched and told the nurse that he'd slipped and broken his nose on the edge of a table. After that, he could have run for camp president, had such an office existed, and won. Backslaps, elbow nudges, and winks showered down on him during his long slog home. There were whispered promises of vengeance and muttered obscenities applied to the camp authorities.

He found himself not liking his allies any better than he did his enemies.

It was a depressing thing to discover. So he went on past his tent to the edge of camp, across the railroad tracks and down the short road that led to the top of the Gorge. The tents were not visible from that place and, despite its closeness, almost nobody went there. It was his favorite retreat when he needed privacy.

The Gorge extended half a mile downriver from the hydroelectric dam to a sudden drop in the land that freed the Aelfwine to run swift and free across the tidewater toward its confluence with the Great River. The channel it had dug down through the bedrock was so straight and narrow that the cliffs on either side of it were almost perpendicular. The water below was white. Crashing, crushing, tumbling as if possessed by a thousand demons, it was energetic enough to splinter logs and carry boulders along in its current. Anyone trying to climb down the cliffs here would surely fall. But if he ran with all his might and jumped with all his strength, he might conceivably miss the rock and hit the water clean. In which case he would certainly die. Nobody could look down at that raging fury and pretend otherwise.

It was an endlessly fascinating prospect to contemplate: Stone, water, stone. Hardness, turbulence, hardness. Not a single tree, shrub, or flower disturbed the purity of its lifelessness. The water looked cold, endlessly cold.

"Don't do it, kid."

Will spun. Standing not far away, so still that if he hadn't spoken

Will would never have noticed him among the rocks, was the dwarf he had spoken with earlier.

"Do what?"

"Yeah, like you wasn't thinking of jumping." The dwarf had a pack of cigarettes in his hand. He tapped out two, offered one. Will took it. "Me neither." He squinted down into the Gorge. "Look at that motherfucker churn! Think of all the time it took to cut something like that, and with only a knife of water too. It makes your life seem brief as a crap, don't it?"

Will had to agree that it did.

"You see all them layers of rock? Them strata? Every layer is a single note that was laid down when the Mother of Darkness sang the world into existence at the fucking dawn of time. You ever been to Dwarvenhelm?"

Will shook his head.

"It's a fucking police state. The Assay has its spies everywhere. Even when you're taking a leak, you're not alone. You can be the most insignificant little turd in the butt end of nowhere and they've got a dossier on you. How do they do that, you ask? Easy. Everybody gets recruited. No fucking exceptions. You get called into Assay HQ and this goat-buggering bureaucrat reads you the juicy bits from your own dossier. Enough to let you know you're facing hard time. Then, when you're about ready to piss yourself, he says, nice and casual, that they need somebody to keep an eye on your friends and family." He spat. "You'd be surprised the things they can make you do."

"Maybe not," Will said. "Maybe I wouldn't."

"What's your name, kid?"

"Will le Fey."

"Hornbori Monadnock." The dwarf stuck out a hand and they shook. "Pleased to meet you, asshole."

"Look," Will said. "You seem like a nice guy, Monadnock. But it's been a long day. My nose hurts. And I've got a lot of stuff to think about. So if you don't mind . . ."

"Keep your fucking pants on. I got something important to relate here. But before I could tell you, I hadda make you understand that I ain't a bad guy. A little rough around the edges, maybe, but what the fuck." He put a hand on Will's forearm. "It ain't like I killed nobody."

Will shook the hand off. "I'll listen," he said. "Just don't touch me, okay?"

"Spoken like a fucking gentleman. You know how they say if you split open a dwarf's skull, you'll find a gemstone deep inside his brain? Well, it's true and it's not. There's many a fucker dead today because he thought some shitfaced dwarf would be easy pickings. And of course there ain't no fucking gemstone. But *metaphorically* it's true. We each got a fucking pearl-beyond-price up there. Only it don't do us no good." Harshly, Monadnock said, "This time tomorrow, I'll be dead."

"What?"

"Some shithead outed me. Generalissimo Lizardo says he'll protect me. Like fuck he will. He might control the camp during the day, but the night belongs to vigilantes. I'll be lucky if they don't necklace me. You know what that is, right? They hang a fucking tire around your neck, douse it with gasoline, and set it afire."

"Listen," Will said. "You can escape. The perimeter patrols are a joke. I can go back to my tent and bring you some supplies. A razor. Shave off your beard and if you get captured again, just give 'em a false name. Forgive me, but nobody can tell you guys apart."

"It's too late for that, kid. That gemstone I was telling you about? Every dwarf got one true prophesy he can make, the day he dies. And I been feeling mine trying to come out for hours. Ordinarily, we save it for our own kind. But there ain't many dwarven-folk in Oberon, and those as are here I wouldn't piss on if their hair was on fire. So I'm gonna give this fucking gift-worthy-of-kings to you."

"I don't understand. Why me?"

"Because you're *here*. Now stop asking fucking questions and listen." Monadnock shook his limbs loose and took a deep breath. Abruptly a shiver ran through his body and he shook as if he were having a seizure. His eyes rolled up so that only their whites showed. In a high, half-strangled voice, he said (and in his head Will simultaneously heard the words translated):

> *"Sol ter sortna,* (The sun blackens
> *sigr fold i mar,* Lands sink into sea,
> *hverfa af himni* The radiant stars

heidar stiornor.	Fall from the sky.
Geisar eimi	Smoke rages against fire,
vid aldrnara,	Nourisher of life,
leikr har hiti	The heat soars high
vid himin sialfan."	Against heaven itself.)

Then the dwarf seized Will's shirt with both hands and yanked down his head so that they were on the same level. His eyes still terrifyingly blank and white, he gripped Will's forehead in one broad hand and squeezed.

It was as if he were struck by a bolt of lightning. All the world turned an incandescent white. For a long still time he stood alone and immobile on a cold and lifeless plain under a starless sky. Everywhere there was rubble. Nowhere was there life. Radiation sleeted through his nonexistent body.

Will had no idea what this vision meant. Yet he knew, with that same sourceless certainty one experiences in dreams, that this was a true seeming and possibly even his destiny. This was unquestionably the single most important moment in his life. All else would be a footnote to it.

Then the dwarf flung Will away as one might a rag doll, bent double, and threw up.

By the time Will had regained his feet, Monadnock was lighting up another cigarette. The dwarf walked to the edge of the cliff. There was a light, erratic breeze coming up from the Gorge. Quietly, he said, "I think I deserve a little fucking privacy now, don't you?"

"What was . . . ? Those words. What did they mean?"

"The words are from the *Motsognirsaga,* which is a text so sacred to my kind that no surface-walker will ever see a copy of it. So you gotta figure that's not good. But what the vision means is for you to find out and me not to give a shit about, jerkoff. Now get the fuck out. I got something I gotta do."

"Just one thing—is this a vision of something that might happen? Or that will?"

"Go!"

Hesitantly, Will walked back toward the camp. At the top of the rise, just before the twist where the road went over the tracks and down again and the Gorge disappeared entirely, a horrid presentiment made him hesitate and look back.

But the dwarf was already gone.

Mother Griet died a fortnight later, not from any neglect or infection but as a final, lingering effect of a curse that she had contracted in her long-forgotten childhood. As a girl, she had surprised the White Ladies in their predawn dance and seen that which none but an initiate was sanctioned to see. In their anger, they had pronounced death upon her at the sound of—*her third crow-caw*, they were going to say but, realizing almost too late her youth and innocence of ill intent, one of their number had quickly emended the sentence to a-million-and-one. From which moment onward, every passing crow had urged her a breath closer to death.

Such was the story Mother Griet had told Will, and so when its fulfillment came he knew it for what it was. That morning she had called to him from a bench before her tent and set him to carding wool with her. Midway through the chore, Mother Griet suddenly smiled and, putting down her work, lifted her ancient face to the sky. "Hark!" she said. "Now *there's* a familiar sound. The black-fledged Sons of Corrin have followed us here from—"

Gently, then, she toppled over on her side, dead.

Esme had been playing inside, building a mud-and-stone dam across a tiny brook that meandered through Mother Griet's memories of the lost forests of her youth. In that very instant, she began to wail as if her heart were broken.

Will thought her to be merely upset at the loss of her playground, which he knew would not survive its creator, and so he did not go to her until the local elders had crowded out of their tents and pushed him away from Mother Griet's corpse and he discovered himself without any other responsibility than to comfort her.

But when he took the child in his arms, she was inconsolable. "She's dead," she said. "Griet is dead." He made hushing noises, but she kept on crying. "I *remember* her!" she insisted. "I remember now."

"That's good." Will groped for the right words to say. "It's good to remember people you care about. And you mustn't be unhappy—she led a long and productive life."

"No!" she sobbed. "You don't understand. Griet was my daughter."

"What?"

"She was my sweetness, my youngest, my light. Oh, my little Griet-chen! She brought me dandelions in her tiny fist. Damn memory! Damn responsibility! Damn time!" Esme tugged off her ring and flung it away from her. "Now I remember why I sold my age in the first place."

The citizens of Block G honored Mother Griet's death with the traditional rites. Three solemn runes were carved upon her brow. Her abdomen was cut open and her entrails read. In lieu of an aurochs, a stray dog was sacrificed. Then they raised up her corpse on long poles to draw down the sacred feeders, the vultures, from the sky. The camp's sanitary officers tried to tear down the sun-platform, and the ensuing argument spread and engulfed the camp in three days of rioting.

In the wake of which they were loaded into railroad cars and taken away. To far Babylonia, the relief workers said, in Fäerie Minor where they would build new lives for themselves, but no one believed them. All they knew of Babylonia was that the streets of its capital were bricked of gold and the ziggurats touched the sky. Of one thing they were certain: No villager could thrive in such a place. It was not even certain they could survive. All pledged, therefore, a solemn oath to stay together, come what may, to defend and protect one another in the unimaginable times to come. Will mouthed the words along with the rest, though he did not believe them.

The train pulled in. The yellow-jackets stood atop barrels on the outside of mazelike arrangements of cattle fences prodding the refugees toward the train cars with long poles. Will moved with the jostling crowd, keeping a firm hand on Esme, lest they get separated.

Ever since Mother Griet's death, Will had been thinking: about her, about the Commandant, about the dwarf and his prophecy. Now everything fell into place. All those events he had witnessed were one and the same, he realized, naught but the harsh white light of justice working itself out in the pitiless court of existence. The good suffered and the wicked were punished. He realized now that he did not have to approve of his own side to take action. In fact, it made things easier if he didn't. He had a purpose now. He was going to Babylon, and though he did not know what he would do when he got there, he knew that ultimately it would put paid to everything he had been through.

I am your War, he thought, and I am coming home to you.

6

Crossing Fäerie Minor

Time did not exist. All the world hung suspended, like a fly in amber, within a medium as airless and unchanging as granite. Then, with the quiet, inexplicable jolt of the first atom popping into existence, the platform stretched and moved slowly to the rear. Light stanchions pulled apart, then bungee'd backward into the past. The station fell away, a flimsy raft of wooden buildings skimmed by, and the train was plowing a furrow, straight and sure, through the golden wheat fields of Fäerie Minor, swift as a schooner on a placid sea.

Alongside the tracks, telephone wires went up and down, up and down, like the ocean ceaselessly rocking. This was the land where horses ate flesh and mice ate iron, if all the tales were true. It seemed too empty to contain a fraction of the wonders attributed to it.

Will watched from a car that was crowded beyond all his prior experience. On the opposite seat, a goat-girl knocked knees with him and held up her chin so her fine, thin beard could be combed out by the russalka alongside her, all the while delicately eating a bouquet of daisies, nibbling the petals one by one so that she might perform a minor divination relative to some future leman, spouse, or back-door lover. An ogreish creature, four hundred pounds if he were a stone and wearing a suit three sizes too small for his bulk, had squeezed beside Will, stuffed a half-eaten sandwich into his breast pocket as if it were a dress handkerchief, and promptly fallen asleep. Drool slid slowly, steadily, down one long and yellowed tusk. There were others in the compartment besides. Though it was built to hold eight, there were dinters and imps, gnomes, a fire-hopper, urchins, and feys, all crammed together like so many pieces of a tromp l'oeil puzzle.

"Are we there yet?" Esme asked.

"No, little one. Go back to sleep."

The smell was extraordinary, too, a rich mixture of Babylonian tobacco, stale sweat, *poudre de riz,* rotting fruit, cinnamon, the clogged toilet at the end of the car, boredom, and simple desperation—and the window, try though Will might, would not open.

Crushed against the glass, Will found escape by staring off into the plains. They were so flat as to be mesmerizing, and stretched, he had been told, all the way to Fäerie Major. (But if there was one thing he had learned in the DPC, it was to put no trust in anything he had been told.) Once, at the extreme arc of a miles-long curve, he thought he saw Babel itself in the distance, a razor-slash arrogantly bisecting the heavens. But he could not be sure, for the tower was too large, too tall, to be easily seen. Its walls and windows took on the colors of the sky. Then the cars swung around with a clatter and the tower, if it had been there at all, was gone.

In his mind's eye, however, he could see the shadow of that unimaginable spire sweeping across the plains, faster than any train, steady as the hand of a clock.

Without his volition, Will's hand rose and traced a word on the window:

!ИUЯ

But Will paid it no mind. He was still staring at the undulating land, feeling small and unimportant and quietly excited. Fear mingled in him with desire. With every passing mile, he experienced a growing emptiness, a gathering tension, a profound desire to be rewritten that was so strong as to almost be a prayer: *Great Babel, mother of cities, take me in, absorb me, dissolve me, transform me. For just this once, let one plus one not equal two. Make me into someone else. Make that someone everything I am not. By the axe and the labrys, amen.*

All prayers were dangerous. Either they were answered or they were not, and there was no telling which outcome would produce the greater regret. But they were necessary as well, for they suggested a way out of the unendurable present. Back in the village, there had been a whitesmith who had won big in the lottery. With the first third of his winnings, he had bought a wife. The second third went to alimony so he could be rid of her. With the last third, he had drunk himself to death. Not long before the end, he'd collided with Will in the street behind the tavern, fallen back on the wall, and then slid to the ground. Looking up, he had smiled beatifically at Will and winked. "Almost there," he'd said. "Just a few drinks more and I'm done."

His hand rose again. This time it wrote:

!!!WON — ƆNIMOƆ ƎЯ'YƎHT

Esme poked an arm out from her wicker basket under the seat and tugged at Will's trouser leg. "Are we ever going to get there?"

"Someday," Will said. "Not yesterday, not the day before, and so far not today. I'll wake you when there's something to see."

"I'm thirsty," Esme said petulantly.

"I'll get you some water."

"I want a soda. An Irn Bru."

Will yawned. "I'll see what I can do." He stood up and the others on the seat expanded to fill the space he'd vacated. Muttering excuses, he squeezed out of the compartment and down the corridor.

The air was stuffy and the rhythm of wheels on rails hypnotic. Plodding along, Will fell by slow degrees first into a drowse, and then into a waking dream so vivid it could only be a true scrying. In this dream he had no sense of self, so that he watched all that transpired with a detached impartiality worthy of the Goddess herself. Had he seen the goat-girl come running after him and, pulling a knife from her purse, plunge it into his neck, he would have thought: Here is a murder. Perhaps the victim will die.

In the dream, something was coming for him.

Three witches had materialized in the final car at the very rear of the train. He knew their kind well. Witches were the self-appointed legislators of the world. They were forever sticking their long noses into other people's business, demanding that a rosebush be replanted, or a child renamed, or a petty criminal taken down from the gallows half-choked but still breathing. It was next to impossible to be born, to lose one's virginity, to plot a murder, to die, or to be reborn, without one or more popping up and uttering gnostic solemnities. Many a time Will had wished the entire race of witches transported to the Southern Seas and there fed to the great water-beast Jasconius.

These three wore cotton blouses with bolo ties and matching gray jackets and mid-length skirts. Their shoes were square-toed, with solid, inch-high heels. Even without the silver lapel pins depicting an orchid transfixed by a dagger, it would have been easy to spot them as political police. Two wore guns in hidden shoulder holsters; the third did not.

"Is he here?" the ranking officer asked.

"Oh, yes. I can smell him. Faint, but certain."

"I hope he's cute," said the rookie. She carried a truncheon at her belt.

They started up the train, bobbing like crows, sniffing the passengers as they went, rubbing canny fingers over sleeping faces. There was a negative glamour upon them so that nobody paid them any mind. The oldest was thrawn as rawhide and stern of face. The middle witch was stolid and heavyset. The rookie was slight and breastless. Dispassionately, Will wondered if she were female at all. She might have been a boy who'd let his hair grow long and liked to dress up as a girl.

"Let's hope he doesn't force us to kill him. That's always unpleasant, and the paperwork is a bear."

"Well, we won't have to kill him *yet*. He's certainly not in this car."

"This one's dreaming of his sister." The maybe-girl pulled a dead mouse by its tail from a sleeper's pocket and, with a moue of distaste, dropped it back in again. "Ew!"

"If you don't want to know, don't look," the plump witch said. "Drive forward. The stench of destiny grows ever stronger."

Passing between cars, Will was stopped by a tall, donkey-eared fey, standing on the platform with an unlit cigarette in his hand, who said, "Yo, hero! Got a light?"

Dreamily, Will patted his pockets, came up with a twist of punk, and conjured it into flame. Donkey Ears accepted it with a nod of thanks, lit the cigarette, and drew in deeply. The punk he tossed away. Then he knocked the pack to Will. "Thanks, son. You're a prince."

Will accepted a cigarette, lit it from the end of the stranger's, and started past him toward the door. But suddenly the man seized his shoulders and shook him violently, crying, "Hey! John-a-dreams! Wake up!"

Will blinked, shook his head, and was abruptly awake. "I know you," he said wonderingly. "You're Nat Whilk."

"So some call me, anyway." Nat had been the camp fixer back in Oberon DPC. Anything anybody wanted, be it a soccer ball, a wedding gown, a semiautomatic pistol, or a blow job, Nat knew where it could be found and for a small fee would share the information. Now his sharp-featured and deeply lined face looked concerned, and he said, "You had the *awen* on you, son. Tell me what you saw."

Will tilted his head back and felt the dream wrap itself around him again. The witches had paused in a familiar-looking car. The rookie knelt to peer under a seat and sniffed the sleeping Esme up and down. "Oh, here's a foul thing!" she cried. "We should strangle it in its sleep."

"And who's going to explain to the Social Services people why we intruded into their territory? You? Don't make me laugh."

Pulling halfway out of the vision with an effort, Will said, "It's the political police. They're after me."

"Shit!" Nat flicked his cigarette to the winds. "Through here. Quickly." He stepped into the next car, pushed open the ladies room door, and shoved Will inside. "I'll be making a racket. Don't do or say anything in response. Got it?"

"Yes."

Nat thrust the pack of cigarettes and a book of matches into his hand. "Whatever you do, don't stop smoking."

Will shut the door and slid the latch and sat down on the toilet. Outside, Nat began slamming on the door with his open palm. "Galadriel! How long does it fucking *take*?!"

While Nat pounded and shouted, Will drew on his cigarette.

When the ashes grew long, he tapped them into the sink. By imperceptible degrees he sank beneath the conscious world, and in his new state followed the witches' slow and methodical progress up the train, until they came to his toilet and were brought to a stop by the red-faced Nat.

"Who's in there, sir?" the first asked.

"My fucking inamorata is who!" Nat kicked the door so hard it shivered. "She must be taking the mother of all dumps. She's been in there for hours."

The middle witch sniffed at the doorway. "Phew! She's smoking up a storm." She waved a hand under her nose. "That's a criminal offense, citizen."

Nat redoubled his pounding on the door. "What did I fucking tell you, Gal, about those fucking cigarettes? Put that fucking thing out and get off your fucking ass and get the fuck out here right—"

"Sir. You're disturbing the other passengers."

"Yeah, well, maybe some of them need to take a crap, too." *Bam bam bam.* "You're breaking the law, Laddie-girl! Now haul your fat butt out here." He turned to the witches. "Shoot the lock."

They looked at him in astonishment. "You've been reading too many detective novels, citizen," the officer said.

"Look, I know you've got a gun. Shoot the lock! You're a fucking public servant, aren't you? What am I paying taxes for?"

The officer looked at the rookie and nodded.

All in one complicated motion, the rookie stepped behind Nat, whipped her truncheon about his neck, and placed a knee in the small of his back. Simultaneously, the stocky witch punched him in the stomach. He fell to his hands and knees, choking.

"Now, *sir*," the rookie said through gritted teeth. "I want you to understand your situation. You've made a public nuisance of yourself. Which means I have the legal authority and some would say obligation to beat you to a bloody pulp. Now I'm going to ease up on your windpipe for just a second. Nod once if you understand."

Nat nodded.

"Good. Now as it chances, we're acting under instructions at the moment and can't afford the time this salutary chastisement would require. However. We will *make* the time to correct and educate you if you force us to do so. Do you intend to put us in that position? I'll ease off on you for a second now."

Nat shook his head.

"Excellent. Now I'm going to release you, and when I do, I fully expect that you will come slowly to your feet, bow once to each of the three representatives of His Absent Majesty's government you see before you, and then silently—silently, mind you!—return to your designated seat. Your lady will join you there when she wishes. If you find the waiting intolerable, you will continue to wait anyway." She stepped back. "Now. Show me that my faith in you was not misplaced."

Slowly, Nat stood. Painfully he bowed to each of the witches, each bow accompanied by three feather-light touches to his forehead, his heart, and his cock. Half bent over, he shuffled away.

The stocky witch snorted. "Asshole," she said.

Then all three moved on.

In his mind's eye, Will followed them up through the cars until they came at last to the locomotive and disappeared. Once gone, it seemed impossible they had ever set foot on the train at all. The past few minutes must have been a hallucination, a passing fancy woven by his brain out of boredom and nothingness.

But then there was a gentle rap on the door. "All right, lad, you can come out now."

Officially, all the space on the train was to be shared equally among the refugees. Yet Nat, typically enough, had arranged for himself a private compartment in the first car. He laughed ruefully as he led Will there. "Oh, I'm going to ache in the morning! Getting rolled by *les poulettes* at my age—you'd think I'd be beyond that kind of adventure by now."

"Listen," Will said. "I've really got to get back to—"

"It's already taken care of." With a flourish, Nat Whilk opened the door to his compartment.

"Papa!" Esme cried. She held up a can of soda. "I got my Irn Bru."

For an instant Will was silent. Then he said, "That was a good trick."

"Oh, you'll find that I'm full of tricks." Nat gestured Will into a seat. Esme climbed into his lap and stared out the window. "But we'll talk about me later. The first question is, why is the government after you?"

Will shrugged.

"Did someone put a curse on you? Maybe you broke a geas? Perhaps you fulfill a prophesy? Were there miracles at your birth? Any runic tattoos, third teats, other signs of fatedness?"

"None that I know of."

"Are you involved in politics?"

Will looked away.

Nat made an exasperated noise. "Look, kid, I took a knee in the yarbles for you. What's with the attitude?"

Esme wriggled in Will's arms, but he did not let her go. "You asked me for a light when you had a pack of matches in your pocket. You knew about Esme. Just how stupid do I have to be not to realize that you were waiting for me? All right, here I am. What do you *really* want?"

Unexpectedly, Nat burst into laughter. "You're quick, lad! Yes, of course I was waiting for you." He held a hand out to show it was empty and then seemingly plucked a card from Esme's ear. While she clapped, he handed it to Will. It read:

ICHABOD THE FOOL
CONFIDENCE TRICKSTER

"Ichabod the Fool?"

"Just one of my many *noms de scène*. That doesn't matter. All that matters is that I'm a fully vested master in the Just and Honorable Guild of Rogues, Swindlers, Cozeners, and Knaves, and I'm prepared to take you on as my apprentice."

"Why me?"

"Why not? I need a partner and you owe me a favor. Also—forgive me for pointing this out—with your problem, you need a steady source of income."

"What exactly is my problem?" Will asked warily.

"Money burns a hole in your hands." Nat took out a billfold, riffled through its crisp contents, and delicately withdrew a hundred-dollar banknote. "Here. If you can hold onto this for sixty seconds, it's yours."

The instant the bill touched Will's fingers, it burst into flames. In less time than it took to yank back his hand, the banknote flared, dwindled, and was gone.

Esme applauded. "Teach me that! Teach me that!"

"Yes. How did you do that?"

"Oh, it's one of my simpler tricks. Work it out for yourself."

For a moment Will sat thinking. Then he said, "When I called up the *lux aeterna* to kindle a flame for your cigarette, you did the same for that banknote. Possibly, you held it folded in your hand. In any case, my own spell would mask the workings of yours. Only you left off the final half syllable . . . a *schwa*, a little puff of breath. Then, when I touched the bill, you quietly made that noise, finishing the spell. Instant fire."

"Bravo! I knew I'd chosen well."

Esme, grown bored with the conversation, ducked out of Will's arms and returned to the window. Outside were enormous hills of trash—mountains almost—with winding roads leading over them. Garbage-laden trucks lumbered up the slopes and disappeared into the interior. Between the hills and the train tracks was a network of streams and shallow ponds fringed with *Phragmites* and rusting machines. An outcrop of rock rose up abruptly, painted over with artless, square-lettered graffiti: LEMURIA RULES and DUPPY POWER and IN-CUBAE SUCK. A vee of barnacle geese splashed down by a line of telegraph poles that staggered drunkenly through the marshland, never quite dipping their lines into the water.

"This place looks strange," Esme said. "What is it?"

"We're passing through the Whinny Moor Landfill, little grandmother. It's the largest artificial structure in the world. If you could fly with the wings of a roc, you could see it from outer space." Nat settled back in his seat. "Well. Now that we're all one happy family, I propose that we shorten the journey by telling stories. About ourselves, and where we came from."

"I haven't agreed to anything yet."

"Ah, but wait until you hear my story. That'll convince you."

"All right," Will said. "I'm listening."

I was a gentleman in Babel once (Nat began) and not the scoundrel you see before you now. I ate from a silver trencher, and I speared my food with a gold knife. If I had to take a leak in the middle of the night, there were two servants to hold the bedpan and a third to shake my stick afterwards. It was no life for a man of my populist sensibilities. So one day I climbed out a window when nobody was looking and escaped.

You who had the good fortune of being born without wealth can have no idea how it felt. The streets were a kaleidoscope of pedestrians, and I was one of them, a moving speck of color, neither better nor worse than anyone else, and blissfully ignored by all. I was dizzy with excitement. My hands kept rising into the air like birds. My eyes danced to and fro, entranced by everything they saw.

It was glorious.

Down one street I went, turned a corner at random, and so by Brownian motion chanced upon a train station where I took a local to ground level. More purposefully then, I caught a rickshaw to the city limits and made my way outside.

The trooping fairies had come to Babel and set up a goblin market just outside the Ivory Gate. Vendors sold shish kebab and cotton candy, T-shirts and pashmina scarfs, gris gris bags and enchanted swords, tame magpies and Fast Luck Uncrossing Power vigil candles, Cupie dolls and 1:6 scale tooled-leather camel figurines with sequined harnesses. Charango players filled the air with music. I could not have been happier.

"Hey, shithead! Yeah, you—the ass with the ears! *Listen* when a lady speaks to you!"

I looked around.

"Up here, Solomon!"

The voice came from a booth whose brightly painted arch read ROCK! THE! FOX! At the end of a long canvas-walled alley, a vixen grinned at me from an elevated cage, her front feet tucked neatly under her and her black tongue lolling. Seeing she'd caught my eye, she leaped up and began padding quickly from one end of the cage to the other, talking all the while. "Faggot! Bed-wetter! Asshole! Your dick is limp and you throw like a girl!"

"Three for a dollar," a follet said, holding up a baseball. Then, mistaking my confusion for skepticism, he added, "Perfectly honest, *monsieur*," and lightly tossed the ball into the cage. The vixen nimbly evaded it, then nosed it back out between the bars so that it fell to the ground below. "Hit the fox and win a prize."

There was a trick to it, I later learned. Though they looked evenly spaced, only the one pair of bars was wide enough that a baseball could get through. All the vixen had to do was avoid that spot and she was as safe as houses. But even without knowing the game was rigged, I didn't want to play. I was filled with an irrational love for everyone and everything. Today of all days, I would not see a fellow creature locked in a cage.

"How much for the vixen?" I asked.

"*C'est impossible*," the follet said. "She has a mouth on her, sir. You wouldn't want her."

By then I had my wallet out. "Take it all." The follet's eyes grew large as dinner plates, and by this token I knew that I overpaid. But after all, I reasoned, I had plenty more in my carpetbag.

After the follet had opened the cage and made a fast fade, the vixen genuflected at my feet. Wheedlingly, she said, "I didn't mean none of them things I said, master. That was just patter, you know. Now that I'm yours, I'll serve you faithfully. Command and I'll obey. I shall devote my life to your welfare, if you but allow me to."

I put down my bag so I could remove the vixen's slave collar. Gruffly, I said, "I don't want your obedience. Do whatever you want, obey me in no matters, don't give a thought to my gods-be-damned welfare. You're free now."

"You can't mean that," the vixen said, shocked.

"I can and I do. So if you—"

"Sweet Mother of Beasts!" the vixen gasped, staring over my shoulder. "*Look out!*"

I whirled around, but there was nothing behind me but more booths and fair-goers. Puzzled, I turned back to the vixen, only to discover that she was gone.

And she had stolen my bag.

So it was that I came to learn exactly how freedom tastes when you haven't any money. Cursing the vixen and my own gullibility with equal venom, I put the goblin market behind me. Somehow I wound up on the bank of the Gihon. There I struck up a conversation with a waterman who motored me out to the docks and put me onto a tugboat captained by a friend of his. It was hauling a garbage scow upriver to Whinny Moor.

As it turned out, the landfill was no good place to be let off. Though there were roads leading up into the trashlands, there were none that led onward, along the river, where I wanted to go. And the smell! Indescribable.

A clutch of buildings huddled by the docks in the shadow of a garbage promontory. These were garages for the dump trucks mostly, but also Quonset hut repair and storage facilities and a few leftover brownstones with their windows bricked over that were used for offices and the like. One housed a bar with a sputtering neon sign saying BRIG-O-DOOM. In the parking lot behind it was, incongruously enough, an overflowing dumpster.

Here it was I fetched up.

I had never been hungry before, you must understand—not real, gnaw-at-your-belly hungry. I'd skipped breakfast that morning in my excitement over leaving, and I'd had the lightest of dinners the day before. On the tugboat I'd watched the captain slowly eat two sandwiches and an apple and been too proud to beg a taste from him. What agonies I suffered when he threw the apple core overboard! And now . . .

Now, to my horror, I found myself moving toward the dumpster. I turned away in disgust when I saw a rat skitter out from behind it. But it called me back. I was like a moth that's discovered a candle. I hoped there would be food in the dumpster, and I feared that if there were I would eat it.

It was then, in that darkest of hours, that I heard the one voice I had expected never to hear again. "Hey, shit-for brains! Aintcha gonna say you're glad to see me?"

Crouched atop a nearby utility truck was the vixen.

"You!" I cried, but did not add *you foul creature*, as my instincts bade me. Already, poverty was teaching me politesse. "How did you follow me here?"

"Oh, I have my ways."

Hope fluttered in my chest like a wild bird. "Do you still have my bag?"

"Of course I don't. What would a fox do with luggage? I threw it away. But I kept the key. Wasn't I a good girl?" She dipped her head and a small key on a loop of string slipped from her neck and fell to the tarmac with a light tinkle.

"Idiot fox!" I cried. "What possible good is a key to a bag I no longer own?"

She told me.

The Brig o' Doom was a real dive. There was a black-and-white television up in one corner tuned to the fights and a pool table with ripped felt to the back. On the door for the toilets, some joker had painted *Tír na bOg* in crude white letters. I sat down at the bar. "Beer," I told the tappie.

"Red Stripe or Dragon Stout?"

"Surprise me."

When my drink came, I downed half of it in a single draft. It made my stomach ache and my head spin, but I didn't mind. It was the first sustenance I'd had in twenty-six hours. Then I turned around on the stool and addressed the bar as a whole: "I'm looking for a guide. Someone who can take me to a place in the landfill that I've seen in a vision. A place by a stream where garbage bags float up to the surface and burst with a terrible stench—"

A tokoloshe snorted. He was a particularly nasty piece of business, a hairy brown dwarf with burning eyes and yellow teeth. "Could be anywhere." The fossegrim sitting with him snickered sycophantically. It was clear who was the brains of this outfit.

"And two bronze legs from the lighthouse of Rhodes lie half-buried in the reeds."

The tokoloshe hesitated, and then moved over to make space for me in his booth. The fossegrim, tall and lean with hair as white as a chimneysweeper's, leaned over the table to listen as he growled sotto voce, "What's the pitch?"

"There's a bag that goes with this key," I said quietly. "It's buried out there somewhere. I'll pay to find it again."

"Haughm," the tokoloshe said. "Well, me and my friend know the place you're looking for. And there's an oni I know can do the digging. That's three. Will you pay us a hundred each?"

"Yes. When the bag is found. Not before."

"How about a thousand?"

Carefully, I said, "Not if you're just going to keep jacking up the price until you find the ceiling."

"Here's my final offer: Ten percent of whatever's in the bag. Each." Then, when I hesitated, "We'll pick up your bar tab, too."

It was as the vixen had said. I was dressed as only the rich dressed, yet I was disheveled and dirty. That and my extreme anxiety to regain my bag told my newfound partners everything they needed to know.

"Twenty percent," I said. "Total. Split it however you choose. But first you'll buy me a meal—steak and eggs, if they have it."

The sun had set and the sky was yellow and purple as a bruise, turning to black around the edges. Into the darkness our pickup truck jolted by secret and winding ways. The grim drove and the dwarf took occasional swigs from a flask of Jeyes Fluid, without offering me any. Nobody spoke. The oni, who could hardly have fit in the cab with us, sat in the bed with his feet dangling over the back. His name was Yoshi.

Miles into the interior of the landfill, we came to a stop above a black stream beside which lay two vast and badly corroded bronze legs. "Can you find a forked stick?" I asked.

The tokoloshe pulled a clothes hanger out of the mingled trash and clay. "Use this."

I twisted the wire into a wishbone, tied the key string to the short end, and took the long ends in my hands. The key hung a good half-inch off true. Then, stumbling over ground that crunched underfoot from buried rusty cans, I walked one way and another until the string hung straight down. "Here."

The tokoloshe brought out a bag of flour. "How deep do you think it's buried?"

"Pretty deep," I said. "Ten feet, I'm guessing."

He measured off a square on the ground—or rather, surface, for the dumpings here were only hours old. At his command, Yoshi passed out shovels, and we all set to work.

When the hole reached six feet, it was too cramped for Yoshi to share. He was a big creature and all muscle. Two small horns sprouted from his forehead and a pair of short fangs jutted up from his jaw. He labored mightily, and the pile of excavated trash alongside the hole grew taller and taller. At nine feet, he was sweating like a pig. He threw a washing machine over the lip, and then stopped and grumbled, "Why am I doing all the work here?"

"Because you're stupid," the fossegrim jeered.

The tokoloshe hit him. "Keep digging," he told the oni. "I'm paying you fifty bucks for this gig."

"It's not enough."

"Okay, okay." The tokoloshe pulled a couple of bills from his pocket and gave them to me. "Take the pickup to the Brig-O and bring back a quart of beer for Yoshi."

I did then as stupid a thing as ever I've done in my life.

So far I'd been following the script the vixen had laid out for me, and everything had gone exactly as she'd said it would. Now, rather than playing along with the tokoloshe as she'd advised, I got my back up. We were close to finding the bag and, fool that I was, I thought they would share.

"Just how dumb do you think I am?" I asked. "You won't get rid of me that easily."

The tokoloshe shrugged. "Tough shit, Ichabod."

He and the fossegrim knocked me down. They duct-taped my ankles together and my wrists behind my back. Then they dumped me in the back of the pickup. "Scream if you want to," the tokoloshe said. "We don't mind, and there's nobody else to hear you."

I was terrified, of course. But I'd barely had time to realize exactly how desperate my situation had become when Yoshi whooped, "I found it!"

The fossegrim and the tokoloshe scurried to the top of the unsteady trash pile. "Did you find it?" cried one, and the other said, "Hand it up."

"Don't do it, Yoshi!" I shouted. "There's money in that bag, a lot more than fifty dollars, and you can have half of it."

"Give me the bag," the tokoloshe said grimly.

By his side, the fossegrim was dancing excitedly. Bottles and cans rolled away from his feet. "Yeah," he said. "Hand it up."

But Yoshi hestitated. "Half?" he said.

"You can have it *all*!" I screamed. "Just leave me alive and it's yours!"

The tokoloshe stumbled down toward the oni, shovel raised. His buddy followed after in similar stance.

So began a terrible and comic fight, the lesser creatures leaping and falling on the unsteady slope, all the while swinging their shovels murderously, and the great brute enduring their blows and trying to seize hold of his tormentors. I could not see the battle—no more than a few slashes of the shovels—though I managed to struggle to my knees, for the discards from Yoshi's excavations rose too high. But I could hear it, the cursing and threats, the harsh clang of a shovel against Yoshi's head and the fossegrim's scream as one mighty hand finally closed about him.

Simultaneous with that scream there was a tremendous clanking and sliding sound of what I can only assume was the tokoloshe's final charge. In my mind's eye I can see him now, racing downslope with the shovel held like a spear, its point aimed at Yoshi's throat. But whether blade ever connected with flesh or not I do not know, for it set the trash to slipping and sliding in a kind of avalanche.

Once started, the trash was unstoppable. Down it flowed, sliding over itself, all in motion. Down it flowed, rattling and clattering, land made liquid, yet for all that still retaining its brutal mass. Down it flowed, a force of nature, irresistible, burying all three so completely there was no chance that any of them survived.

Then there was silence.

Well!" said the vixen. "That was a tidy little melodrama. Though I must say it would have gone easier on you if you'd simply done as I told you to in the first place." She was sitting on the roof of the cab.

I had never in my life been so glad to see anybody as I was then. "This is the second time you showed up just when things were looking worst," I said, giddy with relief. "How do you manage it?"

"Oh, I ate a grain of stardust when I was a cub, and ever since then there's been nary a spot I can't get into or out of, if I set my mind to it."

"Good, good, I'm glad. Now set me free!"

"Oh, dear. I wish you hadn't said that."

"What?"

"Years ago and for reasons that are none of your business I swore a mighty oath never again to obey the orders of a man. That's why I've been tagging along after you—because you ordered me not to be concerned with your welfare. So of course I am. But now you've ordered me to free you, and thus I can't."

"Listen to me carefully," I said. "If you disobey an order from me, then you've obeyed my previous order not to obey me. So your oath is meaningless."

"I know. It's quite dizzying." The fox lay down, tucking her paws beneath her chest. "Here's another one: There's a barber in Seville who shaves everyone who doesn't shave himself, but nobody else. Now—"

"Please," I said. "I beg you. Sweet fox, dear creature, most adorable of animals . . . If you would be so kind as to untie me out of the goodness of your heart and of your own free will, I'd be forever grateful to you."

"That's better. I was beginning to think you had no manners at all."

The vixen tugged and bit at the duct tape on my wrists until it came undone. Then I was able to free my ankles. We both got into the truck. Neither of us suggested we try digging for my bag. As far as I was concerned, it was lost forever.

But driving down out of the landfill, I turned and where the vixen had been, a woman sat with her feet neatly tucked beneath her. Her eyes were green and her hair was short and red. I had the distinct impression that she was laughing at me. "Your money's in a cardboard box under the seat," she said, "along with a fresh change of clothing—which, confidentially, you badly need—and the family signet ring. What's buried out there is only the bag, stuffed full of newspapers and rocks."

"My head aches," I said. "If you had my money all along, what was the point of this charade?"

"There's an old saying: Teach a man to fish, and he'll only eat when the fish are biting. Teach him a good scam, and the suckers will always bite." The lady grinned. "A confidence trickster can always use a partner. We're partners now, ain't we?"

So ended Nat's story. Esme had stopped listening long ago. She was at the window again, staring out at tank farms and pyramids of container-ized cargo sliding backward into the past. A line of high-tension towers leapt out of nowhere, matched speeds with the train, and paced it down the tracks. A second set of rails joined them, and then a third, and then a canal. All the world, it seemed, was converging upon Babel.

"What became of the vixen?" Will asked.

Nat tapped his heart whimsically. "She's right here. Laughing at me." Then, serious again, "I can't say why I should like you, lad, but I do. So let me ask you again. Will you join forces with me? I'll teach you all the lore, the short and clever ways of dealing with the world, and give you a full third share of the swag to boot. What do you say? Are we partners?"

Will felt a tickle on his knee. Looking down, he saw that his fore-finger was tracing invisible letters, over and over, on the cloth of his trousers:

ꙄƎY YAꙄ

ꙄƎY YAꙄ

ꙄƎY YAꙄ

At which very instant the tracks curved and a mushroom ring of natural gas tanks swung away to reveal a wall that rose up to fill the sky. To either side it stretched as far as the eye could see. Will's heart quailed at the sheer size of it—larger, it seemed, than all the rest of the world put together. Abruptly the sheer magnitude of his ambi-tion seemed folly. That fell Tower was bigger and meaner and more ruthless than he could ever hope to be. There was no way he could get revenge upon it.

Not as he was now.

ꙄƎY YAꙄ

And yet, simultaneously, a pervasive sense of destiny filled him. If I am to have my vengeance, he thought, I need to learn deceit and much else besides. Very well. Let this fool be my first teacher.

"Yes," he lied. "Partners."

Esme had grown bored with the passing landscape and was rummaging through Nat's luggage. She hauled out a transistor radio and snapped it on. Music more beautiful than anything Will had ever heard flooded the car. It sounded like something that might have been sung by the stars just before dawn on the very first morning of the world. "What is that?" he asked wonderingly.

Nat Whilk smiled. "It's called 'Take the A Train.' By Duke Ellington."

Faster and faster the train sped toward the featureless stone walls until it seemed inevitable they should crash. Then, at the last possible moment, a tunnel opened in the wall, black as a mouth. The train plunged into it, and Babel swallowed it whole.

7

The Tower of Babel

The walls and pillars of the great hall at Nineveh Station were of snow-white marble, according to a tourist brochure that had passed through so many hands on the train that it was falling apart by the time Will saw it. "Seven pillars on either side bear up the shadowy vault of the roof; the roof-tree and the beams are of gold, curiously carved, the roof itself of mother-of-pearl," it said, and also, "The benches that run from end to end of the lofty chamber are of cedar, inlaid with coral and ivory ... The floor of the chamber is tessellated, of marble and green tourmaline, and on every square of tourmaline is carven the image of a fish: as the dolphin, the conger, the oroborus, the salmon, the ichthyocentaur, the kraken, and other wonders of the deep. Hangings of tapestry are ... worked with flowers, snake's-head, snapdragon, dragon-mouth, and their kind; and on the dado below the windows are sculptures of birds and beasts and creeping things."

Perhaps so. But long years before Will alit from the train, the tapestries and benches had been taken down and dismantled, the floor mosaic replaced with linoleum, and the marble pillars and walls stained a bluish gray by engine exhaust and cigarette smoke.

Nevertheless, the great hall overwhelmed him. Its grandeur came not from the opulence of its materials, however, but from the fact that trains were continually arriving, disgorging passengers, and then proceeding to a further platform to take on more. Such were the numbers of travelers and immigrants that, though individually they jostled and bumped against one another like so many swarming insects, collectively they took on the properties of a liquid, flowing like water in streams and rivers, eddying into quiet backwaters, then surging forward again until finally they formed an uneasy lake behind the long dam of customs desks at the far end of the hall.

"You're my family," Nat said. "Remember that."

"Yes, Pop-Pop."

"Why?" Will asked.

"Because I'm going to have to bluff my way in. The passport I'm carrying wouldn't fool a cow."

"Wait. If you're in such a bad position, then why are you involving us in your problems?"

"*Pfft.* I can talk my way out of anything."

Hoisting Esme in one arm and Will's suitcase in the other, the lanky fey pushed through the crowd. Will hurried after, awkwardly toting two of Nat's bags and dragging a third behind him. He struggled to keep sight of Nat and Esme, fearful that if he looked away for even an instant he would lose them forever in the scurrying throngs.

In less time than he would have thought, a customs agent frowned down at Nat's papers, spoke briefly into a telephone, and shunted all three of them through a side doorway. "You want Immigration Control, room 102, down to the end of the hall. You can't miss it. It's the only entranceway that isn't ensorceled to kill unidentified personnel," he said, and closed the door after them.

Room 102 felt preternaturally still after the hubbub of the train hall. Two Formica-topped tables, overflowing with papers, divided the room, with only a narrow passage between them. Under the tables were cardboard boxes crammed with documents. On the far wall, past overflowing filing cabinets, hung two government-issue prints, one to either side of a closed door. They were, predictably enough, Bruegel's *Tower of Babel* and his *"Little" Tower of Babel,* each showing the city as it must have looked in its early stages of construction. In the foreground of the first, King Nimrod loomed over worshipful stonemasons like the giant that he was, sternly admonishing them to ever more heroic feats of construction. But in the other there were no figures at all, and the Tower was ruddy, dark, and ominous, the conflicted hero of its own complex psychodrama.

Two winged bulls with the faces of men and long, square-cut beards, turned, hooves clattering, when Nat, Will, and Esme entered the room. Their hair, beards, and the ends of their tails were elaborately curled and coiffed. They had no arms, of course, but each was attended by a pair of apes in the red uniform with yellow piping of Immigration Control.

"*Vašu putovnicu, molim!*" one bull-man said sternly.

Nat proffered his passport. An ape held it up for his superior to examine.

"*Imate li što za prijaviti?*"

"No, I have nothing to declare. Other than my not being Croatian, I mean."

The winged bull glowered with disapproval, and switched languages. "And yet you're in this office. Why are you here, if you should be elsewhere? Do you think to make fools of us?"

"No, that's my business—see?" Smiling fatuously, Nat jabbed a finger at the papers. "Ichabod the Fool. That's me."

There was a long silence. Then the man-bull tossed his head in the direction of the rear wall. "You see that door?" One of the apes scampered to the door and opened it. "Once you walk out through it, you'll never need worry about this office again. But to do that, you've got to get past us." The ape shut the door and returned to his station. "So I recommend that you—"

"This document is a forgery!" the second agent roared abruptly. To Will's astonishment, it was not Nat's passport but his own that the agent's ape was holding up. "They are all forgeries!"

"No, no, no," Nat clucked, shaking his head reassuringly.

"The transit codes, the ports of origin—all wrong!" The winged bull turned from the passport ape to another who was holding open a book the size of a telephone directory. "According to this, you should have been taken to Ur."

"It wasn't *my* choice to come here," Will objected. "They put me on the train, and this is where it took me. These are the papers that the

DPC officials at Camp Oberon gave me—if they're wrong, then that's *their* fault and not mine."

"It is your responsibility to make sure that any documents issued you are correct and that you're legally entitled to them." The bull nodded his head and his ape shuffled another passport to the fore. "The girl's papers don't list her year of birth."

"We don't know it," Will said.

"Oh? How can that be?" The agent turned to Nat. "Surely you, being her father, ought to know that."

"I wasn't present when she was born," Nat said smoothly. "I travel a great deal. But it should be apparent that my daughter is nine years old. Just put down Year of the Grasshopper."

Esme sat atop their piled luggage, playing quietly with a corn husk doll. Now she looked up, beaming, and said, "I like grasshoppers."

"It is not our job to assist in your forgeries, but to examine them for inconsistencies. Your own passport, for example, is a treasure trove of such. It is printed on a grade of paper never employed for official instruments. It lacks the requisite watermarks. The typeface is laughable. The transshipment stamps appear to have been applied by an ineptly carved raw potato. Even the photograph is suspect. It doesn't look a bit like you."

"Really," Nat said, looking at his watch, "I don't know why we're still here. You're being unnecessarily obstructive. I'm a citizen, and I know my rights."

"Rights?" The first winged bull snorted. "You have no rights. Only obligations and privileges. I define the obligations, and the privileges are contingent upon my goodwill. They can be revoked without explanation or appeal at my whim. Remember that."

"Further," the second winged bull said, "there is more to being a citizen than mere arrogance. You might as well save the act, auslander. We've seen it all."

For an instant, Nat seemed at a loss for words. Then, with an urbane *tsk,* he said, "This can all be cleared up easily enough." He drew several bills from his wallet and placed them between two mounds of yellow flimsies. "I am certain that if you examine these papers, you'll find . . ."

Will had not thought the bulls' eyes could open wider than they were, nor that their expressions could be any more outraged. Now he saw that he was wrong. As one, the two bureaucrats reared their heads back, nostrils flaring with horror. They stamped their hooves and flapped their wings angrily. One brushed against a file cabinet, almost dislodging the folders stacked atop it.

"Place this really quite insulting attempt at bribery in an evidence envelope," one said to the nearest ape.

"Then place the evidence envelope in an accordion file!" commanded the other.

"Add photocopies of all the paperwork introduced so far."

"Open a new case number."

"Cross-reference and send copies to all appropriate offices."

"Get the forms preliminary to swearing out a criminal complaint."

"Document each step and every form in the case log."

As the apes ran wildly about, slamming file drawers open and shut, working the photocopier, and assembling great masses of paper, one man-bull brought his face quite close to Nat's and menacingly said, "You will find that an attempt to suborn agents of His Absent Majesty's governance is not taken lightly here in Babel."

"'Suborn' is such a harsh word," Nat protested. "I was only—"

"Since you are transparently *not* a citizen," the other bull said, "you do not have the right to a lawyer. Should you have the money for one, it will be removed from you. Anything you say, think, or fail to admit can and will be used against you. You will not be told under what charges you are being detained, nor allowed to confront such witnesses as may be subpoenaed to testify to your guilt, nor be informed as how much they were paid to do so. While incarcerated, you will be required to pay room and board at market rates. If you cannot afford to do so, you will be beaten. You do not have the right to medical care. You do not have the right to convalesce. You do not have the right to a funeral. Do you understand?"

"Perhaps I was insufficiently generous. Should I throw in some silage? I've got excellent connections for some prime alfalfa mixed with clover."

Esme tugged Will's sleeve and, when he bent down to the level of her mouth, whispered, "I smell something burning."

Now Will did, too. Craning his neck about, he saw a wisp of smoke rising from the mound of papers on the table. "Um . . ." The others were arguing furiously. He waved his hand in the air. "I think we've got a problem, here."

With a *whoosh,* the papers burst into flames.

The man-bulls reared up in alarm. Simultaneously, Nat shouted, "Look out!" and lunged at the table, whacking at the fire with his hat. His wild efforts, however, managed only to knock the burning papers onto the file-crammed cardboard boxes behind the table.

The fire spread.

A smoke alarm went off. The apes screeched and leaped from table to filing cabinet and back, kicking piles of forms onto the floor in their animal panic. The man-bulls stumbled blindly about the room, flapping their wings noisily. In the sudden confusion, Will almost missed seeing Nat slip out the rear.

Will snatched up his passport, seized Esme's hand, and followed after, unobserved. Only at the last instant did he remember to close the door softly behind him.

Nat was already down to the end of the hall, where two bronze doors were sliding open. He ducked into a freight elevator and hit a button. "Wait for us!" Will cried—but softly, lest he be heard back in room 102. He and Esme jumped into the elevator, the doors closed, and they began to descend. Nat reached out to hug them both. "Oh, children!" he gasped. "Was that fun or what?"

"You're completely mad," Will said angrily. "There was no reason to travel on forged papers—they were *giving* them away at Oberon. Now we're illegal, undocumented, and guilty of who knows how many crimes?"

"We had a good laugh. That's worth a lot."

"To say nothing of losing our luggage."

Nat flung out his arms. "And what a relief to not have all that baggage to carry around!"

The elevator opened into a drab foyer. They pushed through the swinging doors and stood outside on the sidewalk, blinking at a street paved with blue glazed bricks as mastodons in red-and-orange livery lumbered past, followed by camels, bagpipers, kettle-drummers, and a brace of serpent blowers playing a Sousa march. Esme clapped her hands. "It's a parade!" Nymphs danced naked behind the musicians, ivy woven through their hair and about their horns, short goat tails bobbing. Poldies, haints, and hytersprites darted from sidewalk to sidewalk waving long silk pennants, and swan-mays turned somersaults in the air above. Here was splendor greater than anything Will had ever imagined, and it extended down the street in either direction as far as the eye could see.

"What's all this about?" he asked.

Nat shrugged. "It's always something. A festival or an election campaign, it hardly matters. When you live in the big city, you just have to put up with it." He seized Esme's hand and began striding briskly down the avenue.

The city dazzled Will. It was in equal measures exhilarating and terrifying. Forget the stilt walkers, bell ringers, and sprites with hair aflame tumbling past—he didn't recognize half the races he saw watching the parade from the sidewalk. Also, there were costumed paraders, their part already done, returning down the sidewalk with painted faces and cans of beer in their hands, and viewers who had daubed themselves with blood or dressed for the occasion in seven-league hats and pink feather boas, so that he could not make out who properly belonged to the procession and who did not. It was as if all Babel were one great celebration.

Will wanted to be a part of that celebration—without, he was beginning to think, the inconvenient and troublesome presence of Nat Whilk.

"Why is your hand twitching?" Esme asked.

Will looked down in surprise. His hand was moving with a life of its own. Now both his hands rose up before his face, and the one urgently traced out letters on the palm of the other. There was a *T*, an *H*, an *E*, a *Y*, and an *R* and an *E* . . . "They're coming," Will read.

"Who's coming?" Nat said.

L·A·N·C . . . "Lancers."

A company of mounted soldiers burst through the double doors of the building they themselves had earlier emerged from. They had to duck to get through, and once out they straightened and clattered to a halt. Their high-elven leader stared up and down the street. Will felt an almost tangible thrill when their eyes met. Then the commander gestured with his saber—straight at Will.

"Soldiers!" Esme said happily.

"Shit," Will added.

The soldiers formed ranks, then lowered their lances to clear the walk before them. At a barked order from their commander, they started forward at a light canter. The crowds parted with alacrity. Their leader, who alone among them did not carry a lance, lifted his hand. A bright light shone from his palm and his lips moved in incantation. Will felt his limbs growing heavy, the air thickening about him.

"Don't panic," Nat said. "I have a cantrip worth two of his."

His hand darted into his jacket and emerged with a wad of dollar bills held together with a rubber band. He cocked his arm as if he were holding a hand grenade, and then, snapping the rubber band with his thumb, flung the lot into the air.

At the top of his voice, he yelled, *"Money!"*

Pandemonium.

The parade broke up as the marchers converged to snatch at the bills floating down upon them. Those already on the sidewalk fought for space. Dwarves scurried about on all fours, scavenging the bills that had evaded capture on their way down. And the lancers came to a disorganized halt as the mob surged around them. Some, indeed, had to struggle to keep from being pulled from their mounts.

"Follow me." Nat sped down an alley and ran to its end. A trolley rattled by with a clang of its bell and a blue spark of electricity, and he raced across the tracks. Puffing, because he carried Esme on his back, Will managed to catch up just as Nat ducked down a stairway. He set Esme on her feet and they clattered down in his wake.

At the bottom of the stairs was a public elevator platform. They vaulted the turnstiles and squeezed into the Downtown express.

They emerged in the Lower East Side, a neighborhood that was sunken in a twilight gloom, though outside it was brightest midday. Its streetlights were on, and if they were on now, then surely they were never turned off. The buildings to one side of the street were conventional brownstones but those on the other looked to have been carved from raw stone. "In here," Nat said, and ducked down a dingy stairway under a neon sign reading THE DUCHESS'S HOLE.

The saloon smelled of stale beer. Two video poker machines sat unattended in the empty room, flashing and chuckling to themselves. The walls were roughly dressed stone painted black and hung with neon beer signs and framed posters of Jack Dempsey and Muhammad Ali. A silent TV hung in one corner.

Behind the bar—indeed, filling up almost the entire space behind the bar—sat an enormous toad. She was heavy lidded and thick lipped, with vast, soft, waggling chins, bulging eyes, and an expression that went beyond mere skepticism into outright disdain. One corner of her tremendous mouth twisted upward and she said, "Help you, gents?"

"You must be the Duchess. My name's Nat Whilk." He hooked an elbow over the bar. "You look like a sporting lass."

"Don't let my girlish good looks deceive you, donkey-boy. I'm older than I look and I know every scam, glamour, and tuppenny magic there is."

"Not this one. I just invented it." Nat pulled a metal washer out of his pocket and laid it down on the bar. It was a thick chunk of metal with a hole in it the size of a nickel. Alongside it he plunked down a quarter. "Ten dollars says I can push this quarter through this washer."

The toad squeezed the washer between thumb and forefinger. Then she held it to her eye and stared through it. She examined the quarter with equal care. Finally, she said, "All right. You're on."

Nat picked up the washer and, sticking his finger through it, pushed the quarter.

For an instant the Duchess said nothing. Then she laughed and started to haul out a cigar box from under the bar.

"Just put it on my account," Nat said. "I'm thinking I might eat here on a regular basis. Lunch, to begin with. For three."

"A'right." The Duchess picked up a stub of chalk and wrote "NW: $8.45" on a cluttered slate on the side wall.

Nat leaned forward and erased the forty-five cents with his thumb. "For a tip," he said. "Say, do you happen to have a fresh deck of cards?"

The toad produced a deck from under the bar. "Three bucks."

"No, I mean a cold deck."

"Two bits." She replaced the deck with what looked to be its exact double, and adjusted the tally. Nat borrowed the chalk and changed the final five to a zero.

The Duchess smiled.

She waddled into the kitchen, and after a few minutes emerged with two baskets of toasted cheese sandwiches and drew them a beer apiece. When lunch was eaten, Nat bought a pack of Marlboros, rounding down the tab by an additional nickel. Will lit up gratefully. "First I've had since we hit town," he commented.

"New here, eh? Babel's not how you pictured it, I reckon," the Duchess said.

"I thought it would be a single building."

"Everybody thinks that. But a building isn't flexible the way a city is. Times change, and what's needed changes with them. Used to be, folks got around by horse and carriage and slept nine to a room, winters, to keep warm. Now all the carriage houses have been converted to apartments, because with central heating everybody wants to fuck in private. Nimrod understood that, and so he built not a city but the framework for one—a double helix of interlocking gyres, technically, anchored on this volcanic plug. Buildings are thrown up and torn down as needed, but the city goes on. A man of remarkable foresight was King Nimrod."

"Knew him personally, did you?" Nat said, amused.

"I was not always as you see me now," the Duchess said haughtily. "Long ago, I was young and guileless. To say nothing of being small enough to fit into a teacup. I lived in a crevice in the rock on the upper slopes of Ararat then, beside a narrow path to its top. Every morning King Nimrod strode up that path to sing the mountain higher, and every evening he came down again. Such was his habit, and I thought nothing of it for I was then but a dumb beast and innocent of speech or reason.

"One day Nimrod did not climb the mountain. Oh, what a day that was! Great storms fought like dragons in the sky, and lightning lashed the rock. The earth shook to its very foundations, and the mountain danced. There are no words to describe the fury of it. That was the day—but it was many a century before I figured this out—when, in his direst peril, Nimrod called up the sea to destroy his enemies. Ararat rang like a bell then, when the ocean waters struck it fiercer than any hammer, drowning the marshlands at his command and creating the Bay of Demons, which even now is our port and the source of Babel's wealth. But I suppose you already know that story."

"Yes," Will said.

Solemnly, Nat intoned:

> *"Before history existed, before time began,*
> *King Nimrod led the People from Urdumheim.*
> *Across the stunned and empty world they fled,*
> *To the place of marshes in the time of flood . . ."*

His stentorian boom lapsed into a normal speaking voice, and he said, "If you want, I can recite all eight thousand lines."

"Whose tale is this, yours or mine?" the Duchess snapped. "The next day Nimrod came slowly up the mountain. All discontent was his expression and his glance went everywhere, as if he were looking for something he could not find. Chancing upon me, he stopped and of a whim picked me up. Holding me to his face, he addressed me thus: 'Look upon my works, small natterjack, and despair.' His cheeks were streaked with tears, for the price he had paid for his people's emancipation was death. They had been born immortal and he had made them subject to the great wheel of time.

"I, of course, said nothing.

"But Nimrod was soliloquizing, and the Mighty need only the slightest excuse for an audience—which I was—and no sign of comprehension from it either. 'Diminished,' said he, 'are my powers. The mountain that was to be our fortress, I cannot raise another span. Better freedom and death, thought I, than endless life as a slave. Now I am not so sure. What point is there to building, when all must someday come undone? And if I must die someday, then why wait? Tomorrow is no better than today.' He stopped and eyed me critically. 'You ken not a word of this, d'ye? Brute animals know death only when it comes to them. Well, power enough do I yet retain to make you understand.'

"Then his fingers, which to then had held me lightly, closed about me like a cage. Slowly he contracted his hand, and began to crush the life from me. I struggled but could not escape. Great then was my terror! And in that instant did I indeed comprehend the nature of death."

"What did you do?" Will asked.

"I did what any self-respecting toad would do. I pissed in his hand."

Nat winced. "That was perhaps not the wisest possible action, given that Nimrod was not only a mage but a Power."

"What did I know? I was a fucking toad!"

"So what happened?"

"Nimrod laughed, and put me down. 'Live, little toad,' he said. 'Grow and prosper.' So I crawled as deep into the rock as I could go, and there must have been some puissance yet remaining in his words, for here I've been ever since."

"It must be hard on you to be trapped in a bubble of rock and unable to leave," Will said.

"I have my newspaper. I listen to my little radio. Most years I make enough money to keep myself fed, and when I don't I go into hibernation. It's a life."

At that instant there came a clattering like an avalanche of kitchenware from the stairs. The door burst open, and with a thunder of hooves and a spray of splinters, a spidery black nag pulled itself to a violent stop. Behind it, the stairway was steep and winding. The horse must have had double-jointed legs to run so cannily down it, and sinews of steel to come so quickly still. In one fluid motion, its rider leapt from its back. He was the captain of lancers they had seen before.

Will froze in the act of lighting a cigarette. Across the table, Nat looked shocked and saddened. "You dimed us out, Duchess."

The toad grimaced. "You're a pretty young thing," she said, "and I like pretty things. But the hunt for you was all over the police scanner, and I didn't live to be the age I am by taking chances."

The horse straightened its legs and shook itself. Its rider had lost or left behind his saber in the chase and his troop of lancers as well, but he still carried an automatic pistol at his side, and the effortless way he had unsnapped the holster flap as he dismounted suggested he could draw it quickly.

He bowed slightly. "Captain Bagabyxas at your service." He was elegantly lean, with a sharp and narrow face. "I'm afraid I'll have to take you in for questioning."

Will exhaled a mouthful of smoke. He dipped two fingers into his pocket and drew out his passport. "You'll be wanting this, I suppose."

"I will, thanks." The captain accepted the passport without lowering his glance. He tucked it away in his jacket. "You look to be intelligent fellows, and anybody with half a mind finding himself in your situation would be giving thought to escaping." Esme reached up from Nat's lap to stroke the horse's nose, and Bagabyxas smiled faintly. "I advise you not to try. It will count in your favor if you come along peacefully."

Will glanced at Nat and saw his eyes flick once toward the kitchen door. Out that way, then, there would be a back entrance, and a service passage, and once through that, myriad ways to go. All they needed was a moment's distraction.

Under his breath, he murmured, ". . . *schwa.*"

The lancer's coat burst into flame.

Like leaves before a storm, they blew through the kitchen and out the back door. Nat went first with Esme on his shoulder, her wild laughter trailing behind them. Will followed after. "Are . . . are all your days this exciting?" he puffed when they finally stumbled to a halt. They were in a service corridor whose walls were painted industrial green.

"Too many of them, I fear. It comes with the territory when you're a confidence trickster." Nat chuckled. "Ahh, but how about that Duchess? She was quite the gal, wasn't she? What a pity we couldn't work together."

"Stop! Freeze!"

Far down the corridor stood Bagabyxas, his jacket and hair engulfed in flames, and yet—somehow, madly—still determined to stop their escape. His gun arm rose up.

A bullet sizzled through the air between Will and Nat. An instant afterwards came the gun's report, loud enough in the enclosed space that Will could hear nothing else for several minutes.

Again, they fled.

Bagabyxas followed.

They ran down one nightmarish hallway after another without losing the burning lancer. He fired at least three shots, each one a blow to Will's ringing ears. But then, as Will ran past a steel access door, chained shut but slightly ajar in its frame, his hand of its own accord lashed out to the side and grabbed it, almost wrenching his arm from its socket.

He found himself lying on the floor, staring up at a narrow triangular opening between door and jamb, where the door had been wrenched out of true.

"Freeze!" Bagabyxas cried again.

Frantically, Will squeezed through the space and tumbled down a short set of metal stairs. As he lurched to his feet, he heard the burning man yanking furiously at the door. The chain wouldn't hold long at that rate.

He ran.

Rats scurried away at his approach. Roaches crunched underfoot. He was in a great dark space, punctuated by massive I-beams and lit only by infrequent bare bulbs whose light struggled to reach the floor. Somehow, he had made his way into the network of train tunnels that spiraled up through Babel Tower.

Careful to avoid the third rail, he followed one curving set of tracks into darkness, listening for approaching trains. Sometimes he heard their thunder in the distance, and once a train thundered past, mere inches from where he pressed himself, shivering, against the wall, and left him temporarily blinded. When he could see again, the tunnels were silent and there was no light behind him, such as the Burning Man must surely cast if he were still on Will's trail. He was safe now.

And hopelessly lost.

He'd been plodding along for some time when he saw a sewer worker—a haint—in the tunnel up ahead, in hip waders and hard hat. "What you doing here, white boy?" the haint asked when Will hailed him.

"I'm lost."

"Well, you best get yourself unlost. They's trouble brewing."

"I can't," Will began. "I don't know—"

"It's your ass," the haint said. He faded through a wall and was gone.

Will spat in frustration. Then he walked on.

He knew that he'd wandered into dangerous territory when his left hand suddenly rose up of its own volition to clutch his right forearm. Stop! he thought to himself. Adrenaline raced through his veins.

Will peered into the claustrophobic blackness and saw nothing. A distant electric bulb cast only the slightest glimmer on the rails. The pillars here were as thick as trees in a midnight forest. He could not make out how far they extended. But by the spacious feel of the air, he was in a place where several lines of tracks joined and for a time ran together.

Far behind him was a lone set of signal lights, unvarying green and red dots.

He was abruptly aware of how easy it would be for somebody to sneak up behind him here. Maybe, he thought, he should turn around and go back.

In that instant, an unseen fist punched him hard in the stomach.

Will bent over almost double, and simultaneously his arms were seized from either side. His captors shoved him forward and forced him down onto his knees. His head was bent almost to the ground.

"Release him." The voice was warm and calm, that of a leader.

The hands let go. Will remained kneeling. Gasping, he straightened and looked about.

He was surrounded.

They—whoever they were—had come up around him in silence. Will's sense of hearing was acute, but even now he couldn't place them by sound. Rather, he felt the pressure of their collective gaze, and saw their eyes, pair by pair, wink into existence.

"Boy, you're in a shitload of trouble now," the voice said.

Jack Riddle

The speaker's eyes glowed red. "Well? Bast got your tongue? I'm giving you the opportunity to explain why you have invaded the Army of Night's turf. You won't get a second one."

Will fought down his fear. There was great danger here, but great opportunity as well—if he had the nerve to grasp it. Speaking with a boldness he did not feel, he said, "This is your territory. I recognize that. It wasn't my intention to trespass. But now that I'm here, I hope you'll allow me to stay."

Calmly, dangerously, the speaker said, "Oh?"

"I'm broke, paperless, and without friends. I need someplace to be. This looks as good as any. Let me join your army and I'll serve you well."

"Lord Weary knows you're a fugitive," said a whispery voice. "You can't hide a thing like that. Not here in the dark. There are no distractions here, no sunlight to dazzle the eye."

"Who's chasing you?" asked Lord Weary.

Will thought of the political police, of the lancers, of the Burning Man, and made a wry grimace. "Who isn't?"

"He kinda cute," said somebody female. "If we can't fight, maybe we find some other use for him."

Several of her comrades snickered. One murmured, "You bad, Jenny."

"Lord Weary is amused," said the whisperer, "and thus inclined to be merciful. But mercy does not extend far here. You will be beaten and driven away, lest you bring your pursuers down upon the Army of Night."

A new voice said, "That's bullshit! The Breaknecks sent him here to spy on us. He dies. Simple as that."

"That's not your decision, Tatterwag," Lord Weary said sharply.

"*Siktir git!*" Tatterwag swore. "We know what he is!"

"Are we savages? No, we are a community of brothers. Whatever is done here will be done in accordance with our laws." There was a long pause, during which Will imagined Lord Weary looking from side to side to see if any dared oppose him. When no one did, he went on, "You brought this upon yourself."

Will didn't ask what Lord Weary meant by that. He recognized a gang when he encountered one—he'd run with enough of them as a boy. There was always a leader, always the bright kid who stood at his shoulder advising him, always the troublemaker who wanted to usurp the leader's place. They always had laws, which were never written down. Their idea of justice was inevitably the *lex talionis,* an eye for an eye and a drubbing for an insult. They always settled their differences with a fight.

"Trial by combat," the Whisperer said.

Somebody lit a match. With a soft hiss, a Coleman lantern shed fierce white light over the thronged I-beams, making them leap and then fall as the flame was adjusted down again to a soft near-extinction.

"You may stand now," Lord Weary said.

Will stood.

A ragged line of some twenty to thirty feys confronted him. They were of varied types and races, tall and short, male and female, but all looked beaten and angry, like feral dogs that know they can never triumph over the village dwellers but will savage one who is caught alone and without weapons. The lantern shone through several, but dimly, as if through smoked glass, and by this Will knew that they were haints.

Directly before Will stood a tall figure whose air of command made clear that he could only be Lord Weary. He had the pallor, high cheekbones, and lanceolate ears of one of high-elven blood, and the noble bearing of a born leader as well. Will could not pick out the owners of the other two voices.

But then a swamp-gaunt rushed out of the pack and, pointing a reed-thin arm at Will, cried, "He's one of the Breakneck Boys! I say we kill him now. Just kill him!"

So he had to be Tatterwag.

Will stepped forward, throwing a hard shoulder into the gaunt to knock him aside. "Kill me if you think it possible," he said to Lord Weary. "But I don't think you can. If you doubt me, then name your champion. Make him the biggest, strongest mother you've got, so there won't be any doubt afterward that I could defeat any one of you if I had to. I do not brag. Then, if you'll take me, I will gladly pledge my loyalty and put my powers at your service."

"That was well spoken," Lord Weary said mildly. "But talk is cheap and times are hard." Raising his voice, he said, "Who shall be our champion?"

"Bonecrusher," somebody said.

There was susurration of agreement. "Bonecrusher . . . 'Crusher . . . The big fella . . . Yeah, Bonecrusher."

The figure that shambled forward was covered with fur, wore no clothing, and carried a length of metal pipe for a club. It was a wodewose—a wild man of the forest.

Will had seen wild men before, out in the Old Forest. In some ways, they were little more than animals, though articulate enough for simple conversations and too cunning to be safely hunted. They were stuck forever in the dawn-times, unable to cope with any way of life more sophisticated than a hunter-gatherer existence nor any tool more complex than a pointed stick. Machines they feared, and they would not sleep in houses, though occasionally an injured one might take shelter in a barn. He could not imagine what twisty path had brought this one so far from his natural habitat.

The wodewose's mouth worked with the effort of summoning up words. "Fuck you," he said at last. Then, after a pause, "Asshole."

Will bowed. "I accept your challenge, sir. I'll do my best to do you no permanent harm."

A mean grin appeared in the wild man's unkempt beard. "You're bugfuck," he said, and then, "Shithead."

This was another thing that every gang Will had ever been in had: Somebody big and stupid who lived to fight.

Lord Weary faded back into darkness and returned bearing a length of pipe, much like the one the wodewose carried. He handed it to Will. "There are no rules," he said. "Except that one of you must die." He raised his voice. "Are the combatants ready?"

"Fuck, yeah."

"Yes," Will said.

"Then douse the light."

All in an instant, darkness swallowed Will whole. In sudden fear he cried, "I can't see!"

There was a smile in Lord Weary's voice. "We can."

With a soft scuffle of bare feet, Bonecrusher attacked.

Though Will felt himself as good as blind, there must have been some residual fraction of light, for he saw a pale glint of pipe as it slashed downward at his head. Panicked, he brought up his own pipe just in time to block it.

The force of the blow buckled his knees.

The wodewose raised the pipe again, then chopped it down, trying for Will's shin. Will was barely about to leap back from it in time. There was a *clang* as the pipe bounced off the rail, striking sparks. He found himself panting, though he hadn't even struck a blow yet.

Will knew how to fight with a quarterstaff—every village lad did— but the wild man was not fighting quarterstaff-style but club-style. It was a sweeping, muscular fighting technique the like of which he had never faced before. The club slashed past him again, inches from his chest. Had it connected it would have broken Will's ribs. The wild man followed through, as if he were swinging a baseball bat, and brought it smoothly back, hard and level. Will ducked low, saving his skull from being crushed.

Will swung his pipe wildly and felt it bounce off the wodewose's ribs. But it didn't even slow the wild man down. His club came down on Will's shoulder.

Just barely, Will managed to twist aside so that the club only dealt him a glancing, stinging blow to his arm. But that was enough to numb him for an instant and make his fingers involuntarily release their hold on one end of his weapon. Now it was held only by his left hand.

There was a murmur of admiration from the watchers, but no more. Which meant that Bonecrusher was not popular in the Army of Night, however much they might value his fighting skill.

The pain brought the dragon rising up within Will, a ravening wave of anger that threatened to wash over his mind and drown all conscious thought. He fought it down. Whirling the pipe around his head, he feinted at one shoulder. Then, when the wodewose brought up his own weapon to block it, he shifted his attack. The pipe slammed into Bonecrusher's forehead and bounced off.

Bonecrusher shook his matted dreadlocks and raised his weapon once more.

At that moment, a great noise rose up in the distance. A train! Will tucked his pipe under one arm as if it were a lance and ran full-tilt at his opponent. The pipe struck him in the chest and knocked him stumbling backward.

The train rounded a bend. Its headlight blossomed like the sun at midnight.

Will retreated to the far side of the track. He pressed himself against the nearest support beam, feeling its cold strength under his back. Across from him, Bonecrusher started forward, hesitated, and then turned away, one great hand covering his eyes.

His eyes? Oh.

The locomotive slammed past Will, a wash of air shoving against him like a warm fist. He had a momentary glimpse of astonished faces in the passenger car windows before he threw an arm over his eyes to shield himself from the painfully bright light.

Then the train was gone. When he opened his eyes again, he could see nothing.

Bonecrusher chuckled. "Yer blind, aintcha?" he said. "Mother-fucker."

Now Will was truly afraid.

With fear came anger, however, and anger made it easier for him to draw upon the dragon-darkness within him. He felt it rising up in his blood and clamped down tight. He refused to give it control. It struggled against him, a fire running through his veins, an evil song lifting in his throat. It yearned to be let free.

He heard the whisper of Bonecrusher's naked feet on the railroad ties. He backed away.

Now an inner vision seemed to pierce the darkness. All was still shadow within shadow, but he knew that the shifting blackness directly before him was the wodewose padding quietly forward, raising his makeshift club for one final and devastating blow.

The dragon-anger was straining at its leash. So Will let slip his hold a little, allowing the anger to leap forward to meet the attack. He threw aside his own pipe and stepped into the blow. With one hand, he caught the wild man's club and wrested it from his grasp. With the other, he seized the wodewose by the throat.

Flinging away the wodewose's weapon, he stooped and grabbed his opponent by his thigh. The creature's fur was as stiff as an Airedale's, and matted with knots. Will lifted him up over his head. He tried to curse, but Will's hand clutched his throat too tightly for anything meaningful to emerge.

The bastard was helpless now. Will could swing him around and smash his head against a pillar or drop him down over his knee, breaking his spine. It would be the easiest thing in the world, either way.

Well, screw that.

"I don't have anything against you," he told his struggling opponent. "Give me your word of surrender, and I'll set you free."

Bonecrusher made a gurgling noise.

"That's not possible," Lord Weary said with obvious regret. "Our laws say: To the death."

Frustration filled Will. To have come so far, only to be thwarted by a childish warrior's code! Well, then, he would have to run. He doubted the Army of the Night would pursue him with much enthusiasm after seeing how easily he defeated their champion.

"If your laws say that," Will snarled, "then they're not mine."

With a surge of anger, he flung the wodewose away from him.

"Fucking bas—!" The word cut off abruptly as the wodewose hit the ground. Electrical sparks flew into the air like fireworks. The wodewose's body arced and crisped. There was a smell of burnt hair and scorched flesh.

Somebody whistled and said, "That's cold."

Will had forgotten entirely about the third rail.

Lord Weary picked out four of his soldiers for a burial detail. "Carry Bonecrusher upstairs," he said, "and leave him somewhere he'll be found, so that City Services will take care of the body. Be sure he's lying facing up! I don't want one of my soldiers mistaken for an animal." Then he clapped a hand on Will's shoulder. "Well fought, boy. Welcome to the Army of Night."

When the burial detail had lugged Bonecrusher's body into oblivion, Lord Weary lined up those who remained and led them the other way. "On to Niflheim," he said. Will joined the line and, shivering, managed to keep pace.

He'd walked for what seemed like forever and no time at all when the smell of urine and feces welled up around him so strong that it made his eyes water. Somebody lived down here. A lot of somebodies. Will found himself stumbling up a crumbling set of stairs and onto a cement platform.

A miniature city arose before him. There were perhaps a hundred or so shanties built one on top of the other of wooden crates and cardboard boxes, each one sufficient to hold a sleeping bag and little more. Wicker baskets, large enough to sleep in, hung from the ceiling. There were narrow streets between the shanties down which shadows flitted. The Army of Night wove its way through them into a central plaza, where a cluster of haints and feys sat crouched around a portable television set, its volume turned down to a murmur. Others sat about talking quietly or reading tattered paperbacks by candlelight. High on the walls above was a frieze of tiles that showed dwarves mining and smelting and manufacturing. Deep runes in the stone arch over a cinder-blocked doorway read NIFLHEIM STATION. Judging by the newspapers and old clothes strewn about, it had been closed and abandoned long ago.

A hulder (Will could tell from her buxom figure and by the cow's tail sticking out from under her skirt) rose to greet them. "Lord Weary," she said. "You are welcome here, and your army, too. I see you have somebody new." Most of those who rose in her wake were haints.

"I thank you, thane-lady Hjördis. Our recruit is so recent he hasn't chosen a name for himself yet. He is our new champion."

"Him?" Hjördis scowled. "This *boy*?"

"Don't be fooled by his looks, the lad's tough. He killed Bonecrusher."

Soft muttering washed over the platform. "By trickery?" somebody asked dubiously.

"In fair and open combat. I saw it all."

There was a moment's tension before the thane-lady nodded, accepting. Then Lord Weary said to her, "We must confer. Serious matters are afoot."

"First we eat," Hjördis said. "You will sit with me at the head table."

To Will's surprise, he was included with Lord Weary in the invitation. Apparently the office of champion made him a counselor as well. He watched as tables were built in the central square, of boards set over wire milk crates, and then covered with sheets of newspaper in place of linen. A cobbley set out pads of newspaper for seats and paper plates for them to eat from. Another filled the plates with food. The thane-lady's table was set under the wall, beneath the tiled dwarves. She and her favored companions sat with their backs to the wall, so that the rows of lesser-ranked diners faced them.

The food was better than might be expected, some of it scrounged from grocery-store dumpsters after passing its sell-by date, and the rest of it from upstairs charities. They ate by the light of tuna-can lamps with rag wicks in rancid cooking oil, conversing quietly.

Will commented that the tunnels seemed more labyrinthine and of greater extent than he had thought they would be, and Hjördis said, "You don't know the half of it. There used to be fifteen different gas companies in Babel, six separate sets of steam tunnels, and Sirrush only can say how many subway systems, pneumatic trains, sub-surface lines, underground trolleys, and pedestrian walkways that nobody uses anymore. Add to that maintenance tunnels for the power and telephone and plumbing and sewage systems, storm drains, the summer retreats that the wealthy used to have dug for them a century ago, the bomb shelters, the bootleggers' vaults . . ."

Lord Weary shook his head in agreement. "There is no lore-master of Babel's secret ways. They are too many, and too varied." His sea-green eyes studied Will gravely. "Now. Tell us what drove you here."

"Speak carefully or truthfully," the Whisperer said in his ear, "or you will not survive the meal." Will spun around, but there was nobody there. He looked into Lord Weary's stern face and decided it was the truth.

He told his tale, concluding, "Since that time, I have been cast out of my village and ill fortune has pursued me across Fäerie Minor all the way to the Dread Tower. Perhaps I have been cursed by the dragon's death. All I know is that from that day I have had no place to call home."

"You have a home here now, lad," said Lord Weary. "We shall be a second family to you, if you will have us."

He laid a hand on Will's head and a great flood of emotion washed over Will. Suddenly, and for no reason he could name, he loved the elf-lord like a father. Warm tears flowed down his cheeks.

When he could speak again, Will asked, "Why do you live down here?"

It was a meaningless question, meant simply to move the conversation to less emotional ground. But, "Why does anybody live anywhere?" the Whisperer said in his ear. Will spun around, and there was nobody there.

Then, graciously, Hjördis explained that though those above dismissed the dwellers in darkness as trolls and feral dwarves, very few of them were subterranean by nature. Most of the thane-lady's folk were haints and drows, nissen, shellycoats, and broken feys—anyone lacking the money or social graces to get along in open society. They had problems with drugs and alcohol and insanity, but they looked after one another as best they could. Their own name for themselves was *johatsu*—"nameless wanderers."

"Are there a lot of communities like this one?"

"There are dozens," Lord Weary said, "and possibly even hundreds. Some are as small as six or ten individuals. Others run much larger than what you see here. No one knows for sure how many live in darkness. Tatterwag speculates there are tens of thousands. But they don't communicate with each other and they won't work together and they are perforce nomadic, for periodically the transit police discover the settlements and bust them up, scattering their citizens. But the Army of Night is going to change all that. We're the first and the only organized military force the johatsu have ever formed."

"How many are in the Army, all told?"

The thane-lady hid a smile under a paper napkin. Stiffly, Lord Weary said, "You've met them all. This is a new idea, and slow to catch on. But it will grow. My dream will bear fruit in the fullness of time." His voice rose. "Look around you! These are the dispossessed of Babel—the weak, the injured, the gentle. Who speaks for them? Not the Lords of the Mayoralty. Not the Council of Magi. His Absent Majesty was their protector once, but he is long gone and no one knows where. Somebody must step forward to fill that void. I swear by the Sun, the Moon, and the Stars, and the Golden Apples of the West, that if the Seven permit it, that somebody shall be me!"

The johatsu froze in their places, not speaking, barely breathing. Their eyes shone like stars.

Hjördis laid a hand over Lord Weary's. "Great matters will wait upon food," she said. "Time enough to discuss these things after we eat."

When all had eaten and the dishes had been cleared away, Hjördis lit a cigarette and passed it around the table. "Well?" she said at last.

"When last we were here," Lord Weary said, "I left some crates in your keeping. Now we have need of them."

A shadow crossed the thane-lady's face. But she nodded. "I thought as much. So I had my folk retrieve them."

Six Niflheimers stood up, faded into darkness, and returned, lugging long wooden crates between them. The crates were laid down before the table and, at a gesture from Lord Weary, Tatterwag pried open one with his bowie knife.

Light gleamed on rifle barrels.

Suddenly the taste of death was in the air. Cautiously, Will said, "What do we need these for?"

"There's going to be a rat hunt," Lord Weary said.

"We're hunting rats?"

Lord Weary grinned mirthlessly. "We're not the hunters, lad. We're the rats."

The Niflheimers had been listening intently. Now they crowded around the main table. "We call them the Breakneck Boys," one said. "They come down here once a month, on the Day of the Toad or maybe the Day of the Labrys, looking for some fun. They got night goggles and protective spells like you wouldn't believe, and they carry aluminum baseball bats. Mostly, we just slip away from 'em. But they usually manage to find somebody too old or sick or drugged-up to avoid them."

"It's a fucking *hobby* for them," Tatterwag growled.

"Last time, they caught poor old Martin Pecker drunk asleep, only instead of giving him a bashing like usual, they poured gasoline over him and set it on fire."

"I saw the corpse!"

"This is a mad notion and a dangerous folly," the Whisperer said. "Their sires are industrialists and Lords of the Mayoralty. If even one of their brats dies, they'll send the mosstroopers down here with dire wolves to exact revenge."

"I fear retaliation," the thane-lady said, and then, with obvious reluctance. "Yet the Breaknecks' predations worsen. Perhaps it is time to meet violence with violence."

"No!" Will said. He had eaten almost nothing, for his stomach was still queasy from the stench of Niflheim, and Bonecrusher's death weighed heavily upon him. If he closed his eyes, he could see the sparks rising up around the wodewose's body. He hadn't wanted to kill the creature. It had happened because he hadn't thought the situation through beforehand. Now he was thinking very hard and fast indeed. "Put the guns back."

"You're not *afraid?*" Lord Weary drew himself up straight, and Will felt his disapproval like a lash across his shoulders.

"I can take care of the Breaknecks," Will said. "If you want me to, I'll take care of them myself."

There was a sudden silence.

"Alone?"

"Yes. But to pull this off, I'll need a uniform. The gaudier the better. And war paint. The kind that glows in the dark."

Hjördis grinned. "I'll send our best shoplifters upstairs."

"And explosives. A hand grenade would be best, but—no? Well, is there any way we can get our hands on some chemicals to make a bomb?"

"There's a methamphetamine lab up near the surface," Tatterwag said. "The creeps who run it think nobody knows it's there. They got big tanks of ethyl ether and white gasoline. Maybe even some red phosphorus."

"Do we have anybody who knows how to handle them safely?"

"Um . . . there's one of us got a Ph.D. in alchemy. Only, it was back when. Up above." Tatterwag glanced nervously at Lord Weary. "Before he came here. So I don't know whether he wants me to say his name or not."

"You have a doctorate?" Will said. "How in the world did you . . ."—he was going to say *fall so low* but thought better of it— ". . . wind up here?"

Offhandedly Lord Weary said, "Carelessness. Somebody offered me a drink. I liked it, so I had another. Only one hand is needed to hold a glass, so I began smoking to give the other one something to do. I took to dueling and from there it was only a small step to gambling. I bought a fighting cock. I bought a bear. I bought a dwarf. I began to frequent tailors and whores. From champagne I moved to whisky, from whisky to wine, and from wine to Sterno. So it went until the only libation I had not yet drunk was blood, the only sex untried was squalid, and the only vice untasted was violent revolution.

"Every step downward was pleasant. Every new experience filled me with disdain for those who dared not share in it. And so, well, here I am."

"Is this a true history," Will asked, "or a parable?"

"Your question," Lord Weary said, "is a deeper one than you know—whether the world I sank through was real or illusory. Many a better mind than mine or yours has grappled with this very issue without result. In any event, I'll make your bomb."

It took hours to make the plan firm. But at last Hjördis rose from the table and said, "Enough. Our new champion is doubtless tired. Bonecrusher's quarters are yours now. I will show you where you sleep."

She took Will by the hand and led him to an obscure corner of the box-village. There she knelt before a kind of tent made of patched blankets hung from clotheslines. "In here." She raised the flap and crawled inside.

Will followed.

To his surprise, the interior was clean. Inside, a faded Tabriz carpet laid over stacked cardboard served as floor and mattress. A vase filled with phosphorescent fungi cast a gentle light over the space. Hjördis turned and, kneeling, said, "All that was 'Crusher's is yours now. His tent. His title . . ." She pulled her dress off over her head. "His duties."

Will took a deep, astonished breath. It seemed too awful to kill the wodewose and bed his lover all on the same day. Hesitatingly, he said, "We don't *have* to . . ."

The thane-lady stared at him in blank astonishment. "You're not gay, are you? Or suffering from the Fisher King's disease?" She touched his crotch. "No, I can see you're not. What is it, then?"

"I just don't see how you can sleep with me after I killed your . . . killed Bonecrusher."

"You don't think this is *personal,* do you?" Hjördis laughed. "Blondie, you're the most fucked-up champion I ever saw." At her direction, he took off his clothes. She drew him down and guided him inside her. Then she wrapped her legs around his waist and slapped him on the rump.

"Giddy up," she commanded.

So galloped the chariot-horses of night. Briefly, the first time he came, Will could sense the scryers of the political police searching for him. But half of Babel lay between him and *les poulettes,* and then Hjördis was guiding his head downward to her orchid and he was too busy to think any more.

In the morning (but he had to take Hjördis's word for it that it was morning), Will went out with two of Lord Weary's scouts to look over possible locales for the plan. Then he returned to the box city and sorted through the heaps of clothing that the Niflheimers had brought him, some dug out of old stashes and some custom stolen for the occasion. Carefully, he assembled his costume: Biker boots. Mariachi pants. A top hat with a white scarf wrapped around the band, one end hanging free behind like a ghostly foxtail, with a handful of turkey feathers from the Meatpacking District splayed along the side. A marching band jacket with a white sash. All topped off with a necklace of rat skulls.

With the phosphorescent makeup, he painted two red slashes slanting downward over his eyes, a straight blue line along his nose, and a yellow triangle about his mouth to make a mocking, cartoonish grin:

With luck, the effect would be eerie enough to give his enemies pause. More importantly, the elves would see the glowing lines on his face, the top-hat-feathers-and-scarf, and the necklace of skulls, but they wouldn't see *him*. Once he wiped off the makeup and ditched the uniform, he would be anonymous again. He could walk the streets above without fearing arrest.

"I'll just need just one last thing," he said when he was done. "A motorcycle."

Two days later, the Army of Night's outposts came running up silently with news that the Breakneck Boys had entered the tunnels. Will had already scouted out the perfect place for a confrontation—a vast and vaulted space as large as a cathedral that had been constructed centuries ago as a cistern for times of siege. A far more recent water main cut through it at the upper end, but otherwise it was much as it had been the day it was drained. Now he sent out decoys to lure the Boys there, while he made up his face with phosphorescent war-paint and wheeled his stolen motorcycle into place.

"You stone-souped them," a voice whispered in his ear.

"Yeah, I guess I did," Will said. "But if I'd asked for the motorcycle first, I wouldn't have gotten it. And after this stunt, nobody's going to mind."

"Or else you'll be dead."

"Tell me something, Whisperer. I never hear anybody else talking directly to you. Why is that?"

"Because you're the only one who can hear me." The whisper was soft and intimate, with a mocking edge to it. "Only you, sweet Will."

"Who *are* you?"

Silence. The Whisperer was gone.

Will waited in a niche behind a pillar at the lower end of the cistern. For the longest time there was no noise other than the grumble of distant trains. Then, faintly, he heard drunken elven laughter. He watched as the decoys ran past his station like two furtive shadows. The voices grew more boisterous and then suddenly boomed as the Breakneck Boys emerged from a doorway near the ceiling at the upper end of the cistern.

They began to descend a long brick stairway along the far wall.

They glimmered in the dark, did the elves, like starlight. They carried Maglites and aluminum bats. Some wore camouflage suits. Some had night goggles. They were nine in number, and uncannily young, little more than children. Their leader drained the last of his beer and threw away the can. It rattled into silence.

Will waited until they were off the stairs and had clambered over the water main and started across the cistern floor. Then he kickstarted the motorcycle. It was a stripped-down Kawasaki three cylinder two-stroke, easy to handle and loud as hell. Pulling out of the niche, Will cranked the machine hard left and opened it up. The vault ceiling bouncing the engine's roar back at him, he charged at the elfpack like a banshee with her ass on fire.

It felt great to be on a cycle again! Puck Berrysnatcher, back when he and Will were best friends, had owned a dirt bike and they'd practiced on it, turn on turn, until they'd both mastered such stunts as young males thought important.

Will popped a wheelie and came to a stop not ten yards from the astonished elves.

Throttling down the engine so he could be heard, he cried, "I challenge thee by the *holmgangulog*, if thou hast honor! I am the captain and the rightwise defender of my folk. Present your champion that we may contest at deeds of arms."

A disbelieving look, followed by low, mean laughter passed among the elves. "So you know the politesse of challenge, Master Scarecrow," said the foremost of them. Whatever else he might be, he was no coward. "Very well. I hight Florian of House L'Inconnu." He bowed mockingly. "What is your name and what terms do you propose?"

"Captain Jack Riddle," Will said, choosing the nom de guerre almost at random. "High explosives at close quarters."

The elf-brat rubbed his chin, as if amused. "Your proposal is scarce workable." Casually, his hand crept downward between the lapels of his jacket. Doubtless he had a gun there in a shoulder harness. "For, you see, I have no explosives with me."

"Tough titty," Will said.

With a muttered word, he detonated the bomb that earlier he had very carefully placed for maximum effect.

The water main, which was directly behind the Breaknecks, blew open.

A great wave of water struck the Breakneck Boys from behind, knocking them over and tumbling them helplessly before it. But not—and this was the crucial part of Will's plan—killing any of them.

Will, meanwhile, had spun around his bike and opened the throttle wide. He raced downslope ahead of the cascading water, cut a right so sharp he almost lost control, and was out of the cistern and roaring up a narrow electric conduit access tunnel without a single drop getting on him.

He would have liked to have seen the Breaknecks gather themselves together after the water washed them down to the bottom of the cistern. It would have been worth much to have heard their curses and witnessed their dismay as they pulled themselves up and began the long and soggy journey back aboveground. But you couldn't have everything.

Anyway, he was sure to hear of it. There was a slit-gallery near the top of the cistern that had been used for inspections, which was thronged with silent watchers, soldiers from the Army of Night and potential recruits from Niflheim and possibly even Hjördis herself. They'd have seen and heard everything. They'd have witnessed how he had routed their enemies without the least injury to himself. They'd want a share in his glory. They'd boast of his prowess. No longer was he merely their champion.

He was their hero now.

That evening the johatsu migrated several miles deeper into the tunnels. They moved silently and surely, and when they found their destination—an abandoned pneumatic train tube from an experimental line that went bankrupt in the Century of the Turbine—Lord Weary sent his specialists to tap into the electric and water lines. Even at this distance from the shattered main, the water pressure was lessened. But unlike the citizens above, they'd known to fill plastic bottles beforehand.

"Dockweed," Will said. A hudkin snapped to attention. "Take a couple of likely lads and scout out a good location for latrines. Not too close to the encampment. That's unsanitary." He caught Lord Weary looking at him, and hastily added, "If that's all right with you, sir."

Lord Weary waved a hand, endorsing everything. Then, placing an arm over Will's shoulder, so that it would be ostentatiously obvious to all that they two were conferring with perfect confidence, he murmured, "Dearer art thou to me, after your little escapade today, than meat and drink to a starving man. Stand by me and I shall raise you higher than you can imagine, so that my empire rests upon your shoulders. But if you ever again give orders in my presence without first deferring to me, I'll have you gutted and chained to the bedrock for the rats to eat alive. Do you understand?"

Will swallowed. "Sir."

"I would regret it, of course. But discipline knows no favorites." He released Will. "Tell me something. What exactly have we accomplished today? Other than raising morale, I mean. In a day or three, the main will be rebuilt. The Breakneck Boys are still alive. By now they're probably fast asleep in their feather beds."

"We've cut off an entire neighborhood from water for however long the repairs last. They'll take that seriously up above. If their investigations turn up the Breaknecks' involvement, it will be a political embarrassment for their parents. If not, the Breakneck Boys will still know what a close call it was. The smarter among them will realize they were given a warning. That I could as easily have killed them. We won't be seeing them back again."

"There'll be others."

Will grinned wolfishly. "Bring 'em on."

But his bravado was all bluster and bluff. Nothing here below was as simple as it seemed. While he was waiting in ambush for the Breakneck Boys, the Whisperer had called him Will—yet he had given that name to nobody in the territories below.

So how had the Whisperer known?

9

Great Mother of Horses

William adapted to the darkness. He learned its ways, learned to love the stillness and the silence of it. He grew familiar with the rumor of distant trains, the small dripping and creaking and scurrying sounds that were normal to the tunnels, and the fainter and more furtive noises that were not. He learned how to crouch motionless for hours, his eyes so thoroughly adapted to the dark that when a transit worker or a patrolman went by with a flashlight, he had to narrow them to slits against its glare. He learned how to move silent as a wraith, so that he could follow these intruders from the upper world for hours without them suspecting a thing.

Nighttimes, he went upstairs to dumpster-dive and sometimes to steal. Just to keep in touch with his troops. It was important for them to know that he could do the work of any one of them and did not consider it beneath him. On deep patrols, when it was not possible to go topside for food, he learned to catch and roast and eat rats. Whenever they could spare the time, he sent his forces out to explore and to map, until he knew more of Babel's underworld than any individual ever had before. He would interview any wanderer who passed through Lord Weary's territory, and those who were capable but solitary by nature he organized into a loose confederation of messengers, so that for the first time all the johatsu communities were kept informed of each other's goings-on.

Volunteers arrived daily, anxious to serve under the hero of whom they'd heard so much. Most of them were turned away. Nevertheless, the Army of Night grew. Little by little, their territory was expanding. Bindlestiffs, sadistic cops, degenerate trolls, and other predators learned to avoid tunnels marked with the three-lines-and-a-triangle that had become the token of Captain Jack's protection.

Will knew his work was bearing fruit the day he ghosted up behind a transit cop, squeezed his upper arm in one hand, whispered softly in his ear, "My name is Jack Riddle and if you want to live, you'll place your revolver on the ground beside you and leave," and was instantly obeyed.

That same day, one of his runners brought him a wanted poster from up above. It had a crude drawing of a fey with his grinning face paint, hat, and skull necklace, and it read:

WANTED FOR TERRORIST ACTIVITY, THE DEMON, SPRITE, OR GAUNT KNOWN AS

JACK RIDDLE

Aliases: Captain Jack Riddle, Captain Jack, Jack the Lucky, Laughing Jack

DESCRIPTION

Date of Birth: Unknown	**Hair:** Blond
Place of Birth: Unknown	**Eyes:** Dark
Height: Unknown	**Sex:** Male
Weight: Unknown	**Complexion:** Pale
Build: Slim	**Citizenship:** Unknown

Scars and Marks: None known

Remarks: A flamboyant dresser, Riddle's dramatic persona has led some to speculate that he may have formerly been involved in theater. By his bearing, he may once have been associated with the aristocracy, possibly as a servant.

JACK RIDDLE IS BEING SOUGHT FOR HIS ROLE IN NUMEROUS TERRORIST ACTS PERFORMED IN CONNECTION WITH

> HIS LEADERSHIP OF A SUBTERRANEAN PARAMILITARY
> FORCE THAT HAS COMMITTED ASSAULTS UPON AGENTS
> OF HIS ABSENT MAJESTY'S GOVERNANCE AS WELL AS
> UPON INNOCENT MEMBERS OF THE CITIZENRY OF BABEL.
>
> **CAUTION**
> HE HAS A SAVAGE TEMPER AND SHOULD BE CONSIDERED
> ARMED AND EXTREMELY DANGEROUS.
>
> **REWARD**
> His Absent Majesty's governance is offering the informant's
> weight in gold to any citizen in Categories C through G or a
> statistically derived equivalent for all others, for information
> leading directly to the arrest of Jack Riddle.

"How about that?" Will said, grinning. "And to think that a couple of months ago I was a nobody!"

"Don't you get cocky, Jack," Hjördis said. "That's a lot of money. There are plenty who would turn you in for a fraction of that." She fastened her brassiere over her stomach, then slid it right way around, put her arms through the straps, and shrugged into it. "I'd be tempted myself, if I didn't have obligations to my people." She wriggled into her dress.

"You shouldn't joke like that." Will felt inexplicably hurt.

"You think I'm joking? That's enough wealth to buy anybody's way up to the surface."

"We don't need gold to do that. After we've consolidated the underworld, we can rise up from beneath and seize the neighborhoods above us. Then we'll take the Dread Tower, one level at a time, all the way to the Palace of Leaves."

"I realize that's Lord Weary's plan," Hjördis said doubtfully. "But how likely is it, really? I fail to understand why you would buy so completely into a fallen elf-lord's delusions of glory."

For a second Will did not speak. Then he said, "I have been driven across Fäerie Minor by chance and events, helpless as a leaf in a storm. Well, no more! I needed a cause to devote myself to, one that would give me the opportunity to strike back against my oppressors, and Lord Weary provided me with one. It's as simple as that."

He returned to the poster. "Innocent citizenry. That would be the Breakneck Boys, you think? Or the drug dealers?" Enough of their soldiers were addicted to various substances that it would be foolish to think that drug trafficking could be stopped. But the dealers were territorial and well armed, and prone to sudden violence. Johatsu had been gunned down simply because they'd wandered into the wrong tunnel at the wrong time. So the dealers had been driven upstairs. Those who cared to sell nickel bags of pixie dust or Mason jars of moonshine close by the commonly known exits were tolerated. But when their goods were tainted—when they killed—they were subject to being snatched and hauled below for a trial by the dead user's peers.

There was a polite cough outside the box's entrance. It was Jenny Jumpup. "Sir. Lord Weary's respects, and he say pull your dick out the lady-thane and assemble your raiders. He want his horses."

The clanging began in the distance, regular and unrelenting, the sound of somebody hammering on water pipes with a rock. Beyond and fainter, a second set of clangs joined it. Then a third.

"We been spotted," Jenny Jumpup said.

"Good." Will did not slow his pace. "I want them to spot us. I want them to know we're coming. I want them to know that there's nothing they can do to stop us."

"What's to keep them from slipping through the walls?" Tatterwag asked. "They're haints, after all."

"Their horses couldn't follow. We'd get them all. And these guys practically worship their horses." Lord Weary had sent ambassadors to the horse-folk, offering them full membership in his growing empire, immunity from taxation and conscription, a guaranteed supply of food, and other enticements in exchange for a small yearly tribute of horses. His advances had been rejected with haughty scorn, though the horse-folk were the poorest of all who dwelt in darkness, and possessed neither tools nor clothing.

"Then why don't they just saddle up the horses and run? That's what I'd do in their circumstances."

"They *old* haints," Jenny Jumpup said. She was a haint herself, and proud of it. Her hair was done up in a cascade of slim braids, tied in the back in a sort of ponytail, and she wore a brace of pistols butt-forward in her belt. "They ancestors left the Shadowlands before fire was brought down from the sky. They can't farm, they got no weapons, and they can't ride horses."

"So why the fuck do they care if we take them?"

"They're all the horse-folk have." Will called a brief halt to check the map. A muttered word and its lines glimmered like foxfire. The other raiders gathered about him. They were a good group—in addition to his two lieutenants, he had Radegonde de la Cockaigne, Kokudza, the Starveling, and Little Tommy Redcap. "We're on the bottommost level of tracks—but there are tunnels that delve even deeper, some of them natural and others not." He led them some fifty yards down the track. A black opening gaped to one side. Cool air sighed out of it. "This was an aqueduct once, nobody knows how long ago. Looks like dwarven work."

"It older than dwarves," Jenny Jumpup said scornfully. "My people remember. We built it. And we ain't never been paid for it neither."

"Jenny," Tatterwag said. "Give it a rest."

A train went by and they turned their backs to it. When their eyes had adjusted to the dark once more, they walked some distance into the aqueduct. Will got out the map again. "If everything's gone according to plan, our other troops will be in position *here* and *here*," he said. "That leaves only one way out—right through us. They'll stampede the herd in hopes of trampling us under."

Little Tommy Redcap chuckled nastily. "I'll rip the horses' legs off if they try."

"You were all chosen because you know how to ride," Will said. "Now space yourselves out and let's see if you can climb."

They swiftly scaled the walls. This was a new skill for Will, but one he had picked up easily. There was a narrow ledge just below the vaulted ceiling. The raiders took up positions there, some on one side and some on the other. All save Jenny Jumpup and the Starveling, who swarmed up the ceiling and drove in pitons so they could hang face downward, like bats, waiting.

After a long silence, Kokudza growled, "I don't get it. Horses. Caverns. Call me crazy, but I see a basic conflict here."

"The horses used to be wild," Will said. "Back before Nimrod laid the foundations of Babel, they fed upon the grassy slopes of Ararat. Lord Weary told me he read a paper on this once. Scientists speculate that some of their number would venture into natural caverns to feed upon mosses and lichens. This would have been tens of thousands of years ago, minimum. Something happened, an earthquake maybe, that trapped a small breeding population in the caverns. They adapted to the darkness. You couldn't say they thrived, exactly—there can't be more than a hundred of 'em all told. But they're still here. Albino-pale, short-haired, and high-strung. They won't be easy to catch."

Tatterwag patted his bandolier. "You know what *I* recommend." Now that the Empire of Night was a going concern, they had money enough, extorted from transit workers and the like, to buy materials that had never previously been available underground. Will had been the first to keep a string of magnesium flares with him always, and a pair of welder's goggles in a breast pocket. Tatterwag, who was not only his second-in-command but a notorious suck-up as well, had followed suit. There was no better indicator of how far and fast Will's star had risen.

Will shook his head. "Flares won't work on these horses."

"Why not?"

"They're blind," he said. "Now be quiet."

After a while the clanging stopped. That meant the horses would be coming soon. Some time after that, Will was almost certain that he heard a gentle murmuring noise like the rumor of rain in the distance. It was less a sound than wistful thought. But it was there. Maybe.

"Do not take the lead horse," a ghost of a voice murmured. It was the Whisperer.

"Why shouldn't I?" Will asked, every bit as quietly. "Surely the leader will be fastest and most desirable."

"Not so. It will be fast but callow. The wiser horses hold back and let the young stallions, their heroes, take the foremost with its attendant risks. They are expendable. The queen mare, however, will be found at the very center of the herd and it is she you want. Fleetest of all is she and cleverest as well, sure-footed on wet surfaces, cautious on dry, and alert to danger even when all seems safest."

Far down the tunnel, a gentle luminescence bloomed, faint as the internal glow of the ocean on a moonless night. There was a soft sound, as of many animals breathing deeply in the distance.

"Here they come," Tatterwag said.

Like sea foam, the horses filled the tunnel. Shadowy figures ran among them, as swiftly as the beasts themselves. These were the old haints, the horse-folk, running naked as the day they were born. Even at a distance, they could be sensed, for with them came fear. Though they could not plant or build or light a fire, the old powers were theirs still, and they were able to generate terror and use it as a weapon. Thus it was that they herded their horses. Thus it was that they fought, using the great brutes' bodies against their enemies.

"Oh, baby!" Jenny Jumpup moaned. "I gone get me a young stud. I gone wrap my legs around him and never let go. I gone squeeze him so tight he rear up and scream."

"You're making me horny, Jen," Kokudza said. They all laughed softly.

Then the herd was upon them.

The noise of hooves, near-silent a moment before, rose up like thunder. The horses filled the aqueduct like ocean waters surging. One by one, the raiders dropped down upon them, like ripe fruit falling from the trees.

"Wait," the Whisperer said. "Wait . . . wait . . . not yet . . ." And then, when Will could wait no longer, he spotted the queen mare in the center of the herd, running as quickly as any but clearly not expending herself, holding something extra in reserve. "Now!"

Will leaped.

Briefly, he flew. Then, one incredible second later, he *slammed* onto the back of the mare. He grabbed wildly for her neck and scrabbled to keep his legs on either side of her back.

The queen mare rose up, pawing the air. Will's legs were flung clear, and he was almost thrown. But he clung to her neck, and by the time her forefeet were back on the ground, had managed to get his own legs back in place.

She ran.

Once, twice, she slammed into the horses running to either side of her. Each time, one of Will's legs was crushed briefly between the great beasts. But the impact was not quite enough to numb them, and

Will was determined that he would not be stopped by mere pain. He hung on determinedly.

Then the queen mare had broken free of the herd and was running ahead of them all.

Riding low on her back, concentrating on keeping from falling, Will began to sing the charm he had been taught:

> "Your neck is high and straight,
> Your head shrewd with intelligence,
> Your belly short, your back full,
> Your proud chest hard with muscles . . ."

His mount swung her head around and tried to bite him, but he grabbed her mane high on the back of her skull with both hands and was able to keep her teeth from closing on his flesh. And then the charm took hold and she no longer tried to throw him, though she continued to run in a full-out panic.

They were alone now, separated from the herd and galloping wildly down who-knew-which lightless tunnel. Though she was blind, somehow the queen mare knew where the walls were and did not run into them. Somehow she never stumbled. Whatever senses she employed in the absence of sight, they were keen and shrewd, and equal to the task. Will understood now, as he had not before, why Lord Weary so desperately wanted these steeds. Will's motorcycle was of only limited utility belowground; it could not be ridden along the ties of the train tracks, nor could it leap over a sudden gap in the floor of a tunnel if Will did not spot it in time. This beast could travel swiftly anywhere. It could traverse the distance between settlements in a fraction of the time a pedestrian could.

> "Joy of princes, throne of warriors,
> Hoof-fierce treasure of the rich,
> Eternal comfort to the restless . . ."

There were hundreds of lines to this charm, and if Will were to skip even one, it would not work. He had labored hard to memorize them all. Now, as he neared the final stanzas, Will felt the thoughts of the queen mare like a silvery brook flowing alongside his own. They were coming together now, moving as one, muscle upon muscle, thought on thought, a breath away from being a single shared essence in two bodies.

> *"Riding seems easy to he who rests indoors*
> *But courageous to he who travels the high-roads*
> *On the back of a sturdy horse."*

She was breathing hard now. Horses could only run at a full gallop for brief periods of time, though those who did not know them imagined them continuing thus for hours on end. The queen mare was winded—Will could feel a sympathetic pain in his own chest—and if she did not stop soon and walk it off, her great heart would burst within her.

This was the moment of crisis. Will had to convince her that accepting him as a rider was preferable to death.

Laying his cheek alongside her neck, still singing, he closed his eyes and entered her thoughts. There was neither color nor light in the queen mare's world, but her sensorium was wider and more varied than his own, for she was possessed of a dozen fractional senses. Riding her mind, he felt the coolness coming off of the walls, and the dampness or dryness of the ground before them. Tiny electrical charges lying dormant in the conduits and steel catwalks that flashed past tickled faintly against his awareness. Variant densities in the air slowed or sped sounds passing through it. Smells arrived in his nostrils with the precise location of their origins. Braids of scent and sound and feel wound together to give him a perfect picture of his surroundings.

Now Will thought back to the farmlands outside his old village, and recalled the dusty green smell of their fields and the way that in late afternoon the sun turned the seeded tops of the grasses into living gold. He pictured the cold, crystalline waters of a stream running swiftly through a tunnel of greenery and exploding under the hooves of his borrowed mount. He called up the flickering flight of butterflies among the wildflowers in a sudden clearing, and then an orchard with gnarled old apple trees and humblebees droning tipsily among the half-fermented windfalls. This was something the queen mare had never experienced, nor ever could. But the desire for it was in her blood and her bones. It was written into her genes.

He sang the last words of the charm. Now he found himself murmuring into the queen mare's ear.

"Ohhhh, sweet lady," Will crooned. "You and I, mother of horses— we were meant to be. Share your strong back with me, let me ride you, and I will show you such sights every time we travel together."

He could feel the tug of his words on her. He could feel her resolve weakening.

"I'll take good care of you, I promise. Oats every day and never a saddle, never a bit. I'll rub you down and comb your mane and plait your tail. No door shall ever lock you in. You'll have fresh water to drink, and clean straw to sleep on."

He was stroking the side of her neck with one hand now. She was skittish still, but Will could feel the warmth of feeling welling up within her. "And this above all," he whispered: "No one shall ever ride you but me."

Gently, tentatively, he felt her pleasure at the thought. Joyously, confidently, he showed her his own pleasure that she felt thus about him. Self flowed into self, so that the distinction between fey and horse, he and her, dissolved.

They were one now.

Will discovered that he was weeping. It had to be for joy, because the emotion that filled him now and which threatened to burst his chest asunder was anything but unhappiness. "What's your name, darling?" he whispered, ignoring the tears running down his cheeks. "What should I call you, my sweet?" But horses had no names, either true or superficial, for themselves. They lived in a universe without words. For them, there could be no lies or falsehoods, because things were simply so. Which meant that the task of naming her fell upon Will.

"I shall call you Epona," he said, "Great Lady of Horses."

For the first time since he could not remember when, he felt completely happy.

Will was in no hurry to return to the Army of Night's current bivouac. Epona was the swiftest of her breed; he would not arrive last.

"Take me where I need to be," he whispered in her ear. "But slowly." Then he gave the queen mare her head.

They made their way through the darkness by roundabout and pleasant paths. Occasionally a lone electric bulb or a line of fluorescent tubes flickered weakly to life before them, floated silently by, and then faded to nothing behind them. Downward they went, and then upward again. Once, Epona daintily picked her way up a long-forgotten marble staircase with crystal chandeliers that loomed faintly from the shadows overhead like the ghosts of giant jellyfish. They went down a long passage of rough stone so low that Epona had to bow her head to get through. Twice the ceiling brushed against Will's back, though he clung tightly to his mount. He was just beginning to wonder if they were lost when she emerged into a large empty space.

The roof of the cavern was not visible, but something glowed softly at its center.

It was a ship.

The ship lay near-upright, sunk to the waterline in ancient mud turned hard as rock. It had a wooden hull and its masts lay broken on the ground alongside it where they had fallen. Luminescent white lichen grew upon the wood, glowing gently as corpse-fire. It looked like engravings he had seen of galleons and carracks, and it clearly had been there for a long, long time. How it had come to its final end in a bubble of volcanic rock deep below Babel was a mystery. Doubtless there was a curse involved, a great offense, a mighty spell, and an awesome retribution. Doubtless many had died here in horror and despair . . . But all that was in the past, and everyone involved was dead and gone to the Black Stone long ages ago.

Epona stopped by the stern of the ship and began to graze upon the lichen growing on its rudder.

Will slid off her back.

"Why are we here?" he asked her. "This was not where I wanted you to take me."

The mare tossed her head impatiently. Will's words meant nothing to her, of course, but she caught the note of reproach in his voice and emphatically rejected it. Feeling the tenor of her thoughts, Will cast back to his original command and realized that he had not visualized any particular place but, rather, had told her only to take him where he needed to be.

"Is this where I need to be, old girl?"

Epona crunched on a mouthful of lichen.

"Well, if this is where I need to be . . ." Will walked first one way and then another, looking for an entry to the ship. Finally he scrambled up a fragment of one of the masts that made a kind of bridge from the ground to the gangway.

No lichen grew upon the deck, but an orange glimmer of lantern-light shone from a tiny window in the forecastle. Carefully, for the wood was soft underfoot and he did not trust it not to collapse under his weight, Will made his way to the fore. Something uncoiled within him and he was flooded with a dark sense of foreboding. He took a deep breath to settle himself, and then knocked on the door.

"It's not locked," the Whisperer said. "Enter."

Will stepped inside.

By the light of a single ceiling-hung lantern, he saw a shadowy boy-ish figure sitting at a desk at the far end of the cabin, reading. When Will entered, he put down the book and, rising to his feet, stepped into the light. "Hello, Will," he said. "Do you recognize me now?"

Will cried out in terror. "You!"

Before him stood Puck Berrysnatcher.

"I see you do. Good." The boy nodded to a chair. "Have a seat. We must talk."

One of Will's hands clenched and unclenched spasmodically. He sat. "Are you here as my friend or my enemy?"

The Whisperer cocked his head quizzically, as if searching for a memory in some long-neglected corner of his mind. "I cannot answer that question," he said at last. "I have been dead so long that I am no longer certain that, even to the living, such a distinction exists."

"Why are you here?"

"I have information you need." Puck advanced so close to the chair that his legs touched Will's knees. Bending down, he placed his arms around Will's neck. His breath was warm on Will's face. "But I want something in return."

NO, Will's hand wrote frantically on his thigh. *NO, DO NOT*, and *FLEE!*

- 158 -

Terrified, Will leaped to his feet and shoved the Whisperer away.

With a slam, the boy fetched up against the wall. He smiled. "Who is that writing with your hand? Don't you think you should know?"

"You think I don't know? Of course I know!" Will cried, though up until this very instant he had not dared admit it to himself. "It's the dragon. Night after night, he crawled inside my mind, and when he had what he wanted, he left. But a little bit of him remained, an echo or an imprint. It lives in me still!"

He spun about to flee and discovered that somehow the Whisperer stood between him and the door. They wrestled briefly, but though Will had the advantage in weight and height, the shadowy child was more than his equal in strength. Wrapping his arms tightly around Will, he whispered, "The dragon's growing stronger within you. Isn't he?"

"Yes."

The Whisperer's cheek was cool and smooth against the side of Will's face. "Oh, Will, who has ever been a better friend to you than I? Such gifts I have given you! A horse, terror, and now self-knowledge. Repay me by answering this one simple question: Who am I?"

"When we were both young," Will said carefully, "your use-name was Puck Berrysnatcher. Later, when you rose from the dead, you called yourself No-name. Your true name was Tchortyrion originally, but when you returned you had another that I never learned. Now I know you only as the Whisperer."

"Those are but names," the Whisperer said scornfully. He tugged Will tighter, so that he had difficulty breathing. "From the darkness I came, knowing everything there is to know about you and nothing about myself. Why are you the only one who can see me? Why do I haunt you? Tell me."

"You were my best friend. When the War came to our village, you died in an accident and were brought back by the healing-women. But you'd lost a leg and for this you declared yourself my nemesis, though I swear it was in no way my doing. I was the dragon's lieutenant then and you led the greenshirties in rebellion against him. For this, he entered me and together we crucified you."

"That is what I once was!" the Whisperer cried in anguish. "I need to know what I *am*! You have the key—I can see the knowledge within you but I cannot read it. Tell me!"

"You are a memory," Will whispered. "You are my guilt."

"Ahhh," the Whisperer sighed. Releasing his grip, he slumped toward the floor. But when Will put his arms around him, to catch him and hold him up, there was nothing there.

Despite his detour, Will was the first to return to camp. He had but to picture it in his mind and give the queen mare her head; she knew the fastest and safest way to go. Eventually, they emerged from the catacombs under Battery Park and were home.

Radegonde de la Cockaigne arrived second. She had come from the contested lands of the West, as had Will, but a little of the blood of *les bonnes meres* flowed in her veins and she had grown up privileged. She had been taught to ride, rather than learning on stolen time, and as a result her horse-craft was far superior to his. He was not surprised to see that she had wooed and won a particularly mettlesome steed. After her came Kokudza and Jenny Jumpup, also mounted, and then the Starveling and Little Tommy Redcap, both afoot. Some time later, Tatterwag limped in, looking embarrassed. They had gained four horses and lost not a single life.

Lord Weary came out of Hjördis's box, buckling his belt.

Will made his report.

"Any fatalities?" Lord Weary asked. Then, when Will shook his head, he said, "Let's see the horses."

Will had commandeered a space that was said to have been used once as a holding pen for slave smugglers, and then sent forces aboveground to steal, scavenge, or, in last resort, buy straw to spread on the floor. Lord Weary touched the steel-jacketed door that Will hadn't yet ordered taken off its hinges and muttered, "Good. It'll need a bar, though."

Then Weary saw the horses and a rare smile spread over his pale face.

"They're magnificent!" he said. "I had hoped for five, and been willing to settle for three. *Felicitas in media est,* too, and not just *Virtus* eh? It's a sign."

When seen together, it was obvious that the four steeds were from the same genetic line. The heads were gaunt and narrow, with large blue veins under pale, translucent skin. Their eyes bulged like tennis balls under lids that had grown together and would never open. All glowed faintly in the darkness. Yet equally clear was it that the one was queen and the others her subjects.

Lord Weary went straight to Epona and peeled back her lips to examine her teeth. "This one is best," he said at last. "She shall be mine."

Will trembled, but said nothing.

"First things first. Measure her for a saddle and bit."

"Sir!" His aide-de-camp, a haint named Chittiface, clicked his heels and saluted.

"The others, too, of course. They're still as wild as so many winds, and will need training. Have them broken and gentled. But take care to use no more force than is necessary. For they are my own precious children and I'll not have them scarred or disfigured." He turned on Will and said, "Captain Riddle, I perceive that I have in some way offended you."

"How can a lord offend his captain?" Will said carefully. "One might as well declare that I have offended my hand, or that I act against the best wishes of my left leg. Can the liver and entrails resent the wise leadership of King Head? 'Tis beyond my imagining."

The stables-to-be were swarming with soldiers, many busy, but the greater number merely curious to see the horses. Will noted that all of his fellow raiders were here as well. And every one of them was pretending not to listen.

"Oh, glib, most monstrous glib indeed!" Lord Weary turned a stern face upon Will. "And yet such a litany of sighs and shudders and tics, of soft gasps and shakes of the head, of sudden winces and tightened lips and suppressed retorts have I seen from you as speaks louder than mere words ever could. You are displeased. With me."

"If so, sir, then I apologize most humbly."

"Humbly, sirrah? You defy me to my teeth and plead humility? I'll not have it. Lie to me a third time at your peril."

"But—"

"Kneel!" Weary said, and then, when Will obeyed, "Both knees!"

Lord Weary was Will's liege, and Will had knelt before him often.

But always, as became one of his officers, on a single knee. The ground here was wet and unclean, and the dampness soaked through the cloth where the knee touched it. There was only one reason for Will to be made to kneel on two knees, and that was so that he might be humiliated.

"Now," Lord Weary said. "As I am your liege and you owe me obedience, speak. Tell me what I have done."

"Lord, these words are nothing I would willingly say. But as you command, so must I obey." Simply, then, and without recrimination, Will explained what promises he had made to Epona, and concluded, "What touches my honor is mine alone, and cannot entail yours. I ask only that you consider these matters seriously."

Lord Weary heard him through. Then he said, "Seize him."

Rough hands gripped Will by either arm. The soldier to his left was a new recruit, but the one to his right was Jenny Jumpup. She did not meet his eyes.

"Strip him to the waist," Lord Weary commanded. "Give him five lashes for insolence."

10

Lord Weary's War

William lay on his stomach, eyes closed, marveling at the intensity of his own pain. He had retreated to his spare and soldierly nest, built of stacked cardboard, clothesline, and charity blankets on a rarely used catwalk that swayed and rattled every time a train passed underneath. It vibrated now as footsteps noisily clanged up the metal rungs from below.

"We brought you water." A refilled two-liter Pepsi bottle thumped down by Will's chest. Tatterwag sat down at the tent's entrance, folding his long legs beneath him. Jenny Jumpup sat down beside him. "I couldn't come see you sooner because Weary gave me double-shift guarding his new horses. I was dead on my feet by the time I was relieved, so I just crawled into my box and collapsed."

With a groan, Will sat up. He took a swig from the bottle and waited.

At last Jenny Jumpup blurted, "He got no right to do that to you!"

"He has every right. But he was wrong to employ those rights in this instance."

Jenny snorted and looked away dismissively. Tatterwag's mouth moved silently as he worked out the implications of that statement. Then, quietly, he said, "It's war."

"Eh?"

"Lord Weary has closed the underworld to everyone but johatsu. Not just the police—transit, sewage, water, gas, and electrical workers, too. If they refuse to leave, Lord Weary says, they're to be beaten. Orders are to mark them up good, so that if they return we'll know to kill 'em."

"That's crazy. We've always kept on good terms with the maintenance crews. They can come and go as they wish. Even the cops we don't kill. We let them know who runs things down here, but we don't threaten their safety. That's been the keystone of our polity."

"Not anymore," Jenny Jumpup said. "Lord Weary say that once we seize control of their transit and utilities, the uplanders ain't got no choice but to negotiate a peace."

"They'll have no choice but to exterminate us." Closing his eyes made Will's head spin. When he opened them, he was still dizzy. "Has Lord Weary gone mad?"

"Maybe so." Tatterwag leaned forward, lowering his voice. "Some of us think that. And if he's mad, what loyalty do we owe him? None! Maybe this is an opportunity. Some of us think that maybe it's time for a regime change."

"Regime change?"

"A coup d'état. You think, Will! You're close enough to him. He trusts you. Slide a knife between his ribs and the problem goes away."

"It *sounds* simple," Will said carefully. Particularly, he did not say, for those who need have nothing to do with the deed but to urge him on to it. "But I doubt its practicality. Lord Weary's troops would tear me apart if I pulled a stunt like that."

"You've got backing among the officers. We talked this through, didn't we, Jenny?"

She nodded.

"They're prepared to acclaim you. This is your moment, Will. You call the Army of Night together and give 'em a speech—you're good with words, they'll listen to you—and Lord Weary is done and forgotten."

Will shook his head. He was about to explain that Tatterwag's idea wouldn't work because Lord Weary had just started a war and consequently was more popular now than he'd ever been before or would ever be again. But then a train slammed by underfoot, making speech impossible. By the time the catwalk stopped shivering and the diesel fumes had begun to dissipate, he found that he had slumped down onto his bed again and his eyes were closed and his mouth would not form words at his command.

A random thought went by and he followed it into the realm of dreams.

In his dreams, the commanders of the mosstroopers were gathered around a table, staring down at a map of the underworld that was nowhere near so detailed or accurate as his own, though reliable enough, he could see, on the major and more recent excavations. One of them indicated the mouth of the tunnel where the sub-surface route broke into the outer world and became a trolley line. "We'll enter here"—his hand skipped lightly down the map tapping three of the larger subway stations—"and at Bowling Green, Tartarus, and Third Street Stations. The stations in between we can lock down to prevent Lord Weary's riffraff from retreating to the surface."

"That still leaves his rats a thousand bolt-holes, most of which are unknown to us."

"Let them break and run, so long as we shatter their army and account for their leaders."

They all bent over the map, their granite faces as large as cathedrals, their moustaches the size of boxcars. "What of Jack Riddle? He looks feverish."

Lying helpless beneath their stony gazes, pinned between parallel lines of ink, Will saw a hand come down out of the darkness, growing larger and larger until it filled his sight and then continued to swell so that it disappeared from his ken, all save one enormous finger. It was wreathed with blue flames so that the air about it wavered and snapped like a flag in a gale. "This bug?" said its owner contemptuously. He leaned forward and Will saw that it was the Burning Man.

His finger touched the map and Will felt flames engulf him.

Will's eyes flew open. Tatterwag and Jenny Jumpup were gone and Hjördis knelt by his side. With hands sure and familiar she rubbed balm over his wounds. The pain flared up like fire where she touched him, and sank down to an icy residue where her hands had passed. The smell, flowery and medicinal, lingered.

"You are so good to me," Will murmured.

"It's nothing personal," Hjördis replied.

"Why do you always *say* things like that?"

"Because they're true. There is nothing special or privileged about our relationship. You are our hero and so I have body-rights over you, as I did with Bonecrusher before you, and as I have over Lord Weary even now. You, in turn, take tribute from each new community you conquer, yes? A lei of orchids, freely offered and freely taken. Settle for that."

Will stayed silent until Hjördis finished applying the balm. Then he said, "I hear there's going to be war."

"Yes, I know. Lord Weary came for the crates of rifles we were holding for him. This time there was no brash young stranger to offer an alternative. So it's war. If you care to call it that."

"What else would you call it?"

"Idiocy. But I will not be here to see it. The johatsu are leaving. The tunnels are emptying out as all the communities up and down their lengths desert them for the upper world. I have sent ahead as many of my own folk as have the sense to leave. Now I am visiting the last holdouts, the obstinate and demented, one by one. When I have spoken to them all I will leave myself."

"Where will you go?"

"There are shelters above. Some will sleep in stairwells. Others in the streets. Come with me."

"You can't leave just because there is danger," Will said. "This is your nation!"

"I have never believed in Lord Weary's fantasies. My folk are not warriors, but the weak and the broken who fled down below to find some semblance of safety," Hjördis said. "As their thane, I cannot forget that."

"Tatterwag wants me to lead a revolt against Lord Weary." Said aloud, it sounded unreal. "He wants me to kill Weary, win over the troops with a speech, and then take control of the Army of Night and lead them upward against our oppressors."

"Yes, Tatterwag would, wouldn't he? It's how he thinks."

"Perhaps I should give his plan some thought. It could be tweaked."

"You're overheated." Hjördis rose. "I will leave the balm here; use it when the pain returns. Don't wear a shirt until the welts have healed. Avoid alcohol. Leave before Lord Weary's war begins."

"I can't abandon my troops. I've fought alongside them, I've—"

"My work here is done," Hjördis said. "You will not see me again." She started down the ladder. Before the sound of her feet on the rungs had echoed into silence, Will was asleep.

When he awoke, Lord Weary was sitting beside him, smoking. His pale, shrewd face looked oddly detached. Groggily, Will sat up.

"You could kill me," Lord Weary said. "But what advantage would it bring you?"

He passed his cigarette to Will, who took a long drag and passed it back. His back still burned terribly, but the balm Hjördis had applied took off some of the edge off the pain.

"You're only a hero, after all. I am a conqueror and someday I may yet be an emperor. I know how to rule and you don't. That's the long and the short of it. Without me, the Army of Night would fall apart in a week. The alliances I have formed and the tributes I demand are all imposed by force of my own personality. Kill me and you lose everything that we have built together."

"I don't think I could kill you."

"No," Lord Weary said. "Not in cold blood, certainly."

It was true. Inexplicably, Will's heart still went out to Lord Weary. He thought he could gladly die for the old elf. Yet the anger remained. "Why did you have me whipped?"

"It was salutary for the troops to see you punished. You drew my army's admiration and then their loyalty. Therefore it was necessary for me to establish who was liege and who his hound. Had you not defied me on the horse, I would have found another excuse. This is *my* delusion, not yours."

"Excuse me?"

"You asked me once how I came to this sad estate, living in darkness, eating rats and stale donuts, and bedding gutter-haints, and you did not like my answer then. Allow me to try again. Anyone can see

I'm high-elven. Most of my soldiers think my title was self-assumed, but I assure you it was mine by birth. How could one of my blood and connections ever end up," he gestured, ". . . here?"

"How?"

"It began one morning in the Palace of Leaves," Lord Weary said. "I awoke early to find that the servants had opened all the windows, for it was a perfect day whose breezes were as light and comfortable upon the skin as the water of a sun-warmed lake. I slipped quietly from my bed so as not to disturb my mistresses and, donning a silk kimono, went out onto the balcony. The sun lay low upon the horizon, so that half the land was in light and half in shadow, and at the very center of the world, its focus and definition, was . . . me.

"A vast and weightless emptiness overcame me then, a sensation too light to be called despair but too pitiless to be anything else. The balcony had only a low marble railing—it barely came up to my waist—and it was the easiest thing imaginable to step atop it. I looked down the tapering slope of Babel at the suburbs and tank farms below, hidden here and there by patches of mist, marveling that I could see them at all from such a height. It would be too strong a word to say that I felt an urge to step off. Call it a whim.

"So I did.

"But so illusory did the world seem to me in the mood I was in that it had no hold upon me whatsoever. Even gravity could not touch me. I stepped into the air and there I stood. Unmoving.

"And in that instant I faced my greatest peril, for I felt my comprehension expanding to engulf the entire world."

"I don't understand," Will said.

"There is a single essence that animates all that lives, from the tiniest mite eking out a barren existence upon the desert-large shell of another mite too small to see with the naked eye, to the very pinnacle of existence, my own humble and lordly self. It informs even inanimate matter, a simple I am that lets a boulder know that it is a boulder, a mountain that it is a mountain, a pebble that it is a pebble. Otherwise, all would be flux and change.

"The body, you know, is ninety percent water, and there are those who will tell you that life is only a device which water employs to move itself about. When you die, that water returns to the earth and via natural processes is drawn up into the air, where it eventually joins up with waters that were once snakes, camels, emperors . . . and rains down again, perhaps to join a stream that becomes a river that flows into the sea. Sooner or later, all but your dust will inevitably return to world-girding Oceanus.

"Similarly, when you die your life-force combines with that of everyone else who has ever died or is yet to be born. Like so many lead soldiers being melted down to form a molten ocean of potential."

Will shook his head. "It is a difficult thing to believe."

"No, it is easy to believe. But it is hard, impossibly hard, to *know*. For to recognize the illusory nature of your own being is to flirt with its dissolution. To become one with everything is to become nothing specific at all. Almost, I ceased to be. I experienced then an instant of absolute terror as fleeting and pure as the flash of green light at sunset.

"In that same instant, I spun on my heel and took two steps down to the balcony. I left the Palace of Leaves and went to a bar and got roaring drunk. For I had seen beneath the mask of the world and *there was nothing there*! Since which time, I have distracted myself with debauchery and dreams. I dreamt up the Army of Night and then I dreamt a world for it to conquer. Finally, I dreamt for it a champion— you."

"With all respect, sir, I had a life before we met."

"You were chased into my arms," Lord Weary said, lighting a new cigarette from the butt of the old one. "Didn't it seem strange to you how you were pursued by one anonymous enemy after another? What had you done to deserve such treatment? Can you even name your crime?" He flicked the butt out into the air over the tracks. "I have been, I fear your persecutor-general and the architect of all your sorrows. I am the greatest villain you have ever known."

"If you are a villain," Will said, "then you are a strange one indeed, for I still love you as if you were my own uncle." Even now, he was not lying. "I hate much about you—your power, your arrogance, your former wealth. I despise the way you use others for your own amusement. And yet . . . I cannot deny my feelings for you."

For an unguarded instant, Lord Weary looked old and jaded. His fingers trembled with palsy and his eyes were vacant. Then he cocked his head and a great and terrible warmth filled him again. "Then I shall swear here and now that when I come to power, you shall be paid for all. What is it you want? Think carefully and speak truly, and it shall be yours."

"I want to see you sitting on the Obsidian Throne."

"That is an evasion. Why should that be more important to you than money or power?"

"Because in order for you to reach such a height would require a great slaughter among the Lords of the Mayoralty, such that the Lios-alfar and the Dockalfar and even the Council of Magi would be depopulated."

"Again, why?"

Will ducked his head. In a small voice, he said, "My parents were in Brocieland Station when the dragons came and dropped golden fire on the rail yards. My life was destroyed by a war machine that may have been on that very run. After I was driven out of it, my village was torched by the Armies of the Mighty. All these forces were in the employ of the Lords of Babel and the war itself the result of their mad polity." He looked up, eyes brimming with hatred. "Kill them all! Destroy those responsible, and I shall ask for not a scintilla more from you."

"My dear, sweet Jack." Lord Weary took Will in his arms and stroked his hair caressingly. "I can deny you nothing." He rose to his feet. "Now my war has begun and whether it is real or not, you have your part to play in it. Stand."

"Yes, sir," Will said. Painfully he stood. Bright spots swam in his eyes.

"Put your shirt and jacket on. I'll have the medic shoot you up with witchwart and lidocaine so you can fight."

Lord Weary established his headquarters in the catacombs. In a small room lined with bone-filled vaults and smokily lit by ancient lamps filled with recycled motor oil, he went over the maps with his captains, utilizing a cyclops skull as a makeshift table. They'd placed scouts at all the places where the mosstroopers might profitably begin their attack. There were countless ways in and out of the subterranean world, of course, but very few that would admit military forces in any number.

While the troops assembled rifles, made Molotov cocktails, and folded bandannas and soaked them in water so they could be tied about their faces as a defense against tear gas, their superiors planned an ambush and counterattack. Will had his doubts about the effectiveness of their forces, for he had seen soldiers snorting pixie dust and smoking blunts even as they prepared their weapons. Worse, the more he heard of his commander's plans, the less he trusted them. The tunnels were perfect for guerrilla warfare—wait for the enemy to be overextended and bored, then strike swiftly from the darkness and flee. Direct confrontation meant giving up that advantage. But Lord Weary's compulsion was strong upon him, and in the end Will had no choice but to obey.

So it was that Will found himself upon his motorcycle as part of a small advance force that watched from the shadows as the mosstroopers poured down from the Third Street platform and onto the tracks. The station had been closed, the trains redirected, and the power to the third rail cut. The troopers took up their positions in what looked to Will to be a thoroughly professional manner. They were every one of them Tylwyth Teg—disciplined, experienced, and well-trained. They wore black helmets and carried plexi shields. Gas grenades hung from their belts and holstered pistols as well.

The mosstroopers advanced in staggered ranks, with the dire wolves in the front row, straining at their leashes. It looked for all the world as if the wolves were pulling the troopers forward.

Will watched and waited.

Then, in his distant catacomb sanctum, where he sat scrying the scene in a bowl of ink, Lord Weary spoke a word that Will could feel in the pit of his stomach.

A sorcerous wind came blowing up from the throat of the earth. It lifted the newspapers and handbills littering the ground and gave them wings, so that they flapped wildly and flew directly into the faces of the mosstroopers like so many ghostly chickens and pelicans.

Ragged items of discarded clothing picked themselves up and began to stagger toward the invaders. Coming up out of nowhere as they had, the sorcerous nothings must have looked like a serious magical attack.

Two soldiers, both combat mages by the testimony of their uniforms, stepped forward and raised titanium staves against the oncoming paper birds and cloth manikins. As one, they spoke a word of their own.

All in an instant, the wind died and the newspapers and old clothes burst into powder.

That was Will's cue. He held a magnesium flare ready in one hand and his lighter in the other. Now, before the mages' staves could recharge, he flipped open his Zippo one-handed, and struck a light. Then he pulled the welder's goggles over his eyes and shouted, "Heads down!"

The snipers, who did not have goggles of their own, covered their eyes with their arms. The five cavalry lit and threw their flares.

"Go!" Will screamed.

He opened the throttle too fast and his Kawasaki stalled out. Cursing, he kick-started it back to life.

The plan of attack was simplicity itself. In the instant that their defenses were depleted, they would hit the mosstroopers and their wolves with magnesium flares, then charge the center of their line while they were still blinded. There, the powerful bodies of the horses would break a way through, spreading confusion in their wake. They were to continue onward without stopping and around the bend beyond Third Street Station, disappearing up the tunnel. This would leave the enemy easy targets for Will's sharpshooters. Or so it was planned.

In practice, it didn't work out that way.

Will had lost only seconds by stalling his bike. But in that delay, the horses had outpaced him. Now he saw them overwhelmed by the dire wolves that the blinded mosstroopers had released. Relying on scent rather than sight, those fierce predators met the horses in the air, snarling and snapping, sinking their great teeth into pale throats and haunches.

The first to fall was Epona.

He heard her scream, and saw both horse and rider buried in black-furred furies. The rider, a nonentity named Mumpoker, died almost immediately but his noble steed bit and kicked even as she went down. Not far behind her, Hengroen and Holvarpnia were also overwhelmed. Will saw Jenny Jumpup leap free of Embarr, collide with a dire wolf in midair, and fall with the wolf beneath her and both her hands at its throat.

Will opened the throttle wide. Yelling, he drove toward Epona and the fallen riders, hoping to achieve he knew not what. But then tear-gas canisters fell clattering to the ground and a wall of chemical mist rolled forward and into his troops. The bandanna that Will wore provided little protection. Fiery tears welled up, and he could not see. Desperately he tried to spin his motorcycle about. The bike skidded on its side and almost slid out from under him. His Zippo flew skittering away.

Will struggled to right the motorcycle.

All about him the dire wolves were fighting and hunting. Though the brutes could not see and their sense of smell had been neutralized by the tear gas, they were yet deadly to any combatant they chanced to stumble into.

A wolf's paws landed on Will's handlebars. All in a panic he raised his pistol and squeezed the trigger. Nothing happened.

He had forgotten the safety.

The dire wolf grinned, baring sharp white fangs. "If you're going to piss yourself, best do it now," it said. "Because you're about to die."

The hideous jaws were about to close on Will's face when the wolf abruptly grunted and half its head disappeared in red spray.

"Some fun, huh, Captain?" Jenny Jumpup grinned madly at Will, then stuffed her pistol in her belt and reached out a hand toward him.

Will pulled her up behind him. "Let's get the fuck out of here!" he shouted.

They did.

That was the war's first action. Will's snipers had retreated in disarray before the advancing mosstroopers without firing a single shot.

The horses entrusted him were dead and their riders, all but one, dead or captured. It was a fiasco and, worse, it deserved to be one. Lord Weary's soldiers were only half-trained and their tactics were makeshift at best. They couldn't go up against a disciplined military force like the mosstroopers and expect anything but defeat. That was obvious to Will now.

The guttering flares died to nothing behind them and the dire wolves were called back to their handlers. Will pocketed his goggles. The mosstroopers would continue to advance, he knew, but at a cautious pace. Since they were no longer in immediate danger, he throttled down his bike to a less dangerous speed. Thus, he was able to react in time when Jenny Jumpup murmured, "I think I gone pass out now," and started to slide from the pillion.

Will twisted around to grab Jenny Jumpup with one arm, while simultaneously slamming on the brake. Somehow he managed to bring the Kawasaki to a stop without dropping her.

Pushing down the kickstand with his heel, Will dismounted and lowered his lieutenant to the ground. Semicircles of blood soaked through her blouse and trousers, more than he could count.

"Oh, shit," he muttered.

Jenny Jumpup's eyes flickered open. She managed a wan smile. "Hey. You should see the wolf." Then her eyes deadened and her face went slack.

He bandaged her as best he could and then, mating her belt with his, improvised a pistol-belt carry. Bent over beneath her weight, he staggered onto the cycle and got it going again. He dared not stay in the path of the mosstroopers, and he would not leave her behind.

Into the dark they rode.

Once, briefly, Jenny Jumpup regained consciousness. "I got something to confess, Captain," she said. "When Lord Weary whipped you? I enjoyed it."

Shaken, Will said, "I'm sorry if I—"

"Oh, I don't mean that in a bad way." Jenny Jumpup was silent for a long time. Then she said, "It kinda turned me on. Maybe when this is all over, we can . . ." Then she was out again. Will twisted around and saw that her skin was gray.

"Hang in there. I'll have you to a medic soon."

Will rode as fast and furious as ever he had before.

Some distance down the tunnel, Tatterwag stepped out of the gloom in front of the Kawasaki. And so Will was reunited with those of his snipers who had not simply thrown away their rifles and fled but had retreated with some shred of order. Besides Tatterwag, they were Sparrowgrass, Drumbelo, the Starveling, and Xylia of Arcadia.

Carefully, Will lowered Jenny Jumpup's body to the ground. "See to her wounds," he said. "They were honorably gotten."

Xylia of Arcadia knelt over Jenny. Then she stood and touched her head, heart, and crotch. "She's dead."

Will stared down the corpse. It was a gray and pathetic thing. Jenny Jumpup's clothes were dark with blood and, deprived of her personality, her face was dull and ordinary. Had he not carried it here on his back, Will would have sworn the body was not hers.

After a long silence, Tatterwag stooped over the body. "I'll take her pistols for a keepsake." He stuck them in his belt.

"I'll take her boots," Xylia of Arcadia said. "They won't fit me, but I know somebody they will."

One by one they removed Jennie Jumpup's things. Will took her cigarettes and lighter and Drumbelo her throwing knife. The Starveling took her trousers and tunic. That left only a small silver orchid hung on a chain about her neck, which Sparrowgrass solemnly kissed and stuffed into a jeans pocket. They looked at one another uneasily, and then Will cleared his throat. *"From the south she came."*

"The bird, the warlike bird," said Xylia of Arcadia.

"With whirring wings," said Drumbelo.

"She wishes to change herself," said the Starveling.

"Back to the body of that swift bird," said Tatterwag.

"She throws away her body in battle," Sparrowgrass concluded.

Already, freed of her élan vital and any lingering attachment to her possessions, Jennie Jumpup's body was sinking into the ground. Slowly at first, and then more quickly, it slid downward into the darkness of the earth from which it had come and to which all would someday inevitably return. Haints more literally than others, perhaps, but the truth was universal.

The staging area, when they finally got there, was in an uproar. The platforms swarmed with haints, feys, and gaunts, carrying crates, barrels, and railroad ties to add to the growing barricades, and moving guns and munitions to hastily improvised emplacements. One leather-winged night-gaunt flew up the tunnel from which Will's company had just emerged, with a dispatch box in its claws. Will's heart sank to see how amateurish it all looked.

Porte Molitor Station had seemed a good base because it was located where the A, C, and E lines split from routes 1, 2, and 3 and was not far downline from the sub-surface exit, thus giving easy access to all four potential war zones. But Porte Molitor was a ghost station, built but never used, and so it did not open to the surface. Now, with retreating soldiers converging from every front and scouts reporting that the enemy was advancing through all three tunnels, it seemed to Will like nothing so much as a trap.

"Who's in charge here?" Will shouted. "What are all these soldiers doing on the tracks? Isn't anybody in charge?"

"Lord Weary has placed Captain Hackem in command of the defenses for the left Uptown tunnel," a weary-looking hulder said. "Chittiface is responsible for the right Uptown tunnel. And he himself commands the forces defending the Downtown tunnel. Hello, Jack."

"Hjördis!" Will cried in astonishment. "You're back."

"Everybody's back. All the johatsu who fled have returned to the tunnel. Every last one of them."

"But *why?*" Earlier, Will had urged the lady-thane not to abandon Lord Weary's cause. Now he knew his counsel had been wrong. She had left and been right to do so. She should have stayed away.

"I don't know." Hjördis looked stricken. "It defies all reason. Perhaps there is a compulsion on us. But if so, it is of a force greater than any I have ever known or heard rumor of, for it drives a multitude."

"Where is Lord Weary? If anybody understands this mystery, it will be he."

"Lord Weary charges you to consult with him before the battle begins. On what matter, he does not say." Hjördis turned away. "Now I must leave. I have a field hospital to oversee."

Will watched her leave. Then he turned to Tatterwag and held out a hand. "Give me your combat knife."

Knife in hand, Will clambered over the barricade and kick-started his bike. Then, though it broke his heart to do so, he plunged the knife into the fuel tank. Gasoline sprayed into the air and drenched the ground. Up and down the tracks he rode. The ties made it a teeth-rattling ride and spread the gasoline from wall to wall before the Kawasaki sputtered to a stop.

"There!" he roared when he was done. "Now, when the hell-hounds come sniffing after us, this will render them nose-deaf!"

That done, he strode off to confront Lord Weary, Tatterwag in tow.

The Downtown tunnel fortifications were simpler than the Uptown barricades—a single barrier that reached almost to the ceiling, without crenels or even a walkway along its top—but correspondingly more massive. He found Little Tommy Redcap overseeing the work there in Lord Weary's place. Johatsu carried box after box to the I-beams and duct-taped them to the foot of the supports. Others ran electrical wires from box to box. They could only be explosive devices.

"What the fuck are you doing?" Will demanded.

"What the fuck does it look like I'm doing?" Little Tommy Redcap lifted his voice: "Yo! I need more primers here!"

"It looks like you're preparing to bring half the buildings in the Bowery crashing down on our heads."

The haint who came running up with the box of primers was puffing on a lit cigar. Little Tommy Redcap snatched it from the johatsu's mouth and started to fling it away. Then he stopped and stuck it in his own mouth instead. "If you knew, why did you ask?"

"If this is done by Lord Weary's orders, then he's crazy," Will said. "If you touch those things off, you'll kill us all."

"You think I'm afraid of dying?" Little Tommy Redcap laughed and then tapped the ashes from his cigar onto the primers for emphasis. "It's a good day to die!"

"You're crazy, too."

"Maybe so, but I still got things to do. You got any complaints"— Little Tommy Redcap jerked a thumb upward—"take 'em up with the head honcho."

High overhead was a gallery that Will did not remember seeing before, in a wall that was taller than it could possibly be. (The station seemed larger, too—but he had no time to worry on it.) Lord Weary's face was a pale oval afloat in the darkness like an indifferent moon gazing down upon the wickedness of the world. "I will," he said. "How do I get up there?"

11

The Fall of the Empire

There was a stairwell that Will had never seen before. Two insect-headed guards in green leather armor uncrossed their pikes for him but recrossed them when Tatterwag tried to follow. Leaving his lieutenant behind to argue, Will took the steps two and three at a time. Heart pounding—when had he last rested?—he burst into the gallery.

Lord Weary was leaning over a marble balustrade, contemplating the scene below. He glanced up briefly. "Join me."

A strange lassitude overcame Will and all sense of urgency left him. It was as if in the presence of his liege he had no ambitions of his own. Unhurriedly, he joined the elf-lord. Together they gazed down on the scurrying johatsu. A salt breeze blew up, dispelling the stale air of the tunnels. It seemed to Will that he caught a hint of flowers as well. An unseen sun was warm upon his back. "What place is this?"

"A memory, nothing more. My attention wanders, I fear." Suddenly they stood in a clean, empty room of white marble. A light wind flowed through its high windows. A black absence sat in its center. From some angles it looked like a chair.

"Is that . . . ?"

"Yes. You behold the Obsidian Throne." The air darkened and the vision faded, returning Will to the stale smells and staler prospects of his life underground. Briefly, Lord Weary was silent. Then he said, "The final conflict approaches. Can you hear it coming?"

Will could. "What's that sound?" he asked. "That . . . howling."

"Just watch."

The howling grew until it became a quartet of train whistles shrieking almost in synch. Louder they grew, and louder still. The thunder of iron wheels filled the station. The ground underfoot trembled with premonition.

Then the Uptown barricades exploded. Fragments of beams, barrels, and soldiers were blasted into the air as locomotives smashed through the hastily assembled defenses.

There were four of the great beasts, running in unison, with plows affixed to the fronts of their cabs and they did not slow as they passed through the station. Shoulder to shoulder they sped, grinding troops under their wheels. At the Downtown tunnel, they crashed through the barricade and its defenders and, with final triumphant howls, rushed headlong into darkness, leaving hundreds dead in their wake.

Will clutched the balustrade, his eyes starting from his head. The screams and shouts of the survivors echoed and reechoed in his ears like surf. He could not master his thoughts; they tumbled over each other in meaningless cascades. "You knew this would happen," he said finally, fighting back nausea. "You *arranged* this."

Lord Weary smiled sadly. He leaned over the railing and shouted, "Redcap!"

In the wake of the trains had come the mosstroopers. Somebody fired a magnesium flare at the first squadron to arrive, setting afire the gasoline Will had sprayed throughout the tunnel. But it did not stop them. Burning and ravening, the dire wolves entered Porte Molitor and began killing the survivors. Behind them came the mosstroopers, weapons ready. At their head, Will thought he saw the Burning Man.

Yet amid all this confusion, Lord Weary's voice carried to its target. Little Tommy Redcap looked up from the smoldering body of a dying wolf. "Sir?"

"Are the explosives ready?"

"Sir! Yes, sir!"

"Stand by the igniter and await my command."

"Sir!" Little Tommy Redcap turned and disappeared into the flee-ing, fighting, panicking mob.

So great was Will's befuddlement then, that it did not surprise him to see Tatterwag leap from the stairwell with blood on his jacket and Jenny Jumpup's pistols in his hands. "Traitor!" he cried, and dis-charged them both point-blank at Lord Weary's head.

"Ah," the elf-lord sighed. "Like so many things, this moment was far more pleasing in the anticipation than in its realization." He opened a hand and there lay the two freshly fired pistol balls.

He let them drop to the floor.

"You bore me."

All the color drained from the swamp gaunt's face. He raised his hands pleadingly and shook his head. With neither hurry nor reluc-tance, Lord Weary reached toward him. His fingers closed not upon Tatterwag, however, but around a filthy old greatcoat. With a moue of distaste, he tossed it over the rail.

"What did you just do?" Will asked, shocked. "How did you do that?"

Hjördis stepped from the stairwell, just as Tatterwag had a minute before. "He's a glamour-wallah," she said. "Aren't you?"

Lord Weary smiled and shrugged. "I was the King's Master of Revels," he said. "Not that His Absent Majesty ever called upon my services, of course. Still . . . I had talent, I kept in practice. More than one member of the court was of my devising. Once I threw a masked ball at which half of those attending had no objective reality whatso-ever. The next morning, many a lord and lady awoke to discover their bedmates had been woven of naught but whimsy and thin air."

"I don't understand."

"He creates illusions," Hjördis said. "Very convincing ones. For en-tertainment. When I was living in a shelter near the Battery, the gov-ernment sent a glamour-wallah down for the winter solstice and he filled the streets with comets and butterflies." Then, sadly, "Was Tat-terwag nothing, after all, but one of your creations?"

Lord Weary cocked his head apologetically. "Forgive an old elf his follies. I made him for a grand role, if that makes any difference. He would have shot me just as I was about to take my perilous place on the Obsidian Throne, and then died in reprisal at the hands of our hot-blooded young hero here." He indicated Will. "Then, lying in his arms, I would have begged Jack to ascend the throne in my place. Which, because he was ambitious and because it was my dying wish, he would have done.

"Alas, my interest in this game has flickered to embers long before I thought it would. What can one do?" He looked past Will to Hjördis. "I suppose you are here for some reason."

"Yes. Your munitions teams have planted explosives on the support beams of the buildings above us. If they are set off, all the johatsu and the Army of Night will die."

"And this bothers you, I suppose?" Lord Weary sighed. "Foolish child. They were never real in the first place."

Abruptly the cries, shouts, and other noises from below ceased. Hjördis stared over the balustrade down at the suddenly empty tracks and platforms. There were no corpses, no shattered barricades, no mosstroopers or burning wolves, no rebel army, nothing but the common litter of an abandoned subway station. "Then . . . they were all, johatsu and 'troopers alike, your creations? Only Will and I were . . . ?"

Lord Weary raised an eyebrow and she fell silent.

At last, she spoke again. "I had thought I was real," Hjördis said in a monotone. "I had memories. Ambitions. Friends."

"You grow maudlin." Lord Weary reached for her. His fingers closed about a mop. This, like the greasy overcoat that had been Tatterwag, he tossed lightly away.

"I'm next, I suppose," Will said bitterly. He clenched his fists. "I *loved* you! Of all the cruel and wicked things you've done, that was the worst. I deserved better. I may not be real, but I deserved better."

"You are as real as I am," Lord Weary said. "No more, no less." He was growing older before Will's eyes. His skin was as pink and translucent as a baby's, but loose upon his flesh. His hair was baby-wispy, too, and white. The tremor in his voice was impossible to ignore. "Take from that what comfort you can. For my part, I sought to put off enlightenment through treason and violent adventure. But now I see the unity of all things, and it seems that senility has come for me at—"

Lord Weary's eyes closed and his head sank down upon his chest. Slowly and without fuss, he faded away to nothing. With him went the balustrade, the gallery, and all the light from the air. Will felt the darkness wrap itself about him like the warm and loving arms of Mother Night.

He did not know if he existed or not, nor did he care. Lord Weary's war—if it had ever begun in the first place—was over.

Will awoke to find himself lying on the subway tracks. He staggered to his feet and then had to leap madly backward when a train came blasting down the tunnel at him.

When his vision returned, Will began to walk. He did not know how much of what he had seen and felt and done had actually happened. Friends had died—but had they truly? Were Bonecrusher, Epona, Jenny Jumpup, and all the rest mere phantasms? And if they didn't exist, if they never *had* existed, did that free him of the obligation to care about them? He looked at his hands and recognized scars he had earned during his stay in the underworld. *They* at least were real.

Try though he might, he could make no sense out of what he had been through.

He could not even cry.

For an undeterminable length of time, he wandered in the darkness. Sometimes he slept. Then, finally, he awoke to find that the pain was not gone but manageable.

So Will returned to Niflheim Station and hunted up the cache where he had stashed his old clothes. He'd packed them away in cedar chips salvaged from the trash bin out back of a lumber supply store, so they were still good. He shaved and washed himself in the men's room of the Armory subbasement (it was one of many that he could reach via the steam tunnels without going up to the streets), and he had a new pair of boots from a consignment of hundreds that three of his soldiers had jacked from a sidelined boxcar. When he was finished dressing, he no longer looked like the infamous Captain Jack Riddle. He could pass for a respectable citizen.

He went upstairs and into the street, only to discover that it was spring. He'd passed the entire winter underground.

Will had a pocketful of change, casually extorted from an adventurer who had wandered deeper into the darkness than he ought, so on an impulse he caught an Uptown train to the Hanging Gardens.

Justly famed were the Hanging Gardens, whether considered as park, arboretum, or simply as a collection of horticultural displays. They included a small carnival with a merry-go-round and a Ferris wheel, public swimming pools, and a boardwalk through simulated wetlands where abatwa stalked water dragons no longer than Will's foot with toothpick-sized spears. The aviary had a hundred species of hummingbirds, thirteen of cranes, and a dozen varieties of pillywiggins to be seen nowhere else on the continent. Sullen fauns sold balloons on the greensward. But what Will liked best was the esplanade. Leaning over the concrete railing, he looked down on the far-below docks where giants stood thigh-deep in the water and slowly unloaded containerized cargo from freighters. A salt breeze blew in from world-girding Oceanus. Gulls wheeled over the water, white specks as small as dust motes.

A hippogriff flew past, trailing laughter.

It came so close to Will that he could smell its scent, a pungent mixture of horse sweat and milky pin-feathers, and feel the wind from its wings. Its rider's hair streamed out behind her like a red banner.

Will stared up at her, awestruck. The young woman in the saddle was all grace and athleticism. She wore green slacks with matching soft leather boots and, above a golden swatch of abdomen, a halter top of the same green color.

She was glorious.

The rider glanced casually down and to the side and saw Will gawking. She drew back on the reins so that her beast reared up and for an instant seemed to stall in midair. Then she took the reins between her teeth and with one hand yanked down her halter top, exposing her breasts. With the other hand, she flipped him the finger.

Then, jeering, she seized the reins again, pulled up her top, and was gone.

Will could not breathe. It was as if this stranger had taken a two-by-four to his heart. All in an instant, he was hers.

And he had no idea who she was or if he would ever see her again.

In that fabulous, confused instant, one thought rose up from within Will: *He'd been wasting his life.* Down below, he'd been a hero—but to what purpose? He'd led an army that would not come out of the tunnels, because they feared the light.

He found he did not want to go back.

Instead, he turned his back on the Gardens and walked into the city, sometimes taking an elevator upward, sometimes a stairway down. Lacking purpose, he found himself in a gray neighborhood and on an impulse, he stepped into the nearest bar. It was a dive called the Rat's Nose. He would walk up to the tappie and ask for work. Even if it was just washing dishes and sweeping the floor, it would be a start.

A little girl crawled out from under a table and beamed up at him. "Hello," she said. "My name is Esme. Who are you?"

Nat looked up from his newspaper and smiled. "There you are! I was beginning to think you were *never* going to show up."

12

A Small Room in Koboldtown

Okay, okay, who's it gonna be next?" Nat threw a card down on the folding table. "You give me five, I give you ten. You give me ten, I give you twenty, you're a winner!" He threw down a second card. "Pick the queen, the black queen, *la reine de la nuit,* you're a winner!" He threw down a third card, and flipped them all over. A pair of red deuces, and the queen of spades. "Woddaya got, woddayagot? Forty gets you eighty, fifty a hundred. It's so easy a child could play! Woddaya got?" He switched the cards around once, twice, thrice. "There's always a winner."

A crowd had gathered under the marquee of the derelict Roxy Movie Theater where he'd set up the pitch. They were hobs and haints mostly, with a scattering of red dwarves. Will stood in their midst, pretending to watch the cards but surreptitiously looking for a trout. Haints made good trouts because they expected to be broke at the end of the week anyway and would watch their money disappear with stoic grace. Dwarves liked to gamble but tended to be sore losers. Usually they weren't worth the trouble. Hobs, on the other hand, were tightfisted but they were plungers. Will had his eye on one hob in particular who stood on the fringe of the crowd, scowling skeptically but clearly fascinated.

A haint passed a ghostly gray hand over the card table. Two crumpled dollar bills appeared in its wake. "That one," he said, pointing.

"Not this one, you say?" Nat flipped over the two of diamonds. "Nor this?" The two of hearts. "You chose the queen, you're a winner! Two gets you four. Pony on up, pony on up. Ten gets twenty, twenty gets forty. Woddaya got, woddaya got?"

Flip, flip, flip went the cards. The haint left the four dollars on the table without adding to them, and chose again. Nat turned over the card. "It's not the diamond deuce, no sirree! Two cards a winner, five'll get you ten. Double up, double up, the more you bet the more you win." Nat switched the two cards around and then back to their original positions.

The haint shook his head obstinately and jabbed a smoky finger at his card again. They weren't going to get anything more out of him, Will saw. Nat had obviously reached the same conclusion, for he switched the cards around again, sliding the queen up his sleeve and replacing it with a second two of hearts.

"Final call, double up? No? And it's . . . the deuce!"

Nat pocketed the money. "Who's next, who's next? Bet big, win big, woddaya say?" The hob was starting to turn away now and nobody else was stepping forward, so Will pushed his way up close to the front. "Three cards down, one two three. Three cards over, three two one. Woddaya got? Twenty forty fifty a hundred." The queen was in the middle. Nat swapped the deuces, then switched the queen with one of the twos.

Will threw a twenty down on the table. "That one," he said, pointing to the center card.

The crowd gave out a soft moan as he chose what all of them could see was a losing card.

Nat grinned. "You're sure, now? You don't wanna bet on this one? Double your winnings, easy as pie." He pointed at the facedown queen. "No? All right then, I flip the cards—one, two, and . . . the queen is mine!"

"Oh, man!" a nearby haint said. "The queen, she right there. Anybody seen that."

"Hey," Will said testily. "Bet your own money, buddy, if you're so smart." The hob was watching intently, his body no longer half-turned to leave. He was beginning to think there was money to be won.

He'd taken the hook. Now to set it.

"Twenty gets you forty, forty gets you eighty," Nat crooned. "Pick the queen, you win, black always wins. Twenty forty, fifty a hundred. Easy to win, easy as sin!" He threw down the three cards and flipped them face up.

"Let me see that queen!" Will snatched up the card, examined both sides, and reluctantly set it down again. As he did so, Nat turned his head to the side and sneezed.

Swiftly, Will bent up one corner of the queen. When Nat swept up the cards again, apparently without noticing, Will winked cockily at the haint who'd criticized his last bet. By no coincidence at all, the trout was in a position to notice.

"Luck be a lady, you're a winner! Twenty gets you forty. Woddayagot? Woddayagot?" Cards face up. Cards face down. Nat shuffled them about. "Twenty gets you forty, you're a winner. Fifty gets you a hundred. Woddayagot?"

Will plonked down his entire roll. He could see the hob edging closer, naked avarice on his face. "Two hundred says the queen's in the center." He pointed at the card with the turned-up corner.

"Sorry, kid, fifty's the limit."

The crowd *growled*. Nat looked alarmed and threw up his hands. "All right, all right! Just for today, no limit." He flipped over the cards. "You're a winner!"

Will accepted his winnings and, smirking, strolled jauntily to the edge of the crowd. Nat started up his spiel again, and the hob shouldered his way to the front, shouting, "I got three hundred says I can spot the queen!"

The hook was set. Nat proceeded to reel the trout in.

"You want in? Woddayagot? One hundred gets you two hundred, three hundred six. Pick the queen, you're a winner. Black card, black card, black card. The queen of cards, the queen of night, *la reine d'Afrique,* you're a winner. One . . . two . . . three . . . you choose."

The trout confidently jabbed a finger at the card with the turned-up corner.

Nat flipped it over.

Now came that delicious moment when the trout saw it all: He saw the face of the card whose corner Nat had bent while manipulating it, which was of course *not* the queen whose corner he had smoothed flat again. He saw his money disappearing into Nat's vest. He saw that he'd been cheated, outwitted, and made into a fool. Mostly—and this was the best part of all—he saw that he couldn't unmask Nat as a sharper without admitting to his own dishonesty.

The hob's mouth opened in an outraged O.

With practiced skill, Will slid unnoticed behind the trout, his hand closing about a cosh he kept in one trouser pocket. Just in case. But in the event, the hob indignantly spun on his heel and stormed away.

"Woddayagot, woddayagot?" Will went back to scanning the crowd—and saw that a prosperous-looking haint in a three-piece suit was staring at him, smiling softly. He was too expensively dressed to be bunko, he didn't have the vibe for the left-handed brotherhood, and he for sure wasn't a trout. So what *was* he?

In that instant Will's worried musings were pierced by a shrill, two-fingered whistle. Esme stood atop a trash receptacle at the corner, waving wildly. She pointed at a huaca in the uniform of the City Garda who had just lumbered past her.

All in a breath Nat swept up cards and money, abandoning the folding table, and the crowd, few of whom had reason to love the gendarmerie, scattered. Will made straight for the patrolman, gesturing angrily. "Arrest that scoundrel!" he demanded. "He's a cheat. He took my *money!*" The bronze-faced huaca tried to brush past him, but Will stepped directly in his way. "I demand satisfaction!"

"Get the fuck out of my face," the huaca snarled, and pushed Will aside. Too late. Nat had already slipped down the passageway between the Roxy and the paint store next door and disappeared.

The patrolman rounded on Will. But Will was wearing an Uptown suit with a rep tie, so the huaca couldn't tell if he were somebody who could be roughed up with impunity or not. So he was let go with a chewing-out and a warning.

Will gathered up Esme and because his piano teacher was ill and his fencing master at a competition and so he had no lessons today, they spent the rest of the afternoon playing the pachinko machines in the Darul as-Salam Arcades.

That evening they met as usual in the back room at the Rat's Nose, where Nat regularly held court. Hustlers and trolls, pimps, sprets, thieves, spunks, lubberkins, and hobthrushes came and went, backs were slapped, small favors were promised. Information, much of it minor and the rest dubious, was swapped in voices lowered to the edge of inaudibility. Will nursed a small beer and listened to it all.

He had learned a great deal in the past twelve months. Not just the petty scams and cons by which he and Nat scrounged a living, but the ways of the city as well. He'd learned that in Babel "What the fuck do you want?" meant "Hello," that "I'm going to have to run you in" meant "Give me ten dollars and I'll look the other way," and that "I love you" meant "Take off your trousers and lie down on the bed so I can grab your wallet and run."

He'd also learned that magic came in high and low forms. High magic manipulated the basic forces of existence, and even in its smallest manifestations a badly cast spell could fill every television set for miles around with snow. Hence it was easily detectable by anyone on guard against it. Low magic, however, could be as simple as the ability to deal a card from the bottom of a deck or to pluck a coin from an imp's ear. Done right, it was undetectable. But even if you were careless and got caught, you still had a decent chance of talking your way out of it if your wits were sharp enough. So, in its way, low magic was the more powerful.

Nat was low magic down to the soles of his feet.

But he wasn't exclusively a small-con grifter. Nat was laying the groundwork—or so he swore—for a long con, something big and fabulously lucrative. To which end, Will spent his free time in an endless round of lessons: music, deportment, diction, fencing... This last Will had almost quit after seeing a rank amateur, waving his epee about as if it were a broom, knock the blade out of his fencing master's hand. But "It is a useless skill and therefore valued," the swordsfey St Vier had explained. "If you want to kill a gentleman, use a gun. If you wish to impress him, best him with the sword. The latter is far more difficult, however, so I suggest you apply yourself to your studies."

Now, there was a lull and only they three in the room, so Will said, "Three card Monte is getting old, Nat. It's gotten so that it's a job like any other."

"You've got a point there, son." Nat leaned over and peered under the table, where Esme was reading through her collection of comic books for the umpteenth time. "How's it going down there, little grandmother?"

" 'Kay," Esme said abstractedly.

"So when do we—" Will began.

A haint walked through the wall.

He was portly in the manner of the affluent, and wore a three-piece suit with a brocade vest embroidered with suns, moons, and zodiacal signs. Gold watch chains looped from every pocket. His skin was purple as a plum. "Tom Nobody, you old rascal!" He flung out his arms. "I heard you were back in town."

"It's Nat Whilk these days, Salem." Nat stood and they hugged each other with theatrical gusto. Then he said, "Will, this is the honorable Salem Toussaint, alderman."

The politician had a good handshake and a way of not quite winking as he shook that said, We're all rogues here and so we should stick together. Will liked him instantly. But he did not trust him. "I saw you earlier today," Will remarked.

"I know you did." Toussaint turned back to Nat. "Reason I'm here is, I need a white boy to run errands Uptown, where my usual runners might be a smidge conspicuous. Somebody with his eyes open. Discreet. Able to think on his feet."

"Somebody not terribly honest, you mean," Nat said.

Salem Toussaint smiled broadly, revealing two gold teeth with devil-runes cut into them. "How well you know me!"

"My boy and I are working on something, but it'll take a few months for me to lay the groundwork. You can have him until then."

Will was by now too much the professional to say anything aloud. Nevertheless, he turned and stared. Nat laid a hand on his shoulder. "You've got edge, son," he said. "Now pick up a little polish."

Chiefly, Will's job was to run errands in a good suit-and-haircut while looking conspicuously solid. He fetched tax forms for Toussaint's constituents, delivered stacks of documents to trollish functionaries, fixed L&I violations, presented boxes of candied John the Conqueror root to retiring secretaries, absentmindedly dropped slim envelopes containing twenty dollar bills on desks. When somebody important died, he brought a white goat to the back door of the Fane of Darkness to be sacrificed to the Nameless Ones. When somebody else's son was drafted or went to prison, he hammered a nail in the nkisi nkonde that Toussaint kept out in the hall, to ensure his safe return. He canvassed voters in haint neighborhoods like Ginny Gall, Beluthahatchie, and Diddy-Wah-Diddy, where the bars were smoky, the music was good, and it was dangerous to smile at the whores. He negotiated the labyrinthine bureaucracies of City Hall. Not everything he did was strictly legal, but none of it was actually criminal. Salem Toussaint didn't trust him enough for that.

One evening, Will was stuffing envelopes with Ghostface while Jimi Begood went over a list of ward-heelers with the alderman, checking those who could be trusted to turn out the troops in the upcoming election and crossing out those who had a history of pocketing the walking-around money and standing idle on election day or, worse, steering the vote the wrong way because they were double-dipping the opposition. The door between Toussaint's office and the anteroom was open a crack and Will could eavesdrop on their conversation.

"Grandfather Domovoy was turned to stone last August," Jimi Begood said, "so we're going to have to find somebody new to bring out the Slovaks. There's a vila named—"

Ghostface snapped a rubber band around a bundle of envelopes and lofted them into the mail cart on the far side of the room. "Three points!" he said. Then, "You want to know what burns my ass?"

"No," Will said.

"What burns my ass is how you and me are doing the exact same job, but you're headed straight for the top while I'm going to be stuck here licking envelopes forever, and you know why? Because you're solid."

"That's just racist bullshit," Will said. "Toussaint is never going to promote me any higher than I am now. Haints like seeing a fey truckle to the Big Guy, but they'd never accept me as one of his advisers. You know that as well as I do."

"Yeah, but you're not going to be here forever, are you? In a couple years, you'll be holding down an office in the Mayoralty. Wouldn't surprise me one bit if you made it all the way to the Palace of Leaves."

"Either you're just busting my chops, or else you're a fool. Because if you meant it, you'd be a fool to be ragging on me about it. If Toussaint were in your position, he'd make sure I was his friend, and wherever I wound up he'd have an ally. You could learn from his example."

Ghostface lowered his voice to a near-whisper. "Toussaint is old school. I've got nothing to learn from a glad-handing, pompous, shucking-and-jiving—"

The office door slammed open. They both looked up.

Salem Toussaint stood in the doorway, eyes rolled up in his head so far that only the whites showed. He held up a hand and in a hollow voice said, "One of my constituents is in trouble."

The alderman was spooky in that way. He had trodden the streets of Babel for so many decades that its molecules had insinuated themselves into his body through a million feather-light touches on its bricks and railings, its bars and brothel doors, its accountants' offices and parking garages, and his own molecules had been in turn absorbed by the city, so that there was no longer any absolute distinction between the two. He could read Babel's moods and thoughts and sometimes—as now—it spoke to him directly.

Toussaint grabbed his homburg and threw his greatcoat over his arm. "Jimi, stay here and arrange for a lawyer. We can finish that list later. Ghostface, Will—you boys come with me."

The alderman plunged through the door. Ghostface followed.

Will hurried after them, opening the door and closing it behind him, then running to make up for lost time.

Ghostface doubled as Toussaint's chauffeur. In the Cadillac he said, "Where to, boss?"

"Koboldtown. A haint's being arrested for murder."

"You think he was framed?" Will asked.

"What the fuck difference does it make? He's a voter."

Koboldtown was a transitional neighborhood with all the attendant tensions. There were lots of haints on the streets, but the apartment building the police cars were clustered about had sprigs of fennel over the doorway to keep them out. Salem Toussaint's limousine pulled up just in time for them to see a defiant haint being hauled away in rowan-wood handcuffs. The beads at the ends of his duppy braids clicked angrily as he swung his head around. "I ain't done nothin'!" he shouted. "This is all bullshit, motherfucker! I'mna come back an' kill you all!" His eyes glowed hellishly and an eerie blue nimbus surrounded his head; clear indicators that he'd been shooting up crystal goon. Will was surprised he was even able to stand.

The limo came to a stop and Will hopped out to open Salem Toussaint's door. Toussaint climbed ponderously out and stopped the guards with an imperious gesture. Then he spoke briefly with their captive. "Go quietly, son. I'll see you get a good lawyer, the best money can buy." Will flipped open his cell, punched a number, and began speaking into it in an earnest murmur. It was all theater—he'd dialed the weather and Jimi Begood had doubtless already lined up a public defender—but combined with Toussaint's presence it calmed the haint down. He listened carefully as the alderman concluded, "Just don't attack any cops and get yourself killed, that's the important thing. Understand?"

The haint nodded.

In the lobby, two officers were talking with the doorman. All three stiffened at the sight of haints walking in the door, relaxed when they saw Will restoring the twigs of fennel, and smiled with relief as they recognized Toussaint. It all happened in a flicker, but Will saw it. And if he noticed, how could his companions not? Nevertheless, the alderman glided in, shaking hands and passing out cigars, which the police acknowledged gratefully and stowed away in the inside pockets of their coats. "What's the crime?" he asked.

"Murder," said one of the cops.

Toussaint whistled once, low and long, as if he hadn't already known. "Which floor?"

"Second."

They waited for the elevator, though the stairs were handy and it would have been faster to walk. Salem Toussaint would no more have climbed those stairs than he would have driven his own car. He made sure you understood what a big mahoff he was before he slapped you on the back and gave your nice horse a sugar cube. As the doors opened, Toussaint turned to Ghostface and commented, "You're looking mighty grim. Something the matter?"

Ghostface shook his head stiffly. He stared, unblinking, straight ahead of himself all the way to their destination.

There were two detectives in the frigid apartment, both Tylwyth Teg, golden-skinned and leaf-eared, in trench coats that looked like they had been sent out to be professionally rumpled. They turned, annoyed, when the cop standing guard at the door let the three of them in, then looked resigned as they recognized the alderman.

"Shulpae! Xisuthros!" Toussaint slapped backs and shook hands as if he were working the room at a campaign fund-raiser. "You're looking good, the both of you."

"Welcome to our humble crime scene, Salem," Detective Xisuthros said. He swept a hand to take in the room: One window, half open, with cold winter air still flowing in through it. Its sill and the wall beneath, black with blood. The burglar bars looked intact. A single dresser, a bed, a chair that had been smashed to flinders. A dribble of blood that led from the window to a tiny bathroom with the door thrown wide. "I should have known you'd show up."

A boggart sprawled lifeless on the bathroom floor. His chest had been ripped open. There was a gaping hole where the heart should have been.

"Who's the stiff?" Toussaint asked.

"Name's Bobby Buggane. Just another lowlife."

"I see you hauled off an innocent haint."

"Now, Salem, don't be like that. It's an open and shut case. The door was locked and bolted from the inside. Burglar bars on the window and a sprig of fennel over it. The only one who could have gotten in was the spook. He works as a janitor here. We found him sleeping it off on a cot in the basement."

"Haint." Salem Toussaint's eyes were hard. "Please."

After the briefest of pauses, the detective said, "Haint."

"Give me the story."

"About an hour ago, there was a fight. Bodies slamming against the wall, furniture smashing. Everybody on the hall complained. By the time the concierge got here, it was all over. She called us. We broke in."

"Why didn't the concierge have a key?"

"She did. Buggane put in a dead bolt. You can imagine what the old bat had to say about that."

"Why wasn't there a haint-ward on the door?"

"Didn't need one. Doorman in the lobby. Only one haint in the building."

Will squinted at the wall above the door. "There's a kind of pale patch up there, like there used to be a ward and somebody took it down."

Detective Shulpae, the quiet one, turned to stare at him. "So?"

"So what kind of guy installs a dead bolt but takes down the ward? That doesn't make sense."

"The kind who likes to invite his haint buddy over for a shooting party every now and then." Detective Xisuthros pointed toward the dresser with his chin. A set of used works lay atop it. "The concierge says they were so thick that some of the neighbors thought they were fags." He turned back to Toussaint. "Alderman, if you want to question our work here, fine, go ahead. I'm just saying. There's not a lot of hope for the boy."

"Will's right!" Ghostface said. He went to the window. "And another thing. Look at all the blood on the sill. This is where it happened. So how the hell did he get all the way into the bathroom? Somebody ripped his heart out, so he decided to wash his hands?"

Now both detectives were staring at him, hard. "You don't know much about boggarts," Xisuthros said. "They're tough. They can live for five minutes with their heads ripped off. A heart's nothing. And, yeah, that's exactly what he did—wash his hands. Old habits go last. One of the first things we did was turn off the water. Otherwise, I thought the concierge was going to have a seizure."

Ghostface looked around wildly. "What happened to the heart? Why isn't it here? I suppose you think the haint *ate* it, huh? I suppose you think we're all cannibals."

In a disgusted tone, Detective Xisuthros said, "Get Sherlock Holmes Junior the fuck out of here."

Salem Toussaint took Ghostface by the elbow, led him to the door. "Why don't you wait outside?"

Ghostface turned gray. But he stamped angrily out of the room and down the hall. Will followed. He didn't have to be told that this was part of his job.

Outside, Ghostface went straight to the alley below Buggane's window. There were no chalk marks or crime scene tape, so the police obviously hadn't found any evidence there. Nor was there a heart lying on the pavement. A dog or a night-gaunt could have run off with it, of course. But there was no blood, either, except for a stain under the window and maybe a stray drop or two that couldn't be seen in the dark.

"So what happened to the heart?" Ghostface paced back and forth, unable to keep still. "It didn't just fly away."

"I don't know," Will said.

"You be Buggane." Ghostface slapped a hand against the brick wall. "Here's the window. You stand here looking out it. Now. I come up behind you. How do I rip your heart out in a way that leaves all that blood on the windowsill? From behind you, I can't get at your heart. If you turn around to face me, the blood doesn't splash on the sill. Now, those ignorant peckerwood detectives probably think I could shove my hands through Buggane's back and *push* his heart out. But it doesn't work like that. Two things can't occupy the same space at the same time. If I make my hands solid while I'm inside your chest, I'm going to fuck them up seriously. So I didn't come at you from behind."

"Okay."

"But if you turn around so I can come at you from the front, the blood's not going to spray over the sill, is it? So I've got to be between you and the window. I don't know if you noticed, but Ice didn't have any blood on him. None. Zip. Nada. Maybe you think I could rip somebody's heart out and then make myself insubstantial fast enough that the blood would spray through me. I don't think so. But even if

I could, the blood's going to spatter all over the floor, too. Which it didn't. So you tell me—how could I rip your heart out and leave the blood all over the sill like that?"

"You couldn't."

"Thank you. *Thank* you. That's right. You couldn't."

"So?" Will said.

"So there's something fishy going on, that's all. Something suspicious. Something wrong."

"Like what?"

"I don't know." Abruptly, Ghostface's hands fell to his sides. Just like that, all the life went out of him. He slumped despondently. "I just don't know."

"Ghostface," Will said, "why does all this matter? You called this guy Ice. What's he to you?"

The haint's face was as pale as ash, as stiff as bone. In a stricken voice, he said, "He's my brother."

They went to a diner across the street and ordered coffee. Ghostface stared down into his cup without drinking. "Ice always was a hard case. He liked the streets too much, he liked the drugs, he liked the thug life. That's why he never made anything of himself." He picked up a spoon, looked at it, set it down. "I dunno. Maybe he did it. Maybe he did."

"You know he didn't. You proved he couldn't have."

"Yeah, but that's not going to convince a judge, now is it?"

Will had to admit it would not. "You guys keep in touch?"

"Not really. I saw him a few months ago. He was all hopped up and talking trash about how he'd finally made a big score. He was going to be smoking hundred-dollar cigars and bedding thousand-dollar whores. Maybe he stole something. I told him to get the hell out, I didn't want to know anything about his criminal activities. My own brother. The last time I saw him, I told him to go to hell."

They were silent for a bit. "Nobody said anything about finding anything valuable," Will observed.

"Sometimes the cops will pocket that kind of stuff."

"That's true." Will dipped a finger in his coffee and drew the Sigil of Inspiration on the linoleum counter. Nothing came to him. He sighed. "What would the Big Guy do in this situation?"

"Him?" Ghostface said bitterly. "Probably hand out cigars."

"Hey." Will sat up straight. "That's not a half bad idea. It's pretty cold out there." He counted cops through the window. Then he called the waitress over. "Give me four large coffees, cream and sugar on the side."

Leaving Ghostface hunched over the counter, Will carried the cardboard tray out to where the police stood stamping their feet to keep warm. They accepted the gift with small nods. All four had dark skin, short horns, and the kind of attitude that came from knowing they'd never, ever make detective. The oldest of the lot said, "Working for the spook, are you?"

"Oh, Salem's okay."

The cop grinned on one side of his oak-brown face. "You're what the micks would call his Hound of Hoolan. You know what that is?"

"No, sir."

"It means that if he says he wants to drive, you bend over and bark."

The cops all laughed. Then three of them wandered away, leaving only the rookie. Will took out a pack of Marlboros, offered one, took one for himself, then lit both. They smoked them down to the end without saying much. Will flicked his butt away. The rookie pinched the coal off of his and ate it.

Finally Will said, "This Buggane guy—you know him?"

"Everybody knew him. A real bad character. In jail as often as not. His girlfriend's cute, though. Used to come to the station to bail him out. Skinny little thing, no tits to speak of. The big lugs always seem to like 'em petite, you ever noticed?"

"Some of the neighbors thought he was queer."

"They sure wouldn't of said that to his face. Buggane was a bruiser. Used to fight some under the name of Dullahan the Deathless."

"No kidding," Will said. "His gym anywhere around here?"

"Down the street and over a couple of blocks. Place called the Sucker Punch. You can't miss it."

Ghostface was still in the diner, so Will left a note on the dash of the Cadillac. A few minutes later, he was at the Sucker Punch A.C. If there was one thing Will had learned working for Toussaint it was how to walk through any front door in the world and act as if he had a perfect right to be there. He went in.

The gym was dark and smelled serious. Punching bags hung from the gloom. Somebody grunted in a slow and regular fashion, like a mechanical pig, from the free-weight area. There was a single regulation ring in the center of the room. A trollweight bounced up and down on his toes, shadowboxing.

"Go home, little boy," an ogre in a pug hat said. "There ain't nothing here for you."

"Oh, it's not about that, sir," Will said automatically. By *that* meaning whatever the ogre thought it meant. The alderman had schooled him never to meet aggression head-on.

"No? You don't wanna build yourself up, get the girl, and beat the crap out of whoever's pushing you around?" The ogre squeezed Will's biceps. "You could use it. Only not here. This is a serious club for serious fighters only."

"No, sir, I'm with Alderman Toussaint." By the ogre's expression, Will could see that he recognized the name and was not impressed. "I was hoping you could tell me something about Bobby Buggane."

"The bum. What's he done now?"

"He was murdered."

"Well, I ain't surprised. Buggane was no damn good. Coulda worked his way up to the middle of the card, but he wasn't willing to put in the effort. Always jerking off somewhere with his spook buddy, when he shoulda been working out."

"Somebody said they got into doing crimes together." It was a shot in the dark, but Will figured the odds were good.

"Yeah, well, like I said, I wouldn't be surprised. There's a lot of crap a gorilla like Buggane can pull off if he's got a haint accomplice. You go into a jewelry store and pinch the ward when the guy ain't lookin' and replace it with a sprig of plastic fennel. Looks just like the real thing. Then that night the spook slips in and shuts off the alarm. If you're like Buggane and can rip a safe door off its hinges; you can walk off with a bundle. Somebody pulled something like that at a warehouse down in the Village about six months ago. Got away with a fortune in slabs of raw jade. I remember it because Buggane quit the gym right after that, and I always wondered."

"Raw jade's got to be hard to sell, though," Will said. "I mean, in bulk."

"Not if you got connections. Even if you don't, something big like that could be moved through your regular fence, provided you waited until things had cooled down some. Not that I'd know personally. But you hear stuff."

"Huh," Will said. "This girlfriend of his—you remember her name?"

"Naw. Daiera, Damia, something like that. Maybe Danae. Only reason I recollect at all is that I asked Buggane once was she a pixie or a russalka or what and he said she was a diener. Deianira the Diener, that was it. That's a new one on me. I thought I knew all the ethnics, but I ain't never heard of a diener before. Listen, kid, I really have got work to do."

"I'll be out of your way, then," Will said. "Thanks for your help." He took one last look around the gym. "I guess Buggane should have stayed in the ring."

"Oh, he wasn't a ring boxer," the ogre said. "He was a pit boxer."

"What's the difference?"

"Pit boxing's strictly death-match. Two fighters climb down, only one climbs out. Buggane had a three-and-two record when he quit."

"How the fuck," Will said, "can somebody have a three-and-two record, when he's fighting to the death?"

The ogre grinned. Then he explained.

Less than an hour later, Will, Salem Toussaint, and Ghostface stood waiting in the shadows outside the city morgue. "Okay," Ghostface said, "I thought I knew all the racial types, from Litvak night-hags to Thai shit demons, but you say this girl is a *what*?"

"A diener. It's not a type, it's a job. A diener is a morgue attendant who's responsible for moving and cleaning the body. She also assists the coroner in the autopsy. I made a few calls and Deianira's on night duty this week. Though I'm guessing she might take off a little early tonight."

"Why's that?"

"This is where Bobby Buggane's body wound up."

"I think, boy," Toussaint said firmly, "you'd best tell us the whole story."

"All right," Will said. "Here's how I put it together. Buggane and Ice steal a truckload of jewelry-grade jade together and agree to wait six months before trying to fence it. Buggane keeps possession—I'm guessing it's stashed with his girlfriend, but that's not really important—and everybody has half a year to reflect on how much bigger Buggane's share will be if he stiffs Ice. Maybe Ice starts worrying about it out loud. So Buggane goes down to the basement to talk it over with his good buddy. They have a couple of drinks, maybe they smoke a little crack. Then he breaks out the crystal goon. By this time, your brother's lost whatever good judgment he had in the first place, and says sure."

Ghostface nodded glumly.

"Ice shoots up first, then Buggane. Only he shoots up pure water. That's easy to pull—what druggie's going to suspect another user of shortchanging *himself*? Then, when Ice nods off, Buggane goes back to his room, takes down the ward, and flushes it down the toilet. That way, when he's found dead, suspicion's naturally going to fall on the only individual in the building able to walk through a locked door. One whom he's made certain will be easy to find when the police come calling."

"So who kills Buggane?"

"It's a set up job. Buggane opens the window halfway and checks to make sure his girlfriend is waiting in the alley. Everything's ready. Now he stages a fight. He screams, roars, pounds the wall, smashes a chair. Then, when the neighbors are all yelling at him to shut up, he goes to the window, takes a deep breath, and rips open his rib cage with his bare hands."

"Can he *do* that?"

"Boggarts are strong, remember. Plus, if you checked out the syringe on his dresser, I wouldn't be surprised to find traces not of goon but of morphine. Either way, with or without painkiller, he tears out his own heart. Then he drops it out the window. Deianira catches it in a basket or a sheet so there's no blood on the ground. Nothing that will direct the investigators' attention outside.

"She leaves with his heart.

"Now Buggane's still got a couple of minutes before he collapses. He's smart enough not to close the window—there'd be blood on the outside part of the sill and that would draw attention outward again. But his hands are slick with blood and he doesn't want the detectives to realize he did the deed himself, so he goes to the bathroom sink and washes them. By this time, the concierge is hammering on the door.

"He dies. Everything is going exactly according to plan."

"Hell of a plan," Toussaint murmured.

"Yeah. You know the middle part. The cops come, they see, they believe. If it wasn't for Ghostface kicking up a fuss, we'd never have found out all this other stuff."

"Me? I didn't do anything."

"Well, it looked hinky to me, but I wasn't going to meddle in police business until I learned it mattered to you."

"You left out the best part," Toussaint said. "How Buggane manages to turn killing himself to his own advantage."

"Yeah, that had me baffled, too. But when a boxer picks up a nickname like 'the Deathless,' you have to wonder why. Then the ogre at the gym told me that Buggane had a three-two record pit boxing. That's to the death, you know. It turns out Buggane's got a glass heart. Big lump of crystal the size of your fist. No matter how badly he's injured, the heart can repair him. Even if he's clinically dead."

"So his girlfriend waits for his body to show up and sticks the heart back in?" Ghostface said. "No, that's just crazy. That wouldn't really work, would it?"

"Shhh," Will said. "I think we're about to find out. Look."

A little door opened in the side of the morgue. Two figures came out. The smaller one was helping the larger to stand.

For the first time all evening, Toussaint smiled. Gold teeth gleamed. Then he put the police whistle to his mouth.

After Buggane and his girlfriend had been arrested, Ghostface gave Will a short, fierce hug and then ran off to arrange his brother's release. Will and the alderman strolled back to the limousine, parked two blocks away. As they walked, Will worried how he was going to explain to his boss that he couldn't chauffeur because he didn't have a license.

"You done good, boy," Salem Toussaint said. "I'm proud of you."

Something in his voice, or perhaps the amused way he glanced down at Will out of the corner of his eye, said more than mere words could have.

"You *knew*," Will said. "You knew all the time."

Toussaint chuckled. "Perhaps I did. But I had the advantage of knowing what the city knows. It was still mighty clever of you to figure it out all on your own."

"But why should I have had to? Why didn't you just tell the detectives what you knew?"

"Let me answer that question with one of my own: Why did you tell Ghostface he was the one who uncovered the crime?"

They'd reached the limo now. It flickered its lights, glad to see them. But they didn't climb in just yet. "Because I've got to live with the guy. I don't want him thinking I think I'm superior to him."

"Exactly so! The police liked hearing the story from a white boy better than they would from me. I'm not quite a buffoon in their eyes, but I'm something close to it. My power has to be respected, and my office, too. It would make folks nervous if they had to take my intellect seriously as well."

"Alderman, I . . ."

"Hush up, boy. I know everything you're about to say." The alderman opened a door for Will. "Climb in the back. I'll drive."

One day in early spring, Will returned to the Rat's Nose.

"You're back again," Nat said.

"I, uh, kinda got a haint out of trouble, and somehow the word slipped out. Salem said I was too high profile to work for him anymore."

Esme crawled out from under the table. "Who's he?"

"I'm your Unca Will. You remember me," Will said. "I used to be your papa."

"Oh, yeah." In the accepting way of a child, Esme filed away this new information, to be forgotten as soon as he went away again. Will found, to his surprise, that he felt a pang of regret at not being her father anymore. "Can I have a basket of pretzels?"

"Sure you can," Nat said. Then, to Will, "You've been wearing the ring?"

Will held up his hand to display the cheap pinchbeck ring that Nat had commissioned for him. "Are you finally going to explain the purpose of it?"

"Take it off."

Will did.

Nat indicated the pale circlet of flesh where the ring sat, an indentation that did not recover with its removal. "On such small details is verisimilitude built." He removed something from an inside vest pocket. "Try this on."

The ring was solid and had it weighed so little as a breath more might have been called massive. It was woven of red, yellow, and white gold. A single ruby, bright as a fresh drop of blood, formed the eye in the head of a fanged Wyrm, biting savagely into the ring. On close examination, Will saw that the tricolored gold formed the scales of a body that coiled three times around his finger before ending in the Wyrm's mouth.

It fit the indentation perfectly.

"Tell me," Nat said. "If you're presented to a prince, on which knee do you kneel?"

"Always the right."

"A waiter comes by with a platter of cheese. What hand do you use?"

"Never the left."

"If the music has a time signature of three-four, what should you dance?"

"The waltz."

"If you get into a dagger fight, and your opponent thrusts low and to the right?"

"I parry it in octave."

"If an elf-lady asks you to fondle her breasts?"

Will smiled. "A lady must always be obeyed."

"And if the next time you see her she acts as if it never happened?"

"It never happened."

Nat lifted his glass in a silent toast, and drank. "My little boy is all grown up!" he said. He removed a pasteboard card from an inside pocket of his jacket and laid it on the table before him. It was an engraved invitation. "There is a masked ball next week at House L'Inconnu. It's black tie, so be sure to wear a tux."

"Just what do you have in mind?" Will asked.

"We're going to pull the Missing Prince scam," Nat said. With a mock-salaam, he added, "Your majesty."

13

The Hippogriff Girl

The guests arrived at House L'Inconnu by calishe, stretch limo, rickshaw, hansom cab, and palanquin. They drove Duesenbergs and Harleys and teams of matched white stallions. One came by saddle-owl. A trumpeter and a horn player welcomed each at the main entrance by the turnaround with short phrases of Handel's *Water Music* in place of a fanfare, while the vehicles were whisked away to off-site parking. In the foyer, a string quartet played Mozart to gentle the transition from outdoors to indoors.

Will arrived in a taxi. A storm cloud had washed through the upper levels of Babel, leaving the streets so slick they reflected the neon lights in bright smears. Taking a deep breath and leaving a twenty-dollar tip for luck, he donned his domino; strode past the valets, heralds, and musicians; surrendered his invitation; and allowed uniformed flunkies to deferentially gesture him through a labyrinthine tangle of corridors. He fetched up in an antechamber within earshot of the ballroom, where a monstrous pile of pink chiffon, the matron of the house, lounged on a couch skillfully contoured to hold her enormous bulk. So large was she that, reclining, her pallid flesh billowed up higher than Will's chin. Half elf-lady and half termite queen, she so filled her gown that it threatened to burst with every breath she took.

For a long, silent moment she critically examined his costume and demeanor. In the background, the band was playing "Fly Me to the Moon."

"Monsieur Pierrot, j'observe. Je présume vous parlez français."

"I do, madam, well enough to recognize *le bel accent d'Ys*. My French would pain you to hear."

The matron's eyes glittered. A tiny smile opened in her vast and pallid expanse of face, exposing small, sharp teeth. "That is quite considerate of you, Master"—she glanced down at an invitation held up by a liveried dwarf Will had not noticed before—"Cambion. Quite considerate indeed for someone I do not recall inviting. Did you forge this?"

"Only the name, Fata L'Inconnu. The invitation itself I bought from one of your poorer relations."

"And why would you do that?" Her tone was not exactly frigid but there was no warmth in it, either.

Will bowed ever so slightly. "I am a social climber."

Again that sharp little smile appeared, as if she were a duelist whose opponent had made an unexpectedly shrewd feint. "Are you trying to charm me with the truth?"

"It is all that I have, *madame*."

The matron laughed. "Oh! Oh!" One hand waved feebly in the air and the dwarf placed a tissue in her fingers, so she could dab it daintily at her eyes. "You are a rogue, my gallant young clown, and doubtless you are after either my jewels or some lady's virtue. Were I not old and fat, I would take great pleasure in determining which is the case." She heaved her vast bulk upon the couch, sending ripples running down her flesh and back up again. "But I am conscious of my duties as a hostess. You are a mouthwatering morsel, and the *demoiselles* will enjoy breaking your treacherous heart."

"You do me a disservice," Will said, bending to kiss her puddingsoft hand, "if you think me incapable of appreciating your inner beauty."

"Isn't he cunning, Shorty? Isn't he clever?"

"Too clever by half," the dwarf agreed. "As your chief of security, I recommend his immediate castration. After which, I suggest that he be flogged bloody and then thrown out on his ass."

"You're such a worrywart, Shorty. Let my little pussies have their catnip." The fata turned to Will. "Get on with you! The dancing is through that door and down the steps."

And so Will entered the ballroom.

The ballroom was a semicircular terrace with only a canopy of stars overhead. Apparently spells protected it, for the rain cloud that had drenched the streets outside had not let fall so much as a drop here. A dance band played at the far edge, between two enormous cut-crystal bowls containing mermaids wearing faux-seaweed bikini tops and nothing else. Those guests who were not on the dance floor stood in knots at the railings or sat in scattered chairs set beneath the flambeaux that lined the terrace perimeter. The elf-lords wore holographic costumes like Will's own—phantom jugglers, river gods, and astronauts, through which might be glimpsed formal evening wear if one stared hard enough. The ladies wore costumes that were fantasies of feathers and gems with layer upon layer of overlapping glamour. Will assumed the worst of the ruling classes. However, spoiled though the elf-maidens doubtless were, there was no denying their beauty. They were as glossy and mouthwatering as a basket of poisoned apples. He went to the nearest and bowed. "May I have this dance?"

She looked him over with skeptical hauteur. "Do I know you, Lord Pierrot?"

He responded with his best wise-guy smile. "Does it matter?"

Her gaze paused for an instant at his hands and a new warmth entered her voice. "No," she said. "No, it does not."

She moved as lightly as a feather on the wind. Will enjoyed dancing with her immensely, though he found her costume distracting. It was a Lily St. Dionysée gown that gathered under her breasts, which she had left bare but sprinkled with gold dust. A feathered demi-mask in the shape of a crescent moon had been ensorcelled to superimpose a sow's head over her own. It was a pattern Will recognized from the fashion magazines Nat had made him study, that of Inanna in her pig avatar. The sow's head snapped and slavered soundlessly and when he spun his partner—her name, she confided, was Fata d'Etoile—around, silvery strings of drool flew off into the air.

"You have lovely hands," she commented.

"You have lovely breasts."

"These old things?" she said, pleased. "I've had them forever." Then, returning to her original subject. "That's an interesting ring you're wearing."

"It's nothing special."

"May I ask where it comes from?"

"I wouldn't know. It's just something I inherited. Let's talk about something else. Tell me something about yourself. Something unpredictable and telling."

With a mischievous smile, Fata d'Etoile leaned forward to whisper in Will's ear, "At home I have a godemiché of great antiquity and impeccable provenance. It has known three empresses."

"I don't know what a godemiché is."

"Silly! It's a dildo." She narrowed her eyes and smiled through her lashes. "Do I shock you, my prince?"

"I am no prince."

"Oh? Perhaps I am mistaken." A dangerous look fleetingly possessed her face, as if she were repressing a sudden impulse to slide a knife in his back or a hand down his trousers. "There's only one way to be sure."

"What's that?"

With a hint of a blush, Fata d'Etoile said, "Well . . . you know what they say about the touch of royalty."

Will did not, and would rather have liked to find out. But Nat had directed him to dance with as many partners as possible and so, with a frisson of regret, he returned Fata d'Etoile to the sidelines, thanked her graciously, and extended a hand to another.

"Is your name truly Christopher Sly?" his fourth partner, Fata Kahindo, asked. Her skin was tawny and her eyes were flecked with silver. Firefly lights blinked in the air about her head, like virtual particles popping in and out of existence. "'Tis hardly a royal name."

"I am hardly royal."

She pressed herself closer to him. "And royally hard, to boot."

So the conversation went, from lady to lady. "Have you come to reclaim your throne?" asked Fata von und zu Horselberg.

"I understand you're telling everyone you're not the king," said Fata Gardsvord. "So why, then—?"

"... your hands."

"... your ring."

"... your highness."

"May I cut in?"

A woman in a dark gray uniform with red piping inserted herself between Will and his partner as deftly as a butcher's knife slides between flesh and bone to dejoint a capon. As she danced him away, Will threw a wordless look of apology toward his last partner, standing beautiful and alone and furious at the center of the floor. Then he glanced down and saw a silver lapel pin depicting an orchid transfixed by a dagger.

Will's blood chilled. But lightly he said, "That's an interesting costume. Palace Guard at Brigadoon?"

His partner did not smile. "It's the dress uniform of the political police."

"What an odd choice. Why are you dressed as *une poulette?*"

"Offensive language won't put me off. I've heard what a troll has to say when his nuts are crushed with a pair of pliers. And I wear my uniform because, as I'm sure you've already figured out, I'm here on official business."

Will put on a fatuous, here's-a-line-that'll-get-me-laid expression that had cost him many an hour before the mirror to perfect. "Are you here to arrest me? You might as well—my heart is already in your custody."

"Almost you convince me that you're a complete and utter twit. But then I ask myself, Wouldn't a real twit be trying to convince me that he's *not* a fool?"

Will sighed. "You dance well, lady. You are not uncomely. You are obviously intelligent, which I find appealing, and if you put your mind to it I believe you could flirt as well as anybody here. Yet you do not. Why do you intrude your seriousness into an evening that was heretofore superficial, pointless, and altogether delightful?"

The policewoman's nails tightened on his shoulder. "I begin," she murmured, "to wish that I could take you into custody and interrogate you personally. I believe that with a little care you could be made to last for hours before you broke. However, that is neither here nor there. A concerned citizen has informed my department that you are wearing a ring to which you are not entitled, Master Cambion."

"Again the ring! I begin to wish I'd left the thing at home. It's all anyone seems able to talk about."

"Do you pretend not to know that you wear the signet of House sayn-Draco?"

"It is nothing of the sort. Why worry yourself over it? So the ring is in the form of a Wyrm and the bezel in its mouth is red. Any jeweler can make such a thing."

"So you have emphatically told at least a dozen elf-ladies. Yet oddly enough your denials simply make the imposture more convincing. The entire room gossips about you." Will shrugged. He did not need her to tell him that. Everywhere he looked, eyes stared back, some glaring, others with frank interest, some few simply amused. Knots of young elf-lords discussed him with brooding intensity. Elf-ladies primped. "Florian, in fact, seems obsessed by you."

"Oh? Who's he?"

"Our host." His partner favored him with the coldest of smiles. "The scion and heir apparent of House L'Inconnu." She gestured with her chin and Will spun her around so he could see.

Beneath a crystal bowl in which a gold-and-green-tailed mermaid swam in endless circles, trying not to look bored, an elf-lord in the seeming of a dancing bear was staring fixedly at him. Will stiffened as he recognized the face beneath the muzzled snout.

"You know him," the lady prompted.

"Yes. I doubt, however, that he would recognize me. I was quite a different fellow when last we met."

It was true. Back then, Will had been Captain Jack Riddle, champion of the johatsu who lived in the subways of Babel, and Florian of House L'Inconnu had been leader of the Breakneck Boys, who preyed upon the homeless for their amusement. Will did not even know for sure if they actually *had* met, or if their brief, watery encounter had been undone by the death of Lord Weary. It hardly mattered, however. Whatever the truth might be, he had his memories of the murderous young Master Florian and, based upon them, his opinion of the fellow's worth.

"Well," said the policewoman, "since I have learned all I will tonight, I'll leave you two gentlemen to your conversation." The song ended and without obvious haste, but with no waste motion whatsoever, Will's interrogator deposited him at the edge of the floor. "Thank you for the dance," she said. "I look forward to another—something more lingering next time, I hope. My name is Zorya Vechernyaya. Perhaps someday I will hear you scream it in agony."

"You insist on being unpleasant."

"Trust me—this is an unpleasant town to be caught trying to pass yourself off as undocumented royalty in, kid."

She left.

The music started up again. Zorya Vechernyaya had left him on the same side of the floor as Florian L'Inconnu. So when he saw his host's bear-seeming lumbering toward him, Will quickly turned away to choose his next target from among the smiling many who were subtly jockeying to catch his eye. He fixed almost at random on a lady in sala-mander drag. A mask of red feathers burned from her face in stylized flames and twined into her upswept hair so that it seemed as though her head were afire. Perhaps there was a touch of glamour in that, but if so it was subtle. Her, he thought, and strode briskly forward.

Then Will recognized her and stopped dead.

She wore makeup, as she had not before, lips and nails redder than blood, and her scarlet gown, floor-length with a slit up one side, was a far cry from the hoydenish outfit he'd seen her in (and out of) last. Nevertheless, beyond the least breath of doubt, she was the hip-pogriff rider who'd flashed him the finger on the day he'd emerged from the underground.

She was the stranger he loved.

For a heartbeat that lasted half as long as forever, Will stood para-lyzed. Then he shot his cuffs in a kind of prayer to his tuxedo: I paid enough for you; now give me the confidence I need. He went straight to the elf-maiden, said, "Dance?", and waltzed her out onto the floor before she could answer.

She studied him with frank interest. "You have set the birds a-twitter. Everyone is wondering who you are and whether that ring is real."

"It's real enough. But it's only a ring. Nothing more."

"They also say that you have more names than all the social register put together."

"Forget that," Will said. "Who cares whether I call myself Phobetor or Hotspur or Baal-Peor? It's all bullshit, anyway. The only thing that matters is that I saw you once from a distance, more than a year ago, and lost my heart to you in that instant. I've been searching for you ever since."

"What a load of codswallop! I hope you haven't been using that line on everybody."

"I'm perfectly serious."

"In my experience," the hippogriff rider said, "sincerity is vastly overrated, and only peripherally related to the truth."

"Every word I say is true."

"Being male, you would believe that, of course." Her eyes gleamed as brightly as twin emeralds lit with green lasers. Releasing his shoulder, she slid her fingers into a hidden pocket in her dress. Then she touched his cheek. "Who are you? What are you? Is the ring real?"

"Will le Fey. A confidence trickster. So far as I know it is not." Will's face turned red and he stumbled and almost tripped.

His partner laughed. "Oh, la! If you could only see yourself." Her breath was warm in his ear. "You are not the only one with a ring, 'sieur clown."

With a quick grab, Will closed his hand tight about hers. "This ring?" He saw the hippogriff girl's eyes widen with alarm. "Does it work by contact? Will it work for me? Who and what are you?"

"Yes," she said. "Yes. Yes, obviously, it does. Alcyone. A thief."

She broke away from him. Almost brutally, Will caught her back, and they rejoined the dance. He was terribly aware of the feel and warmth of her waist under his hand, separated from him by only the thinnest scrap of silk. It called to him. He pulled it close. Her body was soft without being fleshy, muscular without being thrawn. It was tense as well; it resisted his embrace, without being able to escape it. "You still wear the ring. If you doubt I love you, just ask."

"If I *cared*," Alcyone said hotly, "I would have asked already."

"Look. We seem to have gotten off to a bad start—"

"Do you think?"

"—but that doesn't mean we can't—"

"Yes, it does. That is exactly what it means." They were at the edge of the dance floor now. She stopped dead in her tracks and held out a hand to the nearest male, a fop in a Green Knight costume. "Thank you," she said, though he had not asked. "I'd love to dance." Perforce, Will surrendered his salamander to her knight.

Away they spun.

For a second, Will contemplated the terrace full of beauties, lovelier than flowers, any of whom would be delighted to dance with him, flirt with him, dally with him till dawn. Save only the single woman he wanted most. What were the odds of that? It was as if he'd been cursed by a Maxwell's imp of the perverse, capable of inverting all probabilities, of turning a cold room hot and a warm one frigid, of making terms of endearment loathsome to the ear of his beloved and rejection only make him desire her the more.

In the distance, meanwhile, the dancing bear waved to get his attention.

Maintaining his outward aplomb, Will ducked and dodged his way through the crowd. Outside the ballroom, at the buffet tables, he asked a servitor for directions to the gent's. "Past the chafing dishes and to the right," the dwarf said with a shadow of a bow.

Will fled, almost blindly.

After he'd vomited into the toilet bowl, Will removed his domino and the Pierrot costume faded to nothing. He rinsed out his mouth, splashed water on his face, and combed his hair. There were two gold smudges on the jacket of his tux. He dabbed at them with a dampened washcloth and tried to regain his calm. He was weary and achy and he suspected he was coming down with a headache.

Will took out his Hermes phoenix-leather rune-bag and removed a razor blade, a cut-down McDonald's straw, and a vial of pixie dust. He chopped the powder on the granite countertop, laid it out in two lines, and snorted up both.

It was as if somebody had opened the Gates of Dawn: Energy flowed back into him. The thought of a moonlit room full of beautiful sylphs all competing for his attention no longer filled him with dread.

Donning his mask again, Will left.

A bear waited for him outside the door. It leaned against the wall, arms folded, alongside a modest Rembrandt etching in an elaborate gold frame. "Caught you at last." It placed its domino in a jacket pocket and became Florian L'Inconnu.

"I saw you talking to the witch from Political Security." Florian took out a silver case and flipped it open. "Smoke?" When Will shook his head, he removed a cigarette, tamped its end against the case, and placed it jauntily in his mouth in a complex and fluid combination of motions that Will was certain he could, with practice, duplicate.

Almost too late, Will assumed his mooncalf/halfwit persona. "Witch? Oh yes, her. Was she really with the polits? I think she wanted to cuff me and haul me off to her dungeon."

"You're safe here, whatever your offense may have been. They wouldn't dare arrest anybody over whom House L'Inconnu has extended its protection—a status that encompasses all our guests, of course."

"I'm not sure I fall under the heading of guest. Shorty implied I did not."

"Shorty? If you mean Hrothgar Thalwegsson, I'd advise you with all my heart not to use one of Mother's whimsical little informalities in his presence. Even I couldn't get away with that. But Hrothgar's made of solid stuff. You'll like him when you get to know him."

"He sicced Zorya Vechernyaya on me."

Amiably, Florian said, "I've already spoken to him about that. I promise it won't happen again." He gestured with his cigarette. "I see you now wear your ring with the stone inward."

"It was attracting too much attention." Will bowed curtly. "It has been pleasant chatting with you," he lied. "But now I must be going."

Behind him, somebody cleared his throat.

Will turned.

Three rows of teeth like daggers. A lion's body. Shaggy red hair. Blue eyes. A hound's ears. A quilled back. The bearded face of a man. A handlebar moustache. The tail of a scorpion. So grotesque were its features that Will could not immediately assemble them in his mind to make up one creature. Then it all fell together.

A manticore.

The manticore grinned a grin as wide as the sun. "You're not leaving just yet, chum." His breath stank of rotted meat. "Not until the boss says you can."

Will stuck his hands in his trousers and jingled the coins insolently. Under cover of this, he reached down deep within himself to where the dragon lay, quiescent but alert, and asked: What should I do?

They've got you boxed in. Pretend you don't notice. Play along. Wait for your chance.

"I'll go where I want and when I wish. As for your threats . . ." He snapped his fingers under the monster's nose. "That for them!"

The manticore snorted.

Despite his bravado, Will was terrified. With the dragon's help, he might be able to take Florian. But not the manticore. Manticores were notoriously savage. Gustave Flaubert had written of one, "The gleam of my scarlet hide mingles with the shimmering of the great sands. Through my nostrils I exhale the terror of solitudes. I spit forth plague. I devour armies when they venture into the desert." No one alive could say for sure that he had meant those words metaphorically.

Will was royally fucked.

Within him, the dragon whispered, *Be patient.*

"Here is our problem," Florian said, taking Will's arm. "We find ourselves in a state of quantum uncertainty. Either you are, as Hrothgar believes, a fraud, or else you are His Absent Majesty's rightful heir." He walked Will down the hall, away from the ballroom. "Perhaps it's the romantic in me, but I should like to believe in you."

"Believe what you wish, I am neither fraud nor heir."

"Yes, yes, yes. There are three possibilities at work here. One is that you are a con man, pure and simple. In which case you will be easily revealed without my having to get involved in the matter. The second is that you're an innocent caught up in the machinations of a con man and in so deep over your head that you can see no alternative but to thrash onward, in hopes of reaching the far shore. In which case, I am prepared to offer you full amnesty and gainful employment. You are obviously a clever fellow, and as you can see"—he nodded toward the manticore—"I have uses for extraordinary individuals. Take my offer and I swear upon my very name that you will not regret it." Will said nothing. "No? Then we come circling back to the third and most piquant possibility. I realize that the odds of your being the true king's by-blow are slight. Ahhh, but if you are, if you *are* . . ."

"If I am?"

Still holding Will's arm tight, Florian touched Will's chest fleetingly, caressingly. "Then we can do great things together," he murmured.

They came to a spiral staircase and went down it. The stairs lit up under their feet and faded back to gloom behind them. The manticore padded quietly in their wake.

"Where are we going?"

"In case you haven't noticed, I'm trying to be your friend—and, believe me, I am a friend well worth having. Your obvious coolness suggests that I have done you some harm in the past. Well, politics is a brutal business. In the pursuit of the public good, I have doubtless done grievous hurt to many. Yet if you do indeed ascend to the Perilous Siege, you will need allies. Nor will you care if their hands are dirty. So it would be to our mutual benefit to come to a rapprochement."

They had come to the bottom of the stairs. To one side were twin doors carved with ithyphallic representations of Grangousier and Falstaff, two perhaps-real, perhaps-legendary heroes of the Khazar Dynasty in Babel's ancient past. "Let me show you something."

The doors opened at Florian's touch, revealing an enormous study, with leather chairs, ashtrays, reading tables, and newspaper racks. Fairy lights lofted into the air at their approach, filling the room with a gentle golden glow.

They crossed a silk Kashan carpet vast as an ocean and woven in a pictographic history of the world and stopped dead center on Babel. Wonderingly, Will stared up at a domed ceiling so high that it required three walking galleries to provide access to the bookshelves lining the walls. It was an extravagant waste of space that—in this neighborhood, particularly—impressed him more than a mound of rubies could have done. Globes of all the worlds, each with its cities, nations, and land masses neatly labeled, spun gently in the air above.

"Here," Florian said, "we shall put an end to all mysteries." He stubbed out his cigarette. Then he picked up a wooden box from a nearby table. This he tossed lightly in the air, caught, and put down again. "It doesn't look like much, does it?"

Will felt the force of Florian's urbane smile with the same intensity as he did the manticore's unblinking stare. He was in terrible peril here. He would have fled, if only that were possible. "No."

"Try to pick it up."

Will did. Casually at first, with one hand, and then with both. It did not budge. He set both feet under him and tried again, with more force. But though he strained so hard that sweat came to his brow, the box did not move.

"That's quite a trick," he said at last. "Electromagnets and an iron bar inside?"

Florian laughed lightly. "Hardly. The box was carved of heartwood from Yggdrasil, the world tree. The combined military might of all the nations could not move or open it. Only those of my family can do so. Yet of itself, the box is a trinket. It serves only to hold something that truly is precious.

"This," he said, opening the box, "is House L'Inconnu's greatest treasure."

The box was empty.

Florian paled. First his skin turned white as snow and then with a crackle of ozone the hero-light blazed about his head. His face seemed a skull, his eyes pools of black savagery. A wind whipped through the room, setting newspapers to flight and their racks clattering to the floor. Elf-brat though he was, Florian was also a Power. He swelled up in Will's sight a full foot taller than he had been before, and correspondingly larger. Rounding on Will in a fury, he seized Will's jacket in one hand and lifted him off the floor. *"What have you done with it?"*

"I don't know what you're talking about!" Will cried.

Florian ripped off Will's domino and studied his face grimly. At last, voice trembling with suppressed rage, he said, "You don't look familiar. How can somebody I don't even know have done such a deed?"

"He didn't do it while I was here, boss," the manticore said. "I was watching the rat-bastard like a hawk."

With a roar of frustration, Florian flung Will away from him. "Stay here. Watch him," he commanded the manticore. "I'm going to fetch Thalwegsson; he'll know what to do." He paused in the doorway. "If he tries to leave, rip his limbs off. But leave him alive so he can face an inquisition."

The doors slammed and he was gone.

After Will had picked himself up off the floor and donned his Pierrot costume again, the manticore yawned hugely and lay down flat on the rug. "You're skunked now," he remarked conversationally. The quills on his back folded down neatly, but his segmented and stinger-tipped tail thrashed back and forth as restlessly as a cat's. "I don't know how you worked it—that box is only supposed to open to a pure-blooded L'Inconnu—but you chose the wrong folks to rip off."

"I have to get back to the dance," Will said.

"I think we both know that's not gonna happen." The manticore closed his eyes. "But if you want to try, I'm willing to give you a ten-stride head start."

His breathing grew slow and regular.

He's overconfident, the dragon murmured. *Let me loose and it's even money he'll be a dead little bug-cat before he knows what he's fighting.*

Will did not think much of those odds. So he thought back to all he had learned since coming to Babel. What would Nat do under these circumstances? Something clever, no doubt. Will wasn't feeling at all clever. What would Salem Toussaint do? That seemed a more productive line of reasoning to pursue.

"There's no reason you and I shouldn't be pals," Will said. "What would it take to convince you we're on the same side?"

The manticore opened his eyes the merest slit. "Nothing I can think of."

"Let me make you a proposition." Slowly, Will slid his wallet out of his pocket. Even more slowly, he opened it and fanned the contents. "I've got thirteen hundred dollars in here." He laid the wallet down at his feet and then stepped back three careful paces. "Let me leave unmolested and it's yours."

Lazily, the manticore stood, arching its back like a cat, and then padded over to the wallet. One claw delicately teased out the bills. He looked up and his piercing blue eyes met Will's. He grinned.

"Pass, friend."

In three heartbeats Will had slipped out of the library and closed the door behind him. Then he ran up the stairs as fast as his feet would take him. *Get the hell out of here,* the dragon advised, and for once Will agreed with him wholeheartedly.

But no matter how Will searched, he could not find an exit. It was as if he were trapped in a labyrinth. Every twist and turn he took sooner or later inevitably took him looping back to the ballroom.

He was in a bad position here. Yet, strangely, he felt elated. The energy that all the dancing and flirtation had taken out of him had returned in force. He was in savage danger and he could handle it. Provided only that he could get away from the ballroom.

As apparently he could not.

Well . . . if he could not, there was only one thing to do.

The moon had risen during his absence from the ballroom. It hung low in the sky, as big and orange as a pumpkin. Ignoring the murmurous regard of the assembled elf-horde, Will scanned the room for Alcyone.

Across the terrace he saw a burst of red.

He went straight to her.

Alcyone's eyes flashed with anger when Will took her arm as if they were old friends about to take a stroll. Her free hand rose slightly as if she would slap him but had restrained herself. It was a warning. "The attentions of a small-time hustler are not required here, sirrah."

"Smile," Will said quietly. "They've discovered your theft."

"That's impossible. They wouldn't—"

"Florian wanted to show off the ring." Will placed his lips by Alcyone's ear, as if he might nibble on the lobe, and whispered, "I'm going to kiss you now. Enjoy it if you can. Otherwise, fake it. Then pull back, take my hand, and tug me out the nearest door. Don't try to be subtle. I'm your trophy. They all envy you. We've got to leave and it's important that nobody guesses why."

There were servants in the hall—dwarves and haints in livery—so they walked without any particular haste until the corridor took a bend and there was no one in sight. Instantly, Alcyone released Will's hand, kicked off her heels and, holding her dress above her knees, fled like the wind.

Will ran after her.

"This isn't the way out," he said.

"All ways to the exits lead past Fata L'Inconnu and her dwarf consiglieri. By now they'll be guarded. Luckily, I foresaw this contingency and I have a way to get myself out."

"Ourselves, you mean."

"Only if I have no choice."

"You don't."

Alcyone stopped at a nondescript door. It unlocked itself at her touch and they went within.

The room was shadowy, but even so, Will noted the canopied bed that billowed invitingly in the night breeze from the open balcony doors. Astarte herself would not have felt disgraced by it. The room smelled of talcum powder, perfume, and roses. Under other circumstances, he would have wanted for the two of them to linger in it.

Alcyone stepped out onto the balcony. "Are you coming, asshole?"

Will did. Outside, Alcyone's hippogriff stood saddled and ready, placidly eating the heads off a potful of geraniums. Its eyes were as large as saucers, as red as garnets. They studied him thoughtfully.

He reached up to stroke the creature's head.

"Watch yourself," Alcyone said carelessly. "He bites."

Will snatched his hand back just as the beast's serrated beak clacked together where his fingers had been an instant before.

Alcyone didn't reach a hand down to help Will up onto the saddle, but neither did she try to stop him from climbing on behind her. Briefly, her dress caught on the horn. With both hands, she ripped the skirt from hem to crotch so she could straddle her mount firmly. "Damn," she muttered. "That was a Givenchy." Then she slapped the reins and the hippogriff launched itself from the balcony.

Enormous wings snapped wide to catch the wind.

They flew.

The hippogriff's surging flight felt nothing like being on horseback; it was simultaneously smoother and more unsettling. But it suited Will's mood, which was ecstatic. He had escaped! He was alive! He could do anything! It was an incredible sensation, the best one in the world. He wanted to go right back in and escape all over again.

Alcyone was laughing aloud and so, Will realized, was he. Meanwhile, the hippogriff was flying strongly, steadily, out over the Bay of Demons. Behind them, the windows of Babel grew steadily smaller, while the city itself did not; it continued to fill the sky. The air was chill and freighted with accents of hyacinth and diesel fuel.

"Tell me something," Will said when their laughter finally died away. "This beast wasn't hobbled. He came when you called. Why didn't you simply call him from the dance floor?"

Alcyone's head whipped around and she fixed him with a hard stare. Then her mouth twisted up in a complicated smile. "What an odd question for a buffoon to ask." She tied the reins to the saddle horn and then lithely swung first one leg and then the other over the hippogriff's back, so that she wound up facing Will. "Let's take off this mask and see what you look like." She flung aside his domino, and his Pierrot glamour whipped away with it. "Hmm. A little rough around the edges, but nowhere near as bad as I was expecting."

"You haven't—what are you doing?"

"Don't be dense." She pushed back his jacket and undid his tie. They went flying off into the night. Then she seized his shirt in both hands and yanked. The studs leaped and scattered. The air was suddenly cold on Will's chest. "I saved your butt back there. So now I'm claiming the hero's traditional reward. Lie back and enjoy it if you can. Otherwise, fake it."

"Hey!" Will cried as his shirt went flying away like a great white gooney bird. The rags of Alcyone's dress were fluttering wildly, stinging his face and arms. Her hair thrashed like a medusa's. "You didn't save me—I saved *you!*"

Alcyone put a hand on Will's chest and shoved him backward, so that he was all but lying flat. Then she ripped open his trousers—by now he was hard, of course—and said, "Let's tell this story my way, okay? Raise your hips off the saddle." Will obeyed and she pulled his trousers off and threw them away, too. He was naked now. Alcyone's gown fluttered and snapped like a flag. Bits of her flesh appeared and were gone too fast for him to be sure of what he had glimpsed.

Slowly, Alcyone bent low over Will. He could feel her mouth approaching his cock.

Then, grabbing one of his legs, Alcyone yanked it up and over her head and down again on the far side of the hippogriff.

He tumbled off into empty space.

There was an instant's pure terror as Will went into free fall. Then water slammed into him, hard as a board. Bubbles surrounded him.

Choking, Will fought his way to the surface.

The hippogriff came skimming in a great circle, its rider howling with delight. "Oh, Will!" she cried. "What a delightful ending to a perfect evening! Nobody ever had a better first date!"

Will shook a fist. "You harpy! You harridan! You bitch!"

Alcyone pulled up and the hippogriff hung in the air, its enormous wings laboring mightily. She'd discarded the shreds of her gown and donned a Hard Rock Cafe T-shirt from her saddlebag. Now, while she held the reins one-handed, she pulled out a pair of jeans, gave them a shake, and struggled into them. "Be seein' ya, chum. Can't say it hasn't been fun."

She shook the reins and headed for the sky.

Will stared up after the dwindling hippogriff with mingled rage and lust, willing it to come back for him. But it did not. It lofted up into the big full moon and grew smaller and smaller until it was a single mote among thousands swarming in his sight.

All this time, Will had been treading water. Now he turned around and saw that he was less than a mile's swim from the shore. Apparently the hippogriff had not headed straight out into the bay as he had thought, but had turned and angled up the Gihon. So, really, it was not so bad as it might have been. Alcyone could have dumped him so far out to sea that he'd never have made it back.

Will took a stroke toward the docks. Then he stopped and stared back over his shoulder at that big watery moon. Somewhere out there was his thief.

"Ah, well," he sighed. "Third time's the charm."

Then he began the long swim to shore.

Starting penniless and naked on the docks, it took Will three days to steal, beg, wheedle, charm, and swindle his way back to Babel. He could have done it in one and a half, but pride demanded that he return home with enough cash in hand to pay for his tux if Nat called him on its loss.

Still, those first few hours had been cold and disheartening ones.

When Will told the story, only lightly edited, of his evening, Nat laughed until he almost choked. "You're good, son! You're almost as good as I am!"

"I thought I'd screwed it all up. The political police are onto us. Florian hates my guts. And Alcyone knows pretty much everything."

"Does anyone have any proof?"

"Uh . . . no."

"Well, then! Don't worry about making enemies—we need enemies to make this scam work anyway. The important thing is that you had fun, after all. And you did have fun, didn't you? Of course you did."

14

The Petrified Forest

Two immense marble lions guarded the steps to the Public Library of Babel. Will sat down between the paws of one to read the books he had just checked out. It was an unseasonably warm autumn day and, because the library fronted on the esplanade, the steps were in full sunshine.

Nat had a cold-water railroad flat not half a block from the El, but it was less than an ideal place for reading. The upbound cog train rumbled by every ten minutes, shaking the apartment like thunder and bringing Esme running to gaze wonderingly out the window. The stairway smelled of cabbages and laundry and ancient lead paint. A clutch of trolls lived on the first floor, a pianist on the second, and lubberkins on the third, and if for a miracle they all fell silent at once, it would not be long before one or another were pounding on the ceiling, angry at some noise he had made. The street outside echoed with the shouts of children playing wall ball, flipping baseball cards, or quarreling over bottle caps. Young elle-mays and their lemans, lacking lodgings of their own, sought out the shelter of the brownstone's doorway in the evening to screw standing up. Delivery trucks rumbled by day and night.

Will began by going through the stack of papers Nat Whilk had saved for him.

Nat's plan was working beyond all expectation. It had taken Will three days to beg, steal, lie, and con his way back home, which turned out to be exactly the length of time it took the media to sniff out the story. On his arrival, the rumor of the king's return was front page news in every newspaper in Babel. RUMORS OF RESTORATION HAUNT CITY stated the *Times*. HIS NOT-SO-ABSENT MAJESTY? asked the *Post*. PREVIOUSLY UNKNOWN PRINCE-APPARENT SOUGHT proclaimed the *Herald Tribune*. And, taking up all the front page of the *Daily News*, was his favorite: HEIR HERE?

The editorial pages were filled with wild speculation. Why, they wondered, had an heir suddenly appeared? Was the king dying? (That he was not dead was certain, an insert explained, by various signs and omens, foremost among which was the quiescence of the Obsidian Throne. So long as His Absent Majesty lived, it would obey none other than he himself or those of his blood lineage, and was death to any other who dared sit upon it, a suite of attributes that even those who supported an absolute monarchy deplored for reasons that the king's absence made manifest.) Why, if the heir had returned, did he not reveal himself? Why, if he wished to remain hidden, had he made so little effort to conceal his identity during his first quasi-public appearance? If, indeed, it was his first. Another special insert of newsroom sweepings and convoluted reasoning argued otherwise.

Will put down the last of the papers and picked up a book.

"*The Care and Feeding of Hippogriffs?*" a stone-deep voice grumbled. "Why read about them? Hippogriffs are nasty beasts. Rats with wings."

Will turned and glared. "Don't you know it's rude to read over somebody's shoulder?"

"I can't help it," the lion said. "I'm a compulsive reader. Newspapers, cereal boxes, anything with words on it. It's my only vice."

"You have no room to complain, then. This has words."

"That doesn't mean I don't have preferences! Sometimes a lounger brings something worthwhile. Faulkner. Woolf. Shelley. One summer there was a knocker who came here every day until he'd read all the way through *War and Peace*." The lion shivered. "That was glorious." Then, delicately raising one toe, he tapped on Will's stack of books with a stone claw. "These, however, are mere compendia of facts. Why on earth are you wasting your time on them?"

"Well, there's this girl . . ."

"There's always a girl."

"You wouldn't understand."

"Oh, no, I suppose I wouldn't. What would a lion know about females? We only keep a pride of seven to ten of 'em happy at a time. Anybody could do that!"

Will put down his book. "And where are they now, this pride of yours?"

"I have the happy honor of informing you that currently they are in labor."

"What? All of them? At once?"

"You wouldn't want me to play favorites!" the lion said indignantly. "Every wife, every night, as often and as long as they please. That is the way to promote marital harmony. Take my word on it, so long as you adhere to this simple regimen, your marriages will never fail."

"If they're in labor, shouldn't you be with them?"

The lion smiled pityingly. "Flesh is transient but stone endures. To us, you guys are as fleeting as the glimmer of moonlight on a summer lake. No wonder you never get anything done! Our lives, however, are long enough to be savored. When I was young, there was only one continent. Imagine my astonishment when a rivulet so narrow I used to hop across it without a second thought widened and became a sea! How dizzied I felt when one land broke into many and went whizzing to all corners of the globe! Sometimes I would have to shut my eyes and clutch the ground with all twenty claws for a few thousand years just to stop my head from spinning.

"Unluckily for me, I was courting at the time, and my intended brides wound up on a different continental plate from me. I was beside myself with anxiety. Had I been as rash as one of you flesh-folk, I would have plunged at once into the water and drowned in a misguided attempt to swim across the ocean floor to rejoin them. But though lionesses demand passion, the one trait they value above all others is dependability and thus they despise impulsiveness. So I was patient. I waited. And after what seemed, even to me, to be an ungodly great deal of time, my continent and theirs closed in upon one another again. I stood by the shore and watched the waters narrow. I saw the lands collide and a mighty range of mountains rise up where they met. When things had settled, I located the least difficult pass between their continental plate and mine.

"Then I sat down.

"The decades passed like ticks on a stopwatch. Centuries flowed like water. No lady likes to appear anxious over a male. Long eons later, nine lionesses came ambling casually by. Eight walked past me without a glance. The last and youngest was about to follow when she noticed me with a start. 'Oh!' she said. 'Have you been here all along?'

" 'Sweet and maneless one, I have,' said I.

"The others came circling back. Their bodies were rangy and tense. Their paws made no sound as they touched the ground. In an offhanded way, the eldest said, 'Perhaps you remember us.'

" 'Oh, tawny goddesses, I have thought of nothing else in all the millions of years of our separation!'

"Closer they circled and closer, until they were brushing casually against each other and lightly bumping against me as they endlessly paced around and around. Their murderous golden eyes flashed. The smell of their privates was intoxicating. Coyly, they showed their sharp white teeth. Here, I knew, was my greatest moment of danger, for they had waited long for me and were I to show weakness or impatience they would turn on me and rend me from limb to limb in their disappointment.

" 'Aren't you going to ask if we've been faithful to you?' asked she who was the best huntress. She nipped me lightly on the flank.

" 'Carnivore of my delight, I would not have fallen in love with you had I needed to ask that question.'

" 'But have you been faithful to us?' asked she who was the most intelligent.

" 'I'm still alive, aren't I?' I said. Oh, I was fearless! I shook out my mane so they could admire it. I stood and stretched so they could see the muscular perfection of my body. 'A glance would have told you I was unworthy. Your teeth would have met in my throat. Your claws would have ripped open my hide, so that my blood would fountain upon the ground. Yet still I live.'

"Great was their arousal at my words. A collective growl rose up from them all. Finally, the shyest of them all stood forward and murmured, 'Then you may have us.'

"I did not move. 'When?' I asked.

"A look of mingled amusement and appreciation passed around the circle and I knew that I had passed their final and most cunning test. The loveliest of the lot lowered her eyes before me. 'Now,' she said.

"So we celebrated our nuptials then and there in that very spot and instant, and long has our marriage been, and happy as well. Then—not long ago as I reckon these things, but beyond the memory of your kind—my ladies became pregnant. Now, the female is at her most vulnerable when she is pregnant and though there are few creatures that would dare attack ones such as they . . . Well, when your gestation period is measured in eons, it pays to take no chances. So in the manner of our kind, they sought out a mountain and dug burrows deep down to its very roots, there to sleep and await their day of delivery.

"I stood guard.

"Sometime I wandered away briefly to hunt or on a call of nature, but never for long. Before I left, I would plant an apple's worth of seeds to measure the time. Always I returned before the resulting orchard had died. Such was my vigilance.

"But one day I returned from a brief excursion to discover the mountain half carved away and masons and carpenters and stonecutters at work on a massive edifice atop the very spot where my beloved wives lay buried! Overseeing it all was a monarch who was large of stature by your standards, though a mere pippin of a creature by mine.

"What's this?" I asked the little king. He was one of the flesh folk and they were new to the world at that time.

Rather nervously—for I had knocked him over and placed a paw on his chest lest he attempt to escape—Nimrod (for such, he said, was his name) explained his great project, its sacred purpose, the many prophesies of its central place to the Thousand Races and inevitable domination of the globe, the elegance of its architecture, and so on and on. During the course of our conversation several of his soldiers loosed spears and arrows, which of course rattled harmlessly off my sides, and I waited until they had drawn carelessly close and crushed them to jelly. But Nimrod I did not destroy, for even in the face of outrage my self-control is absolute.

"With the aid of his draftsmen, the blueprints, and many a fervent oath, Nimrod was able to convince me that the foundations of Babel did not delve deeply enough to harm my sleeping brides. Indeed, upon reflection, it occurred to me that planting a massive city overtop their sheltering-space only made them all the more secure from harm.

"So I stayed my wrath.

"Now at last my wives' time has come. Sometimes you may feel a tremor that lightly shakes the Tower and makes its steel-beam framework moan. That means that one is experiencing a contraction. Someday—tomorrow, perhaps, or a hundred thousand years from now—they will go into the true labor that takes no time to speak of and is over in a week. Then shall they shake off the weight of stone and mortar that lies atop them, and the Dread Tower shall fall and all those who dwell within it will die. My wives will burrow to the surface and feast on the bodies, and I shall lick my cubs into life. But that happy day is not yet, so I abide. I took this job guarding the library, and though the salary is small, my needs are few. It suffices. However long I must endure, I shall. I am patience incarnate."

Will was silent for a while. Then he nodded toward the other lion and said, "And your associate? I assume his story is much the same?"

"Him?" the lion said, surprised. "I wouldn't know. I never asked."

"Ah." Will returned to his reading.

According to the book, hippogriffs ate both grain and flesh. Though there was no shortage of purveyors of each in Babel, Alcyone would doubtless buy from a single provider. Their stables required both access to the open sky and a grassy exercise yard. So there was a second lead as well. A rough-and-tumble elf-girl who could pass as high society shouldn't be as hard to locate as she was turning out to be. So he might want to look for her through her harness-maker. Hippogriffs were far rarer than either the griffins or horses whose crossbreed they were, and thus there were correspondingly fewer artisans catering to the market. Alcyone could be expected to patronize only the best.

It took Will several hours to work his way through to the end of the last book. He put down *The Aristocracy of the Air,* yawned, stood, and stooped to gather up his stack.

Will had only gone a few steps when a child slammed into his legs.

"Unca Will! Unca Will!" It was Esme. She caught her breath and said, "Pop-Pop says don't go home to our apartment." These days she thought Nat was her grandfather. "He says it's important."

Will stooped so he could speak to Esme eye to eye. "Was this recently?"

She shrugged. "I don't know."

"Did he say anything more?"

"Yes, but I forget what."

Will couldn't help but smile. "Of course you do. I—"

There was a sudden weight on Will's shoulders and hips. With a strange sense of discontinuity, he realized that he was wearing a rubberized cloth helmet with a plastic visor. He looked down and found himself clothed in a white moon suit with rubber gloves. A waist unit pumped fresh air through PVC tubing into his helmet.

Inexplicably, Nat Whilk was standing in front of Will. He, too, wore a white biohazard suit. "Whatever you do, don't take off the hood," he said. "Or you'll be frozen timeless like everyone else in the city."

Everything felt odd. "Nat," Will said, "what the hell am I doing in this thing? What's going on here?"

"Take a look." Nat stepped to the side so he wasn't blocking Will's sight.

All the city was motionless. Traffic had ceased. The crowds of pedestrians on the sidewalk were a petrified forest. Flower petals that the wind had blown from a window box were fossilized in the air, like ants in amber. Esme, caught in mid-hop, balanced on one toe.

Nat took a nickel from his pocket and held out before him. When he snatched his hand out from under it, the nickel did not fall. "Major juju, huh? The Lords of the Mayoralty have frozen an instant of time and moved their police and rescue forces into it. This is world-class stuff. You're lucky to be seeing it. A spell of this magnitude is cast only once in a decade, and even then only under gravest need. It's a real budget-breaker."

Nat snatched the nickel out of the air. "Let's go."

"My books . . ."

"I already returned them. One of the advantages of stopping time is that you've got the opportunity to catch up on all those little chores."

"What about Esme?"

"She'll keep."

W ill followed Nat down the street, not asking obvious questions but, rather, answering them for himself. How did Nat know about the time-freeze? Nat had connections. Obviously, he had a mole in the Mayoralty or even the Palace of Leaves. Where had he gotten the moon suits? From the same source. What was he planning now? It was extremely unlikely he knew. Nat always said he did his best thinking on the fly.

The city was silent, and beautiful, too.

A scattering of pigeons was a stairway rising from the street. Nat took one from the air and gently folded its wings. After which he stuffed it down the trousers of a nearby boggart. Gleaming droplets of water were a spreading string of bright diamonds pendant beneath an air-conditioner. Nat plucked them one by one, brushed them into a single sphere of water the size of a child's fist, and slipped it inside a policeman's hat. He snatched a blackfly out of the air and placed it in an ogre's nostril.

"That's very childish," Will said.

"I know. But what can I do? As a fully vested master in and past president of the Just and Honorable Guild of Rogues, Swindlers, Cozeners, and Knaves, I do have certain obligations."

"Tell me something. This guild of yours—are you by any chance the founder and sole member?"

"How well you know me!" Nat lifted a wallet from a prosperous-looking rock troll and, hoisting up a hulder's skirts, slid a hundred-dollar bill in her thong. "*That'll* give her something to think about," he chortled. He danced on down the street, stuffing money into the underwear of every sylph and houri he saw. When the wallet was empty, he flipped it away, leaving it hanging over a trash can like a leather seagull.

"You know, this could be a golden opportunity for us," Will said. "Instead of frittering it away like this, we could be walking out of banks with sacks of gold—for charity if you wish, but at least some of it for ourselves."

Unexpectedly, Nat laughed. "That's not what a trickster does. It's not what he is." He lowered his voice in a caricature of confiding charm, and winked. "It's not what we're *for*."

"Suddenly we have a purpose?"

"Absolutely. We keep things stirred up. Without us, the world would grow stale and stagnant. Every life we've touched today has been made richer and stranger."

"The poor bastard whose wallet you took isn't any richer."

"No! Infinitely richer! He was stuck in a rut and he didn't even know it. He had his head stuck so far up his wallet that he was blind to the wonders of the world. An hour from now, he'll be mourning the loss of his money. But later tonight, he'll reflect on what a fool he was. By morning, he'll be rethinking his life."

"And the young ladies?"

"When a lass finds a C-note in her knickers and no idea how it got there, that's a wake-up call. She has only one possible reaction: To resolve to mend her sluttish ways."

"And what if she's chaste? What if she has no sluttish ways?"

"Then she can take them up!" A police car grumbled by, tracing a tortuous route through the frozen traffic. "It isn't for me to increase or decrease the total amount of virtue or vice in the world—just to keep things stirred up. To keep us all from dying of predictability."

The city, silent until now, began to murmur. Sirens wailed in the distance. A lancer in a biohazard suit galloped by them. But these were exceptions to an otherwise universal state of stasis. "Almost there," Nat said cheerfully.

They passed a line of scarecrows set up on wooden frames whose heads had been doused with gasoline and set afire. The amber flames engulfing them glowed but did not flicker. Nat lifted the yellow police tape that ran from scarecrow to scarecrow, and they both ducked under. They rounded a corner.

"This is our street," Will said. "That's our flat!"

"Look busy," Nat growled. "Act like you belong here."

There were hundreds of emergency workers, investigators, and political functionaries, all vying for preeminence in a situation that had useful work for no more than a tenth their number. Nat and Will wove their way between cars with the insignia of a dozen military and quasimilitary forces, all with their lights flashing. Fire hoses snaked across the pavement. Tylwyth Teg officers stood in amuleted trench coats overlooking the scene bleakly. Sorcerer-elves so old that by rights they should have been declared legally dead centuries ago stood outside the brownstone, staves raised, maintaining the citywide stasis. Poulettes cycled in and out of the building lugging enough cardboard boxes to carry out everything Nat and Will and Esme owned and half the neighbors' possessions as well.

"It looks like they're winding up here," Nat said. He leaned forward so that their helmets almost touched and gestured with short, choppy mudras, as if he were giving instructions. "Now this is just reconnaissance, to see if they've taken the bait. So dummy up, okay? Speak only when spoken to."

"Nat, you madman! This is absolutely bugfuck. What have you gotten me involved in?"

"Everything's happening right on schedule. You should have been expecting this. The return of the king is a big deal. All this fuss was foreseeable." In his most reassuring manner, Nat said, "This is the great game, kid. It's like Aesop's nettle. Approach it timidly and seize it gently and it'll sting like fire. But grasp it boldly, like a man, and it will be painless and as soft as silk to your hand. Also, keep in mind that none of them knows what either of us looks like."

Will had his doubts about the nettle-seizing strategy, whether taken literally or figuratively, but he kept his silence. They were in this thing too deep for quibbles. So he followed Nat to a vantage point in a narrow alley across and down from their brownstone. "They're desecuring the area," Nat said. The emergency vehicles were starting to pull away and the scarecrows were one by one being doused and dismantled. Only the most important players remained to see the operation through to its conclusion. "I don't recognize anybody on the street," Nat said. "How about you?"

"Actually, yeah." Will pointed with his chin. "The one with scarlet lipstick and a warrior's posture. That's Zorya Vechernyaya. She's pretty highly placed in the political police, I think."

"Damn. I've got a rap sheet as long as the Fisher King's dick. She might recognize me." Nat scowled and muttered. "Hey, babe. I need you on deck. You're a better judge of character than I am. Take a look at this dame and tell me what you think."

"Huh?"

"Not *you*," Nat said peevishly. "Yeah, that's what I think, too. You want to take over here?"

"What on earth are you talking about?"

"I've got to step out briefly, kid. There's someone I want you to meet. Tell her everything. Trust her as you would me."

"But I *don't* trust you." Will followed in Nat's wake down the street to the storefront temple at the corner operated by the Cult of Profane Love.

"Smart-ass." They ducked within the temple. The interior might have been an educational tableau demonstrating the cult's varieties of worship: the flagellators with their whips curled in cryptic arabesques above their backs, the self-abusers in a circle about the altar, heads thrown back in ecstasy, and finally the virgin sacrifice strapped down upon the altar, about to receive the priest's chastising instrument. "Watch closely. This is my best trick."

Nat slowly bent over double. For a long moment he writhed as if, within the suit, his body were changing form. Then he straightened.

There was a stranger's face in the helmet.

"So you're the kid. I heard a lot about you." The stranger quirked a sardonic smile. She was one of those women who were beautiful at first glance, then showed their age, and then were beautiful again. Her hair was red and cropped. Her features were sharp and Asian. "I'm an old associate of Tomba's," she said. Then, when Will did not respond, "St. John Malice? Mullah Nasreddin? Tom Nobody? Liane the Wanderer? Nat Whilk? Let me know when I'm getting close."

"Who are you?" Will asked. "And what are you to Nat?"

"He didn't tell you about me? The rat. He'll pay for that." She stuck out a hand. "I'm Victoria il Volpone Sheherazade Jones. Don't call me Vickie. I'm Nat's partner."

"You're the vixen," Will said. "The one who rescued him in Whinny Moor Landfill."

"So he did tell you about me. The bastard. I told him not to."

"You, uh, share Nat's body with him?" Will flushed. "I mean—"

"Fast on the uptake, too." She tapped her chest. "I caught a shotgun blast right here—it pretty much pureed my heart—and had to go to earth for a few months to heal. Let's not get into the specifics about how it's done—they're a little intimate. Bring me up to speed here. What's Nat been up to in my absence?"

Will gave her the short version. How they had met in Camp Oberon and traveled to Babel together. How Nat had saved him from the political police but then, through his disdain of official documentation, made Will an illegal. Lastly, how they were working the Missing Prince scam together.

"Yeah, I know all about the scam." The vixen fleered. "This is another of Nat's overcomplicated schemes. The classics always work best when done simply. But he's an *awrtist*—he needs to rework 'em. Give him a pocket watch and he'll take it apart to see if he can add a few more cogs and maybe a stick of butter to it." Going up to the altar, she said, "Hey, let's give these guys a miracle!" She dipped a finger in a censor of scented charcoal that hadn't yet been set afire, and wrote the rune of celibacy on the sacrifice's stomach. Then she smartly slapped the celebrant's tool between her hands.

"What was that all about?" Will asked as they left the building.

"The priest's dick goes limp, he screams, and the sacrifice is suddenly labeled off-limits." The vixen had a short, barking laugh. "I just created the cult's first sacred virgin."

"You and Nat are two of a kind."

"I'll take that as a compliment." They resumed their posts at the alley. "Not everybody would."

A gong sounded and the mages lowered their arms.

Time resumed.

Will and the vixen removed their hoods and gloves and lit up cigarettes while they waited for Zorya Vechernyaya to finish an interminable conversation with a Teggish agent. The mages dispersed in waiting limousines. Not long after, Esme came running up. "Unca Will! Is this my Auntie Fox?"

"Yes I am, hon." The vixen picked her up and held her upside down until she squealed with laughter. "Pop-Pop told you I was coming, huh?" When she set Esme down, they were both standing in the alley's shadows, out of sight. "We have to be careful here—I don't have Nat's luck."

"Is that how he gets away with all the crap he does? It's all good luck?"

"No, it's *strange* luck. Not good, not bad—just unlikely. Nat must've inherited it from you, eh, little grandmother?"

Esme shrugged. "I guess."

"Wait. Esme's literally his grandmother?"

"Why do you think he was in the refugee camp in the first place? He had a premonition that his mother was going to die, so he went to see her." The vixen pulled a five-dollar bill out of Esme's ear and swatted her on the rump. "Run along and buy some ice cream, sweetie. We'll play later." She peered out onto the street again. "They're breaking up at last. What does it say on the back of my moon suit?"

Will looked. "ATF."

Zorya Vechernyaya strode down the sidewalk, looking grim. She passed by the alley just as the vixen was stripping off her suit, almost but not quite showing more flesh than might be expected. Behind her, Will doffed his suit more circumspectly.

The vixen thrust her bundled suit into the policewoman's arms. "Hey, babe. Be a doll and hold this for me for a sec."

"Do I know you?" Zorya Vechernyaya asked in a tone that said that she did not.

"Kim Freydisdottir, Alchemy, Tobacco, and Firearms." She jerked a thumb toward Will. "This is Dan Picaro. My intern. And today's your lucky day."

The policewoman glanced once at Will, and then glared at the vixen. "Is it?"

"You betcha. You just met me. And I'm a gal like nobody you ever met before."

"How so?"

"I lead your quintessentially charmed life. All these years in ATF and I never been shot. Never been ensorcelled. Never been hurt in love."

"Oh?" Zorya Vechernyaya said. A small, cruel rosebud of a smile bloomed on her mouth. "Let me buy you a drink."

Le Wine Bar's interior was overgrown with jungle vines through whose foliage green and yellow snakes slowly twined. A satyr led them through the foliage to an orchid-strewn table beside a pool of black water from the depths of which corpse-pale faces peered up at them.

"Boodles martini, very dry, straight up with a twist," said Zorya Vechernyaya.

"I'll have a Bloody Mary," the vixen said. "Nothing for my intern. He's on duty."

"You want me to drown a mouse in your drink?" the satyr asked.

"What the hell."

When their drinks arrived, the vixen took a long slug and said, "So. You think this guy is really His Absent Majesty's bastard?"

"We won't know until we find him, of course. But nothing discovered so far contradicts the possibility. Looks to be an innocent fallen in with bad company. The perp he's lodging with is a small-time criminal with so many aliases I doubt even he knows who he started out as. Which explains why the target's so fucking elusive."

"I was talking to a guy who said you'd have the target in custody within three hours."

Zorya Vechernyaya snorted.

The vixen fished the mouse out of her drink and, holding it by its tail, threw her head back, and swallowed it whole. Zorya Vechernyaya watched her intently. Then the vixen swallowed and said, "So what's the next move?"

Zorya Vechernyaya casually placed a hand on the vixen's forearm. "Next we put in for supplementary funding so we can send a compulsion to find this guy back in time two years to get a head start on the investigation."

The vixen whistled. "That's pricey."

"Tell me about it."

"Chancy, too. Suppose they kill him."

"It hasn't happened. So it won't. We just want to get a good, solid start on the investigation—and we have. How do you think we got this close so fast?" Zorya Vechernyaya slugged down the last of her martini and shouted, "Hey! Who do I have to flay alive to get another drink around here?"

Will had had a lot of practice maintaining a deadpan face since taking up with Nat. Now, though, it was all he could do to hide his shock. So this was why the witches from the political police had invaded his train on the way to Babel! They'd been searching for him not because of any crime he had unknowingly committed but because they thought him the rightful heir to the Obsidian Throne. It would also explain why the rumor of the heir's return had spread so quickly and convincingly. The ground had been prepared years ago and doubtless the whispers had since spread beyond the circles of governance. It was all beginning to pull together now. It was all beginning to make sense.

He just didn't know what to think about it.

"Say. You're in investigative, maybe you can help my intern," the vixen said. "The kid's looking for someone."

"Oh, yeah? Who?"

"His father. Only the kid doesn't know much about him. Not even his name. But he does know that he owns a hippogriff."

Zorya Vechernyaya accepted her new martini from the satyr. "Hippogriff or simurgh?"

"Hippogriff," Will said.

"Purebred or mongrel?"

"Considering the owner, probably purebred."

"So your old man's an aristocrat?"

"Blue blood, with a touch of crimson," the vixen said. Mortal blood was red, for it contained iron. "We're pretty sure he's got money."

"You'll be wanting to look into gizzard stones, in that case. A serious 'griffer will have his own distinctive mix. Moonstones, opals, gold nuggets . . . Do you have any idea what colors your rider might favor?"

Emeralds, Will thought. To match her eyes. Rubies to match her hair. He knew it for a certainty. Aloud, he said simply, "No."

"Too bad." Zorya Vechernyaya turned back to the vixen. "Tell me a little more about yourself."

"Not much to tell. I'll sleep with anyone who thinks he or she or they can break my heart. 'Cause I know it can't be done and it's fun to watch 'em try."

Zorya Vechernyaya's eyes narrowed. "I admit to liking a challenge. But to be frank, you're not my usual type and I don't know if I care to get involved."

"Oh, you want me," the vixen said. "My primary orientation is straight, I'm willing to try anything, and I've never been hurt. Emotionally, I mean. I am, to be equally frank, the hottest little weekend you've ever seen."

Under the table, she kicked Will's ankle.

Will looked up to see both women staring at him expressionlessly.

Red-faced with embarrassment, he left.

Dwarf jewelers always set up their shops like caves, with clutters of boxes stacked in the corners as casually as boulders, and rows of tiny little drawers like strata of rock that hid precious stones, rare minerals, and magic rings. You could ask for Charlemagne's sword and, after the mandatory glass of oversweetened hot mint tea, a flunky would appear from the shadows with a canvas-wrapped package whose cardboard tag read, in neatly calligraphic letters faded an almost invisible brown, JOYEUSE.

The firm of Alberecht & Ting, Gastrolitheurs, however, was as posh as they came and almost all the racial signifiers had been scrubbed away. Normally, chairs in dwarf establishments were too small and too low to the floor to be comfortable to sit in. Except for the dwarf. They'd fit him perfectly. Will was ushered into an easy chair that looked no larger than Alberecht's, but was a pleasure to abide in.

Alberecht smiled as though Will were a personal friend. "As I'm sure you know," he said in the easy manner with which the discreet enlighten the ignorant, "the purpose of gizzard stones is to break down the hard parts of your mount's food—the seeds and bits of bone—into smaller pieces to be better exposed to the digestive enzymes. These rest in the muscular gizzard, or true stomach. Now, the opening of the pyloric sphincter is very tiny, which keeps the gizzard stones from escaping. But as the gizzard churns, the stones are ground against each other until eventually they are so small that they escape through the sphincter. Thus, you need to begin with a mix of varied-sized stones, and follow up with a regular replacement regimen."

"I see."

"Our product has been chosen specifically for its gastrolithic qualities and artisan-cut in a manner designed to be both attractive to the eye and safe for your mount. Try one yourself." He lifted up a ruby from the display tray with a pair of tweezers and proffered it to Will.

Will rolled the stone in his mouth as the connoisseurs did. It tumbled over his tongue smoothly. The facets were crisp but did not cut his flesh.

Satisfied, he spat the stone into the discard dish set discretely to one side, as if the stone wouldn't simply be washed and returned to the stock.

"Excellent. You can provide references, of course."

"References?" Never had absolute astonishment been so mildly expressed.

"Satisfied users. For those who have used this particular formulation, I mean. A turquoise-and-sapphire user's acclaim would be worthless. And Schuyler is more than just a racing beast to me. I daren't take chances."

"Hmm," Alberecht said. "Let me see what can be done."

He disappeared into the back room.

Minutes later, he returned with an envelope. Will opened it and glanced down at a short list of four names, nodding with casual recognition. The first was *Pippin Droit-de-Seigneur*. "Oh, yes, old Stinky," he murmured. The second was *Fata Melusine Sansculotte*. He pursed his lips and shook his head slightly, as if she might be beyond his asking, a former lover, say, who knew how to carry a grudge. The third was *Eilrik von Fenris*. He grunted noncommitally. Then he came to the fourth:

Alcyone L'Inconnu.

15

The Rousing of the West

The offices of the Mayoralty coiled like a snake around the air shaft at the core of Babel nine loops up and then another nine down, so that it crisscrossed itself like a parking garage. This meant that there were two floors per level, intersecting and interpenetrating each other in a manner that, when taken in combination with centuries of alterations, subdividings, security glamours, and curses laid down by disgruntled office-seekers, guaranteed that only the cognoscenti could find their way about its endless warren of rooms. All others were lost in a matter of minutes and had to hire a local guide if they hoped to ever get anywhere.

Alcyone had an office on the third gyre of the upward serpent. Will hired a grig who claimed he had originally come to the Mayoralty to obtain a business license, lost his livelihood in the years-long and ultimately futile pursuit of that document, and now never left the building, eating at public receptions when he could and from vending machines and employee cafeterias when nothing better presented itself, and sleeping in the visitors gallery of the City Council caucus chamber. He was a cheerful little cricket of a fellow, and Will tipped him a silver dime when their journey ended safely at an undistinguished door whose brass plate read:

308
A. L'Inconnu
Asst. Director
Signs & Omens

Will opened the door without knocking and stepped inside.

Alcyone looked up from her desk.

For a long moment neither spoke.

At last Alcyone said, "It's you, isn't it? *Tell* me that the bastard prince and heir to His Absent Majesty that everyone is talking about isn't really you."

"Well . . . it is and it isn't, if you see what I mean. May I sit?"

She nodded with chill grace toward a chair.

"I used to have a job that brought me to this building two or three times a week," Will said musingly. The office had good furniture and a grim view. Its window faced across the air shaft to the Criminal Vengeance Division, where the heads of malefactors insufficiently notorious for a place above the city gates were routinely hung from spikes on the windowsills like so many cheeses in a delicatessen. "I had no idea you were so near."

"And why should that matter to you?" Her manner was all business. There was not a scintilla of flirtatiousness to it.

"You know why," Will said. "I'll say it out loud if you like."

"That won't be necessary." Alcyone lifted a stack of papers from her inbox and let it fall again. "There was a rain of snakes two weeks ago. A three-headed calf was born in Hell's Kitchen the day before yesterday. Just last night, a blood-red comet sped across the sky shrieking. Citizens spontaneously burst into flames. Tap water turns to blood. Tatzlwurms infest the Upper West Side. Statues weep and hogs fly. On Sixth Avenue, a merchant tries to give his goods away. There's never been such a season for portents, signs, and plagues of owls. My sleepy backwater office has suddenly become one of the focuses of governance. All of which, apparently, is your doing. And for what?"

"Wealth, obviously."

"But you won't live to enjoy it!" Alcyone slammed her hands down on her desk and stood in a fury. "Yours is a fool's ambition, Master le

Fey. I have seen the death that awaits those who, with whatever rationale, are ambitious enough to seat themselves down upon the Obsidian Throne, and I assure you it is far from pleasant."

"Please," Will said mildly, "don't use that name. I have reason to believe it's been compromised. As for the Obsidian Throne, I plan never to get that far—quite."

"Then what is the point of this elaborate charade?"

"How can I best explain this?" Will cast about in his mind. "Let me tell you a story."

Raven was walking, just walking (Will began). He wasn't looking for trouble. But he wasn't looking to avoid it, either. That's just the kind of guy he was.

Well. He came to Scorpion's house and Scorpion invited him in. Scorpion poured him a drink. "Will you stay for supper?"

"Yes, I will do that thing."

So Scorpion got out his good silver and his best china and served Raven a fine meal. Then he said, "Would you like coffee? Would you care for some tobacco?"

"Oh, I will do those things as well and I will stay the night, too."

Scorpion brewed Blue Mountain coffee in his samovar and gave Raven Turkish tobacco to smoke in his hookah. He showed his guest all the rooms of his house but one. And afterward Raven said, "I hear that you have a room full of treasure. Everybody says so."

"There's nothing special about it," Scorpion said. But he showed it to Raven anyway. The room was full of gold and silver and gems. But Scorpion was right—there was nothing special about it. It was just ordinary treasure.

Nevertheless, Raven's eyes gleamed with avarice. "This is excellent treasure indeed," he said. "But I do not think it is very safe. Somebody could climb through the window at night and steal it all."

"I never thought of that," said Scorpion. This was long ago when everyone was better behaved. "Could such a thing really happen?"

"Oh, yes. I think I should sleep with your treasure tonight to guard it from thieves."

But innocent though the times may have been, everybody had heard about Raven and his roguish ways. So Scorpion said, "No, no, no. That is too lowly a job for a guest. You must sleep in my own bed tonight. It has silk sheets and an Irish lace coverlet. I will guard the treasure myself."

And so it was.

Scorpion went into the treasure room and locked the door and piled all the treasure in a heap, and crouched over it, pincers open and tail raised, ready to sting. He did not sleep a wink that night for worrying about what sort of tricks Raven might be planning.

When morning came, Scorpion emerged from his treasure room to discover that Raven was gone. Along with his bedclothes, silverware, plates, samovar, and hookah.

Will spread his hands to indicate the end of his story. "That's all."

After a brief, tense silence, Alcyone said, "In what sense is this an allegory?"

"Well . . . I have an associate. While I'm being prepped for the coronation, he'll set up an enterprise to sell titles and offices to the ambitious and gullible at prices just barely steep enough to be plausible. Those who suspect I am a fraud—and there will be many such—will refrain from arresting him, lest I become aware they are watching me. I will be housed in the Palace of Leaves, after all, and the treasure there is not at all ordinary. A nimble man could stuff enough in his pockets to make him rich forever. So my adversaries will set traps for me, baited with such wonders as no cracksman could resist. But while they're guarding their glitters and geegaws, I'll skip town. My profits will be relatively modest. But I'll have my life and that's worth something, too."

Alcyone scowled and pinched the bridge of her nose as if she were coming down with a headache. "Oh, you idiot. Why, out of all the denizens of Babel, should you tell *me* these things? I am a functionary in His Absent Majesty's governance. I'm a Lady of the Mayoralty and heir to the female line of House L'Inconnu. There's a legislative seat in the Liosalfar in my future when my brother has moved on to bigger things, as he surely will, and with luck I might even rise to the Council of Magi before my dotage. I am all your enemies rolled into one."

"No." Will stood and took her hands in his. "I don't believe you are. I came here today wondering how much of what I felt for you was but a romantic illusion—the image of freedom I saw in the

Hanging Gardens the day I emerged from the underground—and how much was mere aspiration for the unattainable adventuress I met at your brother's masked ball. You received me coldly, proffering not one kindly word nor a single smile. And yet I find—"

A russalka stuck her head in the office. "Allie, we've just gotten word that the West is moving."

"Yes, thank you," Alcyone said, subtly shifting her stance so that her coworker would not see her holding hands with a stranger. Then, when the intruder was gone, "You find—?"

"I find that—"

A muera rode into the office atop a bureaucrat who walked bent over and leaning on two short canes, so that the saddle on his back was level to the floor. There were blinders on his eyes and a bit in his mouth. She was a goat from the waist down and went naked, save for her tattoos, and with her hair all in tangles and witch-knots as an outward sign of her devotion to the welfare of the city.

"The West is astir!" she cried.

"Yes, yes, I'll get to it soon." To Will, Alcyone said, "You have to understand—"

"It's moving! The West! It moves!"

"*Thank* you, Glaistig." She pulled away from Will just as a black dwarf came in with a crate of chickens and a requisition slip for her to sign. Two haint messengers arrived almost simultaneously, striding through opposing walls, and began speaking at once. A follet knocked on the door and waved a sheath of telephone message slips.

The russalka reappeared. "Allie, the Lord High Comptroller wants to know—"

"Enough!" The battle-light shone about Alcyone's head and her hair whipped in a wind that touched nothing else in the office. Beautiful beyond enduring was she in that instant, and terrifying as well. "Cover your eyes," she said.

She clapped her hands and thunder pealed.

They were flying. The hippogriff swam strongly upward beneath them, and Will's arms were about Alcyone's waist. The crate of poultry was lashed to the back of the saddle behind Will. They were high in the air outside of Babel.

"How did you *do* that?" he gasped.

Alcyone glanced over her shoulder. Her face was stern and strong, like unto that of a warrior. "You're playing in the big leagues now, feyling. If you find this startling, then maybe it would be a good time for you to reconsider the wisdom of continuing in your rash and fraudulent impersonations."

Pale faces stared out from windows that flashed by and were gone. The air was cold and the winds were so strong that they shoved Will like enormous hands one way and another, threatening to tear him from the saddle and fling him to his death. But in the presence of his beloved, Will discovered that, however fleeting the moment might be, he was happy.

The ring of skyscrapers that sat atop Babel like a ragged crown were named after the sacred mountains of the world: Kilimanjaro, Olympus, Uluru, Sinai, McKinley, T'ai Shan, Amnye Machen, Annapurna, Popocatépetl, Meru, Fuji . . . And by tradition, the tallest of them all, whichever it might happen to be at any given time, was named Ararat, after the mountain that had been quarried, shaped, and deconstructed to build Babel. At the very peak of this last and mightiest of buildings was the Palace of Leaves. Wings laboring, the hippogriff flew toward it.

"Where are we going?" Will shouted.

"You'll see."

The palace itself, almost hidden in its arboreal gardens, was a Second Empire wedding cake of gleaming white marble. But the fortress walls beneath it were blank and gray and windowless for the space of many floors. There, four Titans were shackled and chained, one facing each direction: Gog to the north, Magog to the east, Gogmagog to the south, and a fourth giant without a name facing westward. These had been the Guardians of the Four Quarters, who in the First Age held up the world but had subsequently rebelled against Marduk's heirs and so for punishment were imprisoned where operatives of His Absent Majesty's governance could keep a close eye on them—and call upon their divinatory talents at such times as might be politic, as well.

The hippogriff alit on a balcony so small as to be invisible from a distance, located directly beside the western Titan's face. Her head was twice as tall as Will was, but the Titan gave no notice of their presence but continued to stare vigilantly straight ahead of herself.

"Hand me a chicken," Alcyone said. "There's a tape recorder in the saddlebag. Make sure there's a windscreen on the microphone and then perform a sound check. The documentation on this has got to be tight."

Will eased a chicken out of the crate and gave it to her. When the tape recorder was up and running, Alcyone said, "It's the Day of the Kraken, Vendemiaire, Year of the Monolith." She glanced at her watch. "About two-thirty p.m." Removing a small silver sickle from her cincture, she cut off the bird's head. She held the spasming body in the crook of one arm so that its blood sprayed over the Titan's mouth.

The cracked stone lips slowly parted. A tongue as gray as granite emerged to lick them clean. "Ahhhh," the Titan sighed. "It has been long, long since I was fed."

"Show your gratitude, then. You moved in your chains—our observers saw you. What is it you saw that so alarmed you?"

"The sun blackens. Lands sink into sea,
The radiant stars fall from the sky.
Smoke rages against fire, nourisher of life,
The heat soars high against heaven itself."

The Titan fell silent.

"Fabulous," Alcyone said. "They're really going to love this one back in the office."

Will hit pause, so his voice wouldn't be on the tape. "It's from the *Motsognirsaga*. That's one of the sacred books of dwarvenkind. I was told that no surface-dweller had ever read it, though."

"Well, believe it or not, it's more straightforward than the kind of crap they usually feed us. Give me another bird." Alcyone nodded for him to start recording again and repeated the ritual bleeding. "What form does this menace take?"

"And there appeared another wonder in heaven; and behold a great red dragon, having seven heads and ten horns, and seven crowns upon his heads. And his tail drew the third part of the stars of heaven, and did cast them to the earth."

"I don't know that one," Will said.

"I do, and it's never good news," Alcyone snarled. "Another bird!" More blood spurted. "Is it the War that comes?"

"I have seen war. I have seen war on land and sea. I have seen blood running from the wounded. I have seen the dead in the mud. I have seen cities destroyed. I have seen children starving. I have seen the agony of mothers and wives . . . My answer is bring 'em on."

"This just gets better and better. Another!"

"This is the last bird."

"Just record, okay?" To the Titan, Alcyone said, "Is the doom in flight? Or is it something you see in the future?"

"Chicken blood is weak stuff," the Titan grumbled.

"I wouldn't know."

"So long have I hung here, and so dry! How I yearn for something stronger."

"Too bad."

"Once I drained millions of your kind for their blood. The swarming multitudes came to my hand to be crushed to pulp and squeezed for their juice. I drank and drank, so much overspilling my mouth that it stained the hills red and the seas as dark as wine."

"Answer the damn question. Is what you see on its way? Or yet to come?"

Those enormous stone eyes turned slowly to stare down at Will and Alcyone. Then, equally slowly, they moved away. "It is already here." The great stone face once again froze into immobility.

Will turned off the tape recorder.

In a rage, Alcyone kicked the chicken carcasses off the ledge and threw the crate after them. "It's always the same—high-sounding words that mean nothing and ominous warnings of threats they will not define! Now I've got to spend the next three days dummying up reports to make it sound like we've actually learned something from this fiasco. I don't know why we don't just close the whole fucking office down." She swung up into the saddle and thrust out a hand for Will. "Come on."

"Wait." Will took out his Swiss Army knife and cut a large, shallow X in the palm of his hand. He smeared his blood across the gray stone lips. "It's not much," he said, "but it's the best I have and better than you're likely to get anytime soon."

Slowly, the lips were sucked into the mouth and—in a manner that in a being of flesh would have been distinctly voluptuous—slowly they emerged, licked clean. "There is mortal blood in you," the Titan said.

"I know. That's not what I fed you for."

"And a vile power as well. You believe you have mastered it, but you have not. The monster lurks in dark and secret places inside you, gathering its strength."

"Nor that."

A dark glitter of malice entered those vast gray eyes. "Then ask."

"Perhaps I aspire beyond my natural place," Will said. "But I don't give a rat's ass about that. I don't give a rat's ass for anything but Alcyone. Can I win her? Can our love endure? Can we live together to the end of our days? That's all I want to know."

The Titan's mouth twisted up almost imperceptibly, so that its expression took on a sardonic cast. "You do not need to consult an oracle to know that a lady of House L'Inconnu and a pretender to the Obsidian Throne can never wed. Particularly after you have made an enemy of her brother. Yet you asked, and that is my augury. If you want more, you must cut yourself again, and deeper."

Will slashed another cut into his forearm and bent to smear more blood upon those mocking lips. "I'll surrender my claim to the kingship! I'll be her consort, her alphonse, her champion-without-favor, her backdoor man! Can then we be together?"

With an amusement vast and cruel, the Titan said, "No. All of Babel will conspire to keep you apart. Bleed yourself again and ask if there is any hope for you in the larger world."

Will's arm was red with blood. Nevertheless, he slashed himself a third time.

"Anywhere in the world!" he cried. "Offer me hope. Something! Anything!"

The Titan roared with laughter. "Not in all of Fäerie will you find haven together, nor safe harbor in all the world, nor in a thousand lifetimes nor in a thousand worlds will you ever experience peace."

Will went to cut his flesh again and found that Alcyone had leapt down from her hippogriff and was holding back his arm. "Stop!" she cried. "Would you bleed yourself to death because you don't like the answers you hear?"

"Yes," Will said angrily. Then, bitterly, "Yes." Finally, in despairing sadness, "Yes."

She folded him into her arms and they were Elsewhere.

Many rooms were there in House L'Inconnu. After they'd made love in the great billowing bed he'd so coveted the night of the masked ball, Will and Alcyone wandered through them, hand in hand. Aimlessly they strolled down colonnades of ancient Atlantean pillars, past an erotic frieze by Phidias, through jade-tiled baths that had once graced the palace of Prester John, under cave paintings by the hands of the first witch-women. Half the vanished treasures of the world, it seemed, were here amassed. Sometimes they paused to kiss, and from kissing declined to a nearby couch or billiards table or even the floor, after which they rose again, adjusted their clothing, and went onward as before.

They came to light on the lip of a Moorish fountain in a courtyard whose arched windows opened on one side to the sky and the other to the city. Heat lightning played in the distance and ambulance sirens warbled. Alcyone trailed a finger in the water and then flicked droplets at Will and laughed.

"Will you get in trouble for turning in your report late?" Will asked.

"No. Of course I will. Or not. What do I care?" Between bouts of lovemaking, she had clapped her hands thrice to summon a jackal-headed servitor who, ignoring Will's presence and Alcyone's nakedness with equal aplomb, had accepted the audiotape of her interview with the Titan and some hastily composed notes to be couriered to her staff. So Will knew that whatever passions she felt for him, her office was ever in her thoughts.

"Tell me why you stole the ring."

"Why should you care?"

"Because I want to know everything about you. You took an enormous risk depriving your brother of his trinket. Surely your reasons were serious. Surely they mattered deeply to you."

"Surely they were and surely they did. But I will not share them."

Lightly, ironically, Will glanced down at his bandaged hand and forearm, then back at Alcyone. Meaning: *See what I have done for you.*

Alcyone looked away. "You ask too much. I—hark!" A vast bell began to toll, its sound bottomless and unending, from somewhere deep underfoot. Its voice was muffled, as if it came from the center of the earth, yet its vibrations shook the flagstones. She stood. "A compulsion is placed upon me to return to the Mayoralty. I can resist the call of duty for only a moment or two. But I shall leave another in my place to see you safely free of my family's House."

The courtyard darkened and shifted queasily, and Alcyone threw open a pair of doors in a wall that had not been there before. Inside was a shallow closet, empty save for a full-length bronze mirror. She lifted her hands toward it and her reflection, in turn, reached for her. They seized each other's wrists and struggled, the one pulling inward and the other outward.

Alcyone stumbled and lurched forward, her face briefly plunging through the polished bronze interface between realms. But then she pulled back, shifted her grip, and hauled her reflection bodily out of the mirror and into the courtyard.

"This is my fetch," she said, closing the closet doors. To the fetch she said, "Get him out of here alive." Then she spun on her heel and hurried away, fading. With her slowly faded the tolling of the great bell.

Will looked after her and then back at her fetch. They were identical in every detail. He grinned. "Oh, where my imagination has gone."

"Dream on," the fetch snapped. "*She* may love you. I don't."

"You think she loves me, then?" Will said, still grinning.

"If her love is as great as my despite, then you are the worst calamity ever to befall her."

"Hey!"

"Let me explain something to you: There is no future in this. The only thing you and she have in common is your prick, and that only occasionally. You're young and cocky and you think that's enough. But you haven't the education or social standing to walk where she walks. Your experience, outlook, and values are incompatible with hers. You won't like her friends. She wouldn't like yours. You're penniless and she's rich, which means you'd end up parasitic upon her wealth. Even your accent is wrong."

"Obstacles exist to be overcome."

"Love conquers all. Oh, yes." The fetch rolled her eyes. "These high-blooded elf-bitches are aristocratic, inbred, solipsistic, given to sociopathic rages and sudden vendettas, murderous and sentimental by turn, occasionally incestuous, intermittently suicidal, passionate by whim, moody by nature, always unpredictable . . . I can see why you're drawn to Alcyone. But what's in it for her?"

"I can make her happy."

"What makes you think she wants to be happy?"

"What kind of woman exposes her breasts to strangers, knowing they will want her and be helpless to aspire so high?" Will said. "What kind of woman steals a ring she could borrow for the asking? What kind of woman strips her lover naked and dumps him in the Bay of Demons untasted? Makes love and then abandons him to her fetch without declaring her feelings? Not one who values her fate, I think, but one who struggles against it."

"And what have you done for her so far? Tempted her away from her duty, gotten her in bad with her boss, made her the talk of the Mayoralty." The fetch poked his chest with one sharp-nailed finger. "You're a real career-killer, you know that?"

"Now that I reflect on it," Will said testily, "you're not a bit like Alcyone."

"Fool! I *am* her, in all the ways that matter. I—"

The doors to the mirror-closet burst open and the manticore bounded into the room.

"Mistress!" he cried. "We've got a security situation. There's a—" He stopped. "Oh, hello, Enoycla. And you've got the ring-thief with you. This must be Old Home Week."

"*Focus,* you wretched creature!" the fetch cried. "What security situation are you talking about?"

"It seems there's somebody very powerful and covered with flames who wants something inside House L'Inconnu. Hrothgar's having a hell of a time holding him back."

"That would be the Burning Man," Will said. "He's after me, I'm afraid." He should have felt more alarmed than he did, he knew. But he could not. This was simply what his life was like. He'd gotten used to it.

"You don't seem overly upset by this news," Enoycla said coolly.

"And exactly where do you think *you're* going?" This last was addressed to the manticore, who had started to slink away.

"I'm going to have to tell Florian this guy's here," the manticore said sheepishly. "It's kind of my duty."

"Just as my reluctant duty is to keep 'this guy' safe," the fetch said. "You can give Florian a detailed report later."

"Um . . . I should do it now, I think."

"Do you really want to get involved in a fight between my brother and me? Do you think that would be wise? Do you honestly believe things would go any easier on you because I'm the fetch rather than the original?"

The manticore put its head down on its front paws, lifting its haunch in the air submissively. "No," it mumbled, "not really."

"Wise creature. Niceums pussums. Now heel, sirrah! You"—she pointed to Will—"climb on his back."

Will wasn't at all sure this was either wise or safe. Nevertheless he obeyed. "How will I get in touch with Alcyone again?"

The fetch plucked a hair from his head. "I'll give her this for a token. If she wants you, she'll find you."

"But—"

"Scat!"

The manticore surged beneath Will and abruptly they were halfway down the hall and then descending a stairway in long and shallow leaps. The monster looked over his shoulder at Will, grinning a great crescent moon of a grin. "I bet you didn't think I'd recognize you without the clown mask," he said. "But I remember your smell. You oughta lay off the fried foods." He rounded a corner, sending throw rugs flying on the polished wood floor. "Thanks for the bribe, incidentally. It's been spent and Florian made me promise I wouldn't take any more from you, but it was great while it lasted."

"Watch out for the fire pit!" Will shouted.

They flashed through a kitchen, cooks looking up in startlement and scullery lads clambering onto countertops, and vaulted over a roasting oxen. There was a blur of lobby and then they were out on the street.

"I hope you didn't get into any trouble on my account," Will said, holding on for dear life as they soared to the top of a moving autobus and then bounced down onto the sidewalk on the far side. A hot dog cart overturned and a covey of winged schoolgirls scattered and Will and the manticore were speeding down Fifth Avenue.

"Naw. The boss knew what he was getting when he hired me."

The terrifying ride ended at Grand Central Station. Swarms of passengers were boarding Uptown and Downtown express elevators, and a Midtown freight elevator was disgorging fleets of Mercedes and BMWs. Will deemed it safest to be dropped off here, for when the manticore made his report it would give Florian L'Inconnu no hint as to where he might be squatting. "I'm sorry for all the trouble you've been put through," he said when there was pavement safely beneath his feet again. "I apologize for all the trouble I've inadvertently put you through, and I apologize for any humiliation you may have undergone. I didn't want Alcyone's fetch to treat you as she did. It's very wrong of them to behave so shabbily."

The manticore leered. "Yeah, I'd be a socialist, too, only the money's better working this side of the street."

Then he was gone.

Hot date?" the vixen asked when Will sat down at her booth. She'd taken over a dark corner of a diner and, with small bribes to the management and generous tips to the waitstaff, made it her office. Unlike Nat, she did not require that her center of operations serve alcohol.

"I was with Alcyone," Will admitted. The vixen snapped her fingers for the waitress and pointed at Will. An undine nodded and began pouring a cup. "I'm not sure how she feels about me, though."

"Ah, youth!" The vixen accepted a cup of coffee and handed it to Will. "Trust me, she likes you. I can tell because you've got that gingerly way of walking that men get when their dicks are rubbed raw."

"Vickie," Will said irritably, "you're taking something that's sweet and romantic and—"

"Don't let's start passing judgment on an affair until we know how it comes out, eh? It ain't romantic till it's over." The vixen knocked over the saltshaker and muttered a cantrip over the spill. "Let's see what this slut looks like." She blew on the salt. The grains tumbled this way and that and finally formed a recognizable image of Alcyone. She passed her hand over the salt portrait and it took on color.

"Well. The apple doesn't fall from the tree." The vixen sniffed. "A redhead, too. I suppose I should feel flattered." By her tone, Will knew she did not. Yet, looking down upon Alcyone, he could not help but smile.

"She came that close to telling me she loved me," he said.

"Oh, kid, you've got it bad! You do realize that when this scam is over, we'll have to leave Babylon? We'll be traveling fast and we'll be traveling light and we won't dare come back for years."

"I know that," Will said sullenly.

The vixen studied him silently for a moment. Then she lit a cigarette. "Well, enough of that. Listen. You're gonna have to be careful going out in public nowadays. The polits know what you look like. They've got hold of a photo."

"How'd they get that?"

"How d'ya think? I mailed it to them."

16

Moonlight Sonata

The hawk came flying, swift as an arrow, down the center of the street and then straight at Will's face. He flinched away as it snapped out its wings at the last possible instant and, swerving, creased his cheek with the tip of one flight feather. Something fell into Will's hands. A cell phone.

It rang.

"Some friends and I are going clubbing," Alcyone said. "Wait where you are and I'll pick you up."

Will stepped back into the shadowed doorway of a defunct art deco bank building and waited. Not much later, a white stretch limo, longer than life and pale as death, glided up to him. A footman leaped out to open the door.

"Hop in," Alcyone said.

Will did, and the car drove off. He and Alcyone kissed long and hard. "I don't think it would be a good idea for me to be seen in public with you," he said, hoping inwardly that she would suggest they retire to someplace private instead. "My face is known now."

"Tish. I have an invisibility potion." Alcyone led him deeper into the stretch, past masses of orchids and a small waterfall, and flipped down a vanity table. She donned disposable plastic gloves and opened a jar. "Take off your shirt and I'll rub it on you."

Fifteen minutes later, when Will looked in the mirror, a brown-skinned fey stared back at him. Alcyone brushed a pigment into his hair that turned it cobalt blue. "There! Now anybody who looks at you will see a rented escort and give you not a second glance."

"Where are we going?"

"Out." Alcyone gestured just so and a silver bell tinkled. A haint servitor appeared with a bundle of clothes. "Change into these."

Ignoring the haint, who stood unobtrusively ready for any further commands, Will wriggled out of his jeans and into a pair of tight pants. He was coming to realize that a great deal of being high-elven was having a perfect disregard for what one's inferiors—which was to say, almost everybody—saw or thought. The shoes fit perfectly and the socks as well; Alcyone hadn't bothered to provide underwear, so he did without. She handed him a white silken sark and when he had donned it, undid the top three buttons and then leaned back to admire her handiwork. "You clean up good."

"You should see me in morning clothes."

Alcyone handed Will's old clothes to the haint who, upon her saying "Take these away and burn them," vanished as silently as he had come.

"I can't help but notice," Will said, "that you're wearing that which your brother called the greatest treasure of House L'Inconnu." He touched the plain moonsilver ring and smiled. "Ask me if I love you."

"No." She drew her hand away.

"Then tell me that you love me."

Alcyone fixed him with those astounding eyes. "I would do anything for you, Will. For you, I'd do things that would make an ogress blush."

Will's heart soared. Nevertheless, he persisted, "But do you love me?"

She looked away. "I . . . dare not say."

"It's a simple enough thing. Three words and no witnesses to hold you to them."

"Tie me up and whip me if you like. Fist me, piss on me, dress me up as a milkmaid if you must. Ask me anything except that."

"Why?"

"Because I'm a fucking aristocrat, is why!" The limo came to a stop. "We have to put in an appearance at a party first. It's a fund-raiser for the Fata Bloduewedd's reelection campaign, but I'm sure you'll enjoy it anyway."

Two dwarves, one red and one black, fought grimly on the balcony. Their bodies were slick with sweat and their knives gleamed in the floodlights. Their feet kicked up puffs of the sawdust that had been strewn on the flagstones to soak up blood. They were both naked.

Alcyone's friends watched from the roof garden, drinks in hand. They were as tall and glittery up close as their kind always appeared on TV. The males stood with a hand in their slacks pockets jingling coins. The females looked elaborately bored.

"'Lo, Allie. What's the news?" asked the one Alcyone had identified as the war strategist Lord Venganza. The others were the Lords Jaegerwulf and Lascaux, and the Fatas Caldogatto, Misericordia, and Elspeth, all highly placed in offices that mattered.

"You must have heard that the West moved. Pestilence, doom, and universal destruction are imminent. So what else is new? It's been nothing but paperwork for me ever since. And you?"

"There was a minor rebellion in Ys, easily crushed. The War continues and shows every intention of continuing forever. Who's your friend?"

"His name is Tenali Raman." The group's glances traveled briefly over Will and were gone forever, just as Alcyone had foretold. "I'm showing him the sights."

"Nobody cares about the sights anymore." Fata Elspeth pouted. "I've been at this party almost fifteen minutes and nobody's said anything about my tits!"

"If I start praising your breasts, we'll be here all day, 'Speth," Lord Lascaux said.

Fata Elspeth smiled appreciatively. On the balcony below, one of the dwarves grunted as he took a blade in his side, to light applause.

"Heads up, our next lady-mayor approacheth," Lord Jaegerwulf murmured. There was a crackling in the air, and a whiff of ozone. An elf-lady strode toward them, wrapped in an aura of darkness, as if she were a storm cloud. "Time to tug forelocks," she said.

"Tell me I didn't forget Fata Bloduewedd's envelope." Fata Misericordia dug frantically in her purse. "Oh, gods, I did. No, here it is."

"Wait here, Tenali," Alcyone said. "We have some entirely voluntary

and completely legal contributions to make in a venue in no way related to the apparatus of state, for which we will expect no return
whatsoever either in terms of influence or of access. This will only
take a few minutes."

Will watched them go, feeling awkward and out of place. Then he
went to look for the shrimp bowl. In his experience, these functions
always had an enormous bowl of iced shrimp somewhere.

A woman dressed too emphatically high-elven to actually *be* high-
elven stopped him with one outstretched leg. She wore high-heeled
boots and black leather pants. Her red vinyl jacket was zipped low to
reveal a bustier with eye-popping decolletage. It was exactly the kind
of self-mocking, faux-trashy look that Will would have been drawn
to (despising himself for it, but drawn nevertheless), had he not been
here with Alcyone. "Hello," she said. "I'm Fata Jayne."

"I'm nobody in particular. Have you seen the shrimp bowl?"

"No. Why don't we go back to my place and look for it?"

"Um . . . If I'm not mistaken, we just met. Let's not rush things."

"That's exactly what I'm looking for. Somebody who knows how to
take it nice and slow."

"Look. I don't know why you're behaving in this extraordinary
fashion, but I'm here with somebody. So whatever it is you want, it's
not going to happen."

"But you do like me? I mean, you *are* attracted to girls?"

"Actually, no, I'm not," Will lied. "So why don't you go away?"

"Okay, let me give this one last try." Fata Jayne leaned close and
lightly sang the refrain from *The Ballad of Oberon's Arse* in his ear:

> *"Oh, she pegged him high*
> *And she pegged him low*
> *She pegged him where the sun don't go.*
> *She made him do things that a fella don't do . . .*
> *If they could play thus . . . Why not me and you?*

"Try something new, *mon petit serin*. Expand your horizons." Smil-
ingly, she sucked on one red-nailed fingertip and then touched it to
his cheek. Instantly, he was hard as a rock. His face flushed and he
could scarce breathe, so great was his physical desire.

Through gritted teeth, Will said, "Your penny-ante aphrodisiac magicks notwithstanding, I despise your offer. Yet as I am a gentleman and out of courtesy for your gender, I shall simply bow and withdraw."

Lightly, the fata said, "No? Ah, well, then I must find somebody else. But fear not, cheri, I shall always remember you as the One Who Got Away."

A minute later Alcyone swept by with her friends in tow. "Let's go," she said. And, as they left, "I saw you talking with that trashy little man-eater. Did she hit on you?"

"No, we were just talking."

"That's good. Fata Jayne is notorious in our circles. Nobody who leaves with her ever comes back. You have to wonder what she does with them."

Off to the side of the stage, a pianist was playing "Stardust." As the clubbers filtered in and sat at their tables, he spoke into his microphone in a soft and insinuating tone: *"Bienvenido, señors y señoras, a Le Club Frottage."* He was a pencil-thin haint with a garter on one arm and a derby hat cocked to the side. *"Heute abend haben wir eine Festlichkeit für Sie.* A show, a performance, a star unlike any other. *Je vous presente—El Sonámbula! Der Träumengeist! L'Oneiroi des Reves!* The one and only Nanshe!"

He slammed both hands down in a dramatic discord and three cacodemons with needle teeth and malicious eyes pushed and propped up and prodded a slumping figure twice their height onto the stage. It was a large breasted and womanly hipped hermaphrodite in an open silk bathrobe.

"Oh, this is a wonderful show," Fata Misericordia said. "I've been here every night this week."

Nanshe's head, cornrowed in tight Scandinavian-blond braids, lolled on a shoulder. His penis was a slender and shockingly pink tube emergent from the folds of her labia. The cacodemons whisked away his robe and scattered, leaving her standing alone and naked in the center of the stage, bathed in golden light. The pianist segued into Beethoven's Piano Sonata No. 14 in c sharp minor, the Moonlight Sonata.

Briefly, nothing happened. Then a cacodemon returned with a

tube of K-Y Jelly, squeezed a dab into the hermaphrodite's hand, and darted away. Nanshe's eyes opened a crack and the hand floated up to the face, where heavy features studied it puzzledly. Then down it drifted again to delicately anoint the genitalia.

Slowly, languidly, s/he began to masturbate.

"Dance?" Lord Lascaux said.

Alcyone stood and gave him her hand. Caldogatto and Misericordia followed them onto the floor. Elspeth tugged at Jaegerwulf's hand and, reluctantly, he went, too. Which left only Lord Venganza staring fiercely and fixedly at the stage act.

This was as good a chance as Will was going to get. Assuming his generic-exotic-foreigner accent and in the timid manner of someone keenly aware of his lowly status, he addressed the war-elf: "Sir? I was hoping you could tell me something. I've asked this of everybody, but no one seems to know."

Lord Venganza started. "Eh?"

"Why does the War exist?"

"It exists because I work extremely hard to bring together billions of dollars and hundreds of thousands of soldiers requiring supply lines half a continent long and enough medical facilities to service a medium-sized nation. You should be grateful it's not *you* charged with such a task."

"No, I mean what caused it?"

"Arrogance," Venganza said. "Laziness, greed, lack of foresight, bad intelligence, an unwillingness to negotiate, a disinclination bordering upon an outright refusal to listen to reason, a reflexive undervaluing of the enemy's resources and resolve, an unseemly haste to resort to force—and I suppose there may have been faults on our own side as well."

"But what is it meant to accomplish?"

"Hum. Well, I suppose the West wants us to pull out of their territory. We can't do that, of course, or they'd advance their armies across our borders, looking for vengeance. So ultimately we have no option other than to seek complete and total victory." He shrugged. "Which, given the lockdown on our most powerful weapons occasioned by His Absent Majesty's abdication of his duties, isn't likely to happen anytime soon."

"But...if there's neither reason nor purpose for the War, why can't you simply put an end to it?"

"For the same reason an avalanche can't be stopped. These things must play out their natural course." Lord Venganza smiled faintly. "At any rate, war is required in order that we may exercise our talents to their fullest. Should I be moving tankers of oil about the world, or speculating in wheat harvests? That's a bloodless and ignoble game."

"Then exercise your talents to end the War! That would surely be noble. If you—"

The dancers chose that moment to return, swooping down on their seats like a flock of roosting birds. They chirped and twittered, continuing a conversation that seemed to have no proper beginning and to be in no danger of ever reaching an end.

"...find it harder and harder to care."

"Darling, nobody cares anymore. Not anybody who matters, at least."

"What do you make of the rumors about the king's heir? Who's putting them out?"

"It's a grassroots thing, for certain. If it were a conspiracy surely one of us would know."

"Perhaps one does and isn't speaking," Fata Elspeth said, with a significant glance at Alcyone.

"Oh, please."

"Your, um, friend," Lord Venganza said, not-looking at Will, "thinks we would be best employed bending all our efforts to end the War."

"One cannot address all the ills of the world," Misericordia said. "There is only so much time, money, compassion, hours in the day. Only the king could address everything at once—and pray the Seven he never returns to try!"

Shocked, Will said, "But everyone yearns for the king's return."

"Everyone is an ass, then. What possible purpose does it serve to put all the power we have into the hands of an individual of uncertain morals and competence, idiosyncratic enthusiasms, and unknown temperament merely because his father was king? None whatsoever."

"He could end the War, for one thing."

"Yes, but at what cost? In a representational democracy, even one as clotted and corrupt as our own, all groups are represented and, from self-interest, defended. Do you honestly believe that a king would understand the needs and interests of a venture capitalist, a kobold, or a small businessman as well as they do themselves? The abuses of tyranny more commonly arise from ignorance than from malice. And if you think that a monarchy is any less prone to foreign adventure than a democracy, then I suggest you need to reread your Herodotus."

"At least one person can be held accountable."

"No, one person can be killed. The entire society is held account-able."

"Yes, but—"

Alcyone had been staring moodily at the stage act for some time. With sudden decisiveness, she stood and said, "We're leaving."

"Already? Are you sure?" Fata Misericordia asked. "It's considered good luck if Nanshe spurts on you."

At the exit, a red-skinned devil with short horns and a tuxedo jacket bowed slightly to Alcyone and said, "The show wasn't to madame's liking?"

"I liked it fine. But I'm looking for something a little more . . . sordid. Squalid? No, sordid *c'est le seul mot juste*."

"Ahhhh. Something low and vile for the highborn and genteel lady." He rubbed his chin thoughtfully. "Well. For a thousand dollars I can offer you the decaying corpse of a sea lion. For three thousand—" He looked down at the bundle of bills Alcyone had slipped into his hand and his eyes widened. "I think I know what you want."

They followed him through a door marked PRIVATE and then down a warren of back ways and narrow stairs. The farther they went, the shabbier the halls, the older the paint, the worse the lighting. Will's skin itched with the memory of his days as Jack Riddle.

They emerged in an alleyway beside an overripe and overflowing dumpster. In the wall opposite was a blue metal door with stenciled letters reading:

FORBIDDEN

"What's in there?" Will asked when the devil started to unlock it.

"Why, whatever you want, sir!" the devil said ingratiatingly. "Every-thing you fear most, oh, yes—atrocities and meaningless cruelty,

alienation and despair. Very loathsome, very disgusting, very pleasant, a distinctly refreshing change of pace." He held it open for Will.
"Through here."

Will could not make out the any details of the interior for the
murkiness within. But there were flames inside and the smell of gasoline and cold iron.

Stark terror gripped his heart and squeezed. But he could not bear
to display cowardice in front of Alcyone.

He took a deep breath and stepped forward.

"Oh, no, you don't." Alcyone slammed the door shut before he
could pass through. "You're only here for support." To their cicerone,
she said, "This has nothing to do with him, understand? It's my own
worst fear I need to confront."

With an apologetic smirk, the devil unlocked the door with another key. It opened onto an entirely different space.

Alcyone stepped within. The door shut behind them.

Will almost gagged from the mingled stench of stale urine, feces,
and physical decay that rose from a hospital bed at the center of the
room. But the room itself was clean and well-appointed, with blue
rose-patterned wallpaper and lace curtains so thick that only a joyless
gray light shone through. To one side of the bed was a table with a vase
of dried flowers and a bowl of dusty wax fruit. At its foot was an aquar-
ium in which a lone Siamese fighting fish swam around and around a
ceramic castle in slow and unvarying circles. A clock on the wall ticked
steadily, its slimmest hand twitching in place once a second, perpetually
three hacks from the hour and never quite reaching two.

At first Will thought that the crone lying in the bed was but a
shadow or a trick of the light. Then, with the slightest shift of per-
ception, there she was: transparent, like a glass filled with water.
Straps had been tied about her waist and chest to keep her in place.
Her mouth hung open in a frozen gasp of pain. "Who is she?" Will
asked.

"My Aunt Anastasia."

"What's wrong with her?"

Alcyone looked stricken. "Early onset enlightenment."

She sank gracefully down at the side of the bed and placed a hand
on the smudged rail. "Oh, Auntie, speak to me."

Almost inaudibly, the crone whispered, "The gods of the valleys . . . are not the gods of the hills."

"What?"

"Ethan . . . Allen said that." Her voice gained strength and her body took on the faintest tinge of color. "Forthwith a hideous gabble rises loud. The whale is a mammiferous animal without hind feet. We sing, but oh the clay is vile. And there the lion's ruddy eyes shall flow with tears of gold. This certainly has to be the most historic phone call ever made. No job too dirty for a fucking scientist. Milton Cuvier Dunbar Blake Nixon Burroughs said that. Here also lie the rainbow gardens of the Lady. Nobody knows who said that. It wasn't me."

"Auntie, you're not making any sense."

"No, Hardy! No, Hardy! It is a very interesting number."

Alcyone took her Aunt Anastasia's hands in her own, so that the moonsilver ring touched the old lady's fragile and translucent skin. "Come back to the world," she said. "I need your advice, Auntie. Come back to me."

"Mary McCarthy said that Venice is the world's unconscious, a miser's glittering hoard, guarded by a Beast whose eyes are made of white agate, and by a saint who is really a prince who has just slain a dragon. But surely she meant Babel? Babel is the mile high city, the city of light, the big apple, and the hog butcher of the world. All roads lead to it, and he who is tired of the Worldly Tower is tired of life. I am so very tired of Babel. I am so very desirous of a road that leads somewhere else."

"Speak to me no more in riddles and citations!" Alcyone said sternly. "I command you by the authority of this ring, forged on a continent that no longer exists, before the Thousand Races arose, to address me in clear words and with a lucid mind."

There was a faint flutter of the crone's eyelids. They opened narrowly and the eyes beneath them drifted from side to side. "You've brought me back to consciousness?" The crone's hands plucked feebly, uselessly, at her restraints. "How hateful. You always were a cruel child."

"Yes, dear, I'm afraid I have. But my need was great. You have information that I can get from no one else."

The eyes closed. "Then ask."

"You had a lover," Alcyone said. "It was the scandal of the family. Nobody would talk about it. But I overheard enough to know that you had a lover for decades before you succumbed to enlightenment. Tell me how you did it."

"It is a long story. Ask me something briefer."

"Oh, Auntie. You know I can't."

"Very well. I was a precocious child," Anastasia said, "much as you were, dear. I walked, as they say, before I could crawl, and I levitated before I could properly stand. All places were one to me and I was anchored to any given locale only by my desire to be there rather than elsewhere. By age seven I could read the thoughts of those dear to me as easily as I could my own. Yes, yes, you could as well at an earlier age, sweetie, I know that, and who's telling this story, you or me?"

"Sorry."

"So my guardians put me on a discipline of cold-water treatments and corporal punishment. My rank was such, of course, that nobody dared touch me, and so I acquired a whipping boy. Hodge was a common fey, like your friend, but like your friend he was a comely thing. And of course a whipping boy must be personable, the sort of individual who will quickly become one's best friend, or else punishing him would be ineffective.

"So we grew up together. Alas for Hodge, I was a hellion and could not modify my ways, and so he was scourged almost every day. Afterward, to hide my shame at what I was responsible for, I would laugh at him, and lick the tears from his face.

"Do I need to say that he loved me? Of course he did. How could he not? But I, of whom such behavior was not to be expected, fell in love with him as well."

"What's wrong with that?" Will asked.

One eye opened and moved slowly to stare at him. A few seconds later, the other joined it. "We high-elven are like bubbles which, rising, dissolve before reaching the surface. Our power is spiritual in essence and so as we gain strength our attachment to the world grows increasingly weaker. This is why we have affairs, why we interfere in the lives of others, why we involve ourselves in the machineries of governance. Sex, gossip, and bureaucracy are the three great forces that bind us to the world."

"I knew one who claimed to stave off dissolution with treason and violent adventure," Will said.

One eye drifted away from him. The other stayed. "It was a male who told you that—and an elderly one, or he would not have forgotten to throw in sex. But to answer your question, the problem with love is that it has the potential to make one happy. Pure, undiluted happiness, how many days of that could one such as I or Alcyone have before it destroyed us?"

"Twenty-seven," Alcyone said quietly.

"Yes, that sounds about right. And how swiftly pass the days when one is in love. One loses count so easily. So you see, young romantic, if you were to take up with our little Allie, she'd be as I am now within a month."

"But you lived with your lover. You found a way around it," Alcyone said.

"Oh, I was cunning, all right. I was most careful not to be happy. I was cruel to my Hodge and I encouraged him in a thousand ways to be cruel to me. We bickered constantly. I nagged and scolded. And every time he began to make me joyful, I whipped him until he bled.

"So it went, for many a long and miserable decade. But as with anything that is used as a substitute for sex, the punishment became eroticized. Pain became an expression of my passion for him. He understood this and egged me on to greater and greater exertions. Until a day came when my pleasure in his suffering became so perfect that I did not stop and I beat him to death."

Will cried out in horror.

"Perfection is death," Anastasia said. "The world is imperfect, but if it weren't, who would love it?" Her eyelids closed, absolutely solid now and pale as old paper. "Our symposium has come to an end. Leave me go back to courting oblivion."

"Yes, dear." Alcyone's voice was almost inaudible. "I'm sorry I disturbed you."

"The goddam sands run out . . ." Anastasia mumbled. "You're lucky if you get time to sneeze in this goddam phenomenal world. Salinger."

As they were leaving, Will glanced back over his shoulder. He saw in the hospital bed not an old woman but a blaze of light.

In the stretch afterward, Alcyone said, "Do you believe what they say about Nanshe?"

"What do they say?"

"That she-and-he is the psyche—the ka—of Babel. That our world is nothing but his-or-her dreams, in which we live and love and fight and aspire, all the while thinking ourselves the center of the universe. But that the day will come when Nanshe wakes up and we will all suddenly and painlessly cease to be."

"I don't know. I hope not. What do you think?"

"I wonder. The reason I left the club so suddenly? I thought I heard him-and-her moan your name, and I feared what she-and-he might say next." She took the ring from her finger and put it away in her clutch purse. There were tears on her face, and Will desperately wanted to kiss them away. "Which is ironic, considering."

"Alcyone, I—"

"Shush," she said fiercely. Then, in control again, "When I was a child, I bought my first hippogriff and learned to fly because I wanted to be free. Then, as I grew older and more aware of the constraints put upon me, I flew to test the limits of my cage. Finally I flew in order to pretend that freedom might someday be possible." The limo's tires hummed on the pavement. It was late enough that there was almost no traffic in the streets. "Tell me. Can you see any way that you and I could be happy trogether?"

"No," Will said after a long pause. "No, I don't."

"Nor do I."

She dropped Will off on Broadway, a good forty blocks from where he needed to be. He walked home through a cold drizzle that blew through Babel from the sea.

17

A Prince in Ginny Gall

The rumor spread like wildfire through Harlem and Ginny Gall and into the fringe neighborhoods of Beluthahatchie and Diddy-Wah-Diddy: A cloaked prince had come, barefoot and alone, to consult with Salem Toussaint and to obtain the alderman's blessing preparatory to claiming his throne. Haints came out into the streets, flowing down the tenement steps and pouring from the pool halls and juke joints, stumbling up from the opium dens and storefront joss houses, stepping from the doorways of the barber shops and hair salons and social clubs, abandoning the night classes and soup kitchens, their eyes bright with strange hopes, and found his footprints glowing on the tarmac.

Will and the vixen had painted them earlier with phosphorescent paint overlaid with a suppressor spell timed to wear off shortly after sundown, but of course only they knew that.

In the alderman's office, Will doffed his hood and for an instant gloried in the complete and utter bafflement of his former employer.

Salem Toussaint reached out a hand and squeezed Will's forearm, as if to assure himself that it actually was him. "Are you *really* the king?" he said dubiously. Then, reverting to his usual decisiveness, "No, of course not. What in the world are you up to, Will?"

"Well, I'm pretty sure I'm not the heir, at any rate," Will said. "But folks started coming up to me and telling me that I was, and . . ." He shrugged. "I dunno." He should have felt bad, lying to his old mentor. But the truth was he strangely enjoyed the sensation of power it gave him. "Nowadays I'm just winging it. Going with the current and seeing where it takes me."

"Don't you try to bamboozle me, young fella. The city talks to me. What Babel knows, I know." Toussaint put on his sternest face. "I sure hope you know what you're doing, boy. Because if you don't, let me warn you proper: Politics is a meat grinder. Don't go sticking your head into it unless you're damned sure you know what you're doing. And even then. Now tell me why you're here in my office."

"I came to ask for a favor, Salem."

Toussaint's face relaxed into a smile. He was on familiar ground now. "It's what I'm here for, son."

"Nat needs an office. Someplace that looks official but that rents to private citizens. Someplace that's both grandiose and just a little bit seedy. One that can handle a lot of foot traffic without drawing attention. And one where somebody like you could arrange for an off-the-books cash rental on short notice." He gestured at the building about him. "Old City Hall would be perfect."

"What on earth would you need such a thing for?"

"See . . . the way we figure it, if there's going to be a new king, there'll be a lot of individuals who'd like to have access to him, in order to present their complaints or schemes, who might be willing to prime the pump in exchange for that access."

"Ahhh," Salem Toussaint said. "You'll be selling titles and offices."

"How well you know me! So can we do business?"

"Well, now. Much as I like Nat personally, he's just a wee bit too well known locally for me to—"

Will held up his hands. "Oh, Nat wouldn't set foot in the building. I mention his involvement only so you'll know I'm not trying to hide anything." He went to the door. "Contessa, you can come in now." To the alderman he said, "This is Contessa Victoria il Volpone. She'll be acting as Nat's office manager."

The vixen was wearing a man's suit, tieless, with an orchid pinned to the lapel. The top shirt buttons were undone and the shirt itself folded back to reveal the tops of her breasts. It was an ensemble that made her look roguish and fetching while its eccentricity rendered her assumed title seem almost plausible. "I feel honored to meet you, alderman," she said. "Will has said so many fine things about you."

"Milady." Salem came around his desk and, bending low, kissed her hand.

The vixen colored prettily. "Oh, my!" She fanned herself. "I hope you're taking notes, Will. This is one gent who, I swear, need never go to bed alone."

Toussaint beamed like all the world's favorite uncles rolled into one.

Jimi Begood chose that instant to come out of the side office. When he saw Will, he whistled long and low. "Well, I'll be damned." He raised his voice. "Ghostface, get your butt out here!" Then, "He isn't the—?"

"Well, now," Salem Toussaint said. "Let's keep our options open on that one. We'll just wait and see what turns out to be the most advantageous thing for us to believe. Right now, this lovely lady needs an office."

So they talked. Numbers were named and percentages haggled. Terms were put on the table and taken off again. There came a brief magical moment when all were in accord and Will stepped in to declare the deal accepted, lest the vixen and the alderman rush past it, going on and on into the night for the sheer pleasure of negotiating with a fellow professional. Toussaint gave the vixen the key to a room not too close to his own, but certainly not so far away that he couldn't keep an eye on her. The vixen put her hands together and bowed formally. *"Domo arigato."*

"De nada," Salem Toussaint said. Then, "What's that noise?"

Jimi Begood opened the window to discover that the street outside was thronged with haints. They were all staring up at the building. Seeing movement at the window, they began chanting, *"Give-us-the-king. Give-us-the-king."*

"Holy fuck," Ghostface said.

"Hear that, kid? They love you," the vixen said. "Step out on the balcony and give 'em a wave."

But against all expectations this show of devotion seemed strangely sad to Will. "Why should they care?" he asked. "Were things ever any better for them when the king sat over Babel, Babylonia, and the Contingent Territories? Why should folks who never benefitted from the monarchy welcome its return?"

"*Give-us-the-king.*"

"His Absent Majesty is the personification and embodiment of justice," Salem Toussaint said. "So naturally every honest citizen awaits his return, and all who exploit them fear it." One gold tooth caught the light. "As you can hear, my constituents are all honest citizens."

"*Give-us-the-king. Give-us-the-king.*"

Jimi Begood had been tugging on the French doors that opened onto a small and long-neglected balcony. Now they banged open.

"Put that hood back on," Toussaint said. "Then go out there and let them see you."

Will stepped out onto the balcony, feeling light-headed and almost dizzy. He looked down on a sea of upturned faces. Then he raised a hand.

As one, every haint in the street cheered and applauded. Pinpricks of light twinkled as flash cameras took picture after picture. A great wash of love surged up from the crowd, filling Will with an incredible energy. He felt strong enough to lift a bus and deft enough to walk on water. It was a wonderful sensation. He turned from side to side, waving with one hand and then the other, grinning madly. It did not seem possible he could feel this alive.

After all too short a time, hands seized his arms and shoulders and tugged him back inside. He was gasping with exhilaration.

Salem Toussaint was saying something. "*Listen* to me, boy!" The alderman shook Will. "Are you listening? I sent Ghostface out to bring the car around. We're going to get you out of here." He turned to the vixen. "This proposition is way too dicey for me to be directly associated with it. But I'm getting a funny feeling about it. Take Jimi Begood with you. Everyone knows he's one of mine, but if things turn sour I can always say he went along as an observer."

Then, to Will again, "Good luck, kid. I still think you're a fool to be doing whatever it is you're doing. But I hope you come through it okay."

"Thanks, Salem. You're a mensch."

"I'll hammer a nail in the nkisi nkonde for you."

There were throngs of gawkers standing around the front steps of Old City Hall and almost as many around the back, so Will slipped out a side door. But he was spotted anyway.

Somebody he didn't remember said, "It's the white boy."

Embarrassed, Will shook the haint's hand. "Hi, good to see you." He clapped another on the shoulder. "How are you doing?" More and more haints appeared, murmuring in wonder, reaching out to touch him, ghost-soft whispers of fingers stroking his arms, his shoulders. He shook hands and slapped backs like a younger version of Salem Toussaint. "I'm with you," he said, and "Thank you for your support," and "Don't think you're forgotten, because you're not."

Ghostface pulled up in the alderman's Cadillac. He leaned over to unlock a door and Will, Jimi Begood, and the vixen squeezed into the back. Then, slowly, they pushed their way through the gathering crowds. Hands hammered against the hood and roof and young haints climbed up on the trunk. They pulled far enough ahead for Ghostface to stop briefly and pull off the riders, and then they were free.

Sitting in the back seat alongside Will, the vixen abruptly bent over double.

"Are you all right?" Will asked. He saw her ears lengthen and sprout hair. "Oh."

Nat straightened and, reaching into his shirt, pulled out a brassiere which, with a wink to Jimi Begood, he stuffed into a pocket. Then he buttoned up the shirt, threw away the orchid, and donned a tie that he removed from inside his jacket. "Drive as fast as you like," he said. "They've got the license number. They'll find us."

Ghostface turned around, startled. "Where's the fox?"

Nat touched his heart. "In here." Then he rubbed his palms together. "Okay, we've got one ethnic bloc of voters behind you. Let's line up another." He checked his pocket planner. "The Cluricauns! Perfect."

"Nat," Will said, "I'm not sure I can do this."

"It's too late to stop it now. You're in the saddle, son, and it's either ride or be trampled underfoot." Nat flipped open his cell. "Get the big guy in place," he said. "It's showtime. What do you mean when?

When do you think? Right now. Yeah. Yeah. You know where the Society of Cluricauns has their hall? Good. They're having their annual awards banquet tonight. We'll meet you outside."

A graffito on a pedestrian overpass declared *he is coming* in letters of fire and then drifted behind them and out of sight. Another blazed on the side of a bank. *He Is Coming* burned across an entire block in letters a story high and *HE IS COMING!* snapped and sizzled in blue flames on kiosks and redbrick walls and elevator stations. "Look at them," Will said wonderingly. "They're everywhere. Where did they come from?"

"Kind of gives you the shivers, doesn't it? I've had twenty taggers working their humps off for the past three nights. Cost a bundle. They really got the message out, though. It's the talk of Little Thule."

The Society of Cluricauns was a social and cultural organization providing for the welfare of those descended from the original population of the Blessed Isles. Which was to say, it was a drinking club. But over the years, through the success of its component members, it had acquired significant political clout. Which meant that Salem Toussaint was a familiar visitor there, and that consequently Ghostface had no trouble finding it.

They pulled up in front of a former opera house, onetime movie palace, temporary burlesque parlor, and occasional catering concern, union hall, and furniture warehouse, which the Cluricauns had restored to something like its original splendor and made their own. There was a construction giant slouched in the street outside, cradling a rusty heating-oil tank in his arms. Nat went to speak to the troll who stood, smoking a cigar, in his shadow. When he came back, he showed Will his empty wallet. "That's it," he said. "We are now officially penniless. If this scam doesn't work out, we are royally skunked."

But he smiled as he said it, in a way that told Will he was sure the night would go their way.

There was a sprig of fennel over the door. Nat took it down so that the two haints could enter. Jimi Begood led them straight to the banquet hall and they waited outside its double doors. "Patience is a virtue," Nat said when Will glanced at his watch. "And timing is everything."

Boom!

Out on the street, the giant had picked up a length of steel girder and slammed it into the oil-tank drum. The sound crashed through the building and stilled the babble of voices inside the banquet hall.

Boom!

The drum sounded louder than thunder. "We three are the entourage," Nat told Jimi and Ghostface. "We hold ourselves proudly, stay a pace behind Will and to the side, and no matter what happens we show no emotion whatsoever. Can you do that?"

"Man, I work for Salem Toussaint!"

"What he said."

"That's good enough for me, lads."

Boom!

Then, as Nat had arranged, the giant lifted his hands to his mouth and shouted in a voice that rattled the floors, "HE . . . IS . . . *HERE!*"

As one, Nat and Ghostface slammed open the doors to the banquet hall.

Will strode in. All heads turned to look at him.

To absolute silence, Will walked up the center aisle between the banquet tables, with Jimi Begood flanking him to the right rear and Ghostface to the left with Nat behind him. He climbed the stairs to the dais at the head of the room, and went to the podium. Then he put down his hood, so that everyone could see his face. Nat lifted the gray cloak from his shoulders as unobtrusively as a butler, and Will stood revealed. He was wearing white slacks and a loose white shirt. The light dazzled from him as he stepped to the microphone.

"Hello," he said. "Before I introduce myself, I'd like to say a few words.

"I'm going to talk about a young dragon pilot—I'll mention no names—who, like so many others, volunteered to serve in the military in order to defend his country and his tower from foreign aggression. He served well and proudly in the War, and great was the mourning among his comrades when his beloved war machine was shot down over the jungles of an obscure rural province known to its inhabitants as the Debatable Hills. But though he was grievously injured, he did not die. The local folk found him, tangled in his chute, and brought him back to their village, where the healing-women labored long and hard to bring him back to life.

"As you probably know, dragon pilots are half-mortal, because only those of the red blood can withstand the proximity of so much cold iron. The blood of kings flows in the veins of every one of them. So perhaps it was this that the villagers responded to, or perhaps they recognized a certain innate nobility in him. But their own lady-mayor had recently died and so they had need of a leader.

"They made him their liege lord.

"It was a fine thing for a young pilot to rule over a small and peaceful folk. His work was far from onerous. Perhaps once a fortnight, he would be called upon to mediate a dispute, and his decisions were always praised by all, for he dispensed wisdom and mercy in equal measures. Village life was simple but wholesome. Perhaps, too, there was a lass who . . . well, let's not speak of that.

"But, pleasant though his life might be, the pilot was still an officer in His Absent Majesty's Air Force, and loyalty required that he return to duty. The day came at last when he was strong enough to leave, and so—though his subjects wept to see him go—he did.

"Across the ravaged lands of war he made his way toward the border. In stealth and fear and hunger, he slipped through the enemy's territory. Once he had an encounter with a small troop of centaurs. Great hairy, black-bearded brutes were they, who would have slain him in total disregard of the laws of civilized combat. It was a close thing, yet somehow he managed to outwit and kill them all.

"Alas, his heroism was for naught. He was captured and placed in a prison camp. You can imagine the conditions there: the filthy water, the scanty food, the forced labor, the torture. Yet once again, the pilot knew his duty. He rallied the dispirited inmates under his leadership. He faced down the camp commandant, and demanded adequate treatment for the prisoners. Finally, he organized a mass escape.

"Thus it was that after many a great hardship, he found himself in Babel again. There he discovered that his term of service had run out while he was in the camp and an honorable discharge had been issued in his absence. I may not have mentioned this, but the pilot was an orphan and, having no family to return to, he found himself at loose ends. So, what with one thing and another, he ended up making a pilgrimage to an oracle who dwelt deep in the darkness in the roots of Babel.

"Was the pilot's way difficult and dangerous? Did he see the sun rise at midnight? Of these matters and much else as well he is sworn not to say. Yet in the end, he won through to the oracle, paid her a price that he may not divulge, and discovered the one thing that he most yearned to know: The secret of his parentage.

"Up from the darkness our pilot rose. He emerged in the Hanging Gardens, and was moved almost to tears by the natural beauty that presented itself to him there. Yet though he now knew that he had a rightful claim to a great inheritance, he did not reveal himself. For he was without personal ambition. Instead, he worked with the under-privileged and established a small business, doing his wee part—as do so many here—to increase the wealth and welfare of the country as a whole.

"Nevertheless, one cannot live in a city without seeing the ills that afflict it. The poverty, the injustice, the lack of leadership and vision. So in his spare hours, the pilot went looking for answers. Up and down the city he walked, meeting with the high and the low, citizens of every class and race, and listening to what they had to say. Until finally he knew what needed to be done.

"Babel is sick for lack of a king. There is the simple truth, which not a man-jack or lady-jill here will deny. All our woes stem from the fact that the Obsidian Throne sits empty. There is no one to make the hard decisions. Expediency and compromise rule the land. The poor are neglected, the businessfolk are overtaxed, and the nobility grow fat and indolent. Babel needs a king! Yet where can one be found?" He paused for a long moment. Then he leaned into the microphone again.

"My name is Will le Fey. His Absent Majesty was my father."

As one, everybody in the hall stood up and *roared*.

The Sons of the Blest surged forward and raised him up on their shoulders and paraded out into the street, where the first of the haints from Ginny Gall were just pouring in. As the two currents met, there were swirls and eddies of dark and pale faces, all smiling, ecstatic, friends linking arms and strangers hugging strangers.

Vines sprouted in the streets and covered the sides of buildings. Trees burst into flower and birds into song as Will passed. Somebody ran out of a furniture store with a Chippendale side chair and suddenly he was plonked onto its cushion and the makeshift throne was floating up the West Side like a cork on a river. Somebody else ran into a furnishings shop and emerged with an armload of garden flambeaux that were lit and passed along hand to hand.

It became a torchlight parade.

The sea-elves had come to town, and if there was a lass anywhere in Babel who remained unseduced, she hadn't been interested in the first place. Now they emerged from the bars and strip joints, still crisp in their dress whites, saw the procession, and joined in, forming ranks and marching in time to ancient songs of glory. *Let rogues and cheats prognosticate,* they sang

> *Concerning king's or kingdom's fates*
> *I think myself to be as wise*
> *As he that gazeth on the skies*
> *My sight goes beyond*
> *The depths of a pond*
> *Or rivers in the greatest rain*
> *Whereby I can tell*
> *That all will be well*
> *When the king enjoys his own again.*

At which all the street united to sing the chorus:

> *Yes, this I can tell*
> *That all will be well*
> *When the king enjoys his own again.*

Meanwhile, a flatbed truck had somehow materialized under Will's throne. Citizens threw flowers until the truck was half-buried in them. Egret-headed bird maidens flew in loop-de-loops overhead, corkscrewing bright silken banners behind them.

All the emotion welling up from the crowd flowed through and into Will until he was intoxicated with it. He waved and blew kisses, while confetti snowed down on him and maenads and fauns tumbled naked in the street. The experience was much like waking up and discovering that the dream was still ongoing—and then waking up again and again, always with the same result.

It felt wonderful.

A pair of donkey ears sprouted from the bobbing heads of haints and Cluricauns jogging alongside the flatbed. Will looked down and saw Nat smiling up at him. "You're on your own now, son! This is your time. Grab the bastard by the throat and strangle it."

"Nat, this is incredible. You've got to—!" But his words were smothered by the immense throng. He wanted to tell Nat that he should come along, to advise him and make sure he didn't overplay his hand. All the cons he had ever pulled taken together were as nothing compared to this.

But Nat had already fallen behind and disappeared.

There was no time to think about that, however, for the television cameras had arrived at last. Their trucks paced him and their floodlights made his image blaze like a terrestrial star as it went out to every set in the city. The sea-elves, still lustily singing, came once again to the chorus, and once again all joined in to sing:

> *Yes, this I can tell*
> *That all will be well*
> *When the king enjoys his own again.*

Had hours passed? Or was it only minutes? Never afterward was Will able to decide. Yet now the hordes of Babylonians, millions it seemed, came crashing up against a line of crones and wizards, all dressed in their robes of office and holding their staves of power. They dammed the street leading to the city's topmost skyscraper Ararat upon whose uppermost floors rested the Palace of Leaves, and though they were old and frail and the procession slammed into them like a mighty wave against a seawall, not all the throng put together could prevail against them.

The oldest crone of the lot spoke, and though she spoke softly her words sounded forth loudly enough that none need not hear. "Stand ye forth, Pretender, and surrender yourself to our custody that you may be tested."

The crowd made an ugly noise of disapproval. But Will put up his hands and silenced them.

"Be calm, my people!" he cried. It was a spontaneous decision not to employ the royal we, but it felt right that their new monarch should impress them with his natural and unaffected humility. "It is just and proper that the Council of Magi should demand proof of my parentage. Nor is Pretender an ignoble title, for it does not mean that my claim is false, but only that it has yet to be tested. Which tests I not only submit myself to but demand—for the kingship of Babel is not a petty thing, to be given up lightly, but a solemn responsibility that falls only upon the blood line of Marduk. So I am well pleased with these, my loyal crones and wizards. Faithfully have they guarded my throne, and for this shall they be richly rewarded when I have ascended to it. As shall you all, my dear and loving subjects. As shall you all!"

All cheered.

"Now I leave you to be taken to the Palace of Leaves and there put to such tests and questions as shall prove my legitimacy. Such things are prescribed by custom, and are not to be hurried. They may well take weeks."

The crowd groaned.

"But I am not impatient. Nor should you be, knowing well the happy and inevitable outcome of these tests. Meanwhile, you can follow my progress through the media, so that in this manner we are not separated, you and I, but united in our common purpose and determination. We are together now and will remain so forever."

Then, as the crowds cheered and cheered, Will gestured and an aisle opened up stretching from his makeshift Chippendale throne to the distant mages who stood motionless and grim, their faces burning as bright as magnesium flares.

He stepped down from the flatbed (a kneeling ogre served as a step, and this he acknowledged with the faintest of sideway nods) and, still barefoot, began to walk toward the Council of Magi. Those to either side of the aisle knelt and bowed their heads.

Somebody screamed.

There was an abrupt change of tone and cadence of the sounds to one side of Will, as jarring as might be were the sea itself to abruptly change its voice. A red warmth sprouted and in its wake a wash of dread as well. Will turned.

He saw.

How and where had the Burning Man acquired a horse? How had

he regained his lance? How could he have gotten so close without be-ing detected? Such were the irrelevant and distracting questions that filled Will's thoughts, leaving him with neither a sensible under-standing of his situation nor any proper notion of what he should do.

Briefly, the Burning Man filled the doorway of a hotel, the ex-ploded shards of the doors themselves lying at his feet.

Then, eyes bulging and nostrils wide with terror, his charger ran straight toward Will.

The crowd screamed and scattered before it.

Will stood frozen.

He was all alone at the center of the street, empty tarmac appear-ing before him as if by magic. The Burning Man had his head lowered and his spear set. He spurred his mount forward.

"Bastard!" he cried. "You die at last!"

The lancer swelled in Will's vision. Deep inside him, Will heard the dragon screaming, demanding that he let loose its reins and sur-render control to it. Which seemed a reasonable thing to do. He just couldn't bring himself to take action. He was like a deer caught in the headlights or a moth entranced by the flame, save only that for him the paralyzing light was the shocked awareness that his life was about to end.

Out of nowhere, hands seized Will and flung him out of the horse's path.

As Will stumbled and fell, he saw Nat standing in the precise space that Will had just vacated. He saw the spear run through Nat's body. He saw Nat's face screw up with pain. He saw blood spurt.

He saw Nat die.

But then the crowd had surged back upon Will and triumphantly lifted him up, so that all might see that he lived. Capering with joy, they delivered him to the waiting mages, who bowed and with utmost deference slid him into a waiting sedan chair. Uniformed officers of the political police formed an honor guard about him. Ranks of high-elven dignitaries, Lords of the Governance all, fell into place behind them. Then four of the oldest and most revered crones hoisted the chair onto their shoulders and all processed into the lobby of Ararat where elevators waited to lift them up to the Palace of Leaves.

Behind him, sirens shrieked and wailed like so many banshees. Camera flashes strobed. Police fought to keep the reporters at bay and the camera operators struggled to break through their lines. Will did not care. He threw his head back and howled.

Nat Whilk was dead.

To the music of bodhran, flute, and sackbut, the procession carried Will helplessly away from the body. Rage and shout as he might, nobody listened.

Outside the building a band of duppies was playing reggae and citizens were dancing in the street. The king's heir had been found and the monarchy was restored. The stewardship of the Council of Magi, the Liosalfar and the Dockalfar, and the Lords of the Mayoralty was over. Democracy was no more. The king had returned to set everything right, and everyone who lived in Babel, it seemed, was mad with joy.

For them it was the happiest day in the world.

18

In the Shadow of
the Obsidian Throne

A train whistle at night was a word that meant the same thing in all languages. It was compounded of loneliness and otherness and the futile desire to be anywhere but here, anybody but one's own wretched self. What made the heart ache at the sound of it was the knowledge that the locomotive was pulling out without you and always would. You were never going to catch that imaginary train that would carry you to the faraway land containing the solutions to all your problems. You were never going to arrive at the impossible city where all the things for which you secretly yearned were given away free in the streets.

Sitting on a carved serpentine bench in the midnight garden, listening to the whistle fade, Will almost wished that the train would come and carry him away to his death.

He heaved a sigh.

"Sir? Is there anything you want?" the disembodied voice of his majordomo asked.

"No. Of course not. I have everything. What could I possibly want?"

"Sir?"

"Go away, Ariel."

At Will's feet was a pond as black as ink. Above him was the moon.

He looked from one to the other. There were fish in the pond as strange as anything to be found in the crystal cities of the moon. Yet in all the universe he could think of nothing as strange as he himself, a king apparent who wanted only to escape his servants, wealth, and palace, a con man who had scammed himself into the most opulent prison in the history of the world.

"The Master of the Tests approaches."

"Shut up, Ariel."

A shadowy figure came down the garden path, his feet almost silent on the gravel, and sat down on the bench alongside Will. "You understand things better now, I imagine, than when first we met." It was Florian L'Inconnu. He didn't exactly smile, but his expression was nowhere near so unfriendly as Will would have expected it to be.

"I understand that I'm trapped here."

"You shouldn't feel that way. Not when the tests have gone so well."

So they had. The blood work had proven Will to be part mortal, which had not surprised him, and the ring that Nat had given him had been declared sufficiently old and plausibly similar enough to the recorded aspects of the king's signet to pass muster, which, given Nat's attention to detail, was only to be expected. But he had also passed tests—the spontaneous cure of a scrofulous imp after Will touched him, the wizards' approval of a humble wooden spoon plucked at random from a trove of hundreds of gaudy trinkets—that he had expected to fail. That very afternoon, the sibyls had thrown seventeen coins minted of virgin silver and they had all come up heads. Which convinced Will as nothing else would have—for he could work that same trick in a dozen different ways—that the tests had been rigged in his favor.

"So what? There's only one way this can end."

"I know that you believe you are not the true heir," Florian said. "I ask only that you consider the possibility that you might be wrong. Enough survivors from your former village have been interviewed to establish that your parentage is . . . clouded."

"I'm a bastard, you mean."

"Which is no shameful thing when the biological father is the king! The monarch is numinous. His touch ennobles. His sperm breeds true."

"It'll make a great pickup line, anyway." Will was silent for a long moment. Then he said, "How is she?"

Florian did not pretend not to understand. "Well enough. She has her work, and that's something. You may have noticed how well prepared everybody was when you showed up at Ararat with the rabble at your back—the entire Council present and accounted for, with no laggards. That was Alcyone's doing. She got a plaque for it."

"I'm glad."

"She always asks after you. Guardedly, of course. Are you being cared for properly?"

Will snorted. "I asked for a sword so I could keep in practice with my fencing. I was thinking of an epee, though I could've made do with a foil, but I didn't actually specify that." He raised his voice. "Light!" A line of garden torches burst into flame, making the silk party canopy behind them flutter. "Take a look at what they gave me."

He held out both hands flat and a sword appeared in them. Drawing the blade free of the scabbard, he gave it to Florian.

"A Masamune!" Florian held it up so that the torchlight glittered from the martensite crystals in the habuchi. "Look at the nie! Like stars! It is a privilege just to hold it."

"Yet they gave it to me."

"Who better?"

"My skill is mediocre at best and I've only ever practiced with a European blade. Before they gave me this, I'd never even held a katana. Surely it belongs with somebody who can appreciate it."

"You're in quite a mood tonight." Florian put a hand on Will's knee.

Will looked at him in astonishment. "Is *that* what you want?"

"What? No," Florian said. "Oh, I'm perfectly willing, of course. But what I really want is a king. An absolute monarch is a weapon finer than anything Masamune ever crafted, and I want to wield one with my own hand." He gestured with the sword. "One stroke to cut through the bureaucracy and red tape that keeps Babel from ever accomplishing anything. A second to behead the lawyers. A third to strike down the traitors who return from the War and spread tales that it is bogged down and unwinnable. Another for subversives and activists fueled by class envy, labor unions, intellectuals, defeatists . . ."

"There are good reasons for laws and lawyers and truth-tellers."
Will stood. "Nor do I value action for its own sake." He walked in
among the trees and Florian followed.

Twelve trees grew in the garden of the Palace of Leaves. These
were the Birch, the Ash, the Alder, the Willow, the Hawthorn, the
Oak, the Holly, the Hazel, the Vine, the Ivy, the Water-Elder, and the
Elder. The Vine was a tree only by courtesy, of course. But taken together, the garden formed a grimoire written in the runes in the Al-
phabet of Trees, and thus to one who could read them (and there was
no shortage of such in His Putative Majesty's service), all auguries
were implicit therein. Further, in accord with the quantum-astrological
law, "As Above, So Below" and the principle of reverse causation,
its foretellings must inevitably bring whatever they predicted into
existence.

"Behold." Will plucked an elder leaf from a limb hanging over the
edge of the garden and dropped it over the railing. It twisted and
looped in the night wind and then was lost to sight. "I have raised a
storm half a world away," he said. "Or perhaps I have quelled an
earthquake. A child will be born with two extra fingers. One who was
meant to be lame will be whole. There's no way of knowing, is there?"

"No."

"So is it wise to meddle blindly?"

"Not blindly, lord, but boldly." Florian fluidly moved into a fighting
stance. With a stroke of the katana too swift for the eye to track, he
lopped a limb from a birch. The blade struck a glancing blow off the
trunk of an oak. Bark flew. "A ship sinks! A city declares bankruptcy!
Revolutionaries launch rocket attacks across a previously quiet border!" Twigs showered down upon his head and he laughed. "Glory
falls from the sky!"

"For the love of the Seven, stop—you don't know what you're doing!"

"Why should I care?" Electrical fires crawled about Florian's face
and hair. "For me, anything—even if it entailed my own death—
would be preferable to peace and stagnation."

Will felt the dragon-anger rising up in him and choked it down.
"Put the katana away," he said, and the sword disappeared from Florian's hand and its scabbard from the bench. And to Florian: "Your

scheme, then, is to replace a functioning democracy with the rule of force. 'Tis brute anarchy and nothing more."

"Why should you defend the old regime? A democracy is a bovine thing that wants nothing more than to be left alone to endlessly chew its cud and fertilize the fields. It has no taste for blood. It lacks the capacity to endure hardship, nor does it welcome pain. Only in extremis, and at the urging of the elite, will it rise to greatness, and when the crisis is over it inevitably sinks back down into the muck of inaction and petty corruption."

"You had best pray that I am *not* the king. For I would never trust one such as you."

"No, Majesty. I am the only one you can trust, for I have revealed myself completely to you. Think you the others are saner or less ruthless than I? Pfaugh! They will smile and flatter and lie, all from the same mouth, and you will know they are misleading you but not to what purpose. But I am a tiger—you understand me. So when need comes, you will turn to one whose biases you know."

"Then I suppose that there's a bright side to the fact that the situation will never come about." Will leaned heavily on the garden rail, feeling the exhausted breath of the city warm on his face. A thousand windows gleamed on the skyscrapers below. Almost whimsically, he said, "I could leap over the edge here and now and fly away."

"If you had wings, you mean."

"Even without them, I'd be free. For a time," Will said darkly. He turned back to face Florian. "I am weary and I am going in to sleep now. You may retire from my presence."

"My liege." With only a hint of a smirk, Florian withdrew.

Will remained, staring out into the darkness, thinking thoughts he would not have cared to share with anyone. After a time, a polite voice said, "Sir? Will you be needing your bed turned down?"

"Fuck off, Ariel."

A Pretender did not wake himself up. The music of fairy flutes entered his dreams to warn him that his sojourn in the lands of sleep was come to an end. Then a soft and deferential voice informed him that it was morning. Twin yakshis eased him from the bed. A dwarf in red velvet read him the day's schedule as he was being dressed.

"... immediately following the test by fire and oil. After which you will oversee the installation of the new garden furniture."

Will stretched and yawned, sending the yakshi who was fitting him into his brocaded vest dancing after his hand. "Is that really necessary?"

"If you'll recall, it was your own request, sir. You were deeply involved in the design."

"Oh, yeah." Will absently scratched his stomach, earning a small but fetching pout from the second yakshi, who was kneeling before him, buttoning his trews, and now had to undo them again in order to tuck his blouse back in. He flapped a hand negligently. "Pray, continue."

"There will then be an hour's free time, which may be spent napping, or in light sports, or in educational pursuits."

"I'm in the mood for a monoceros hunt."

The dwarf smiled indulgently, as one might at a willful but fundamentally sound child who didn't know how transparent his attempts at deception were. "There would scarcely be the time, sir. Also, while you're on probation, you can't leave the palace. If you wish, you could go up on the roof and hawk for pigeons."

"It's not the same thing, is it, Eitri? I think I'll spend the hour in the cabinet of curiosities."

Half the palace was forbidden to Will because it was taken up by the the living quarters of the servants needed to make it function, and it would be wrong to embarrass them by barging in unannounced. Half of what remained was closed to him at any given time because it was being cleaned or stocked or restored or disenchanted, and it was not proper for the help to labor in his presence. Of the rest, a great deal was not to his taste, and even more served no function that he could understand. Yet what finally remained was enough to occupy anyone. Will was particularly fond of the library and the sauna and the roof garden, with the orrery, the saurischian pit, the Victorian fernery, and the observatory not far behind. The picture gallery was, admittedly, a bit of a disappointment (all the finest paintings were on loan to public museums, he was told, but could be recalled upon his coronation), but the smoking room with its Whistler peacocks and gold trim, and the Frank Lloyd Wright lounge, rescued from a house demolished during the last teind, were first-rate. However, what he enjoyed above all else, the only thing that he out-and-out loved, was the cabinet of curiosities.

Or so he'd made certain that all the staff knew.

So that afternoon, immediately after he'd approved the new rattan tables and chairs (the tables looked more like overturned bushel baskets than he'd anticipated, but that was all to the good) and the rose-hedge plantings to either side of the garden canopy, he allowed himself to be taken to his most cherished possession.

"Sir," the docent said with the smallest and stiffest of bows when he entered the cabinet.

"Dame Serena," Will said. Alone of all the staff Dame Serena refused to permit the Pretender to address her familiarly. Yet Will could never resist trying. "You're looking as lovely as ever, today."

"Piffle," she said. "Age has laid its hand upon my shoulder and left me hunchbacked, skinny as a twig, and so wrinkled that even prunes shudder at the sight of me. A gentleman—which is an estate that even a king would do well to aspire to—would not have brought up so painful a subject."

"Eitri says you were a king's mistress when you were young."

"Does he."

"He says you were mistress to two kings and the terror of every monarch since."

"Eitri is a verminous little gossip, and a backstabbing snitch. If you had any self-respect, you wouldn't listen to him. Now. What is it that you want to see today?"

Though the original cabinet may have been a single piece of furniture, the collections had long since metastasized to the point where they required a vast, barrel-vaulted room stuffed with cases and vitrines. A Conestoga wagon, a whaling boat, and a Soyez spacecraft hung from the ceiling. There was a Scythian lamb growing in a pot alongside a stuffed capricorn. Hidden away within drawers were comprehensive selections of stone flowers from the Urals and dried mushrooms from the Fôret de Verges; on the walls were the only portraits of Queen Lilith and Lord Humbaba known to have been painted from life; elsewhere were to be found the cauldron of Ceridwen, a vast table whose polished top was made from a cross-section

sliced from a single horn of Behemoth, endless shelves of Japanese
shunga, a crystal skull that could talk, though not to any purpose, seven
coral-encrusted brass bottles in which Solomon had imprisoned rebel-
lious djinni—only one of which had been obviously breached—and
much else besides.

"The amulets of power, I was thinking," Will said.

"Follow me."

Dame Serena glided down the aisles, not bothering to look to see if
Will was keeping up. She stopped before an exhibit case and one by
one its drawers glided open at her glance, each containing hundreds
of amulets. Will pointed at random to an amulet that was set with
garnets. "What does this one do?"

"Place it around the neck of whosoever you desire and he or she
will fall completely and immediately in love with you." She sniffed. "I
imagine that makes your eyes light up, eh?"

"Alas," Will said, "getting someone to love you is the easy part."

"Quite right," the docent said crisply. "Though where in the world
one so young as yourself learned such a salutary lesson is more than I
wish to know." She nodded and the drawers slid closed. "What else
would you like to see?"

"There was another drawer with some interesting amulets. . . ."

"You'd be thinking of the unicorn-ivory amulet with the secret
name of fire carved into it. The one you tried to snitch the last time
you were here. No, I don't think that you need to look at that. What
else?"

Will drew himself up. "Dame Serena. I am the king apparent, not
only of this tower but of all Babylonia and half the civilized world
beyond. So that amulet is properly mine. You may doubt the legitimacy of my claim, if you wish, but even if I were an imposter—what
conceivable difference would it make? Where could I possibly go
with it?"

The docent's face grew taut with anger. Old though she was, there
was no denying that she had great cheekbones; it was easy to imagine
what her dead lovers had once seen in her. She jabbed him hard in the
chest with a long, bony finger. "Don't you try to pull rank with *me*, you
young jackanapes. I've got tenure. And it's been a long time since
I was impressed by mere royalty. Once you've seen an absolute

monarch drunk, covered in his own puke, and weeping because he can't get it up, you lose all sense of awe for the institution. Now. At the risk of repeating myself, what next?"

"Um . . . winds?"

The cabinet of winds held a suite of shallow drawers divided into partitions like typesetters' trays. Each partition in turn contained a short length of rope tied into a witch-knot, and each witch-knot different. Dame Serena lightly touched four knots at the cardinal points of the tray. "These are the Anemoi, according to the Greek system: Boreas the North wind, Zephyros the West, Notos the South, and Euros the East, which are also known as Tramontana, Ponente, Ostro, and Levante in the medieval compass rose system, whose octave is completed by Maestro, Libeccio, Siroco, and Greco. The subdivisions are theoretically infinite, of which this collection contains several hundred particularly select exemplars."

"These are from Lapland, right?" Will said, fingering the tray. He lifted a knot. "What happens if I untie one?"

"We shan't ever know, shall we?" Dame Serena slapped his hand. "Drop it," she said, adding, "You're a regular font of mischief today."

"It was only a zephyr," Will said placatingly. He placed the witch-knot back in its rectangle with such exaggerated care that Dame Serena didn't notice that he had palmed the original knot, while leaving a carefully tied duplicate of it in its place.

The hour went quickly. ("Ten minutes, sir," Ariel said, and "Get stuffed," Will replied.) As Will was turning to leave, however, Dame Serena slid open yet another drawer. "There's something in here you'll want to see," she said. "This is Your Majesty's smallest territory. It'll take no time at all to inspect." Within the drawer were blue ocean waters with spouting whales smaller than earwigs and a mountainous island no more than a yard across, complete with harbors, a bustling port, and wee stone cities.

Holding his breath to avoid afflicting its inhabitants with a tempest, Will bent low to examine the tiny prodigy. But when he did, the land blurred before his eyes and he looked up to discover that he was standing in a pavilion by a white-sand beach. Bright tropical foliage blossomed all about him. "Where am I?" he asked. An elf-maiden, tall and lissom in a turquoise sarong, lounged against the railing. She was beauteous even beyond her kind.

"You can stop staring at my tits now," she snapped. "You'll wear your eyes out."

Will recognized the cheekbones then and gasped. "Dame Serena?"

"You needn't act so astonished," the elf-maiden said. "It's hardly flattering that you find it so hard to believe that I was once a looker. As to where we are—this is the Land of Youth. We can't stay here long."

"Is this some kind of allegory?"

Smiling, the elf-maiden leaned forward and pinched him hard. "Does this *feel* allegorical?"

"No, I suppose not. Why are we here?" Will said, rubbing his arm.

"The Palace of Leaves may be an architectural wonder, but there's no expectation of privacy to be found in it. It's quite the fascist state, actually. There are spies and hidden microphones everywhere. But in the Land of Youth there are no such hazards. Marduk XVII and I used to come here to . . . well, never mind. But if his subordinates had known, I'd not have lived to such a disgustingly old age. We can talk safely here."

"Uh, okay, I suppose. What about?"

"They know you want to escape. Please don't try."

"I am a prisoner in the palace, Dame Serena," Will said quietly, "and the first duty of a prisoner is to try to escape."

"Well, if you must, you must. Far be it from me to stand between an idealist and his conscience, however disconnected from reality they both may be. But not this afternoon. They're expecting you to try something then, and they'll be ready for you."

"How do you know this?" Will asked.

"I told you that Eitri was a gossip. We get together for tea in the afternoons. It's the only vice I have left to me."

The Land of Youth wavered and was gone, and Will found himself standing in the cabinet of curiosities again. Dame Serena, old once more, pressed something into Will's hand. It was the ivory fire-amulet he had failed to steal the other day. "Take this," she whispered. "Just in case you need it."

"Why, Dame Serena!" Will said in astonishment. "You *do* like me after all."

"Oh, zip your lip, or I'll give you the back of my hand. You're a fool, like every other king I've ever known, and I'm doubly a fool for trying to help you." Her look softened. "But I've always had a soft spot for kings."

They were expecting him to make his move that afternoon. So of course he did.

Will was taking the air in the garden when Ariel said, "The Master of the Tests wishes to see you, sir."

"Florian? Send him to the reception room. Make him wait."

"He says it's urgent, sir."

"Then tell him I'll be with him as soon as possible, and an hour from now remind me that he's waiting."

Will stuck a cigarette in his mouth and lit up. It was a deliberately provocative gesture, and one that engendered a response almost immediately. Eitri came running up, wringing his hands in alarm. "Sir! Sir!" he squeaked. "You can't smoke here."

"Why not?"

"There's a city ordinance against smoking in a government park. Which your gardens, technically, are."

"You have a smoking room, sir," Ariel said. "It's rather well appointed."

"Yeah? Well, I can't be bothered to go there." Will blew a mouthful of smoke in the general direction of his majordomo's voice. "So what're you gonna do about it?"

"I can't touch you, of course, sir. But I can dock all of the palace staff a day's pay for every incident." Eitri, who had a gambling problem he fondly imagined wasn't common gossip, looked stricken. "If that is what you want."

Will cursed and threw the cigarette down on the ground and stomped on it. In a flash, Eitri was on his knees, sweeping the ashes into his hand. "Just . . . bugger off, all of you, okay? Leave me alone. If I can't smoke, at least let me have five minutes alone. Go away, both of you, and take the rest of the staff with you."

"Yes, sir. Thank you, sir," Eitri said fervently.

"As you wish, sir."

The creepy feeling that Will always got when Ariel was near evanesced.

As soon as he was sure he was alone, Will flipped over the wicker table so that it made a basket shape with a short pedestal-well at the center, rather like the mold for a bundt cake. He dumped the fruit from a large copper bowl on a nearby table and placed the bowl snugly atop the pedestal. Then he tossed the fire-amulet into the bowl and activated its rune with a muttered word. Heat washed up from it, not enough to make the canopy lift free of the ground—that would come later—but enough so that it tugged lightly against its guy lines. These Will untied from their stakes and retied to the edges of the basket. The tent poles he let fall to the ground.

He was ready!

Will hastily set several armfuls of potted plants into one side of the basket to balance it and then climbed into the other.

"Sir? What are you doing?"

"My duty," Will said. He muttered a second word that brought the fire-amulet to full power. Heat gushed up from the copper bowl and with a great *whoosh* the canopy overhead billowed as it filled with hot air.

Will untied the witch-knot and a brisk west wind sprang up, scattering napkins across the patio and pushing at the swollen canopy.

Alarmed servitors came running out on the roof just as the makeshift balloon lifted up into the air. Some crashed into the rose hedges and others ran around them, vaulting or stumbling over the new garden furniture. They leaped up, trying to catch at the basket, and failed. Will laughed into their upturned faces and—

"Enough."

The air grew cool. The canopy-balloon ceased to flutter. In the center of the garden Ariel had manifested in his physical form: a slim figure with a chalk-white face, lank black hair, and a rooster's coxcomb. His mouth was twisted and bitter. Yet his voice was calm and dulcet.

Ariel raised an arm and twisted a hand and the balloon returned without fuss to its point of origin. Servitors ran up to hasten away the fire-amulet, to right the wicker table, to restore the scattered fruit to the copper bowl, to reerect the canopy. In seconds all was as it had been before.

They had caught him. But of course, there had never really been any question of that.

Now that Ariel stood before him in visible form, eyes cold and mouth cruel, Will found himself more convinced than ever that the creature was his household's spy-master, the one that Eitri and the yakshis and for all he knew Dame Serena as well, reported to.

Slowly Ariel faded back into insubstantiality.

"Sir?" his voice said out of nowhere. "This is perhaps a little early, but . . . you wished to be reminded that Florian L'Inconnu is waiting."

Like most of the rooms in the Palace of Leaves, the reception chamber was far too big and far too ornate for Will to feel comfortable in. The ceiling was white with rose-colored plaster swags of fruits, ribbons, and medallions. If Fabergé had made a pink Wedgwood teapot the size of a bus depot and turned it inside out, it would look much like this.

Florian, of course, looked right at home. He rose gracefully from a leather chair at Will's approach, stubbing out his cigar in a nearby ashtray.

"I must speak to you in absolute confidence," Will said without preamble. "The other evening in the garden you said things I am certain would not have been spoken had you thought one of the palace spies might overhear them. So I presume you have means of ensuring our privacy."

Florian removed a BlackBerry from his jacket, tapped several keys, and pocketed it again. "You may speak your mind freely."

"Tell me," Will said. "Am I truly the king?"

"Yes," Florian said, "I honestly believe that you are."

"Then kneel."

"What?"

"Kneel!" Will repeated with force.

Florian L'Inconnu, Master of the Tests, holder of a permanent seat in the Liosalfar, and scion-and-heir of a great house though he might be, went down on one knee and bowed his head, just as the merest peasant or byre-slave would have. "Your Majesty."

"Both knees!"

Florian's face hardened, but he obeyed.

"Touch your forehead to the ground."

Flushed with humiliation, he did so.

So, thought Will, this is what true power feels like. He could grow to like it. It would be the easiest thing in the world to abuse. Which in and of itself was another compelling reason for him to leave this place immediately. "Stand," he said, "and take off all your clothing."

Warily, Florian did as he was told. "May I ask what all this is about?"

"Absolutely." Will casually picked up a heavy crystal ashtray. Then he smashed it into the side of Florian's head. "While you're in the hospital recovering from that concussion, I'll be making my way out of Babel."

The spell Will used to disguise himself as Florian was the flimsiest of things, cobbled together from tissue paper, moonlight, cobwebs, and filched fingernail parings. If an inmate in a state penitentiary had employed it, it would have worked no better than a gun carved out of soap and blackened with shoe polish. Which is to say, well enough to get him in trouble, but no so well as to get him over the wall. But the Palace of Leaves was unique among prisons in that its wardens had forgotten that it was one, and thus were not prepared for a break.

Wearing Florian's stolen face and his clothing as well, Will walked unmolested to the main elevator bank where a haint so deferential he almost wasn't there at all, rang for a car. The great bronze doors opened and he got in. "Ground floor," he told the operator. Downward they went. The car stopped only once, at the seventieth floor, to let on a passenger.

It was Alcyone.

Will's heart lurched. Nevertheless, he maintained an icy exterior.

"What news, my brother?"

"Babel endures. The testing goes well. We should have the Pretender on the throne within the week."

"So you still think that the Obsidian Throne will accept him?"

"What matters it to me? Either way, I am content. If he is the true king, I have a puppet, and if not . . ." Will hesitated a second. "If not, I will find it mildly amusing to watch his torments as he slowly dies."

Alcyone looked at him puzzledly. "You did not speak so passionlessly on this subject the other night. You said that you practically had your hand halfway up his . . ." She stopped and stared into his face hard. Her eyes widened. "Will?" she breathed.

Will held a finger to his lips in a shushing gesture and glanced quickly at the elevator operator. Who, thankfully, stared straight ahead of himself, either having heard nothing or being too discreet to think about it. Carefully, Will reached to the side and took Alcyone's hand. She squeezed it without saying a word.

So she was with him. For a moment—no more—Will's spirits soared.

Then the elevator doors opened into Ararat's lobby. A line of lion-headed demon guards stood between him and the street. At their head was Florian.

For an instant Will was speechless with astonishment. Then he saw it all. "You shit. You set me up with your fucking *fetch!*"

Alcyone's cheeks were as pale as marble, and as hard as stone.

"There are many reasons to test a potential king, you know," Florian said. "The legitimacy of his claim, of course. But it is also important to be certain that the candidate is fit to rule. On this point, I admit to having had my doubts about you.

"You pretended to be suicidal in order to distract attention from your escape attempt. A child could have seen through that ploy. As for the escape itself . . . well, it was witty, I'll give you that. But it was not convincing. Even with the aid of a following wind, you could not hope to out-fly even something so common as, say, a hippogriff. Nor was it sound judgment to trust so rickety a craft to the notoriously fickle winds generated by the Dread Tower's mere presence. So when Ariel uncovered your plan, I was not impressed.

"Almost, I gave up on you.

"But then I thought of the time you spent as a confidence trickster, apprenticed to a master so sly that all the combined efforts of the political police have not sufficed to locate him. Would one with such an education come up with so obvious a plan? No. You meant your balloon-escape to be discovered and prevented, for it was only a distraction from your true escape—and *that* was truly clever. Indeed, it would have worked had I not been on the lookout for something unexpected."

Florian's eyes glowed like a wolf's. "You have proved yourself to be deceitful, treacherous, and ruthless. You will make a fine ruler. You've passed the final test. You are fit to sit upon the Obsidian Throne."

19

The Dragon King

William went to the coronation as to a beheading.

The Obsidian Throne was located deep in the heart of the same building that the Palace of Leaves perched atop. So the procession ran widdershins around Ararat seven times, with the Lion Guard clearing the way and brass bands, ranks of wyverns, spider-legged daliphants, sword dancers, and fire jugglers following. Will sat upon a horse whose strength and beauty were second only to those of Epona herself, flanked by a security force of scorpion-men.

Nymphs danced before him in flowing white, scattering rose petals and twirling batons.

The sidewalks were filled with spectators and the windows of all the buildings as well, while those who could fly perched on rooftops and thronged the sky. Shouts and cheers merged into a constant background pandemonium. Banks of bright balloons were released as Will rode by and tumbled upward through downfalling multicolored confetti and flocks of newly freed pigeons slanting skyward like mad whirligigs. It was infinitely better organized than his Acclamation had been, but it felt prepackaged and over-rehearsed. The mood on the street was uglier, the cheers less spontaneous. Bucentaurs trotting a pace behind Will threw handfuls of gold soleils and silver lunars, fresh minted with his profile on the obverse. The gesture was meant to start off his reign with a burst of goodwill, but the crowds scrambled frantically for the coins so that fights were constantly breaking out in Will's wake.

Will kept his head down, for his thoughts were dark and he did not wish anyone to read them in his eyes.

"Smile, sir," Ariel murmured in his ear. "Wave."

Halfheartedly, Will managed to wave. It seemed only fair to the citizens. Yet he could not manage a smile. Nor could he feel the same love for them he had when they had spontaneously carried him all the way from Little Thule to the top of Babel. He felt nothing for them but a distant, emotionless disdain.

And then, all too soon the procession was over.

Will had arrived back where he had started. Three ranks of gleaming horns played a heroic fanfare composed for the occasion as he dismounted. The satraps of vassal states lay down before him, forming a carpet with their backs. Celebrities vaulted from their limos to fling open the doors to Ararat.

He entered.

Though his bodyguard and the politicians nearest him in the procession poured into the building along with Will, only a fraction of the procession made it into the lobby. Fewer could squeeze into the first elevator car with him. And somehow, more still were lost on the long walk down narrow corridors to the throne room. When its metal doors slammed shut behind him, Will looked up, startled, to realize that his entourage had been reduced to two ogres, who held him by the arms, and Florian L'Inconnu, leading the way.

"Now comes the moment that pays for all," Ariel said. "Sir."

Will looked back to discover that nobody was following him.

"Where is everybody?" he asked confusedly, as he was forced down onto the throne. Leather straps were cinched over his arms and legs. Another was tightened about his chest. He couldn't move.

The room was dimly lit and it had cinder-block walls. There were stains, or possibly scorch marks, on the floor, radiating out from the throne. A burnt smell lingered in the air. In one wall was a long window. Through it he could see a line of high-elven dignitaries watching him impassively. They all wore cobalt-blue goggles and lead X-ray vests.

"What's going on here? Why are they wearing protective gear?"

"It's only a precaution." Florian opened an equipment chest and lifted out a tangle of cords and wires. The ogres set to work unsnarling them and plugging them into wall sockets and unidentifiable electrical equipment. A featureless metal ring, about half a hand wide, was screwed tight about Will's head. "Your crown," Florian explained. He took a set of jumper cables and clipped one end to the crown and the other to what looked to be a generator.

"I don't understand," Will said, trying to fight down panic. "This is nothing like I expected it to be."

The ogres applied electrodes to the sides of his neck with dabs of gel. "If you throw up," Florian said, "try to turn your head to the side so that you don't short out any of the equipment."

"Am I likely to throw up?"

"There is a season for everything, sir," Ariel said primly. "It's possible you may also soil yourself."

To his horror, Will felt tears welling up. He tried to blink them away. "Please," he said. "Not like this. Let me die with some shred of dignity."

Wordlessly, his escort withdrew. Florian L'Inconnu bowed formally before closing the doors from the outside.

Will was alone.

A minute later, Florian entered the room on the other side of the window. He donned vest and goggles and joined the line of observers. An elf at the opposite end of the line turned briskly to the wall. Will saw for the first time that there was a large knife switch there, bolted open by two flanges. The elf took out a screwdriver and unhurriedly but efficiently removed the fail-safes. He put his hand to the switch.

Ariel's voice sounded from a staticky wall-mounted speaker.

"Try to relax, sir. There may be some slight discomfort."

A flash like an incandescent lightbulb exploded behind Will's eyes. He fell.

Showering sparks, Will fell through infinite darkness. The darkness was virtual, so in a sense it did not exist, but the sensation of falling was quite real, for he was plunging deeper and deeper into the spirit world. Will spread his arms so that in his mind's eye he looked like a William Blake watercolor of a falling star.

He fell and, falling, understood the nature of the Obsidian Throne for the first time. It was more than a symbol of power and more than the ultimate test of the legitimacy of the king. Those functions were incidental to its true purpose. For it was the controlling node for all electronic and thaumaturgic data ever assembled by the governance of Babel. All the lore and secrets of the Tower of Kings were here to be discovered. Will could learn anything he wished.

But where to begin?

Will found himself sitting by a small stream, feet in the water, talking with his best friend, Puck. Dragonflies darted busily about the reeds. There was a pleasant marshy smell. For one dizzying instant he thought that he was back in the village and that all his adventures in the wider world had been nothing but a timeless vision vouchsafed him by the Seven, whose capriciousness was notorious and whose motives were unfathomable. But then two abatwa trudged by with a water dragon's carcass hanging from a twig slung over their shoulders, and he realized that he was in the Hanging Gardens of Babel.

"...suffered greatly to get here, and so you must be given a gift," Puck was saying. "Here it is: When you die, you'll find yourself standing in a kind of field or meadow with short green grass, almost like a lawn. There'll be a bright blue sky overhead, but no sun. There's a path and you'll follow it because there's nothing else you can do. Eventually it comes to a stone—a big thing, set up on its end like a menhir. Most folks go around the left-hand side. The path is well-trodden there. But if you look closely, there's a way around to the right. You're of the second blood so you can go either way. If you go around to the left, you'll be reborn again. What happens if you go around to the right, no living wight knows."

"Am I dead?" Will said carefully.

"No, of course not. Trust me, if you were dead you'd know it."

"Then why do you tell me this?"

Puck Berrysnatcher leaned forward and fixed Will with those dark, intense eyes. His face was pale and puffy, as if he'd drowned some time ago and his body only just now been hauled from the water. "Not to tell you which way to go—that's your decision. But to let you know that when the time comes, you have a choice. You always have a choice."

Will remembered then that Puck was dead, and his skin crackled with dread. "Are you really here?" he asked. "Or am I just imagining you?"

"Such distinctions do not matter in the Inner World. Perhaps I am only a mental artifact, cobbled together from your memories and emotions. Perhaps—and I personally think this is more likely—I am a messenger from a distant land." He grinned a grin as wide as a bull-frog's. "You have sat yourself down on the Obsidian Throne, and thus we can converse freely. That's all."

"How is that possible? Why didn't it kill me?"

"Because you are the one true king."

With those words, the Obsidian Throne unlocked itself completely. In the language that was spoken in the dawn-times before the invention of lies, which had been forgotten a million years ago but was so lucid that to hear it was to comprehend it perfectly, the Throne told him that he was the legitimate and undisputed heir to the throne and thus, now, the king. Then it told him exactly how this strange fact had come to be.

Thus it was that the first words spoken by Marduk XXIV, by the Grace of the Seven, King in Babel Tower and Monarch Over All Babylonia and Its Contingent Territories, Defender of Fäerie, Protector of Fäerie Minor, Clan-Chief of House sayn-Draco, Titular Prince of Coronata and the Isles of Avalon, and Hereditary Laird of the Western Paradise, were, "Oh, you *bastard!*"

Nat Whilk was Will's father.

Once said, it was obvious. Nat had been waiting for Will on the train to Babel, and had used all his wiles and cunning to bring Will under his influence. When Will proved reluctant to join forces with him, he had lost Will's luggage, rendering him paperless, a pauper, and an outlaw. Nat had been an aristocrat in Babel, he'd said, and had escaped—but what aristocrat, other than the king, would be so obviously lacking in high-elven genes? What aristocrat, other than the king, *needed* to escape?

Nat had isolated Will, taught him cunning and deceit, and bought him the social graces. He had aimed Will, swift and true as an arrow, straight at the Obsidian Throne. And all the while, in his arrogance, he had not spoken a single untruthful word. He had deceived Will by acting as if he were an inveterate liar while speaking always the simple and unvarnished truth.

How many times had he called Will son?

Will's head throbbed, his stomach was queasy with nausea, and his wrists were so cold they ached. He remembered those sensations well from the dark nights when he had been the dragon's lieutenant. The familiarity of which filled him with despair, for it made him feel as if he had escaped nothing.

From the corner of his mind, Will saw the high-elven dignitaries in the observation chamber smiling with relief and removing their goggles. They came ambling into the throne room, chatting casually with each other. They were going to disconnect him from the Obsidian Throne now while he was, as they assumed, still stunned from his first exposure to it. The next time he sat upon the throne, however, would be a different matter. They would be prepared for him to attempt to use its power for his own purposes. They would have neuromancers monitoring his thoughts, and a thick-witted but loyal ogre holding a cocked gun to his head to ensure he did as he was told.

It had been so long since they'd had a king that they'd forgotten what one could do.

Will had lost track of the Hanging Gardens and was adrift in raw information. All the Outer World was recorded here, every gas pump, weed, and nobleman of it, rendered in binary mana and tracked in real-time emulation. Which meant that, in accordance with the quantum-alchemical principle of similarity of effect most often rendered by the phrase "As Within, So Without," any model he created in the Inner World would have its corresponding doppelgänger in the physical universe.

Will imagined a wind and let it fill the throne room, buffeting and pushing the elf-lords out into the hall and then chivying them, squeaking and flapping their arms, through the corridors of Ararat, down the stairwells, and out into the street. The doors he shut and locked behind them. At one point Ariel managed to slip aside and crawl behind an alabaster planter. But Will had not forgotten him, and his invisibility only operated in the Outer World. Effortlessly,

Will exploded the planter outward, taking care that its blast pattern did not intersect the majordomo's body. Then he picked up his erstwhile jailor by the scruff of the neck, floated him through a window, and dropped him into a decorative thorn hedge.

This was fun.

Swiftly, Will ran his thoughts through the Palace of Leaves, locking doors and securing corridors. When he was sure he was safe from interruption, he withdrew his attention from the palace.

It was time he saw just what powers he had inherited.

Will let his consciousness go skipping from mind to mind through the streets and apartments of his city.

He was a stone lion rerereading with neither haste nor admiration *Aristocrats of the Air,* a book on the natural history of hippogriffs that he'd stolen from an inattentive hick outlander. For the umpteenth time he cursed the little git for his deplorable taste in reading matter.

He was a Tylwyth Teg treasury agent closing in on a petty embezzler named Salem Toussaint. For decades, the alderman had been redirecting public monies to private (and sometimes one-person) charities under the supremely self-assured conviction that only he knew best how it should be spent. Will had the accountant carefully gather up all the paperwork that had been assembled over the past three years and then make eight trips out to the incinerator chute. After which he left a compulsion in the investigator to go to the nearest bar, drink until he passed out, and wake up with no memory of the case whatsoever. Meanwhile, Will erased all the electronic records incriminating his onetime mentor. While he was at it, he rewrote the voter regulations which artificially depressed the haint turnout on election days, and enacted legislation to make certain discriminatory banking practices illegal.

He was a rail-thin shellycoat creeping out of the mouth of the subsurface line on a twilight scavenging mission. His johatsu community had been driven out of their old squat by the transit police and their thane-lady had sent him upstairs to seek out much-needed bedding material—shredded newspapers, scrap wool, whatever came to hand. He sank back into the shadows as a truck pulled up to a vacant lot directly opposite him. Then his eyes widened as a ginger dwarf hopped down from the cab, double-checked an invoice, shrugged, and began dragging new, plastic-wrapped mattresses from the truck and flinging them into the lot.

He was one of the horse-folk, gaunt and naked, but proud of their herd. Because they neither had nor wanted any possessions other than their blind cave-horses, there was nothing Will could give them. So he moved swiftly on.

He was, briefly, Dame Serena. Will was astonished to learn just how wealthy she was. Every king over the last two centuries, it seemed, including those who had ostensibly lived in fear of her, had left Dame Serena well provided for. He glanced into her memories, blushed, and fled.

Up and down the seventeen boroughs of Babel Will let his consciousness flow from haint to troll and dwarf to stickfella, through hobthrushes, nocnictas, and night-gaunts, street-corner wise guys, traffic cops, kitty-witches, milchdicks, a russalka pretending to hump the pole in a titty bar, cynocephali, onis, a cluricaun dying in a small room above a bar, mawkies, coin clippers, pastry chefs, rogues and innocents, opportunistic weaklings, corrupt lawyers and saintly plumbers, clabbersnappers, vodniks, longshoreman-poets, a street-sweeper spending his last thirteen dollars on lottery tickets, igoshas, itchikitchies, muggers and remittance men, red-diaper babies, bricklayers, heartbreakers, commodities brokers, a desperate klude changing into her dog form before raiding a restaurant dumpster, haberdashers, fishmongers, bouncers, lexicographers, a korigan dreaming of bygone days on the Broadway stage, Ukrainians and Ruthenians, laboratory inspectors, proud hags and war-scarred battleaxes, nixies, nymphs, heiresses, kinderofenfrauen, foolish virgins, doting grannies, hopeful monsters...

He saw the vixen riding a Vespa down a two-lane road with the Tower of Babel at her back and could not enter her mind. Will thought at first that it was a function of distance, a matter simply of how far she was from his siege of power. But then she abruptly swerved her scooter into a pull-off area. "You're here," she said. "I can feel you."

The vixen unbuckled her saddlebag and dug out a gun and a doll so small that it disappeared when she closed her hand around it. "You and I were never exactly friends," she said with a crisp flash of sharp white teeth. "But you're Nat's kid, so I'll cut you some slack." She opened her hand to reveal a crude effigy made of tar and straw with hanks of blond hair stuck to its pate and a button from one of Will's blazers sewed onto its shirt. "Guess whose hair and blood and snot went into this?" She put the muzzle of the gun against the doll's stomach. "Try to sleaze your way into my head one more time, laddy-buck, and the little guy buys it. You'll never know what hit you." Then she smiled sweetly. "Or maybe I'm just bluffing. You can call me on it, if you like."

The vixen got back on her scooter and drove away. But just before she disappeared around the bend, Will saw her look back, wink, and tap her heart. *He lives,* she meant. *In here.* Then she blew him a kiss and was gone. *Good luck.*

He had a complete picture of Babel now, from its demon sewer-workers to the gargoyles that haunted its rooftops. Will turned his thoughts to the War. First, he leaped into the mind of Lord Ven-ganza, the war strategist he'd met when Alcyone took him clubbing, and there determined that the proximate causes of the War—boundary disputes dating all the way back to the Treaty of Hy-Brasil, the sinking of a gunboat by a sea serpent off the coast of Magh Mell, and the refusal of the Daughters of the West to offer tribute in the form of a purebred bull of the lineage of Fennbennech Ai—were less important than control of North Sea oil, strategic supplies of man-ganese, and access to the Straits of Hyperborea. Indeed, the deeper Will looked, the less clear it became who was the original aggressor or how the conflict could be peaceably resolved. But when he looked into strategy and logistics, Will saw immediately that the entire Western campaign would fall apart without adequate air support.

He set about changing the access codes to every war-dragon in His Present Majesty's Air Force so that, once landed, they could not be ordered into the air again.

"Oh, Will. What have you done?"

Will looked up and found himself standing on a dark and windswept plain. Mountains glittered in the distance. No stars shone in the sky. Before him stood a figure who looked exactly like Puck Berrysnatcher but was not. "I know who you are," Will said. "Reveal yourself."

With a smirk, the fey grabbed one of his ears and pulled, peeling the water-bloated flesh from his head so that it came off like a fat, rubbery mask. Underneath, raw and pink, was Will's own face.

"You cannot fool me, old mocker," Will said sternly. "I recognize you, Dragon Baalthazar."

"You think I'm trying to deceive you? I'm a part of you now, re-member?" the dragon said. "You and I shall never be free of each other." But he took on his spirit form, sinuous and veined with light. It made Will's heart ache to remember how beautiful the creature was. "You wish to end the War—fine. But will shutting down your air forces do it? More dragons can always be built."

"Silence, Worm! I know whose side you're on."

"I care nothing about sides—destruction is my all. The question is, whose side are *you* on? You swore once to bring the War to Babel. Have you forgotten? Do your youthful ideals mean nothing to you anymore? Let me show you how it could be."

The noise was deafening, as if all existence had screamed. So primal was it that only after the fact did Will's mind register it as the shock of a tremendous explosion. A warm hand made of air pushed him backward a foot and he suddenly realized that his ears were ringing. Something has changed, he thought, and simultaneously he felt all of Babel shift uncomfortably underfoot.

Will twisted around to either side but saw nothing out of the ordi-nary. There were strollers on the sidewalk and hummingirls in the air. A faun sold roasted chestnuts from a pushcart.

Then there were bodies leaning over the railing of the esplanade and fingers pointing upward to where, high above, billows of smoke poured from the side of the city. "It crashed!" somebody said. "I saw it!"

Will leaned over the rail as well, craning to see. Smoke was gushing outward from the Tower. It seemed impossible that there could be so much smoke. It poured from the city in a rush, as if it were eager to fill the sky. Surely it would have to use itself up soon, he thought—there couldn't possibly be anything left to burn. But it just kept com-ing and coming and coming. . . .

A presentiment was building deep within Will. It was nothing so crude as a hand writing letters on his palm. Nevertheless, what he felt was so profound and certain that he could not deny its truth: Something bad was about to happen.

"Look!" a haint cried. "There!"

He turned just in time to see a dragon slip across the sky like a dark shadow. For a flickering instant, Will felt a pulse of kinship. Then the dragon flew into the side of Babel.

The noise was beyond thunder, a physical presence so great that the explosion of the war machine's fuel tanks was no more than a continuation and amplification of it. For a second time, Babel shook under him.

Other dragons, small as gnats, were swimming lazily through a heartbreakingly blue sky. He saw them converging upon the Dread Tower from every direction. There must have been hundreds of them within sight. Meanwhile, a part of Will's mind accessed the Air Force registry and discovered that for every dragon he could see, there were hundreds more over the horizon. Every dragon in his empire that was capable of flight had launched itself into the air. They were all on their final mission, jets throttled wide open, straining to reach Babel while some of it yet stood.

A third dragon crashed into the side of Babel, and a fourth. Sirens rose from all parts of the city. The street rose and fell in a wave. Will felt terrified and elated, all at one and the same time.

"Is it not brave to be a king?" the dragon exulted. "Is it not passing brave to be the last king of Babylon, and watch the fall of the Tower?"

No, Will wanted to say. But he could not. It was impossible for him to lie while he was in the spirit world. He could not deny the black delight that rose up in him at the thought of an all-encompassing vengeance. "I . . ." Will swallowed. "I mean, I . . . I think that . . ."

"Claim your revenge! Start with the king who seduced your mother and cuckolded he who should have been your father. The aunt who neglected you and then feared you when you came into power. The friends who turned on you. The village that cast you out, the bandits who tried to kill you, the informants who framed you, the camp commandant who blackmailed you, the refugees who tried to make you what you weren't, the petty officials who forced you into outlawry, the authorities who hunted you like an animal, the lovers who betrayed you, the followers who deserted you, the nobles who thought you beneath their contempt, the mediocrities who ordered you about, the aristocrats who wanted you for what you were not, the elf-lady who dared not love you, the populace who all against your will made you king! What do you owe any of them but pain to match your own? They all—all!—made you suffer when the power was theirs. Why should you refrain from responding in kind now that you have the upper hand? What have you ever known in this world but ugliness and wickedness and violence? You tried kindness, and what did that get you? The world responds to nothing but the whip. Lay on, then, with all your might, and make it bleed!"

Will looked around vaguely. "What is that sound?" he wondered. "I hear a sound."

"Pay it no mind!" the dragon snapped. "We have more important—" But Will had already opened his eyes.

Somebody was crying.

Will looked around groggily and saw nothing. Then he turned to the side and there was a small child tugging at the leather strap that held his left arm fastened to Obsidian Throne. It was a little girl.

"Esme?"

The strap came undone and Will lifted his arm. He could move both arms, he realized. The strap about his chest was gone. So was the one around his legs. He was weak as a kitten, though. It was all he could do to reach up and push the crown off his head. It fell to the floor with a clatter.

"Come here, child." Will patted his leg and Esme climbed into his lap. "Don't cry. How in the world did you get in here?"

"I know how to do things. How to slip past guards. How to pick locks. How to walk through walls. How to . . . I forget what else. But it wasn't hard for me, I know how to do almost everything."

"Yes, I remember." It seemed like something from another time, another world. Then a thought came to Will. "Why are you still here? With your luck, you should have left Babel days ago, Esme. This isn't a safe place to be."

"I know. You want to knock down the city. You want to kill my toad!"

"You have a toad?"

"She's big. I think you know her. She's so big she can't leave her bar and she listens to the radio and reads the newspaper all day. She said something about you, but I forget what."

"Do you mean the Duchess? Esme, you should stay away from her—she's a treacherous creature."

"Wait, I remember what my toad said now. She told me you don't like her. But I *do*! She's nice to me. She gave me pretzels."

"You've got to leave, Esme. You've got to go someplace safe. The city is burning." But then Will realized that it was not. The war-dragons he had seen smash into it were a vision that Baalthazar, his dragon-aspect, had shown him. The city was yet whole, and the mighty metal war-drakes were all locked down, unable to fly until he himself released them. With a convulsive shudder he hugged the child to him. He had almost killed her! The thought filled him with revulsion. How could he have thought to destroy an entire city when he hadn't the stomach to kill even a single child? "All right, Esme," he murmured through his shame. "I'll be good."

She struggled out of his embrace and put her forehead against his, staring solemnly into his eyes. "Promise?"

"Promise. But it's still not a good idea for you to stay here. Can you get out of the palace without being caught?"

"Of course I can. I'm lucky."

"Can you take me with you?"

Esme looked doubtful. "I don't think it works like that."

"No, I was afraid not." Will kissed the child on her forehead, then set her down on the floor. He was about to swat her behind and send her off when something caught his eye. "Why is there a safety pin clipped to the front of your sweater?"

"Oh, yeah. I had a letter I was s'posed to give you. Only it got in my way, so I put it somewhere." Esme dug into her jeans and emerged with a wadded-up envelope. "Here."

"Thank you," Will said solemnly. The envelope said READ IMME-DIATELY on the outside. He pocketed it without looking inside. "Now, go! You'll be fine."

"I know," Esme said. "I'm lucky like that."

She scampered away.

Now Will had to decide what to do with himself. He dared not sit on the Obsidian Throne ever again, lest his dragon aspect overcome him. Nor did he care to be used by the Lords of Babel as a weapon against the lands of the West. The power he had inherited was simply too great to be safely employed by any single person. As king, he was a constant threat to the safety of his city and of the world, and thus he must absent himself.

One way or another.

Two twists, one turn, and a flight of stairs upward, and Will was lost. To be lost is a wonderful thing if one is in a position to appreciate it. Everything is new and surprising. The spittoons startle. The existence of a warren of access corridors to keep the servants unobtrusive astonishes. Will would have lingered to marvel at the stenciled ROYAL SERVICE ONLY on the scuffed backside of a door whose front was surely distinguished, had he not heard voices echoing up the stairwell. The staff had regained the building. He plunged through the doorway and found himself surrounded by alabaster statuary and ormolu clocks.

A hunted animal does not run full-out until the predator is in sight, but saves its energy for the crisis. So, now, Will. He loped down a hallway and, when the doorway he had passed through slammed open, slipped into the nearest room.

It was yet another conference space with too-high ceilings and mahogany trim carved into life-scaled nymph heroines in Greek helmets. There was a kitchenette to one side, but only the one door. The stentorian clamor of booted feet grew louder.

Will threw open the windows and climbed outside.

The ledge was narrow. The wind was cold. Will closed the windows behind him and edged to the side, out of sight. Then he looked down and almost fell.

It was a vertiginously long way down. From here, the ground was half-obscured by clouds. It looked distant and impossibly romantic. He wished he were down there now, by the side of one of those gossamer-thin roads, thumb out and about to hook a ride that would carry him halfway to Lemuria.

There were muffled sounds from the room he had just left. Will held his breath. But nobody looked out the windows, and after a minute or so the sounds died away.

He was stuck. He dared not go back inside, and he was physically incapable of moving anywhere on the ledge. Will stuck his hands in his pockets against the cold, and discovered the letter that Esme had given him.

He took it out and began to read.

Dear Son:

So now you know! I'm sorry to have played such a shabby trick on you. But what choice did I have? Babel needed a king and I've grown a little too long in the tooth and independent-minded to play the part. Nor was it my decision to involve you. The Throne had been empty too long, and so it began searching for you. It drew you to itself. Without my interference, you would have been found on the train from Camp Oberon—and when they made you king, you wouldn't have been prepared to make the decision you just have.

Of course I can't know what you decided. That choice was yours to make. But I think I know the kind of person you are. So, if I'm right—and when am I ever wrong?—you're looking for a new line of work, and trying to figure out exactly what you should do with the world.

But here's a secret that only you and I know: The world doesn't need doing.

The world is not perfect, nor can it be made so. But despite all the pain and heartbreak, it's a fine place to live. It gave me your presence, however briefly, and as far as I'm concerned that pays for everything. Learn to praise the imperfect world. You're a trickster, like me. Only achieve joy, and you'll be a great one.

Love,

Your Father, (Nat), Marduk XXIII, by Grace of the Seven, Absent

Will let go of the letter and the wind whipped it away. Then he took a long and ragged breath. The air was cold up here and invigorating as iced wine. He felt more alive now than he ever had before. Life was correspondingly more precious to him as well. He looked down the side of Babel. It looked so fragile from this perspective. So beautiful.

It would not be an ignoble thing to die protecting.

There was a small dark speck in the air in the distance dancing against a cloud. Something about it felt vaguely familiar.

Will wasn't sure he was going to be able to jump. All his body resisted the thought. Against all expectations he realized that what he had thought at the time to be an unending cascade of misery and calamity had actually been a pretty good life. He was sorry to be leaving it.

He took a deep breath.

Alcyone swept down out of nowhere, her hippogriff screaming under her, and reined up just below the ledge. "Get on, you idiot!" she cried. "They're going to be after us in another minute."

Will blinked.

Then he leapt down behind her and put his arms about her in a hug. "How did you know I'd be here?" he said gratefully.

"I head up the gods-be-damned Division of Signs and Omens," she said. "If I didn't know, who in seven hells would?"

Ararat grew slowly smaller behind them. Ahead, the sky was vast and unending, with continents of clouds adrift in it, and on them harbors and cities and billowing castles. "We can't stay together. A month would kill you."

"Don't talk like a fool. I know all that. But I don't suppose you can make me too happy in a week or three. And after that . . . well, there's always next year."

"I bet I could make you too happy in three weeks if I tried. I bet it would only take me ten days—tops."

"Asshole!" Alcyone laughed and wheeled her beast up and around in a great arc, and they were flying, and he was young and joyful and in love and his sweetie was here with him, and she loved him, too. All the world was theirs and bright with possibility.

So it couldn't last. Who the fuck *cared*?

20

The End of the Story

Returning to Babel was, for Will, like returning to a beloved book that one has all but memorized. It of course contained a thousand thousand stories—its very name meant "book" in the primal tongue, though some scholars interpreted that to mean "library"—and those stories were always changing, always coming to an end, always beginning again. But if one could sit upon the Obsidian Throne and be given the power of the Dragon King to comprehend everything in the city at once, he would see that it was all one glorious and heartbreaking tale and that tale as recurrent as the seasons.

It had been about two decades since Will was last in Babel. Its every brick and smell tugged at his heart. He was young when last he had trod these streets. Nobody could say he was young anymore. But what he had lost in years, he had gained in guile. Old Nat would have been proud of how he'd turned out. Nobody, seeing him now, could have guessed that he was waiting for somebody, nor how anxiously. Had anyone happened to glance his way (but they did *not* glance, not when he had decided that they shouldn't), they'd have thought him a boulevardier loitering for a moment before proceeding on to a destination of no discernable importance. The facial scar they would dismiss as resulting from some youthful sporting accident.

He had been waiting for hours. He was prepared to wait forever.

Suddenly, his heart leaped up.

The tenement door he had been surreptitiously watching opened. A girl came out of it. She was lean and dressed in punk leather, but she had the foliate ears of one with noble blood in her veins. There was mortal blood in her as well, though it took one like Will to see it. She wore black lipstick. Half her head had been shaved. She looked like she could use a meal.

Will smiled a smile so faint that it would not have shown up in a photograph. It was her! It had taken him years to track her down from the scant clues that her mother had provided him. But an instant's glance told him who she was, and locked her tight in his heart forever.

He waited until she was about to brush past him, and then extended an arm with a pack of Marlboros in it.

"Say, princess," he said pleasantly. "Got a light?"

Made in the USA
Lexington, KY
14 December 2015